**A high-risk procedure . . .**

Yanking open the heavy metal door that accessed the stairwell, Alex bolted up the stairs. Breathless from terror more than the climb, she charged out of the stairwell and into the ICU.

The moment she reached the nursing station, she could see a procedure in progress in the fluoroscopy room. Feeling the tightness in her throat, she marched across the ICU and stopped in front of David's room. It was empty. Her eyes flashed back to the fluoroscopy room. At the very last moment and on the brink of losing control, she collected herself enough to approach the room.

Wearing a sterile surgical gown and standing over David with a syringe in his hand, Victor Runyon slowly lowered the needle . . .

*Titles by Gary Birken, M.D.*

**FINAL DIAGNOSIS**
**PLAGUE**
**EMBOLUS**

# EMBOLUS

## GARY BIRKEN, M.D.

BERKLEY BOOKS, NEW YORK

**THE BERKLEY PUBLISHING GROUP**
**Published by the Penguin Group**
**Penguin Group (USA) Inc.**
**375 Hudson Street, New York, New York 10014, USA**
Penguin Group (Canada), 90 Eglinton Avenue East, Suite 700, Toronto, Ontario, M4P 2Y3, Canada
(a division of Pearson Penguin Canada Inc.)
Penguin Books Ltd., 80 Strand, London WC2R 0RL, England
Penguin Group Ireland, 25 St. Stephen's Green, Dublin 2, Ireland (a division of Penguin Books Ltd.)
Penguin Group (Australia), 250 Camberwell Road, Camberwell, Victoria 3124, Australia
(a division of Pearson Australia Group Pty. Ltd.)
Penguin Books India Pvt. Ltd., 11 Community Centre, Panchsheel Park, New Delhi—110 017, India
Penguin Group (NZ), Cnr. Airborne and Rosedale Roads, Albany, Auckland 1310, New Zealand
(a division of Pearson New Zealand Ltd.)
Penguin Books (South Africa) (Pty.) Ltd., 24 Sturdee Avenue, Rosebank, Johannesburg 2196, South Africa

Penguin Books Ltd., Registered Offices: 80 Strand, London WC2R 0RL, England

This is a work of fiction. Names, characters, places, and incidents either are the product of the author's imagination or are used fictitiously, and any resemblance to actual persons, living or dead, business establishments, events, or locales is entirely coincidental.

EMBOLUS

A Berkley Book / published by arrangement with the author

PRINTING HISTORY
Berkley edition / January 2006

Copyright © 2006 by Gary Birken, M.D.
Cover design by Pyrographx.

ISBN: 0-425-20735-8

BERKLEY®
Berkley Books are published by The Berkley Publishing Group,
a division of Penguin Group (USA) Inc.,
375 Hudson Street, New York, New York 10014.
BERKLEY is a registered trademark of Penguin Group (USA) Inc.
The "B" design is a trademark belonging to Penguin Group (USA) Inc.

PRINTED IN THE UNITED STATES OF AMERICA

10  9  8  7  6  5  4  3  2  1

*To the memory of Jeffery Resnick, M.D.*

*And for Barbara, with my heartfelt*
*appreciation of her unfailing support.*

# Prologue

*Swimming frantically through the frigid January water of the pond behind the house she had grown up in, Nancy Olander stopped only long enough to slam her palms against the dense ice that blocked her ascent to the surface. Looking up through the glistening mass, she could vaguely make out the silhouette of a small child staring down at her. Desperate, and with her last bit of air almost spent, she again began to swim. Pounding the ice between each stroke, she finally found a thin patch and exploded through to the surface.*

It was the same terrifying nightmare that Nancy Olander had experienced dozens of times—but this time, when she emerged from the dreaded night terror, the euphoric feeling of filling her lungs with a huge breath of air was distinctly absent.

She was now wide awake and gasping as her eyes darted wildly around her hospital room. Suddenly she was consumed by a piercing pain that took root deep in her left shoulder and then shot obliquely across the left side of her chest. Turning her head, she saw a fleeting splash of light disappear from the middle of the room, and then out of the stark silence she heard the sound of the door being gently pulled closed.

Rapidly becoming faint and disoriented, Nancy ran her hand along the top of the bed rail, looking for the button to summon her nurse. But the call button, which had always been coiled around the rail, was strangely absent. Wheezing with each gasp, she lacked sufficient breath to call out for help. As her grip on the rail weakened, her eyes rolled up and her oxygen-starved brain lulled her into a state of unconsciousness.

For a minute she lay peacefully in her bed, but then, out of the fragile stillness, her chest heaved spastically, marking her body's last futile attempt at survival. The end was accompanied by an agonal quiver that consumed her entire body, and at exactly two-twenty A.M., Nancy Olander, a thirty-four-year-old social studies teacher with an angelic face and a tender nature who only hours ago was well on her way to recovery, died needlessly and for no apparent medical reason.

# PART
## One

# Chapter 1

As a responsible journalist, David Airoway felt compelled to meet personally with the physician who had just promised to provide him with the most shocking story of his career.

Arriving a few minutes early for their meeting, David meandered along the Potomac River until he reached Washington Harbor. Continuing on the riverside promenade, he strolled by its many eclectic restaurants and shops. As he gazed out over the river, taking in the crisp April afternoon, a young man wearing a blue denim shirt approached. Average in appearance, he sported a faint raven-colored mustache that hung neatly beneath a bladelike nose.

"Mr. Airoway?"

"Yes," David acknowledged.

"My name's Robert Key. We spoke earlier. Thank you for meeting me."

"Where are you in practice?" David asked.

"I'm on the faculty at John Adams Medical School. I'm a radiologist."

"How long have you been there?"

"I finished my residency at Adams two years ago; I was offered a position and decided to stay on."

"You said on the phone you'd be able to recognize me but you didn't say how."

"I've seen your photograph a number of times. I'm quite familiar with your work. You're an exceptional investigative journalist."

David, slender in contour with lank, curvy shoulders, was three months shy of his thirty-sixth birthday. With short curly brown hair that barely covered the tops of his ears, he was polished in both appearance and manner. He continued to stare out over the Potomac at the Kennedy Center, which loomed in the distance.

Outwardly the young man seemed calm, but David wasn't convinced that he was as collected as he appeared.

"How can I help you?" David asked, noticing that Robert's eyes never stopped scanning the area.

"Do you mind if we walk?" he asked, gesturing toward the promenade.

"It's your meeting," David answered with a shrug.

They hadn't taken more than a few steps when Robert said, "Before we begin, you'll have to agree that I remain a confidential source. You can never mention me by name or disclose who I am to anyone."

David half smiled. "That conversation generally takes place after I've decided to do the story. Why don't you start by telling me what this is all about?"

Robert's expression never changed, but his pace became more brisk. "I assume you're familiar with the Gillette Trauma Center?"

"I am."

"A number of patients have died there over the last year or so. Their deaths have been intentionally covered up by certain members of the medical staff."

David grinned and then shook his head. He placed his hand on Robert's shoulder, bringing them both to a halt. "Look, I'm not trying to rain on your parade, but if this is another malpractice story, I'm not interested. The medical liability crisis has been beaten to death and I have no interest in doing another tired piece on some incompetent doctor. Maybe you should be talking to the medical board."

"I'm not talking about malpractice or medical errors, Mr. Airoway. I'm talking about premeditated murder for political gain. Now, do you agree to my terms or not?"

David paused for a few seconds to study the young man's face, and then with a short sigh he removed a small spiral notepad and a pen from the inside pocket of his sports coat. "Okay," he said. "I'll agree for now but I may want to speak to you about this again. Now, can you give me the names of these patients?"

"I'm afraid I can't do that," Robert said categorically.

"Okay then, who's killing them and for what specific purpose? You said something about political gain. What did you mean?"

Robert shook his head again and for the first time appeared a little flustered. "Let's just say that I'm not in a position to fill in every last detail for you."

David looked up and then flipped the pad closed. "Look, Robert, I'm not exactly asking you about minute details here. Are you saying that you don't know or that you're afraid to say?"

"What's the difference?"

"Nothing, except that you're making it kind of tough for me to buy into any of this," David explained.

"I have to move slowly and see how things develop. I'll walk you through it but for now I guess you'll just have to take a leap of faith."

"I'm an investigative journalist. Going out on a short limb is one thing but if I spent all my time taking leaps of faith, I'd never publish a thing."

"If you're not interested in what I have to say, just say so and I'll walk away right now. It's your call. I promise you'll never hear from me again."

David took a few seconds to gather his thoughts before responding. With the kind of answers he was getting, the smart thing to do would be to take Robert up on his offer and say a polite good-bye. He had certainly spoken to enough crackpots over the years to know when he was in the presence of one, but the well-spoken young man standing next to him hardly fit that profile. He lacked the detached and omniscient eccentricity of the usual psychos who called him about man-eating Martians living in the president's rose garden.

"You realize that you're making some pretty serious allegations," David said.

"I understand that, but that fact doesn't make them any less true."

"Look, Robert. I've never met you before in my life. You call me up a couple of hours ago and set up this meeting. I'm here and I'm listening, but you haven't given me a single fact

I can verify or any leads that I can pursue. Before I commit to a story I have to know my source is credible."

"My credibility's not the issue here, Mr. Airoway. I'm telling you the truth but there's just so much that I know, so if you want to put this story together, you're the one who's going to have to do the legwork."

Realizing that Robert was not going to elaborate, David said, "Then at least tell me where to start."

"You'll want to look into an organization called the Caduceus Project—especially their leadership."

"Okay. How are they mixed up in this thing?"

Robert smiled. "You're an investigative reporter—investigate. I'll help when and where I think I can."

"How come you just don't take this to the police?" David asked.

After a short but nervous laugh, Robert said, "Because I'd like to continue practicing medicine."

"You could speak to them anonymously," David pointed out.

"Something tells me they wouldn't take me very seriously."

"How many deaths are we talking about?"

"Several."

"What does that mean? Three . . . four . . . five?"

"What difference does it make? Look, Mr. Airoway, a number of patients at the Gillette Trauma Center who were well on their way to recovery suddenly died. Their deaths were not the result of their injuries and should have initiated a comprehensive investigation, but it never happened."

David watched as Robert turned and looked over his shoulder. His eyes seemed to lock on two men dressed in dark suits leaning against a railing about fifty yards away.

"Who are they?" David asked. "Do you know them?"

When Robert turned back around, the shadow of fear was plain to see on his face. "I've got to go," he said, ignoring David's question. "Don't try to contact me or the deal's off. I'll call you when it's safe. There's one other thing, Mr. Airoway—these people are ruthless and they aren't finished." And with that, Robert started walking toward M Street.

"Wait a minute," David called out to him, to no avail. He

then quickly looked back at the two men, who had now started off in the opposite direction. Ignoring them for the moment, he turned back to Robert. "Did you know that my sister's a trauma surgeon at Gillette?"

Without breaking stride, Robert glanced back at David. A knowing look crossed his face as he said, "We both better pray that I'm the only one who does know that."

# Chapter 2

It was four minutes before midnight when Robert Key coaxed his Jaguar into the driveway of his brick manor home in McLean.

Exhausted from a sixteen-hour shift, he sat behind the wheel for a minute, dreading the fact that in exactly six hours he'd be on his way back to the hospital. After a long sigh, he tossed his cell phone into the center console and slowly climbed out of the car.

He wasn't more than a few steps down the tree-lined gravel driveway when the working end of Simon Lott's nine-millimeter Beretta came crashing down across the back of his skull.

Before Lott could hit him again, Robert's knees buckled and sent him staggering forward. Stunned but still conscious, he desperately tried to stay on his feet by lunging for his car. But his reach fell short and he was only able to make a wild swipe at the corner of the hood before the momentum of his fall carried him to the ground. As he struck the driveway face down, his cheeks and forehead were impaled by the coarse grit and tiny stones of the driveway.

From the darkness, his head was suddenly filled with brilliant javelins of light that crisscrossed his mind in sudden bursts. The luminescent projectiles soon began to fade, and just as quickly as they had appeared they vanished, leaving him in a silent black void.

It was only a minute or so but Robert had lost all sense of time and, at first, didn't feel Lott's boot pressing down on his shoulder. But as his mind began to clear, he was able to force his eyes partially open, and in the dim light of a near moonless night he could still make out the silhouette of a man with an indistinct object in his hand standing over him. Oblivious to the blood streaming down the back of his neck, Robert turned his head to the side and wiped the blood from his eyes.

"Can you hear me?" When there was no response he kicked Robert in the shoulder and then renewed his question. "I said, can you hear me?"

"Yeah," Robert mumbled, still trying to shake his head clear.

"Good. I've been asked to speak to you about your recent indiscretions."

Lott, a rugged, soft-spoken man with penetrating olive green eyes, leaned over, grabbed Robert by the shirt, and yanked him to a sitting position against the English sedan's wheel well. Robert braced himself with his arms, trying to prevent himself from sliding back to the ground. "I don't know what you're talking about," he said, staring at the black blood on the back of his hand.

Lott shoved the Beretta under his chin and then twisted it into the soft tissues of his neck. "I think you do. You see, Robert, we've been watching you and I'm sorry to say you've disappointed a lot of people who had very high hopes for you."

"I swear, I've only done what I was supposed to," he said in a cracked voice.

Lott repositioned the gun, snugging it up against his Adam's apple. "You're a bloody liar and a poor one at that."

Even in the marginal light, Lott could see the fear creeping across Robert's face. It was a look he had seen before on other men's faces—one that invariably betrayed their weakness. Lott took a step forward and straddled Robert's legs. He had wasted enough time and now regretted that he hadn't shot

Key when he got out of the car. But Lott enjoyed the drama his work sometimes created, and watching someone's reaction when he knew he had only moments to live was an exhilarating experience.

He slowly lowered the barrel of his Beretta until the sight was squarely on the young man's forehead. As Lott tightened his finger on the trigger and was just about to finish what he had come to do, his attention was suddenly drawn to the sound of raucous laughter. He turned and carefully peered over the roof of the car. About fifty yards away, on the opposite sidewalk, a young couple walking their dog passed under a streetlamp.

"Shit," he muttered with his eyes drawn on them. Pausing to think, he ran his fingers through his full head of silvery white hair. It was a premature phenomenon that he shared with his maternal grandfather, a man he admired for his independent spirit and strength of character.

Distracted by the unexpected intruders, Lott barely noticed the shadowy movement from below him. When he realized what was happening, it was too late. The heel of Robert's shoe struck him squarely in the groin. The force of the blow immediately folded him over across his belt line. The extreme pain fanned out across his lower abdomen in pulselike waves, robbing him of his ability to draw a breath.

Lott managed a couple of steps backward before squatting like a baseball catcher to ease the excruciating cramps and refill his lungs with air. He smothered the urge to vomit by gritting his teeth and covering his mouth with the back of his hand. Finally, after a dozen breaths or so, the pain and nausea subsided enough for him to come to a standing position.

By this time, Robert had found the door handle of the Jaguar and was struggling to pull himself to his feet. Lott realized that if Robert screamed or the couple came close enough to observe what was going on, he'd have to either kill all three of them or flee without killing Robert. Unfortunately, none of those eventualities would sit well with the people who were paying him.

Lott had but one option. While Robert was still fighting to get up, Lott moved forward. As he did so, he rotated the gun in his hand and grabbed it by the barrel. Raising it high over his head and using one powerful motion, he brought the Beretta down, striking Robert directly above his forehead. The blow was intentionally much harder than the first, delivered with extreme precision, and sent the young doctor crashing back to the driveway—this time leaving him silent and motionless.

Lott limped toward the car, leaned his shoulder against it, and then craned his neck to look over the roof. Still talking loudly and laughing, the couple stopped and waited for their dog to explore a patch of thick shrubbery. But when the animal lost interest, the couple continued to approach slowly. Lott knew there was a chance they would walk right by without noticing Key on the driveway, but it was too risky to chance. With self-preservation calling the shots, Lott decided to slip away. Even if Robert Key wasn't dead, it wouldn't be long before he was. If, by some miracle, he did survive, it wouldn't matter. With the extreme power of the second blow, Lott was sure he'd be a vegetable for life.

He slipped the Beretta back into his ankle holster and then quickly reached into Robert's back pocket and slid his wallet out to complete the facade of a mugging. He then turned and, using the car for cover, went down the driveway and across Robert's backyard.

Parked at the end of the block was a black Tahoe that he had stolen only a few hours earlier, which he would dispose of before the sun came up. Once behind the wheel, he wasted no time in starting the engine and pulling away. He checked his watch. In spite of the unexpected snag, the entire operation had taken only four minutes.

Based on their usual lack of imagination, Lott expected the police would arrive on the scene and conclude that Robert Key had been attacked and robbed. Not a very pleasant occurrence for such a quiet law-abiding neighborhood, but certainly lacking in the shock value necessary to attract major media coverage.

Opening the center console, he reached for his cell phone and tapped in a number. The call was picked up on the second ring.

"Yes."

"I think the project has ended in the desired result," Lott said.

"You think?" asked the man whom Lott knew only as Morgan.

"I'm sure," he said.

"Good. Call me tomorrow at the usual time."

There were no accolades or congratulations on a job well done. Lott snickered as he tossed the phone onto the seat next to him. Fortunately, he was not the type of man who needed a pat on the back or an encouraging word—both unrealistic expectations in his world. What he did expect was to be paid promptly and handsomely for providing a unique service.

As he headed for the spot that he had selected to dump the SUV, Lott thought about what he had told Morgan. Hopefully, by the time somebody found Key, he would be dead. If that wasn't the case, he'd have some explaining to do to Morgan, but he'd think of some way to handle it.

As Lott slowed the Tahoe and then came to a stop at a red light, an arcane smile covered his face. It was so obvious, he couldn't understand why it hadn't occurred to him sooner. Although it was not his assignment nor intention to leave Robert Key alive, if by some miracle the doctor did survive, he just might be worth a lot more to the project alive than dead.

# Chapter 3

## APRIL 21

Had it not been for the unexpected arrival of a fifteen-year-old boy with a gunshot wound to the chest, Dr. Alexandra Caffey might have been on time for her lunch date with her twin brother, David Airoway.

An attractive woman by virtue of her lustrous nut-brown

hair, soft features, and willowy figure, Alex was generally un-flappable, remaining steadfastly reflective and calm under fire. After finishing five years of general surgery residency and then a one-year fellowship in trauma at Jackson Memorial Hospital in Miami, she had been heavily recruited by several of the leading trauma centers in the country.

After giving the matter the same degree of careful consideration she did most important decisions, she chose to take a position at the Gillette Trauma Center. If anybody had asked Alex the day she was accepted to medical school whether she'd eventually wind up as the first female surgeon at one of the country's most prestigious trauma centers, she surely would have laughed.

The first thing Alex noticed when she walked into the main trauma bay was the look of terror in the boy's face. One of the nurses centered the overhead surgical spotlight on him, revealing his bleach-white skin.

"It's a little early in the day for this kind of thing," she said.

"The knife and gun club's opening for business earlier and earlier," came a voice from among the team of responders who had already assembled and taken up their assigned positions.

"When did he get here?" Alex asked, looking across the stretcher at Dr. Theo Hightower.

"About sixty seconds ago," he answered. Theo, a first-year trauma fellow and second in command under Alex, peered out from under the brim of his Baltimore Ravens cap at the monitors. He was baby-faced with cropped brown hair and stubby fingers, and his signature science fiction paperback protruded from his back pocket. His rumpled green scrubs and a fresh crop of peach fuzz attested to the end of another busy thirty-six-hour shift. He was four years behind Alex in his training; they had first met in Miami as residents and had been friends ever since.

"And how are you?" Theo asked Alex as he quickly lifted the blood-soaked dressing from the boy's chest. As he expected, the outer edges of the entrance wound were jagged and black.

"What do we have?" Alex asked as she quickly put on a yellow surgical gown and a pair of examining gloves.

"He's a fifteen-year-old who was shot by his girlfriend at school during their lunch break. From the looks of this entrance wound I would say it was a fairly low-caliber round and at close range. His blood pressure and pulse have been normal—no evidence of shock."

Alex walked over to the X-ray viewboxes. Being only five foot three, she got up on her tiptoes. "Is this his chest film?"

"No. That one's from the last patient," came the response from the hoarse-voiced X-ray technician as he rolled the portable machine past her. "His is cooking. It'll be out in two minutes."

"How's he doing?" Alex asked Theo.

"I'm sure he's got some blood in his chest and a collapsed lung. He'll be a lot better as soon as we get a tube in."

"Are we going to the operating room?" she asked, knowing it probably wouldn't be necessary but interested to see what Theo's assessment was.

"Right now I'd say no but I'm not dismissing the possibility. I'm hoping the chest tube will be all that he needs."

"No chance of a cardiac injury?"

"I doubt it," he said, joining her at the viewbox. "The entrance wound's pretty far over to the right, but we'll get an ultrasound just to be sure."

"Why did she shoot him?" Alex asked.

Theo leaned forward and explained, "Evidently the young lady was less than thrilled about his suggestion that they explore the possibility of dating other people."

Together they crossed the room. Alex walked over to the head of the bed while Theo reexamined the wound.

"How's it going, young man?" Alex asked, watching the frightened boy's eyes hurtle from side to side.

He grimaced a little and said, "I'll be okay."

"What's your name?"

"Chris."

"Okay, Chris. Are you having much trouble breathing?"

"Some," he confessed.

"Don't try to talk anymore. We're going to give you some medicine to make you sleepy and then put a little tube right here," she explained, pointing to his chest. "You'll feel much better after we do." Alex took his hand and then gave it a gentle squeeze for reassurance. Still holding his hand, she turned to Theo. "Who's going to put the tube in?"

Theo stopped what he was doing and looked over at Kim Linzer, the surgical intern on the service. She took a couple of steps forward, her eyes betraying the usual apprehension that accompanies performing a procedure for the first time.

"I assume you'll be supervising," Alex whispered to Theo.

He immediately shook his head. "C'mon, Alex. How long have we been working together?"

"It seems like a lifetime."

"The chest tray is right behind you. I'll prep," Elena Mercado, the nursing team leader, said as she quickly finished up threading in a second IV.

"I thought you were out of the hospital?" Theo asked as he washed his hands and motioned Kim to do the same.

"I was just about to leave to meet David for lunch, but I think I'll hang around for a while. I want to see the chest X-ray after the tube's in and make sure he doesn't need to go to the OR."

"Yes, Mother," Theo said as he slipped on a pair of sterile gloves. "When you were a fellow, did your attendings hover over you like you do to me?"

"Who remembers? It was so long ago."

Theo's scanty eyebrows rose halfway up his forehead at the same time that his lower lip curled. "It's only been four years since you finished your fellowship, Alex. This is me you're talking to. I was your junior resident—remember?"

Alex turned and headed for the large sliding glass door that separated the trauma bay from the main corridor.

"Oh yeah. I remember now. You were that cocky guy who thought he knew everything. Put the chest tube in. I'll be right over there making a phone call."

Alex barely had time to leave a message on her brother's cell phone that she'd be late when Kim and Theo joined her at the nursing station.

"The tube's in," Theo said. "They're taking the film now."

The three of them walked back into the trauma room to wait for the X-ray. As inconspicuously as she was able, Alex walked over to the bedside to check the tube and have another look at Chris. Her efforts were in vain, and when she looked up Theo was only a few feet away with his arms crossed and a scowl on his face.

"The film's here," Kim said, throwing it up on the view-box and pointing to it with confidence. "The lung's completely expanded and the tube's in perfect position." Theo remained silent, allowing her to take center stage.

"I agree. Nice job, Kim," Alex said. "How much blood was in his chest?"

"We got about two hundred cc's when we first put the tube in and that was it. There's no more coming out."

"That's not too bad. He should be out of here in a few days. Is he going to the ICU?" Alex asked.

Theo jumped in. "Even as we speak, they're getting him ready to transport."

"Are his parents here?"

"Mom got here a little while ago. I've already spoken to her," he answered.

"How's she doing?"

"Better than most. I hate taking care of kids," he complained. "There's nothing worse than facing the parents of a pediatric trauma."

Alex took off her white coat and hung it on the back of the door. "It's part of the job. Is there anything else cooking?"

"Nope. It's pretty quiet right now, but it may only be the calm before the storm."

Alex said, "Hopefully, things won't get too crazy until tonight. I've got my beeper and my cell phone. I'll only be a few blocks away. I shouldn't be gone for more than an hour or so."

"Tell Dave I said hi," Theo said.

"I will. Let's make rounds with the whole team at about three," Alex said making sure her pager was clipped to the strap of her purse. She then checked her watch for the third time before shaking her head and heading for the door.

# Chapter 4

Simon Lott relaxed on a braided cane lounge chair on the balcony of his fourth-floor apartment that overlooked Connecticut Avenue.

It was a cloudless afternoon with just enough wind to make sitting outside pleasant. It had been a busy few days and he welcomed the opportunity to unwind for a few hours. A native of Ireland, Lott grew up in the west of Dublin in a suburb called Ballsbridge. The only child of a very successful industrialist, he was raised in affluence and was educated in the same traditional manner as other privileged children of Dublin. Beginning early in his childhood, and for reasons that his family and teachers could never understand, he found a diabolical delight in rebelling against authority.

In spite of a gifted mind and limitless potential, he became an increasing embarrassment to his family. He did manage to graduate from Trinity College, but by that point had been shunned by his parents for his rebellious behavior and repeated minor scuffles with the law. Lott found violence to be an intoxicant and, as a result, he never found his moral compass. It didn't take him very long to learn that there was considerably more excitement and money to be made on the wrong side of the law than the right.

Placing his wineglass on a small glass table, Lott stood up and walked over to the railing, where he stared down at Connecticut Avenue. Basking in the tranquility of the afternoon, he savored another swallow of his white wine.

The serenity of the moment came to an abrupt end when his phone rang. Without checking the caller ID, he had a pretty good idea of who was calling. After ignoring the first two rings, he finally walked over and answered it.

"Yes."

"I'm afraid I have some rather disturbing news for you," Morgan said.

"Really," Lott responded, indifferent to the annoyed tone in his voice.

"Contrary to your assurances, it seems that Robert Key has survived."

"That's rubbish."

"Hardly, Mr. Lott. Less than an hour after you left Dr. Key, he was stumbled upon by a late-night jogger who called 911. He was taken immediately to Gillette and at this very moment is being attended to by the finest physicians they have to offer. Fortunately for us, he remains in a rather deep coma. At least that's what my sources tell me."

"I don't see the problem. Even if he is alive, he'll be a vegetable for the rest of his life," Lott pointed out.

"The people I represent aren't prepared to take that chance. They would prefer it if Dr. Key was added to the list of the other unfortunate victims of the Gillette Trauma Center." Morgan's suggestion came as no surprise to Lott—it was the obvious move. "I remind you, Mr. Lott, that I'm being held accountable for your performance. It wasn't an easy matter to explain away your failure. Your instructions were quite clear regarding Key."

"Why don't you let me worry about Key. That's what you hired me for."

"I'm not sure that the people I represent would be measurably reassured if I conveyed that message to them. At the moment, they aren't very pleased with your work."

It always amused Lott that Morgan never spoke of the people he represented other than to refer to them as just that. Lott rubbed his chin and then switched the phone to his opposite ear.

"Let's keep this civilized, shall we?"

"You came highly recommended, Mr. Lott. I certainly hope your efforts on our behalf in the days to come will be somewhat more practiced."

"I appreciate the advice."

Lott could see no reason to say anything further so he simply hung up, set the phone back on the table, and returned to the railing, where he took a long slow swallow of the Riesling. He had known other men like Morgan, pompous and haughty in their manner, but for the most part, they operated in the blind, unaware of how dangerous it could be to treat a man such as himself with such careless disrespect.

He watched overhead as a single-engine plane banked gently over the Potomac, while in the distance an imposing group of thunderheads gathered. The thought of returning to Ireland for no other reason than to merely relax and clear his mind suddenly seemed quite appealing. Life was easier there and as long as he kept his head down, he probably wouldn't have any problems with the authorities. Unfortunately, in view of the phone call he'd just received, a pleasure trip to Dublin did not seem like a very practical idea at the moment. Dr. Robert Key was becoming a thorn in his side and he knew he'd have to redouble his efforts and take care of the matter sooner rather than later.

After a few more minutes on the balcony, Lott strolled back into the living room. An ornate grandfather clock with bold roman numerals chimed rhythmically. As he listened to the last few tones, he considered calling Morgan back, but after giving the idea a second thought, he decided to let the man founder in his own ineptitude.

# Chapter 5

Walking down N Street, Alex gazed around at the usual lunchtime bustle of Georgetown.

It was a warm day but paled in comparison to what lay ahead in the depths of July and August. A frustrated architect at heart, Alex slowed her pace just long enough to gaze down a small side street at a beautifully maintained brick rowhouse with elaborate bracketed cornices, typical of the late 1800s. Every minute or so she checked her watch, hoping that her brother had received her message and that he wasn't sitting in the restaurant steaming about her habitual tardiness.

As soon as Alex walked through the door of Furin's, David's favorite restaurant for lunch, she spotted him seated at a small table toward the back. The unique family restaurant was small and also one of Alex's favorite spots for lunch. When she caught his attention, she smiled and waved. In response, he folded his arms, a gesture of disapproval that Alex could remember as far back as grade school.

As she approached the table, he was still frowning and pointing to his antique gold watch that his father, Jim Airoway, had passed down to him when he was a senior in college. At the time, he was terminally ill from leukemia and died a few weeks later without having the joy of seeing Alex and David graduate.

Before sitting down, she stopped at his side of the table and kissed him on the cheek. "I'm sorry," she said, setting her cell phone down on the table. "Just as I was leaving we had a trauma alert."

"I got your message, so I'll forgive you this time," he said with a wry grin.

"So when I walked in you were just torturing me with that stupid glare on your face?"

"Pretty much," he confessed.

Alex noticed that, as usual, David was casually dressed. It had always meant a great deal to her that his deep affection for her was surpassed only by genuine concern for her well-being. She never found his overbearing nature too intolerable and loved the time they spent together. He was a gifted investigative writer, and his talent for injecting perspective and proportion into his exposés had won the admiration and praise of dozens of critics across the country.

"How's everything? Any news on the book?" she asked, unfolding her napkin and placing it on her lap.

"I spoke with my agent yesterday. We already have two pretty good offers,"

"Not bad. First a slew of nationally recognized articles and now your first book. So what are you going to do about the offers?"

"Whatever she recommends."

"It's hard for me to believe that anybody would be interested in reading an entire book on Medicare fraud."

"That's because you're a doctor and probably in denial that it even exists."

She chuckled briefly as she reached for her water. "So, to what do I owe the pleasure of this lovely invitation?"

"Can't a guy ask his sister out to lunch without having a hidden agenda?"

"A normal brother maybe, but not mine," she answered simply. "You're a hopeless creature of habit and just as predictable."

He interlocked his fingers and placed his elbows on the table. "Creature of habit, huh?"

"Absolutely. How many of those stupid football games did we miss in four years at Dartmouth? When was the last Saturday morning you didn't wash your car and pay bills? Sorry, David. Dinners are your social time. Lunch is strictly reserved for conducting business. So why don't you cut to the chase and tell me what's on your mind?"

David picked up his fork and tapped the table a couple of times. "May I ask about my favorite niece first?"

"Jessie's fine," Alex said without elaborating.

"I have something really special for her birthday."

"Her birthday's not for three months," Alex said, shaking her head. "If you and Mom don't start controlling yourselves, my daughter's going to be the most spoiled five-year-old on the East Coast."

"Have you heard from Chuck recently?" David asked, knowing the mere mention of her ex-husband's name would probably dampen her mood.

"No, thank God, but I heard he was living in Europe with one of his ex-grad students. What a shock," she added sarcastically.

"I still think you guys didn't have to get divorced so fast."

"Not this again," she moaned. "You know, for someone who's never been married, you sure seem to be an expert on the subject."

"I didn't say I was an expert. I'm just saying I think you two could have worked things out."

"Worked things out? Would that have been before or after

he emptied our bank account, ran my credit cards up to their limit, and then disappeared for six months with one of his college playmates. The man led his life between his legs, David. I see enough kids at the hospital—I don't need to come home to one at night. Besides, he never calls his daughter or pays a nickel of child support."

"He must have some redeeming qualities," David said.

"Oh, he can be charming when he wants to be and he fooled me for a long time, but deep down he's got no substance or character. I'm just glad I finally figured him out. Now, do you think we can talk about something besides my personal life?"

David had never been a big fan of Chuck, but was still disappointed when he and Alex announced they were splitting up. He raised his hands over his head in capitulation. "Let's," he said.

"What happened with the condo?" she asked.

"Didn't I tell you?"

"I don't think so," Alex said.

"I put a deposit down on it yesterday."

Alex reached across the table and grabbed his wrists. "Congratulations. Welcome to the world of homeowners. When do you move in?"

"Sixty days."

"That's great. How does Samantha fit into all of this?"

"Now who's prying?" he asked with a wink. "Anyway, I'm not sure I understand the question."

"Oh, I think you do. Are you guys going to live together?"

"We're still in negotiations."

"Give it some serious thought. You could do a lot worse than Sam."

An unenthusiastic waiter, moving as if everyone in the restaurant had two hours for lunch, meandered over to the table. Before Alex had a chance to even look at the menu, David turned to the man. "I'll have the Tex-Mex salad and the lady will have the Vegetarian Odyssey."

The waiter looked at Alex to give her the opportunity to say something. "That sounds perfect," she said, sending him away with a faint grin. "So what's going on? Why were you so mysterious on the phone last night?"

David exhaled slowly and then glanced around the restaurant. "There's something I'd like to talk to you about," he said.

"Shoot."

"What I have to tell you is totally confidential."

Alex pushed back in her chair. "Okay."

"I'm serious, Alex," he said, expecting her to tease him a little more about being so melodramatic but before she could, he asked, "What do you know about the Caduceus Project?"

"The medical society?"

"Yeah."

"Not too much, really. It's a political organization made up of doctors. As I recall, they're kind of old-fashioned and elitist, maybe even a little silly."

"Why do you say silly?" David asked.

"I don't know. I guess because in this day and age those types of organizations seem just a tad corny and anachronistic."

"Do you know who's calling the shots?"

"I imagine they have a chapter president but I don't know who it is."

"I've done a little research. Would it surprise you to hear that the Caduceus Project is a highly organized and a very rapidly growing group? They're becoming more and more politically influential, especially on a national level. From your comments, I assume you're not a member."

She laughed. "Are you kidding? Of course I'm not a member. What's this all about, David?"

Moving his fingertips to the table's edge, he said, "Supposing I were to tell you that I have reason to believe that there are some very bizarre things going on in your hospital."

"What kind of things?"

"Patients dying who shouldn't be," he answered.

"We're a trauma hospital. The leading cause of death in this country in children and young adults is trauma. We're practicing high-quality medicine, David, but we can't save everybody who comes through our doors."

"I'm not talking about medical errors or malpractice. I'm talking about patients who are being intentionally murdered."

"That's absurd," she said with a wave of her hand.

"How can you be so sure?"

"Because I'm living in the real world and not some TV movie."

"That's not an answer," he said.

"And you think the Caduceus Project is involved in this . . . this conspiracy?" she asked.

"Maybe."

"Are you serious?"

"As a heart attack," he assured her, lifting his glass but then setting it back down before taking a sip. David paused for a few moments and leaned back in his chair. "One of your colleagues at Adams called me a few days ago. He told me that he wanted to talk with me as soon as possible."

"And he was the one who told you this nonsense about Gillette?"

"Yes."

"How did he get your name?" she asked.

"He said he was familiar with my work." David stopped, trying to decide whether to elaborate. He glanced up and saw Alex studying him.

"What did you say his name was?" she asked.

"I didn't," he began, but his words were largely drowned out by the annoying alert of Alex's phone. "His name is Robert Key," he said, doubting whether she had heard him. "My God, it sounds like we're in a lifeboat drill. Why do you have to set that damn thing so loud?"

Alex was still studying the display on her cell phone when she asked, "What did you say?"

"I asked, why do you keep your phone so annoyingly loud?"

"For the obvious reason, David—I don't want to miss a call. Take it easy, this will only take a sec," she said, holding up her index finger. But after about a minute, she looked up toward the ceiling and shook her head. She then looked across the table at him and mouthed, *I'm sorry.* "Okay, Theo, I'm on my way. You better let the operating room know. It sounds like we're going to have to explore his abdomen." Giving David her classic apologetic look that he'd seen many times before, she tossed her phone back into her purse and stood up. "I'm sorry, David. I have to go. There's a bad gunshot wound coming in. The guy's only about ten minutes out but I want to hear more about this. I'll call you as soon as I get home tonight."

"Don't worry about it," he told her.

"Listen to me," she said, coming to her feet. "Physicians can become stressed out and say all kinds of bizarre things. We have a few flip out every year."

David nodded but was unconvinced. "You must keep pretty accurate records of all the deaths at Gillette," he said casually as she threw her purse over her shoulder.

"As a matter of fact we do, but something tells me you already knew that."

"Do you think I could have a look at them?"

Alex looked around, leaned toward the center of the table, and then spoke in a distinct whisper. "Are you crazy, David? I could lose my job. How could you ask such a thing?"

He smiled and then winked at her. "It was just a thought."

"An insane one. Don't get up." Alex leaned over and kissed him on the cheek. "I love you." David took a deep breath and watched as she disappeared through the door.

The restaurant was a little warmer than he would have liked, but he hardly noticed as he was lost in thought about the very reason that had brought him there. He barely looked when the waiter returned with their lunch.

"My sister had to leave," he said. "She's a trauma surgeon over at Gillette."

"A lot of their doctors eat here. We're kind of used to seeing them fly in and out of here. Do you want the salad?" he asked indifferently.

"I guess so," he answered.

For the next few minutes, David picked at the salad. Unfortunately, whatever appetite he had had was now gone and eating was the last thing on his mind. Finally he tossed his fork on the plate, stood up, and signaled the waiter for the check.

As soon as he stepped outside he spotted a cab and managed to flag it down. As the late-model Ford took him through Foggy Bottom, David tried to ignore the driver's endless prattle, made even more annoying by his constant changing of the radio station.

David Airoway embraced fact, not fiction, and even though things were a little unclear right now, he felt there was a story in what Robert Key had told him. What was clear, however, was that if he were to pursue the story he'd have to get Robert to feel comfortable confiding in him. If he had learned anything from researching his book it was that gathering information about medical organizations could be extremely difficult.

Filling his lungs with a deep breath, he held it for a few moments before allowing it to escape. He again thought about the wisdom of sharing what he knew with Alex. One saving grace was that if he did have a change of heart, it wouldn't be too difficult to backpedal his way out of any further discussions on the topic of Gillette.

As the cab followed the traffic down Pennsylvania Avenue, David Airoway reclined his head and wondered if it were really possible that a number of unsuspecting patients had been murdered within the walls of one of the most prestigious hospitals in Washington, D.C.

# Chapter 6

### FALLS CHURCH, VIRGINIA

Before tonight, Marc Gilbert had never had a reason to call 911.

While waiting behind the Windsor Gate Apartments for the Metropolitan Police Department to arrive, he held his rambunctious golden retriever, Tyne, on a short leash. Every few seconds, Gilbert, a long-limbed man with close-set eyes and a conspicuous chin, glanced over at the unconscious man who was lying face up in a puddle of dark blood.

Five minutes passed and the first Metropolitan cruiser

rolled up. The man behind the wheel, Officer Al Carlisle, a veteran, was the first to exit the car.

"Mr. Gilbert?" he asked as he approached.

"Yes," he answered, wrapping the leash around his hand a few extra times, trying to quell Tyne's friendly but rambunctious nature.

"I'm Officer Carlisle. Where's the man?"

"He's right over there," Gilbert said, gesturing toward the corner of the parking lot.

Carlisle's rookie partner, Gino Vaccaro, joined them.

"I'd appreciate it if you could hang around for a few minutes. I'd like to get your statement," Carlisle told Gilbert as the two officers started toward the man.

The far end of the parking lot, which was only about twenty paces from where Gilbert was standing, was relatively well lit by paired spotlights mounted on the corners of the five-story building. The lot ended at a short barren knoll that extended about twenty yards away, eventually blending into a grove of young trees.

The two officers approached the man with caution. When he was a few feet away, Carlisle took a knee and studied him, thinking to himself that he couldn't be more than forty. From the smear of blood on the pavement, it appeared as if he had dragged himself across the cement for a good fifteen feet before finally losing consciousness. There was a large jagged gash across his forehead. The edges were widely serrated and formed a crescent over the dry blood that had trickled down over the victim's right eye and cheek.

Suddenly, out of the silence, the man's chest heaved. The result was a coarse gurgling sound created by the rush of air down his blood-filled windpipe.

Carlisle stood straight up. "He's alive, Gino. Where the hell are the paramedics?"

"They're here," he answered, pointing to the ambulance as it rounded the corner of the apartment building.

Carlisle took a second look and shook his head.

"Somebody at Gillette's going to have their work cut out for them tonight. Look at his face. I don't think his own mother would recognize him."

"I'll bet you anything he jumped," Gino said as he bent over and slid the man's wallet out of his back pocket.

Just as Gino stepped back, the paramedics came running up. They worked quickly, and as soon as they had inserted a breathing tube in the man's windpipe and started an IV, they loaded him into the ambulance and sped off. By this time several dozen tenants had filtered out of the building and were rubbernecking from several feet away.

With nothing more to see and at Vaccaro's urging, the crowd slowly dispersed. It was all over in ten minutes.

"Thanks for your help, Mr. Gilbert," Carlisle said. "You didn't by any chance see what happened?"

"I'm sorry. I didn't. If it weren't for my dog, I probably wouldn't have even noticed him."

"You didn't see anybody else back here?"

"Nope."

"Did you hear anything?"

Gilbert shook his head.

"Do you walk your dog around here often?"

"Not usually, but I thought I'd give her a little run in the field."

After several more questions, Carlisle thanked Gilbert and reminded him that as their investigation proceeded, the police might want to speak to him again.

Gino walked over from talking to the apartment manager and smiled at his partner. "I was right," he said pointing to the far end of the building. "That's the guy's balcony right up there."

"Where are they taking him?" Gilbert asked.

"Gillette Trauma Center," Carlisle said. "Thanks again."

Gilbert watched as Carlisle and his partner got back into their cruiser and slowly made their way out of the parking lot. He then turned and gave Tyne a gentle tug. She immediately jumped out in front of him. As they started to walk off, Gilbert reached into his pocket and pulled out his cell phone.

# Chapter 7

The planning and construction of the first dedicated trauma hospital in Washington, D.C., took almost seven years. The initial gift from the Gillette family to John Adams University exceeded fifty million dollars, a sum of money that was instrumental in making the hospital a national showcase of modern trauma care.

Marcus Gillette, a fussy old curmudgeon, had become a multimillionaire by amassing a number of smaller companies into an international pharmaceuticals empire. In spite of his many shortcomings and peculiar quirks, he was an extremely philanthropic man who had taken painstaking measures to set up a large foundation that was particularly interested in pouring money into medical research.

It had been one of the busiest shifts Alex could remember working since coming to Gillette. She was just walking out of the operating room after repairing a lacerated spleen in a Dutch tourist who had stumbled into the wrong section of Washington. An unfortunate victim of a brutal mugging, the man was at the moment without any cash or credit cards but still in possession of his life. It was ten minutes shy of one A.M.

With her hands pushed deep into the pockets of her white coat, Alex stood in front of the elevator, feeling relieved that her shift was finally over. Halfheartedly, she smothered a burgeoning yawn with the back of her hand.

When the elevator doors opened, Theo Hightower stood in front of her with a somber expression. Alex stepped on, turning shoulder to shoulder with him. She purposely said nothing, but it didn't take Theo long to glance over at her with a pained look of gloom on his face.

"Whatever it is, I don't want to hear about it," she said, pointing to her watch. "My shift was over hours ago. I should be home in bed."

"I wasn't going to say a word."

As the elevator descended, the two of them stood in silence, staring straight ahead. Just as they reached the ground floor, she growned and said, "Okay, tell me about it."

"A jumper, male in his thirties. The ambulance should be pulling in right about now. The paramedics were so busy working on him they didn't have a chance to radio us until about five minutes ago."

"Who's the attending on call?"

"Unfortunately, it's Dr. Runyon."

She arched her eyebrows. "Be careful what you say, Theo. Keep your opinions to yourself. I'm talking to you as a friend now, not your attending."

"C'mon, Alex. He's a nice guy but he's the third rail of surgeons. He's killed more patients than cancer."

"He's competent, Theo."

"Well, I guess that depends on your—"

"Has he been notified?" she interrupted, having no further interest in discussing Victor Runyon's skill as a surgeon.

"Yeah, but it generally takes him about twenty minutes to get here. But don't worry about it. Your shift is over. Go on home. We'll be okay until he gets here."

"Spare me the martyr routine, Theo. I'll help you until Runyon shows."

He smiled. "Well, if you insist."

"Were the paramedics specific about his injuries?" she asked him as they walked down the short corridor toward the emergency room.

"They were too busy but they did say he had a bad head injury and that they suspected internal bleeding."

"Well, Dr. Hightower, I guess we're going back to work."

"You know," Theo said, "after you left Miami, I got friendly with one of the cardiac surgery fellows who once told me something about working around the clock for days at a time. I didn't believe him but after working in this place for the better part of a year I think I'm starting to understand what he was talking about."

"What did he say?" she asked.

"He told me he knew he had lost his humanity when he found himself wishing one night that one of his critically ill patients would die so that he could get some sleep."

Theo tapped the metal plate on the wall and the two huge metal doors swung open with a *whoosh*. Alex could see the multicolored flashing lights of the ambulance as it backed into the receiving dock. Already assembled in the main bay were the on-call trauma team consisting of two nurses, a respiratory therapist, a radiology technician, a lab tech, and a host of medical students and residents. Two husky paramedics wheeled the victim into the room and transferred him to the bed.

"What do you have?" Theo asked in a voice that rose above the constant buzz of the controlled pandemonium. "Quiet down, everyone, I don't want to hear anybody except the paramedics."

The paramedic at the head of the bed responded first. "The report we got was that he jumped from his balcony."

"How high?"

"Fourth floor. We tubed him and got two good IVs in. He's completely unresponsive and his blood pressure's never been above sixty."

"How much fluid has he gotten?" Alex asked.

"He's already had two liters of saline. It looks like he has pretty bad skull and facial fractures and his abdomen is getting larger. He must be bleeding in there."

"No fractures of the arms or legs?" she asked.

"No obvious ones," he answered.

"He's still in shock. Give him two units of O negative blood," Theo ordered. "I agree about the facial bone fractures," he added as he palpated the man's jaw.

By this time the whole team was working feverishly. The third-year resident, Chet Alden, placed an additional IV in the jugular vein and threaded it down until its tip was just outside the heart. While the lab technicians were drawing blood, the respiratory therapist rolled a ventilator into the room.

"I need that two units of O negative right now," Theo yelled again. "Get the Level One hooked up. We'll need it for high-speed transfusion and to warm the blood."

Ten minutes after his arrival, the young man had received a rapid infusion of two units of blood. One of the nurses stepped forward and looked up at the monitor. "He's doing better. His blood pressure's up to one-ten over seventy."

Chet was rapidly completing the portable ultrasound examination of the patient's abdomen. "It looks like this guy's got a belly full of blood," he announced.

Theo checked the man's pupils by flashing a small penlight into his eyes. His pupils were both sluggish but clearly reacting. "This guy's still alive. Call the OR and let them know we're coming up. Get neurosurgery and plastics on the phone and tell them that we may need them later. Okay with you, Alex?"

"Let's do it," she stated as she peered over his shoulder at the ultrasound monitor. "The bleeding's probably coming from his liver. Are you sure you don't want neurosurgery to see him before we go to the OR?" she asked.

"No, I say we get him to the operating room right now. We'll get a CT of the head afterward."

"Why not now?" Chet asked.

"No way," Theo insisted. "We could lose him in CT."

"Theo's right," Alex told Chet.

Just at that moment, the X-ray tech returned with the initial films of the young man's neck, chest, and pelvis and put them up on the viewbox.

Alex and Theo stood next to each other in front of the films, with the rest of the team behind them like ducklings imprinting on their mother.

"I can't believe it," Alex said, studying his chest X-ray. "His chest looks normal. I can't believe he doesn't have any rib fractures or bleeding in there."

"I think his neck's okay—no fracture," Chet said, running his finger slowly down the film, checking each vertebra.

Alex made her way closer to the patient, taking up a position at his feet. "The guy falls four stories and doesn't break his legs or pelvis?"

"It's a little unusual," Theo said.

"A little?" she responded. "Let's finish up here and get him upstairs."

Cindy Farrell, a seasoned professional who was the nursing team leader, kicked the release locks on the stretcher, but before she gave the go-ahead to wheel the patient out she stopped to transfer the IV bags. As she did so, Alex caught a glimpse of the man's watch. At first she didn't make the connection and looked away. But a moment or so later, her eyes widened as she was suddenly riddled with terror.

While Cindy was still fiddling with the IVs and the monitors, Alex took a few cautious steps forward. Picking up a small white towel, she slowly wiped the man's wrist to better see his antique gold watch. The images of the last few minutes started to merge in her mind: his athletic physique, his estimated age, and now the old and very distinctive watch he wore on his left wrist.

She tried to swallow but her mouth was already as dry as cotton. Barely able to move, she forced herself to the head of the stretcher, where she slowly dabbed the blood away from above his mouth and around his eyes. The multiple fractures of his jaw and other facial bones had already caused a great deal of swelling, which dramatically distorted his appearance.

"Alex, what are you doing?" Theo whispered in her ear. "We've got to get this guy upstairs right now."

With a few more sweeps of the towel, Alex was sure. In spite of his disfigured facial features, she knew it was her brother, David.

# Chapter 8

Unable to control her rapid breathing, Alex quickly became lightheaded.

Suddenly taken by the fear of passing out, she struggled to regain her composure by concentrating on one breath at a time. She hadn't even noticed but there was now a conspicuous hush in the room. She took an unsteady step backward.

Weak-kneed, she lost the strength in her legs and they began to buckle. Fortunately Theo was only a step away and was able to grab her around the waist and steady her in place.

"Alex, are you okay? Get a chair in here," he yelled.

She never heard the question and just looked across the trauma bay with a blank stare. Theo reacted immediately by gently escorting her to the other side of the room and then helping her into the chair. With his hand still on her shoulder, he then turned to Chet and said in a calm tone, "Listen to me. I want you to get this guy up to the operating room right now. You're in charge until I get there. Get him on the table and prep him from his neck to his knees. Keep giving him plenty of IV fluids. He'll need it to keep his pressure up. Anesthesia will help you. I'll be right up." Without asking any questions, Chet nodded, moved to the foot of the stretcher, and helped guide it out of the room. "I want everyone else out of here," he said, continuing in the same composed voice. He waited until everyone complied and then turned back to Alex. "Alex? Are you okay? What's wrong?" She slowly lifted her chin and then raised her hand. Her bloodstained fingers were quivering like feathers in the wind.

He was just about to renew his question when she spoke. "It's David," she began in barley above a whisper as her gaze dropped to the floor. "That man is my brother."

"Are you sure?" Theo asked, watching as the stretcher disappeared down the main corridor.

She nodded slowly. "I'm sure."

"My God," he whispered. He closed his eyes for a few seconds but then opened them and said, "Listen to me, Alex. I have to go upstairs with David. Will you be okay for a few seconds? I'm going to get Cindy."

Alex gazed up at Theo and nodded very slowly. "I'll be okay."

Walking backward, Theo made his way to the hall without taking his eyes off her.

"What the hell's going on in there?" Cindy asked as soon as he was out in the hall.

"Do we have a name on this guy or is he a John Doe?"

"The police just gave me his name. It's David Airoway," she answered.

"I can't believe this. Where's Dr. Runyon?" he asked.

"He called in sick about an hour ago. Dr. Calloway's covering for him."

"How far out is he?" Theo asked.

Cindy frowned. "We had a little communication problem because of the change."

"What the hell's that supposed to mean?"

"Nobody told the unit secretary. She just got hold of Calloway a couple of minutes ago. He'll be here in about fifteen minutes."

Theo looked into the trauma bay, shook his head, and then turned his attention back to Cindy. "Look, I'm going up to the OR. As soon as Calloway gets here, tell him to come straight up."

Cindy peered over Theo's shoulder at Alex. There was no disguising the bewilderment on her face. "What the hell's going on here, Theo? I've never seen Alex act like that."

"That's because the patient we just sent to the OR is her twin brother."

Cindy closed her eyes and then covered her mouth. "Are you sure? His face was so swollen . . . I mean—"

"It's him."

"I'll call Dr. Calloway again. Maybe we can reach him in his car," she said.

"Listen, let someone else do that. I need you to take care of Alex. Stay with her. I don't know what she'll need, but just stay with her."

Cindy raised her hand. "Just go to the OR. I'll look after her." She then waved the unit secretary over and asked her to see if they had a cell phone number for Dr. Calloway. After taking a deep breath, Cindy walked back into the trauma bay and made her way slowly across the room.

"Alex. Let's go into the lounge and wait. Everything's going to be okay. Theo's great and Dr. Calloway's on his way in. There's nothing you can do right now."

Her lips pressed together in silence, Alex looked up at Cindy. When their eyes met, Alex began to sob uncontrollably. Cindy assisted her to her feet and they made the short walk to the lounge, where Cindy helped her to the couch. Two aides on break who were watching TV had no trouble sizing up the situation. They turned off the television and tiptoed out of the room.

Sitting down next to Alex, Cindy put her arm around her shoulder. The two of them had always had a wonderful working relationship. Similar in personality and both single mothers, they had shared many of the same life experiences. During some quiet hours in the emergency room, they had shared a cup of coffee, talked about relationships, and just generally enjoyed each other's company.

"It'll be okay, Alex. You'll see. David's going to make it."

When Alex didn't answer, Cindy leaned forward to get a better look at her face. For the next thirty minutes, the only sound that disturbed the silence was an occasional soft whimper from Alex. Finally, with several moist tissues clenched in her hands, she stood up and looked at Cindy.

"I want to go upstairs and wait in the OR lounge." Even though she spoke in just above a hush, her voice still trembled.

"I'll go with you," Cindy said.

Together, the two women went upstairs. They sat on a long leather couch in the operating room lounge. Cindy tried to be optimistic and give Alex encouragement, but in reality neither of them had the first clue what news Theo and Tom Calloway would soon be bringing them.

# Chapter 9

Alex stood at the foot of David's bed studying his peaceful but otherwise expressionless face. It was ten A.M. and he'd had been out of surgery for almost nine hours.

He was heavily sedated and still dependent on the ventilator to breathe for him; his chest rose in the same rhythmic manner each time the machine clicked and inflated his lungs with highly concentrated oxygen. The operation to save his life had lasted only about an hour. Dr. Calloway and Theo had packed David's abdomen with a dozen or so huge sponges to stop the torrential liver bleeding with the plan of bringing him back to the operating room in about twelve to twenty-four hours, after David had been stabilized and they were sure there was no further bleeding.

Even though David had required eight units of blood during the operation, indications were that all the bleeding had now stopped. Carol Preston, an ICU nurse for fifteen years, hovered over him like a guardian angel, simultaneously keeping an eye on the monitors, administering medications, and sending off blood tests.

The injury to David's head was a serious one. The amount of swelling the brain had suffered was substantial and the direct cause of his coma. Carol finished checking David's abdominal dressing and then sat down on a small chair at the foot of the bed to catch up on her charting.

"What time are they planning on taking him back to the OR?" Alex asked even though Theo had already told her twice.

"Later this afternoon. If he does well they'd like to get another CT scan of the head right afterward." Carol placed her pen down on the clipboard and stood up. "I have two brothers myself but I've always wondered what it would be like to be a twin."

"It's very special," Alex said with a warm smile, taking a couple of steps forward and then reaching down to slide David's blanket a little higher on his chest. Alex had always been stumped when someone had asked her what it was like to have a twin. She could never quite find the words to accurately portray the shared instincts, unspoken language, and singular closeness of it.

"I'm not going to leave him," Carol promised, handing her a small box of tissues. Alex didn't answer. She watched David for another minute or so and then finally stepped away from the one person in the world she knew better than anyone else.

Feeling completely helpless as both a physician and a sister, Alex gathered herself by mustering all the optimism she could and said to Carol, "I know he's going to make it." Leaning over, she whispered in his ear, "Don't give up."

Carol put her hand on Alex's. "Why don't you go home for a few hours? You must be exhausted."

Alex took a deep breath and nodded. "I should see my daughter. I'll be back later."

As she started across the ICU, Alex was overcome with fatigue. She had just passed the nursing station when a voice called out to her. "Dr. Caffey," the unit secretary said, holding up the phone. "I have your secretary on the phone. There's a police officer in your office who'd like to speak with you."

After a soft groan and a few seconds of deliberation, Alex said, "Fine, tell Joyce I'll be right there."

# Chapter 10

When Alex walked into her office, Detective Maura Kenton of the Metropolitan Police Department was gazing out her window.

Alex waited a moment, assuming the woman would sense her presence and turn around, but when she didn't, Alex said, "It's quite a view of Georgetown University."

"It's spectacular," she said, turning around.

"When I first saw it I told the chief of our department that I had to have this office. Please sit down."

"My name's Maura Kenton. I'm a detective with Metro," she said, pausing just long enough to open her purse before sitting down. After rummaging around for a few seconds, she finally found her identification and held it up for Alex to see. "I know what you must be going through so I'll try not to take up too much of your time."

Outside the office, those who knew Maura might affectionately think of her as a bit of a scatterbrain, but that was hardly the case in her professional life. A police officer for ten years, she possessed an uncanny instinct for the job. A tireless plodder, she was single-minded when it came to the importance of details. She maintained an optimistic nature through the grimmest of times and, for the most part, managed to do her job while sidestepping most of the political pitfalls of being a police officer.

Instead of sitting behind her desk, Alex took a seat in the matching chair across from Maura's. "How can I help you?" she asked, taking note of the slight amber tint of Maura's skin, especially around her eyes. Alex guessed they were about the same age. Maura was much taller.

"Let me first ask you, how's your brother doing?" Maura inquired.

"He's stable right now but he's lucky to be alive. I'm trying to remain optimistic."

"I'll keep my fingers crossed with you."

Alex tried to smile. "I spoke to two of your officers earlier this morning," Alex said. "I'm a little surprised to hear that another wanted to speak with me."

"Really? Why's that?" Maura inquired, reaching into her purse and pulling out a small notepad and a pen.

"It seemed pretty obvious that your colleagues were convinced that David tried to commit suicide. They appeared quite satisfied to leave it at that."

"I read their report and then spoke with the officers. They both felt that it was a straightforward suicide attempt, but they mentioned to me that you weren't so sure that's what really happened."

"My brother didn't try to kill himself, Detective Kenton, and I doubt very seriously that he accidentally fell from his balcony."

"I see. Then you are saying he was assaulted."

"I don't see any other possibility," Alex maintained.

"What makes you so sure?"

Alex stood up and walked around to the back of her chair. "Because I know him as well as I know myself. If he were contemplating suicide, I would have known about it."

"When was the last time you saw your brother?"

"I had lunch with him the day he was attacked," Alex answered.

Maura reflected for a few moments, tapping her pad with the pen as she did. "Could he have been suffering from a severe illness? Perhaps something so serious that he didn't want to share it with you?"

"Are you asking me if my brother was terminally ill?"

"I mention it only as a possibility."

"I'm a physician. I think I would have seen signs of a grave illness, and besides, if David were ill, he would have told me."

"How can you be so sure?" Maura asked.

"Because he's my twin brother," she answered in a manner that called for no further explanation.

"How about his love life?" Maura asked.

"He's in a committed relationship."

"With a woman?"

"Yes, with a woman," Alex said, a little taken back.

Maura then asked, "Are you sure that's the type of relationship he really wants?"

Alex tipped her head to one side. "Are you asking me if my brother attempted to take his own life because he was deep in the throes of depression about being gay and conflicted about coming out?"

"I've seen it before—more often than you might think."

"The notion is preposterous," Alex assured her, moving back around the chair and again sitting down.

"Really? Why?"

"Do you have any brothers or sisters?" she asked Maura.

"Actually, I have a brother. He's two years older than me."

"Are you close?"

"I think we are," Maura answered.

"What's his favorite color?"

Maura thought for a few seconds. "I have no idea."

"How about his favorite restaurant or vacation spot?"

"I'd be guessing," she admitted.

"David's favorite color is sky blue and he'd move to New Zealand tomorrow if he could. What gets to your brother? I mean from an emotional standpoint."

"That one I can answer," Maura said with a laugh. "Absolutely nothing."

Alex leaned forward, fixing Maura with her eyes and said, "You're probably very wrong."

"What about David?" she asked. "What gets to him?"

"He is deeply saddened by anything that involves cruelty to animals and cries at any movie where long-lost family members are reunited or the athletically challenged triumph in the end. He's as predictable as the phases of the moon."

"I think I get your point," Maura said. "Let me try something else. Do you know of anyone who might have wanted to harm him—somebody who might be harboring a grudge or have some other reason to hurt him?"

The pause was long enough to make Maura look up from her notepad. "I'm not sure," Alex finally offered.

"You've lost some of your conviction."

"My brother is an investigative journalist. It's easy for him to step on the wrong toes or snoop around in places that ruffle people's feathers. It's an occupational hazard."

"Do you think that's what happened?" Maura asked.

"I . . . I don't know anything for sure."

"Do you know what he was working on?" It was already obvious to Alex that Maura was trying to keep an open mind regarding David's injuries. If she should tell her that he was trying to expose some diabolical hospital conspiracy that involved the murder of innocent patients, she might close the door on any possibility of eventually convincing Maura that David had been attacked. Maura again asked, "Do you have any idea what David was working on?"

"I'm sorry. I don't," Alex answered.

Maura again took note of Alex's hesitation, getting the feeling that she wasn't being totally forthcoming with her. She asked several more questions before she finally closed her pad and said, "I'd like to help you, Dr. Caffey, but without more to go on, there's really nothing I can do. Unfortunately, we live in a violent city and have a lot more allegations of assault and other violent crimes than people to investigate them. We're forced to be selective regarding the ones we pursue or else we'd be chasing a lot of dead ends."

Alex wasted no time in countering, "I wonder how the

public would feel if we told them that the trauma surgeons at Gillette were shorthanded and that we could treat only some of the critically injured patients that the paramedics wheel through our doors on a daily basis."

"I appreciate your frustration, Dr. Caffey. If it will make you feel any better, I can tell you that many of us in MPD feel the same way." Maura reached into her purse and pulled out one of her business cards. She waited for Alex to stand and then handed it to her. "I have to be honest with you. From what you've told me I think I'd have a hard time convincing my captain that we have enough to pursue a violent crime investigation."

"Supposing it weren't up to your captain?" Alex asked.

"Unfortunately, that's not the case." Maura fell silent for a few moments. Alex noticed that she was looking at one of the framed pictures on her desk. "Is that your daughter?" she asked.

"Yes, her name's Jessie. She's five."

Maura smiled. "I have a six-year-old with the same color hair." Alex noticed that Maura stole a quick glance at her hands while she was speaking.

"I'm divorced," Alex said.

Maura grinned again. "You're a pretty observant lady. You would have made a great cop. I'm single too," she said.

"How long have you been divorced?" Alex asked.

"Actually, my husband was a cop. He was killed on the job a few days after my daughter's first birthday."

"I'm so sorry," Alex said.

Maura looked away briefly. "We're doing okay," she said, stepping away from the chair. "I may want to speak with you again. You have my phone numbers. If any new information comes your way that might change things . . . or if you just want to talk, give me a call."


Turning down her street, Alex was again swept with a wave of extreme fatigue. Now that David was stable for the moment, and as she had had no sleep in well over twenty-four hours, the only thing on her mind was getting home and curling up on her favorite couch.

# Chapter 11

After what seemed to be a catnap at best, Alex was suddenly awakened by the sound of the front door opening. Checking her watch, she was astonished to find that it was almost three P.M.

The next sound she heard was the *clip-clop* of rapid footsteps across her hardwood floors.

"Hi, Mommy."

Alex sat up and pulled Jessie into a tight bear hug. "Hi, baby."

Healthy, bright, and an endless bundle of energy, Jessie Caffey was a pleasant handful. With a cherubic face and a devilishly seductive grin, she was an outspoken, inquisitive child who always had something on her mind. The picture of optimism, she loved everyone, especially her Uncle David.

Jessie said, "Grandma called. She's coming tonight."

"I know. You must be so excited," Alex said, tightening her grip until Jessie started to squirm and giggle uncontrollably.

Standing right behind Jessie was Olivia Mills, her au pair from Australia. Nothing short of a lifesaver, Olivia was a mature and competent young woman who loved Jessie dearly.

"You mother said that she'd take a cab from the airport," Olivia said.

"That's fine. I'll probably be at the hospital when she gets here. Just call me. By the way, I haven't told Jessie anything as yet."

"I understand," she whispered. "How's David doing?"

"He's stable. I should know more later today after surgery."

With a reassuring smile, Olivia held her crossed fingers in the air for Alex to see.

"Come with me downstairs, Mommy," Jessie yelled as she

ran down the hall. As tired as Alex was, she got up and headed for the basement door to spend some time with Jessie in her playroom.

As she descended the steps, Alex knew that the next twenty-four hours would be critical for David. For now, her focus had to be on his initial recovery. But once he was out of the woods that focus would change. She didn't care how positive the police were about what happened—they were dead wrong.

She was not by nature a confrontational person and could go along with the flow as well as anyone, but the matter of how David was injured was different. He didn't accidentally fall from his balcony, nor was he trying to kill himself.

He was deliberately attacked, and her best guess was for a specific reason—a reason she might have learned had she not been urgently paged back to the hospital in the middle of their lunch. Time was not an issue for her, and it didn't make a particle of difference how long it took. Eventually she would find out who was responsible for assaulting her brother.

# Chapter 12

**APRIL 23**

At least once a week, Simon Lott would take a brisk walk through Glover Archbold Park, a beautifully cared-for area situated on the west side of Georgetown.

Reminding him of Green Park in Dublin, the serene setting, slender in its layout, contained some of the prettiest and most secluded woodlands in the D.C. area. Beginning at an old stone tunnel, Lott followed the historic canal towpath as it meandered through the park. A haven for joggers and young parents with strollers, the park had long been one of the best-kept secrets in Washington. Lott wandered down the path for about ten minutes before taking a seat on a wooden bench that had recently been repainted a dark shade of green. As he faced west, the late-afternoon sun caused him to squint.

Lott first saw Morgan approaching when he was about twenty yards down the towpath. With Morgan's assistance, Lott had been able to extract an excellent flow of information from Gillette. He received reports twice daily and as of eight A.M., Robert Key was still unconscious. Without a word the rangy man with a sallow complexion dressed in a camel sports coat brushed off the bench and sat down.

"We still have some concerns that Dr. Key will regain consciousness before we are able to complete our business with him," he said as he looked in one direction and then the other. Apart from a middle-aged couple dressed in matching warmups who loped along in silence, no one was in sight.

Lott said, "I've already told you. Key will never cause a problem for you."

"Really? That sounds to me like a pretty authoritative opinion. I wasn't aware you had any medical training."

Lott's response was measured. "Spare me your sarcasm."

"We would just like some reassurance that the entire project hasn't become jeopardized."

"Then be reassured."

"What does that mean exactly?" Morgan asked.

"It means that he will never become a problem. Just leave the matter of Robert Key to me. That's why you hired me."

Morgan flicked a small bug off his sleeve. "Nobody's trying to trample on your independence. We would just like to remind you that we're making excellent progress and would like things to continue as smoothly as possible."

"As long as your money holds out and my personal safety is not at risk, I'm happy to comply with your wishes."

Morgan cast a dubious glance in Lott's direction. "I'm glad to hear that. Now, I want to talk to you about Alexandra Caffey."

"Who?" Lott asked, reaching into his coat pocket and pulling out a small paper clip.

"She's one of the trauma surgeons at Gillette. She's also David Airoway's twin sister."

Lott just gazed out over the park, untwisting the paper clip until it was straight, a habit he had developed as a boy in Dublin. He was expressionless for a time and then simply shook his head.

"David Airoway has a twin sister who works at Gillette. A doctor, of all things. Now, that might have been something worth knowing a few days ago."

Morgan made a rasping sound as he cleared his throat. "Let's just call it an oversight."

"If your reckless oversight should threaten to become my undoing," he said, "nobody in your organization will be safe."

"I said it was an error, Mr. Lott. Let's not dwell on the matter or make irrational threats. We're on the same team."

Feeling his abdominal muscles squeezing down, Lott cut a thin line in the bench with the paper clip. "Perhaps this would be a good time for you to tell me just how Dr. Caffey figures into all of this."

"We're not sure, but we have reason to believe that she doesn't think her brother tried to kill himself."

Lott asked, "And how would you know that?"

"Does it matter?"

"I can't work in a vacuum, Morgan."

"Let's just say we've been able to find out what she told the police."

Lott shrugged his shoulders. "As long as the police are calling it a suicide, who cares what she believes?"

"You may be right, but apparently she can be quite tenacious about things, and since she's in a position to create problems for us, she bears close watching."

"Close watching? Now, there's a definitive solution if I've ever heard one."

"You can't kill everybody who crosses your path," Morgan said impatiently. "For the time being, we just want you to keep a very close eye on her. Call me with a daily report. I want to know exactly where she's going, what she's doing, and especially who she's talking to. If she becomes a problem, well, there will be ample time to rethink our approach."

Lott patted his thighs a couple of times and then asked, "Are you asking me to baby-sit this woman?"

Morgan stood up; Lott did not. "If you have a problem

with that, tell me now and we can make arrangements to re-place you."

Lott dug the paper clip deeper into the bench. "I'll do it your way . . . for now," he said calmly.

"Good," Morgan said as he buttoned his sports coat.

"Is she married?" Lott asked.

"I beg your pardon?"

"I asked if she was married."

"I believe she's divorced."

"What about her family?" Lott asked.

"Her father died about twelve years ago. Her mother lives in Florida and Airoway's her only sibling."

"No kids?"

"She has a five-year-old daughter," Morgan said.

Lott grinned. "Now that's the first good piece of news you've given me. Kids can make for excellent leverage."

Morgan mumbled something under his breath and then said in a manner that left no room for ambiguity, "Listen to me. Why don't you just put those types of ideas on the back burner for now?"

"I was only thinking about the security of your project," Lott said.

Rolling his eyes, Morgan answered. "Why don't you leave that to me? As we discussed, just keep an eye on her for now and see if she's up to anything."

Morgan then turned and started back down the towpath in the same direction from which he had approached. If the man was foolish enough to think that Lott was going to leave a lot of witnesses around who could someday come back to haunt him, he was sadly mistaken—especially some officious woman doctor who was on a crusade in search of justice for her brother. Lott didn't know very much about the people Morgan claimed to represent, but he did have a strong inkling that they were well connected at the hospital and controlled a great deal of money.

Lott's attention was suddenly diverted by a leggy young jogger with curly strawberry blond hair. They exchanged a flirtatious smile. When she had gone down the path about ten yards, she stopped and began jogging in place. Lott watched, suspecting that she would steal a peek at him over her shoulder. He had long since made the self-admission that he was incapable of love, preferring the solitary life and avoiding any relationship he couldn't walk away from at the drop of a hat.

A few moments later, the young woman casually turned to sneak a glimpse of him. With a smug smile, he got up and strolled down the path to introduce himself.

# Chapter 13

When Morgan reached his car, he stopped before getting in and pulled out his cell phone. He took a quick look around and then tapped in a number.

"Yes."

"This is Morgan. I've just had a long chat with Mr. Lott. I think he understands what he needs to do."

"Are you sure?" the man asked.

"In spite of his recent performance, he came to us with an outstanding record. I'm confident he won't disappoint you any further."

"I hired you for a specific reason, Morgan. I'm paying you a small fortune to make sure my plans progress without any problems. Lott was your choice, not mine. I told you I thought he was a bit of a loose cannon and that you should handle these matters personally."

"You hired me for my brains, not my muscle. Lott brings certain unique skills to the table that I, frankly, don't have. There are plenty of Lotts in the world but people like me are a lot harder to come by."

"I guess that remains to be seen. I assume you've given him my latest instructions."

"I have," Morgan answered.

"And he still believes that you represent a group of people?"

"I think he does but as long as he's paid on time, I don't think he cares."

"But I do," the man said. "He's your responsibility. Make sure you keep a very careful eye on him."

Morgan flipped his phone closed and gazed out in the direction of the Washington Monument. In spite of his reassurances to his employer, he was starting to have doubts of his own about Lott's abilities.

# Chapter 14

Standing at the foot of David's bed studying his face, Alex was amazed at how much he had improved in the last twenty-four hours.

His facial swelling, especially around his eyes, had already started to diminish and there was just the hint of color back in his cheeks. David's second operation had been a complete success. A very encouraged Tom Calloway had spoken with Alex for almost an hour afterward, assuring her that David's prognosis was a good one.

"How's he doing?" came a worried voice from behind her.

Alex recognized it as belonging to Samantha Frost, David's girlfriend. A political analyst and consultant for an up-and-coming D.C. firm, Sam was a Vassar graduate who had endless patience for most of David's harmless peccadilloes. She had a classic face, a smile to match, and docile gray eyes.

Alex had gotten to know Sam quite well since David had begun dating her about a year ago, and from the beginning she thoroughly enjoyed her carefree and winsome manner. Alex knew how attached Sam was to David. Calling her to tell her about David's mishap was one of the hardest things she'd ever done.

Alex turned and took her two hands in her own. "He's going to make it, Sam."

"I was here earlier," she struggled to say. Behind her small glasses, her eyes began to fill with tears. "I . . . I tried but I couldn't stay with him very long. His face . . . I could barely recognize him."

"All of that swelling is going to go away in a few days. It looks a lot worse than it is. He's made it through two big operations. That's what's important."

With pursed lips, Sam tried to force a smile. "I'm going to sit with him for a while."

"I'll be in my office," Alex said. "Why don't you stop by before you leave? We'll go get some coffee."

"Okay," she said sitting down in a small wooden chair. "Give me about an hour."

Alex had taken only a few steps toward the exit when she saw a nicely dressed man craning his head to the side to look into David's bay. At first Alex was going to ignore him, but it occurred to her that he might be someone David worked with.

"My name is Alex Caffey. I'm David's sister. Can I help you?" she asked.

The man extended his hand. "My name's Marc Gilbert. I was the one who found your brother and called the police. How's he doing?"

"He's stable right now," Alex said. "It was very kind of you to check on him personally."

Marc's complexion turned a little red. "I felt kind of bad because I have absolutely no training in CPR. Maybe I could have done something."

"I don't think so, Mr. Gilbert. I'm very thankful that you found him when you did and called 911. If much more time had gone by . . . well, I don't think he would have made it."

Marc's expression suddenly changed to a more encouraged one. "I hadn't thought about it that way," he said. "I'm going to get going now. I'm glad your brother's doing well. Would you mind if I visited again?"

"Absolutely not. I don't think David would mind a visit from the man who saved his life."

Marc's color became even more red. "It was nice talking to you," he said.

Alex walked with Marc across the ICU, thanked him again, and started for her office. She was about halfway there when her pager went off. She recognized the extension and stopped at the information counter in the main lobby to use the physicians' phone.

"Dr. Goodman's office. Eileen speaking."

"Hi, Eileen. It's Dr. Caffey."

"He asked me to page you and see if you had a few minutes for him."

"Of course," she answered. "Tell him I'll be right there."

Dr. Owen Goodman was Gillette's nationally renowned chief of surgery and the one who had recruited and hired Alex. There was no one she respected more. As soon as she hung up the phone she was on her way to his office.

# Chapter 15

Five minutes after Alex left Sam in the ICU, she found herself in Owen Goodman's wood-paneled office, which was at least twice the size of hers.

"I truly appreciate your concern, Owen, but I prefer to get back to work as soon as possible. I'm not on call again until Wednesday and I see no reason why I can't take my normal turn in the rotation."

"Don't you think you might benefit from a week or two off?" he asked.

Waiting for her response, Goodman steepled his thin fingers and then placed his hands on an old faded black blotter that some said he had purchased the day he took the job at Gillette ten years earlier. Being of meager stature, Goodman almost looked like a child sitting behind his enormous pedestal-style mahogany desk. With slumped shoulders and cauliflower ears, he was hardly an attractive man, nor did he fit the mold of the typical high-powered trauma surgeon, but there was very little in the realm of traumatic injuries that Owen Goodman wasn't quite adept at treating. Soft-spoken, he was a man who was cautious in his ways but decisive when he needed to be.

"The worst thing for me is to sit idly at home," Alex went on. "I need to get back to work," she insisted as Owen fiddled with a stack of surgical journals.

He took a deep breath, looked at her in a reassuring manner, and then stood up. He walked slowly across his office and then stopped in front of his bookcase and looked with pride at the collection of perfectly spaced antique microscopes that occupied the middle shelves. "I hand-picked you for this job, Alex. I've always been impressed by your sound judgment. I've shared those feelings with the dean of the medical school. So I'm going to make this your call. As long as you feel that you're able to work, it's okay with me."

"Thank you."

"But remember, I'm still the boss around here and it's my responsibility to ensure the highest quality of patient care. If you even feel for a second that you're not up to working then I assume you will take yourself off the schedule and contact me at once."

"You have my word."

"Okay, as of now, you're back in the rotation."

"Thank you." Owen returned to his desk and took a seat in a high-backed upholstered chair that faced Alex. She glanced over at his credenza, where he displayed many of his awards for his prize-winning roses. Having long been an avid enthusiast and grower, he had become a well-recognized authority on the subject. "It looks like you've added another award," she said pointing to the plaque.

Slightly red-faced, he smiled with pride. "I'm particularly proud of that one. The competition was brutal."

Alex pressed her lips together to fight back a giggle. When she was sure she was sufficiently composed she said, "I'm sure you deserved it."

After gazing proudly at the award for a few more seconds, Owen turned back around and asked, "Have the police come up with anything yet?"

Alex moved forward in her chair, cleared her throat, and said, "At the moment they're calling it an attempted suicide, but I don't believe it for a second."

Owen crossed his right leg over the left. "How can you be so sure the police are wrong?"

"I just am," she said, pausing for a moment to study his reserved expression that revealed nothing.

"Theo mentioned to me that the police found no signs of a struggle or a break-in at David's apartment."

"It doesn't matter what they did or didn't find. David's a stranger to them. If they knew him the way I do, they'd know that there was no way he tried to take his own life."

"Suicide's a strange phenomenon, Alex. I don't think any of us truly understand it. You love David. He's your brother. Perhaps you're not being totally objective."

She paused to make sure her response sounded controlled. "If you accept the premise that David fell from his balcony, then how do you explain the fact that he suffered no broken bones except in his face? And with a deceleration injury of that magnitude, why didn't he tear his aorta in half and bleed to death? Patterns of injuries resulting from falls have been studied over and over again. How many people have you seen who have fallen four stories, landed on concrete, and lived to talk about it?"

Owen nodded. "Sometimes injury patterns don't make sense, and I guess if you've been around as long as I have, you've seen just about everything." Alex could detect the uneasiness in his face. His response was unscientific and conciliatory and it was clear to her that she had said enough, but before she could change the subject, he asked, "Has your mother arrived yet?"

"She flew in last night."

"How's she doing?"

"She's a strong lady. I've been painting as rosy a picture as I can for her. She's holding up pretty well."

"Is there anything I can do?" he asked.

Alex smiled. "Not right now, Owen, but I appreciate your concern." She paused for a moment, rethinking his offer. "There is something I'd like to talk to you about. Do you have another few minutes?"

"Of course," he said.

"What can you tell me about the Caduceus Project?"

With a puzzled expression, Owen ran his fingers through his thinning salt-and-pepper hair. "With all that's going on in your life right now, why in the world would you be interested in the Caduceus Project?"

"The day David was injured, I had lunch with him. He was considering doing a story on organized medical societies with major political agendas. He specifically mentioned the Caduceus Project."

A shadow of uncertainty inched across Owen's face. "Are you sure this isn't something that can wait?" His manner was supportive, not patronizing, but Alex knew that nobody knew more about Gillette and its medical staff activities than Owen. If anyone was in a position to enlighten her, it was him, but she was reticent to disclose too much of what David had told her at lunch, especially after his specific instructions to the contrary. Alex was trying not to overreact, but she couldn't ignore the possible connection between David's interest in the Caduceus Project and the fact that he was now lying in an intensive care unit clinging to life.

She explained, "David got hurt before we could finish our conversation. I'm just trying to find out a little more about the Caduceus Project."

"They've been around about ten years. They don't have the long history that many of our other national fellowships and organizations do, but they're very aggressive with respect to their political agenda and have managed to gain considerable support and momentum. The first chapter was founded right here at John Adams and is by far the largest and most influential in the country."

Alex asked. "I know that they're very conservative, but what's the thrust of the organization?"

"According to Victor Runyon, who's the president of the Adams chapter and an influential member of the national board, they are principally interested in major medical issues, especially national health insurance."

Alex was surprised by Owen's comments. She'd known Victor Runyon since she started at Gillette. He was regarded by most of his colleagues as a marginal trauma surgeon. Aloof in many ways, he had never struck her as a political activist.

"I didn't realize Victor was so involved in political issues."

"He's passionate about the project, and, as I said, a major player at a national level. In fact, he may very well be the next national director. There are many who might not agree with their politics but they're certainly to be commended for their energy and passion."

"Why do you say that?" she asked.

"Because most societies are made up of a pretty diverse group of physicians with a broad range of political persuasions. More often than not, they're largely social and poorly organized when it comes to political issues. The Caduceus Project is just the opposite. They're highly organized and single-minded in their philosophy, which is ultraconservative and opposed to any progressive changes in our health care system. Some fairly enlightened people believe they are destined to become the most influential medical-political group in the country."

"I had no idea. What other issues have they focused on?" she asked.

"As I mentioned, their main initiative is opposing the implementation of any form of national health insurance, but they're also very much involved in managed care reform, stem cell research, and tort reform with respect to malpractice."

"How can I learn more about the specifics of their agenda?" she asked.

"I'd speak directly to Victor. I'm sure he'd be happy to bend your ear until it broke on the project's initiatives. It's his favorite topic of conversation, especially if he felt he might be able to persuade you to join."

"Join?" Alex asked with a curious grin.

"Be careful," he advised with a fatherly grin and a raised index finger. "Victor can be very convincing, and if you do decide to get involved in the Caduceus Project, don't be surprised if the next call you get is from the membership chair of the John Birch Society."

"I'm not sure, but I doubt very seriously that I'd fit the Caduceus Project profile. What about you?"

"Me?" Owen replied with a short chuckle. "I've never been a political person. My supreme goal is to offend nobody and the best way to do that is to stay out of politics."

"I thought you were a member of . . . uh . . . that organization I can never remember the name of."

"It's called the Partnership for a Healthy America and we're not exactly political. We support programs that address child abuse, infant vaccinations, teenage drug abuse, and prevention of nursing home abuse. So far we've managed to offend nobody and that's the way we'd like to keep it."

"Which would be a little different from the Caduceus Project," Alex added.

"I would hope so." Owen stood up and Alex followed. Taking her by the arm as if they were attending a presidential dinner at the White House, he escorted her across his office and out into the hall before saying good-bye.

On her way back to her own office, she began second-guessing her decision not to be more open with Owen. It would be nice to have someone like him to confide in, and he had always been a straight shooter and very supportive of her efforts. But the last thing she wanted to do was appear irrational—and that's exactly what might happen if she shared her suspicions regarding David's injuries with him. If he felt she was pursuing some ludicrous conspiracy theory, it might give him serious reason to doubt his decision about agreeing to let her go back to work.

Fortunately there was someone else, however, in whom she could comfortably confide. As opposed to Owen, she had absolutely no reservations about being totally direct and candid with Micah Henry.

# Chapter 16

Micah Henry, the chief operating officer of the Gillette Trauma Center, sat in the main lobby of his hospital watching Jessie Caffey marvel at the exotic fish as they darted about in an elaborate saltwater aquarium. The tank, which had been donated by a grateful family, was a nice addition to an already beautifully decorated lobby.

Micah, an exceptionally talented hospital administrator, had been named as the COO four years earlier. Some felt he lacked sufficient seasoning at age thirty-four for the job, but he was appointed above their protests and promptly silenced the naysayers by proving that he was a forthright man who led by example. His six-foot-two frame was barely accommodated by the Corvette convertible he insisted on driving. His cheekbones were edged and projected outward. A widower of several years, he was physically fit and good-looking and was still high on Gillette's heartthrob list even though he had recently become engaged.

While keeping a careful eye on Jessie, Micah glanced across the lobby as the elevator doors opened, allowing Jeanette Airoway, Alex's mother, to step off. As soon as he made eye contact with her, he smiled broadly and waved. They met in the middle of the lobby, where Jeanette immediately gave him a huge hug.

Jeanette was a commonsense, level-headed woman with an undying passion for children. For the last fifteen years, she had served as the principal of a small private school in Fort Lauderdale. Trim with an aristocratic face, a pearly complexion, and a florid voice, she was an erudite woman who had often confessed that raising twins had been no easy matter, but to her it was a labor of love and she had accomplished it with complete fairness, patience, and devotion.

"How are you doing?" he asked, noting how spent she appeared.

"I still don't understand how such a horrible thing could happen," Jeanette said before pausing for a few moments to collect herself. She tried in vain to smile and then added, "The last time I saw David, Alex, and you together was in high school." Looking past him, she added, "I guess these aren't the circumstances under which I was hoping to see you all together again. I remember the day Alex interviewed here and told me you were the hospital administrator."

"I guess it was quite a surprise to both of us. We should have tried harder to stay in touch over the years." Micah moved forward and put his hands on her shoulders. "Everything's going to be fine, Jeanette. David's getting great care. He's going to make it."

"Alex told me that David's going to be okay. For now, that's all I need to know." Jeanette reached out and took Micah by his wrists. "It's so good to see you again. I feel so much better knowing that you're here. I just pray he's not in too much pain," she said just above a whisper, struggling with each word.

"Alex said that David's getting a lot of medication for pain and sedation, which means that when he's better, he's not going to remember any of this."

"I hope so," she said, closing her eyes briefly. "I recall how I felt when my Jim died. I'm not ready to go through that again." Jeanette opened her purse and removed a moist, crumpled tissue. "Jim was so proud of you when you were appointed to the naval academy. I'm sorry he didn't get to see you graduate."

"It would have been my great honor to have him there."

"Thank you, Micah," she said. "I know there's nothing I can do for David except pray, but I'm worried about Alex."

"Alex is a tough lady. She'll get through this okay. Try to stay positive."

"Grandma," Jessie said, running over and grabbing her wrist. "Come see the fish."

"I'll be right over, honey, but I want to talk with Micah for another minute or two first."

"Okay," she said with a pout, "but hurry up."

Jeanette waited until Jessie ran back across the lobby to the aquarium before continuing her conversation with Micah. "David didn't have an enemy in the world. I just don't understand why anyone would do such a thing."

At a loss for words, Micah just nodded. It was obvious that, just as Alex had done, Jeanette had dismissed the possibility that David might have attempted suicide.

"When will Alex be down?" he asked.

"In a few minutes. Just as we were leaving the ICU, one of David's doctors came in. Alex wanted to talk with her for a few minutes." Jeanette glanced over at Jessie and without looking back asked, "So tell me the truth, Micah. How's my daughter doing?"

"She's come a long way in the last two days."

"I worry about her."

"You don't have to. I've got my eye on her," he said.

"Just like you used to do in high school?"

Micah's face flushed. "Not exactly, Jeanette."

"Don't you think a mother knows when a young man has a crush on her daughter?"

"That was a long time ago, Jeanette." Micah hesitated for a few seconds, noted the skepticism in her eyes, and then asked, "Was it that obvious?"

"Maybe not to everyone, but I always suspected that Alex was a little smitten herself."

"Well, if she was, she was a master at concealing it. Maybe all of those boyfriends were just a clever way of disguising her unbridled love for me."

"Well, you can joke about it but I still say the only reason Alex took this job was because you were running the place."

Micah averted his eyes and then pushed his hands into his pockets. "I appreciate the compliment, Jeanette, but I think it had a lot more to do with Gillette and the fact that David worked mostly in D.C. than anything else."

"How's your son doing?"

"Gabe's doing just fine but I think he's fallen hopelessly in love with Jessie. The kids are great together. Alex and I try to take them out together at least a couple of times a week."

Micah glanced across the lobby just as the elevator doors opened to see Alex step off behind an elderly couple. Catching her eye, he motioned her over.

When she was about halfway across the lobby, Jeanette quietly tugged at his sleeve and whispered, "You still look at her the same way."

"Really, and how's that?"

"Like she's the most elegant woman you've ever seen."

"Just like her mother."

"Don't tease an old woman, Micah."

"You do know that I'm engaged?" Micah asked.

"I think Alex might have mentioned it," she said, dismissing his question.

As Alex neared, Micah watched her perplexed eyes scan the lobby. Before she could say anything, Jessie came flying across the floor and grabbed her around her legs.

"Where's Olivia?" Alex asked as she patted Jessie on the back and then kissed the top of her head.

"Micah told her to go home," Jessie said.

"Is that so?" Alex asked, casting a dubious glance Micah's way.

"She had to leave," Micah said with authority.

Alex furrowed her brow. "Really? How come?"

"I saw Jessie and Olivia sitting in the lobby and I came over to say hi. Olivia looked frantic. She told me that one of her close friends had just been in a car accident in Arlington, so I told her to go. I was going to call you in the ICU but I decided not to bother you." Micah paused, searching Alex's face for some sign of how his explanation was being received. When there was none, he went on. "I told her not to worry and that I'd watch the Jessie monster," he cried, reaching over and grabbing the little girl under the arms, which immediately caused her to shriek and burrow herself even deeper into her mother.

"Now wasn't that nice of Micah?" Jeanette piped in.

Alex crossed her arms. "Yes, Mom. That was very nice of Micah."

"Excuse us for a moment," Jeanette said. "Jessie and I are

going to look at the fish." Jessie immediately let go of Alex and ran off to join her grandmother.

"How long have you been waiting?" Alex asked.

"Only about fifteen minutes," he answered. "How's Dave doing?"

"A lot better than I expected. There's no evidence of any further bleeding and all of his vital signs are right on the money. Right now, I'd have to say things are looking pretty good."

"What about his head injury?"

The half smile that Alex had managed vanished from her face. "The repeat CT scan still doesn't show any hemorrhage but he has a lot of swelling." In a voice that had lost some of its optimism she said, "Time's the only thing that's going to tell us how bad his head injury is, but I'm hopeful."

Micah realized that Alex was speaking as David's sister and not his doctor. "Your optimism must be contagious because your mother's spirits seem to be okay."

"Well, it's not like he's out of the woods but he's come a long way in two days, which is an encouraging sign," she said, returning Jessie's wave. By the time Alex filled Micah in on the details of David's condition, Jessie and Jeanette had returned.

"So what were you and Micah doing while you were waiting for me?" Alex asked Jessie as she parted her bangs.

"Micah told me a story."

"Really," Alex said, mimicking Jessie's enthusiasm and animation. "And what was the story about?"

"Well, I wanted him to tell me *The Giving Tree,* but he didn't know that one, so he told me about these men on a big boat who had a monkey."

Alex glanced over at Micah, who immediately frowned and looked away.

"A monkey?" Alex asked. "Boy, that sounds like quite a story."

"Uh-huh. It was on this boat called the . . ." Jessie stopped for a moment and looked up at Micah, who tried to nonchalantly shake his head at her. When he didn't answer, she took a few steps forward and tugged at his sports coat.

"The *Caine,*" he whispered.

Alex nodded a couple of times and then smiled as if she were just about to advance her queen and declare checkmate.

"Jessie said *monkey*. I don't suppose what she really meant to say was *mutiny*."

"Maybe," Micah confessed.

"You told my daughter the story of the *Caine mutiny*?" she asked with a giggle. "She's only five years old, Micah."

"It's a great saga of the sea, and anyway, I don't know any stories for girls. Gabe loves my navy stories," he added with conviction.

"I don't believe you. I guess you can take the man out of the navy but you can't take the navy out of the man."

"Very funny, but I'll have you know that Jessie was really interested in that story, and, by the way, you shouldn't limit her horizons. Maybe she'll grow up to be a Navy SEAL."

Alex hoisted her purse a little higher on her shoulder. "I guess what I envision for my daughter is her saving the seals, not being one."

Micah pointed his finger. "That's just the type of horse-and-buggy thinking that's dragging women down in this country." Micah's voice changed to a more serious one. "You're not mad, are you?"

"Let's just say I'll forgo convening an admiral's mast for the time being."

Micah glanced down at his watch. "I better get going or I'll be late. I have to pick Maxine up at the airport. She and her boss are getting in from Hong Kong."

"Hong Kong? I thought they were in Italy."

"That was last week."

"I see," Alex said. Micah knew she had very definite opinions regarding his fiancée but was very diplomatic in how she expressed them.

"I guess that's what you have to expect if you're engaged to a talented fashion designer," Micah said.

"Give Maxine my best."

"I certainly will."

Alex then said, "I'm going to come by your office. There's something important I want to talk to you about. How's your schedule for the next couple of days?"

"Not too bad. I should be there most of the time," he said

before saying good-bye to Jessie and Jeanette. As he headed for the exit, Alex watched until he disappeared.

"It's too bad that he may be spoken for, Alexandra," came a familiar voice from behind her.

The warm feeling Alex was experiencing disappeared as she turned around with an affectionate jeer. "Cut it out, Mom. Micah's a wonderful man but we're just very good friends—and please don't call me Alexandra."

"Excuse me, dear. I just think someone of your age and gender should have a woman's name."

"Fine, I'll go along with the Alexandra thing if you promise not to torture me ever again about Micah."

"I'm not the type of mother to interfere in her children's lives."

Alex rolled her eyes. "I'm glad to hear you say that."

"I know you too well for that. For goodness' sakes, I remember when Micah would come around pretending he wanted to see David when it was really you he was looking for."

Alex gave her mother a quick hug and then a peck on the cheek. In spite of her direct nature, Alex could never stay annoyed at the woman she adored for too long.

"I think your imagination's working overtime again, Mom."

"Did you know that Dad wrote Micah a beautiful letter in support of his application to the naval academy?"

"I think you've mentioned that to me a couple of hundred times."

Undaunted, Jeanette studied her daughter's face and then squeezed her hand. "Be patient, dear. I know you'll meet the right man some day. There are other men out there just as wonderful as Micah."

Alex counted silently to five before responding. "You've been watching too many old movies on TV again, Mother. My life does not revolve around finding a man. I'm busy with my career. You act like I never go out on a date."

"Well, it seems like lately you've had a lot of first dates."

"You know what they say, Mom—you have to kiss a lot of toads." Alex reached down and kissed the top of Jessie's head.

"C'mon, baby. Grab Grandma's hand. It's okay to squeeze it as hard as you want."

"Where are we going?" Jessie asked.

"How about pizza?" Jeanette asked.

"I'd rather have shrimp," Jessie said flatly.

"Shrimp?" Jeanette asked, casting a critical eye at her daughter. "It's always so lovely to encounter a young child with such sophisticated tastes."

"Well then, shrimp it will be. Let's go, honey. Grandma's buying," Alex said with an affectionate smile as she took Jessie's hand. She looked over toward the exit, thinking about Micah and just how much she valued his friendship. The thought lingered for only a few moments because in the next instant, Jessie extended her other hand to her grandmother, and together the three of them marched across the lobby.

# Chapter 17

**APRIL 25**

After finishing three hours of tedious paperwork in her office, Alex decided she needed her sacrosanct afternoon caffeine boost.

Outside her office, at the end of the corridor and next to the stairwell, the hospital had arranged for a bank of food and beverage machines. Alex popped four quarters into the coffee machine, barely noticing a young man wearing a dark baseball cap who approached from behind her.

Scanning the selections of the machine next to hers, he said in a calm voice, "I know what they're up to."

"I beg your pardon?" Alex said as she turned and looked at the man.

"Please don't look at me," he said. "Just look straight

ahead at the machine." When she complied, he went on. "What happened to your brother was no accident."

Alex remained calm, tapping the button for black coffee.

"Who are you?" she asked.

"I'm a friend of Robert Key, the doctor who met with your brother."

The name was vaguely familiar to her and she now seemed to recall that David had mentioned it at lunch. She looked over her opposite shoulder to make sure nobody else was around.

"I'd like to speak with Robert," she said, making sure to proceed with an abundance of caution.

"You might find the conversation a tad one-sided. You see, he's in a coma downstairs in your ICU probably being watched by more than his nurse, so if you're thinking of running down there . . . well, I'd think again."

Struggling to remain composed, she asked, "Why are you so interested in my brother and Robert Key?"

"I don't know . . . justice, retribution for a lifelong friend. I guess there are a lot of reasons."

Alex watched as the coffee cup filled but didn't reach for the cup. "I'm not sure what you—"

"Listen to me, Dr. Caffey. Robert Key wasn't mugged and your brother didn't try to commit suicide. We need to talk."

"My office is right down the hall. We could go—"

"I don't think that's such a good idea," he said. "Are you familiar with Tryst?"

Having been at the art-filled café a number of times, Alex cleared her throat and answered, "Yes, I am."

"Meet me there Thursday night at nine. I'll be at the bar. There are some rather grim things you should know about your hospital and what's going on with the Caduceus Project."

"The Caduceus Project?" Alex demanded with a sudden intensity in her voice. "What do you know about the Caduceus Project?"

"Take it easy, Doctor. I'm not answering any questions now. Just meet me at Tryst." When Alex didn't immediately respond, he stated, "This is a onetime offer, Dr. Caffey. If you're not there by nine, I'll assume you're not coming and you'll never hear from me again."

"What's your name?" she asked.

"Kurt," he answered. "Enjoy your coffee."

With that, he looked down the hall, marched straight toward the stairwell, and disappeared.

Standing about fifty feet away, Simon Lott stood with his arms crossed, pretending to read one of the numerous announcements that were haphazardly posted on a large bulletin board. Having seen Kurt make his exit, he smiled and shook his head. He had always found that dealing with meddlesome amateurs was nothing more than a boring chore, but at the moment he could see no alternative.

When he heard the chime of the elevator across the hall from him, he turned, smiled at the two young students in white coats, and stepped aboard. As the elevator started down, Lott realized that Kurt had spoken to Dr. Caffey for only a minute or so and couldn't have revealed too much. He assumed that Kurt's main reason for coming to Gillette was to set up a meeting with her, which hardly concerned him because he was quite confident that no such meeting would ever take place.

Still numb, Alex absently lifted the piping-hot cup of coffee to her lips and started to take a sip. The pain reflex was instantaneous as she pushed the cup away. Turning immediately toward the water fountain, she bent over and took a long swallow.

Returning to her office, Alex tried to remember every word Kurt had said, but her heightened anxiety dealt a blow to her memory and she found herself wondering whether he was nothing more than a crackpot. It was a moot point. She was going to show up at Tryst. Her next thought was to call Micah, but she feared he'd insist on going with her to the meeting. She was tempted to go downstairs to the ICU to see what she could learn about Robert Key, but Kurt's admonition echoed in her mind and she quickly decided that at least until after their meeting, she'd heed his advice.

In the meantime, there was one thing she could do and that was make sure that he'd given her accurate information. She spun her chair around, stopping in front of her flat-screen monitor. Bringing up the hospital census, she typed in Robert's name. The screen changed and confirmed that he was indeed a patient at Gillette, currently in the ICU.

Alex edged forward in her chair. Staring at the screen in deliberation, she decided that patience was the best approach and that she wouldn't speak with anybody until after she'd met with Kurt. *How much difference could a couple of days make?* she thought to herself as she reached forward and turned off the monitor.

Her impatience aside, Alex tried to take solace in the fact that in a little over forty-eight hours, the man who had just spoken to her at the coffee machine might unlock the door to what had really happened to David.

# Chapter 18

As Kurt Findlay proceeded north on I-270 toward his motel in Rockville, he was having second thoughts about his meeting with Alex Caffey.

His initial impression was that she would definitely meet him, but now, and for reasons he couldn't quite pinpoint, he had his doubts. He had known Robert Key since grade school. They had remained best friends for the majority of the ensuing years even though personal circumstances had separated them. Kurt was a physically unfit individual with a mustard complexion and a prematurely wrinkled brow. A high school math teacher from Altoona, Pennsylvania, he was an unpretentious man with solid values who had never been consumed by lofty ambitions.

Robert had begun seriously confiding in Kurt about two months ago. Most recently, Robert had given him careful instructions what to do if anything unexpected happened to him. Had it not been for the extraordinary relationship the two men had, Kurt probably wouldn't have believed a word of what Robert told him about what was going on at Gillette.

The last time they had spoken was early on the day that Robert was attacked. Kurt's clear recollection was that Robert sounded concerned but not desperate. Over the next four days, Robert didn't return any of his phone calls. Only after calling every hospital in D.C. did Kurt find out that Robert was in the ICU at Gillette. Acting on Robert's specific instructions, Kurt came to Washington and attempted to contact David Airoway. Failing that, he was to locate Alex Caffey and arrange a meeting with her.

The traffic was heavy and by the time Kurt reached his motel outside D.C. it was five-fifteen. He dreaded the idea of sitting in his room all night and decided to go out to an early movie and then grab a quick dinner. As it turned out, the movie wasn't much better than the dinner and at nine-thirty he was back in his motel room.

After a leisurely shower, he climbed into bed. Staring at the ceiling, he again wondered whether Alex Caffey would show up for their meeting. He hadn't slept very well the night before and the cool jet of air from the vent above the bed was a welcome hypnotic. It usually took him at least thirty minutes to fall asleep but on this night it took only five.

"Mr. Findlay," came a voice and then a knock from outside Kurt's door. He awakened and was instantly wide-eyed. Rolling over, he looked at the small digital clock on the night table. It was ten after eleven. "Mr. Findlay?" the voice repeated, again followed by a loud rap.

"I'm coming," he answered. "Who is it?"

"My name's Brad Tolliver. I'm the assistant manager. I'm afraid someone's broken into your car."

"Shit," he muttered under his breath, having just gone through the same thing six months ago in Altoona. It wasn't as if he were driving a Ferrari, for God's sake. What was all the interest in a three-year-old Taurus, he wondered as he approached the door. He pressed his eye up to the observation port. A man with a full head of white hair, dressed in a button-down dress shirt and a striped tie, stood at the door with an easy smile. Kurt opened the door.

"I'm sorry to have to have to be the one to bring you this bad news, Mr. Findlay," he said.

"Come in."

Stepping into the room, he advised Kurt, "I've already called the police. They should be here anytime."

"What the hell happened?" Kurt asked as he closed the door.

Instead of an answer, his inquiry was met with Simon Lott's pistonlike fingers penetrating squarely into both of his eyes. The intense pain sent him sprawling backward into the middle of the room. The agonizing burning crescendoed as it cleaved behind his eyes and then fanned out across his temples. Completely blinded, Kurt began groping for the wall to reclaim his balance but before he could, Lott was on him. Using a five-hundred-pound monofilament line as a garrote, Lott stepped forward, looping it around the front of his throat. Before Kurt could react, Lott quickly slid by him, first passing shoulder to shoulder and then taking up a position behind him.

Now almost back to back with him Lott crisscrossed the garrote around Kurt's throat. When the line was as tight as Lott could make it, he snapped himself forward. As he bent forward at the waist, Kurt came flying off the ground until his back was parallel to the floor as if he were in the middle of a back flip. His momentum and Lott's strength carried him further backward until he completed the somersault. When he struck the floor, the result was as predictable as the outcome of a shell game. His skull was fractured in three places and his neck was fatally snapped. The entire sequence took less than ten seconds. Kurt Findlay was dead before Lott could remove the line from around his throat.

Before leaving, Lott took a few minutes to go through Kurt's pockets and search the room. Finding nothing of interest, he made his way over to the door, cracked it, and then checked the hall. There was nobody in sight.

As he rode the elevator down, he was pleased that everything had gone off as planned. He smiled in anticipation of what that dolt Morgan would find to complain about this time.

# Chapter 19

As Alex came through the line of the doctors' dining room, she spotted Victor Runyon eating alone and reading the morning paper. After her conversation with Owen Goodman, she had planned on talking with him later in the week but the present opportunity seemed too good to pass up.

Victor had joined the faculty at Gillette about five years earlier than Alex. Wiry in form with a pencil mustache, he had a distinct penchant for avoiding extra work. Alex found him a tad on the pompous side and, at times, annoyingly arrogant.

"Do you mind if I join you?" Alex asked as she approached his table.

Victor looked up, pushed his black reading glasses down toward the tip of his nose, and, with no warmth in the gesture, pointed to the chair across from him. "Have a seat," he said. "Where's your usual mob of students and residents?"

She shrugged as she pulled out the chair across from him. It was well known among the faculty that the residents and students didn't care much for Victor and had little if any rapport with him. "I guess they must be on rounds," she said.

"How's your brother doing?" he asked, as if he were inquiring about any patient on the service.

"He's been rock stable. If you had asked me that first night if I thought he'd look this good so quickly, I would have said no way."

"Is he starting to wake up?"

"Not yet," she said with a sigh. "I spoke with Milt Sawyer from neurosurgery earlier today and he told me not to expect too much for several more days."

"I guess under the circumstances that's understandable,"

he said, folding the business section of the paper in half and then sliding it under his tray. "Any clue about how all this happened?" he asked just before popping a piece of melon in his mouth.

"That depends on who you ask. The police are convinced that David tried to kill himself."

"It sounds like you don't agree."

"Let's just say I'm not sure what happened."

"I see," he said, obviously having little interest in pursuing the conversation.

"I'm glad I ran into you. There's something I've been wanting to ask you about."

Victor's eyes were watchful. "Sure, go ahead."

"Owen told me that you're very involved with the Caduceus Project."

"I would say that's a fair statement," he answered after a moment's hesitation.

"He mentioned that you were an advisor on the national council. How many advisors are there?" she asked.

"Only twelve. We're trying to keep the key leadership limited."

"I'd like to hear more about the organization," Alex said, sensing that Victor was responding in a guarded fashion to her questions. His manner surprised her a little in light of what Owen had said about his unbridled enthusiasm regarding the Caduceus Project.

After a few seconds of silence, he reached down, pulled his pager off his belt, squinted as he read the display, and then frowned. "As much as I'd like to talk to you about the project, I'm afraid we'll have to do it some other time. I have to go," he said, rising to his feet.

"Maybe I'll stop by your office later this week," Alex said, noticing that he had barely touched his breakfast.

He threw her a courtesy nod and then stepped away from the table. As she watched him walk away, she doubted that he had really gotten a page, assuming it was more likely that she had strayed into an area that he had no interest in discussing. Whatever his reasons, Alex was quite perplexed that the mere mention of the Caduceus Project made him so ill at ease that he felt compelled to invent some ludicrous pretense for leaving.

# Chapter 20

After a grueling night in the operating room, Theo Hightower was just about to try to grab a couple of hours of sleep before six A.M. rounds when he got a stat page from the floor.

Putting his fatigue aside and without wasting the time to call, he sprinted up the three flights of stairs, arriving at the nursing station in less than two minutes. Babs Clancy, the charge nurse, was waiting for him.

"What's going on?" he asked, still puffing.

"It's Kyle Dolan. He looks awful."

"What do you mean?"

"He can barely breathe. I put some oxygen on him but he's not showing any signs of improvement."

"When did all this start?" Theo asked.

"It must have just happened. I checked him forty minutes ago and he was fine. I went back to his room because I left my stethoscope in there and he looked like he was about to code. That's when I called you."

Kyle was a seventeen-year-old center fielder from De-Matha High School who had high hopes of playing for Rutgers in the fall. In a freak accident during practice, he had collided with one of his teammates, catching the brunt of the fall on his neck. The result was two fractured vertebrae. He was taken immediately to Gillette but in spite of intensive therapy, the injury proved to be irreversible and he was left a paraplegic. No longer requiring an intensive care setting, Kyle had been transferred to a private room on Four West only three days earlier. With his immediate care now completed, he was awaiting transfer to the rehabilitation unit.

Theo was generally the type of physician who preferred to

remain detached from his patients, but Kyle was the exception. Kyle reminded him of his younger brother, and Theo had taken an immediate liking to the young man mainly because of his undying optimism and faith in the face of such a devastating injury.

"Is he having any chest pain?" Theo asked as he headed for Kyle's room.

"I'm not sure. He was having a lot of trouble responding to my questions."

"What about his vital signs?"

"I got a full set right after I called you. His pulse is one-sixty and his pressure's eighty."

"Shit," he muttered more to himself than anyone else.

When they entered Kyle's room, one of the other nurses on duty was attempting to tighten an oxygen mask on his face. Theo glanced at the oxygen saturation monitor, a device that measured the amount of oxygen in a patient's bloodstream. It read sixty percent, the normal range being from about ninety-five to one hundred.

"Get me another blood pressure," he told Babs as he approached the bed. He then turned to her and whispered, "Get the crash cart in here right now. We need to get a tube in him, and get respiratory therapy up here—we'll need a ventilator." Babs signaled the other nurse, who immediately ran out of the room and wheeled in the large red cart that contained all the emergency supplies and medications that would be needed in the event of a full-blown cardiac arrest.

At that same moment, Payton Waverley, the third-year surgical resident on call, and her medical student came crashing through the door. Payton was a late entry into medical school, having taught high school biology for ten years before deciding to finish premed. Always willing to work, she was a promising resident and one for whom the department of surgery had high hopes.

"What's going on?" Payton asked.

"I think Kyle's had a pulmonary embolus," Theo told her. "We need to get a tube in him right now."

Payton turned to her first-year medical student, Emily Jeffcoat, who looked hopelessly in the dark. Trying to help her through her first clinical crisis as a medical student, she explained, "A pulmonary embolus is a blood clot that has broken off from a vein and traveled to the lungs. The clot blocks the blood from getting to the lungs, so the body quickly becomes starved for oxygen. The large ones are usually fatal."

"Kyle? Can you hear me?" Theo asked.

When there was no answer, Theo ordered the appropriate medication to heavily sedate him and then inserted a lighted scope deep into his mouth. The scope allowed him to see the vocal cords, which mark the entrance to the windpipe. When the cords were clearly in view, Babs handed him a plastic tube and Theo quickly slid it between the cords and down into Kyle's windpipe.

Using a bag that fit on the end of the tube, the respiratory therapist began delivering large breaths about every three seconds. Even though Kyle was receiving the highest possible concentration of pure oxygen, he showed no signs of improvement. In spite of the respiratory therapist's attempts to force as much oxygen into Kyle's lungs as possible, his lips were becoming more blue, his cheeks were now sallow, and his eyes were taking on a sunken, inanimate quality. Theo checked the oxygen saturation monitor. It had dropped to forty.

"How much oxygen are you giving him?" Theo asked.

"We're still on a hundred percent," the therapist answered.

"His pressure's dropping," Payton said. "It's sixty over palp. His pulse is forty. We're losing him."

"Let's start CPR. Call a code," Theo instructed.

Within a matter of seconds, the code blue alert had gone out over both the beepers and the overhead paging system, bringing several more nurses and other ancillary personnel rushing to Kyle's room. Even though only a few minutes had elapsed, Kyle was now deeply unconscious from the lack of oxygen. His eyes remained open but his pupils now drifted up. His heart slowed to twenty beats per minute.

"Give him two amps of bicarb and an amp of epinephrine," Theo ordered. "I want a chest X-ray as soon as possible and tear me off a rhythm strip so we can see what his heart's doing." One of the nurses reached up to the monitor, tore off a long strip of paper, and handed it to Theo. After studying the tracing for a few seconds, he said, "Give him another amp of epinephrine and mix up a dopamine drip."

In spite of Theo's efforts, Kyle continued to deteriorate. Another minute passed and he went flat line. Even with absolutely no heartbeat, Theo didn't give up. He again tried several medications to get Kyle's heart going, but they all failed. Finally Babs put her hand on his shoulder. Her expression was all too familiar to Theo, who, after taking a deep breath, fell silent and took a step back.

The room seemed warmer to him than when he'd first walked in, and that strange odor that always seemed to accompany a code blue hung in the air. All eyes in the room were on him—the way it usually was right before the physician who was running the code contemplated calling it off.

"That's it," Theo said as he placed his hands on his hips. "I'm calling it. We're done here. Somebody note the time."

Theo bent over and picked up a couple of empty medication boxes before falling into the only chair in the room. With a vacant look in his eyes, he squeezed one of the boxes until it crumpled. Apart from Babs, Payton, and her medical student, everyone in the room slowly filed out.

"They're calling Kyle's parents," Babs said. "They should be here soon."

"I'll speak to them," he said. "I've gotten to know them pretty well."

"What do you think happened?" Payton asked Theo.

"It had to have been a pulmonary embolus."

"How's that possible?" Babs asked.

"What do you mean?" he asked.

"Don't you remember? He had a caval filter put in last week."

Theo raised his hands in the air in frustration. "Nothing's a hundred percent."

"I've been here a long time," Babs said. "We've put in an awful lot of filters and I've never seen a single patient flip a pulmonary embolus."

"I don't know," Theo said, without really thinking about what she was saying.

"I'm going back to the nursing station. Do you need me for anything?" Babs asked.

"No, go ahead. I'll be out in a minute." Theo stood up, looked over at Kyle for one last time, and then slowly walked out into the hall.

"What's a caval filter?" Emily asked Payton.

"It's a metal device specifically designed to prevent pulmonary emboli," Babs answered. "Do you remember from your anatomy course that the inferior vena cava is the main vein of your abdomen that leads back to the heart?"

"Yes."

"Well, a caval filter kind of looks like a metal birdcage. It's placed inside the inferior vena cava to trap any blood clots that have broken off from the leg veins and stop them from traveling to the lungs."

"He was pretty young," Emily said, trying to appear unshaken by what she had just observed.

Having first-year medical students in the hospital was a new program and Payton could see that Emily was shaken up. Thinking it would be easy to say something that would make her feel better, Payton actually found herself at a complete loss for words.

By this time, Theo had made his way to a small booth at the nursing station to dictate a death note on Kyle. It took him only about five minutes to complete it. He was no longer exhausted, but he sat with his eyes closed in utter dismay for a time before finally getting up and walking back to the nursing station. "Call me as soon as Kyle's parents get here," he told Babs.

He had just started down the hall when he noticed a muscular man with a full head of white hair coming toward him. The man, wearing a pair of blue Gillette surgical scrubs and a nurse's aide identification badge bearing the name of Hal Newcomb, smiled.

"Tough night, Doc?" he inquired.

"They're all tough," Theo answered without giving the man a second thought.

# Chapter 21

Once a week Alex made rounds without the students and residents. Early on she had discovered that seeing her patients alone from time to time allowed her to get to know them a little better and gave them the opportunity to speak with her without her usual entourage.

She had just returned to the nursing station and started to make a note on one of her patients when a voice from behind her asked, "Are you interested in joining?"

Alex turned in her chair just as George Murray, one of the fourth-year residents on the trauma service, sat down next to her. George was a well-meaning and hardworking resident but was totally devoid of any social graces or bedside manner.

"I beg your pardon?" she asked the slovenly dressed young man.

"The Caduceus Project," he said. "In the cafeteria yesterday, I was sitting at the table behind you and Dr. Runyon. I wasn't eavesdropping but I heard you asking him about it."

"Let's just say I'm a little curious," Alex said. "Are you a member?"

"I sure am. It took me three years of pounding on the door but I finally got in."

"What got you interested in the organization?" Alex asked.

"When I was an intern, I went to a meeting with a bunch of the residents just to see what it was about, but I never expected anything to come of it."

"But something did?"

"Dr. Runyon's speech was so powerful and inspiring that I knew I had to join. He's an amazing speaker. Everything he said made perfect sense." George stopped for a moment and then with a profoundly serious look said, "Did you know that he's even been quoted in *Time* magazine?"

"You seem to think quite highly of Dr. Runyon."

"Everybody in the project does. He's a nationally recognized authority on a whole host of medical issues and a shoo-in to be the next national director of the Project."

"How do you know that?" Alex asked.

"Because they wouldn't have asked him to help preside over the big national meeting in Boston this month unless he was part of the inner circle."

"The inner circle?"

"The elite of the elite," George said reverently. "Let's just say that Doctor Runyon knows everything that's going on in the country that has anything to do with health care, and he knows how to get things done."

"What do you mean?" she asked.

With an insider's grin, he winked and said, "Let's just say that Victor Runyon's not about to let anyone steamroll over him or the Caduceus Project." George stretched his legs out and crossed his ankles. His sneakers looked older than he was. "It's not enough anymore just to be a clinician. Doctors have to take an active role in the shaping of our professional destiny. As physicians we have lost all control of our profession. We no longer make policy—we're the victims of it." He stopped only long enough to cast a smug grin in her direction. "We've also learned that the people who oppose us don't always play by the rules."

"Does that mean Dr. Runyon doesn't play by the rules either?"

George smiled with a measured degree of caution. "He's prepared to play hardball if that's what it takes." George continued to drone on until he was suddenly interrupted by the alert of his beeper. He reached down, slipped it off his belt, and checked the number. Coming to his feet, he paused just long enough to slide his chair back under the counter. "I better get going," he said as he started away. "The students are waiting for me in X-ray."

Alex shook her head and then reached for another chart. She didn't know whether to feel sorry for George for his naiveté or to be furious at Victor for filling his head with such unabashed drivel. If nothing else, she had certainly learned something interesting about Victor, and that was that he was obviously a militant on medico-political issues.

Alex slid the chart back into the rack and stood up. Before heading home, she decided to stop in the ICU. Sam had telephoned her earlier and mentioned that she might be visiting David in the late afternoon and Alex was hoping to run into her. Leaving the nursing station, she took the elevator down to the lobby in order to go to the gift shop before heading up to the ICU.

She had just stepped off the elevator when she saw Victor and George standing near the information counter. Victor's back was facing her, but she could see George plainly and his eyes were trained directly on the floor. She stopped and then stepped back against the wall to avoid being seen. Victor was gesticulating as he was talking. She saw George nod a couple of times as if he were being browbeaten in an extremely one-sided conversation. Finally, Victor walked away in a huff, leaving George standing there.

Alex stepped away from the wall and watched George for a few moments. Wanting to catch him before he left, she started across the lobby, hoping to make their encounter seem coincidental. Before she had taken more than a few steps, George looked up and spotted her coming. Red-faced, he immediately looked away and marched off in the opposite direction.

Alex stopped and watched him vanish. She considered going after him but quickly decided against it. She could only guess, but whatever Victor was chastising him about must have been pretty intense to leave poor George cowering like that.

# Chapter 22

Micah Henry's office was large and smartly decorated but paled in comparison to the corporate suites of some of his colleagues who were employed by more flamboyant health care systems.

As soon as Alex arrived, Micah's new secretary, Lisa, showed her in. She couldn't have been more than twenty-five and dressed like a pop diva, looking as if she subsisted on about fifty calories a day. Alex guessed she spent every waking minute outside the hospital at her fitness center.

Micah got up from behind his desk a soon as he saw Alex and met her in the middle of the office. She was silent until Lisa had withdrawn from the office and closed the door.

"Have a seat," he said.

"Does Maxine know about that?" she asked, pointing to the door as she sat down in a soft leather chair.

"Actually, she's the niece of one of the bigwigs at the university. I got my arm twisted to hire her."

"Poor you," Alex said. "Can she type?"

"Who cares?" he answered, opening his eyes wide. Alex couldn't help but laugh. "How's David doing today?"

"I just got back from the ICU. He looks better every time I see him."

"What about you?" he asked directly.

"It's been a stressful time, Micah, but I'm okay," she answered with an awkward smile.

"You mentioned the other night in the lobby that you wanted to talk to me."

"I had lunch with David the day he was hurt. He was telling me about a new project he was working on. He seemed unusually anxious about it."

"What do you mean?" Micah asked.

"Well, David's generally pretty calm about his work, but then he told me that he had been contacted by a physician on staff at Adams to set up a meeting to discuss a possible story."

"When did all this happen?" Micah asked.

"A few days before he got hurt. It seems that this doctor made some pretty serious allegations about Gillette."

"What kind of allegations?" he asked with a heightened sense of concern.

Alex shook her head. "I don't know, but it had something to do with the Caduceus Project."

"What about the Caduceus Project?"

Alex sighed. "I'm not sure. Just as David was about to fill me in, Theo called with an emergency and I had to run back to the hospital."

"Did you speak to David later?"

"I was supposed to call him after my shift, but that obviously never happened."

"That's kind of a bizarre story," Micah offered, suspecting that perhaps Alex wasn't telling him everything she knew.

"I found out later that this physician who met with David is a patient in our ICU. His name's Robert Key. He's a radiologist over at Adams."

"What happened to him?" Micah asked with a degree of reservation in his voice.

"His admitting diagnosis was head trauma. He was supposedly mugged."

Micah thought for a few moments before saying, "I guess it could still be just a coincidence."

Before Alex could respond, the door opened and Lisa appeared.

"Doesn't she knock?" Alex whispered more to herself than Micah.

"I'm sorry, Mr. Henry, but your next meeting is off campus and if you don't leave right away, you'll be very late."

Micah cleared his throat. "Thank you, Lisa."

After a short dismissive glare in Alex's direction, Lisa withdrew.

"She's very efficient," Alex said, raising her eyebrows.

"You'll have to give me a break on this one, Alex. It's out

of my hands. Look, I have to get going but let's meet for lunch. I want to talk more about this."

"I'm not sure if I can make it. Give me a call when you get back from your meeting. I'd check with Lisa but I'm afraid she'll scratch my eyes out."

Micah moaned. "You're not going to let go of this, are you?"

"I'm not the one you have to worry about. It's your fiancée."

"My guess is that Maxine couldn't care less."

"Really? Now I know what we can talk about at lunch."

Micah got up, stepped behind his desk, and removed his sports coat from the back of his chair. When he came back out, Alex was already on her feet.

She walked him to the lobby, keeping the conversation light. Without knowing why or giving it a second thought, she watched him until he disappeared out the door.

# Chapter 23

Alex was just finishing rounds when she received a call from Micah that he'd be back from his meeting at around one o'clock. Her noon conference had been canceled, so they arranged to meet in the doctors' dining room at about one-fifteen.

Alex arrived a few minutes early, grabbed a diet soda, and found a table against the far wall. Most of the doctors on staff preferred to avoid the hassle of leaving the hospital for lunch and ate in the dining room. The smartly decorated room was well staffed, had a fairly diverse menu, and served pretty good food.

Alex didn't exactly regret speaking to Micah about David, but afterward she did realize that she had to avoid being too pushy for fear of coming across as irrational. She knew Micah would ask how she knew that Robert Key was the doctor who had met with David, but if she filled him in about Kurt, she knew he'd want to accompany her to their meeting. When Micah walked through the door, Alex had already decided that it would be better to keep things vague for a while.

He spotted her immediately and waved her over to go through the line with him.

"How was your meeting?" she asked.

"Somewhere between going to the dentist and writing a check to the IRS," he said, pulling two trays off a large stack and handing her a silverware setup. They went through the line quickly, Micah deciding on a turkey club, fries, and a piece of pie while Alex chose a small portion of stir-fry.

"Why do you eat so much for lunch?" she asked as they sat down.

"Because it's free," he said.

"So how's Maxine?"

"She's okay. I thought we were going to talk about David."

"Do you mind if we do that later? My new rule is no stressful conversations during meals."

"Then we shouldn't be talking about Maxine." Alex gave him an encouraging look. He studied her for a few moments, nodded, and then said, "Maxine left for L.A. this morning. I've barely seen her since she got back from her last trip. She told me that her boss called at the last minute and that he needed her to go."

"So what's the problem?" Alex asked.

"What's the point of being engaged if you never see your fiancée?" Micah was obviously upset and Alex decided to let him keep venting. "Don't get me wrong," he went on. "Maxine's a great person. She's smart and attractive . . . it's just that—"

"She works too hard?" Alex asked.

"We all work hard but Max is consumed by her work. Even when we're together, which hasn't been very much the last few months, we always wind up talking about her job."

"Not to state the obvious, Micah, but have you tried changing the topic?"

"Sure, but as soon as I do, something eventually reminds her of work and we're right back on it."

"C'mon, Micah. We've all made the mistake of getting too wrapped up in our work. I'm no expert on relationships, but have you considered having a heart-to-heart with Max about all this?"

"I've tried to delicately broach the topic a couple of times but . . ."

"Well, if the subtle approach hasn't worked, then be more direct and just tell her how you feel," Alex said.

"And get my head bitten off? No thanks."

Alex nodded as Micah spoke and then asked, "How are the wedding plans coming?"

"Max suggested we put them on the back burner until she feels really secure in her professional life."

"That sounds . . . practical."

"You really think so?" he asked.

"Definitely."

"This whole thing isn't easy, you know."

Alex looked up from her stir-fry. "What isn't easy?"

"Getting married for a second time. Have you ever thought about it?"

Using her fork as a pointer, she said, "Well, seeing as how I haven't been faced with that decision yet, I'm not sure my opinion would be valid, but I can say this—our circumstances are completely different. I wanted out of my marriage and you . . . well, you're still passionately in love with Beth."

Micah answered, "I'll always love Beth. And we did have a great marriage, but I also realize that she's gone, and I think I could have a great marriage with someone else." Micah didn't have to elaborate; his doubts weren't about the institution of marriage. They were about Maxine.

"Are you asking me how you know?" Alex asked.

"I was so sure with Beth. Maxine's great, but . . ."

"Maybe you're being too analytical about the whole thing," Alex said, before pointing out with a brief smile, "Romance isn't quite the same as planning a naval battle."

"In other words, I'm an unromantic pragmatist who's shallow as a puddle," he said.

"I'm not saying that."

He smiled and crossed his arms. "Okay, then. Since you're so sensitive and a die-hard romantic, how would you know?"

"I believe in the first-kiss theory."

"I beg your pardon?"

"I can't necessarily speak for you or men in general, but I believe that the first time you kiss someone, you know."

"You know what?"

"If you've found the love of your life."

His eyes narrowed as he tapped his fingertips together in profound doubt. "No offense, Alex, but you wound up divorced."

"My case rests."

"Really? That's very interesting. So you knew Chuck wasn't the one but you married him anyway?"

"You got it."

"And you knew this the first time you kissed him?" he asked.

"Without a doubt."

"I've always thought of you as this hard-ass trauma surgeon. I never realized how insightful and romantic you are," he teased.

"I gotta go," she said, picking up her tray and shaking her head at him. "The students are waiting for me to make rounds with them, and, by the way, you're the same idiot I knew in high school."

"I'll speak with you later," he said. "I think I'll have a cup of coffee and give this first-kiss theory of yours some very careful thought before I face my afternoon schedule."

Returning to his seat with a cup of decaf, Micah began to think about the things that he and Alex hadn't talked about at lunch. There was no question in his mind that she knew more than she was letting on about David's injuries. He also knew that she'd almost certainly confide in him in her own good time. The problem was that he doubted seriously that her suspicion about David and Dr. Key was anything more than a strange coincidence.

Hopefully, she'd see that before embarking on anything that might prove professionally embarrassing.

# Chapter 24

Alex arrived at Tryst at eight forty-five and went directly to the bar.

When she didn't immediately see Kurt, she took a careful look around to see whether he was sitting at one of the tables. When she realized he wasn't, she took a seat at a small table with a good view of the entrance. She hadn't been there for more than a minute when a waitress appeared and took her order for a glass of white wine.

When the waitress returned and set the glass of pinot grigio on the table, Alex noted the time. It was exactly four minutes to nine. She took the first sip and decided that she would use a simple strategy for the meeting. She would let Kurt do the majority of the talking and pick her moments to ask questions.

For the next ten minutes, Alex kept her eyes fixed on the entrance while she slowly finished her wine. As she placed the glass down, a man approached her table. At first she assumed it was Kurt, but as soon as he was close enough to have a good look at his face, she knew it wasn't him.

"Good evening," he said. "You've been sitting here alone for about twenty minutes staring at the entrance. I've been hoping the person you're expecting won't be coming."

Alex used her most formal doctor's voice to respond. "The person I'm waiting for should be here momentarily."

"Are you sure?"

"Positive."

"I guess that's bad luck for me. Here's my card," he said, placing it on the table. She averted her eyes, hoping that he wasn't the persistent type. "I hope you enjoy your evening." The man returned to the bar, where he had been sitting alone.

Alex glanced at his card. It read *Kevin Granger.* He was an attorney.

Alex was tempted to order a second glass of wine but she resisted. By nine-thirty her patience was drawing thin, but she decided to give Kurt another five minutes before leaving. She considered a multitude of explanations for his failure to show, but none of them did much to allay her disappointment. It more than crossed her mind that something of a violent nature had happened to Kurt, but Micah's warning echoed in her mind and she cautioned herself about being too melodramatic.

Exasperated and irritated, Alex motioned the waitress over and paid her bill. Not knowing why, she grabbed Kevin Granger's business card and dropped it into her purse.

As she walked by the bar, she noticed he had turned in his chair and was watching her. It occurred to her that perhaps he had been sent by Kurt, but if that were the case, why didn't he say something?

# Chapter 25

As soon as Alex arrived home, she went directly to her study, kicked off her shoes, and sat down on a leather loveseat.

In the midst of a sea of puzzling events, one clear fact emerged and that was that there was no longer anything keeping her from going to the hospital and having a look at Robert Key's chart. Her first thought was to go in the morning, but after a little more reflection, she changed her mind and decided to go immediately.

Reaching for the phone, she called the main number at Gillette and asked the operator to page Theo.

"Hightower," he answered.

"Hi, it's Alex."

"I know why you're calling and I just saw Dave an hour ago. He looks fine. There are no changes."

"Thanks for checking on him, but actually I called about something else."

"Shoot."

"Have you been involved in Robert Key's care?"

"Of course," Theo answered.

"What can you tell me about him?"

"I assume you're aware that he's a physician."

"I am," she told him.

"Basically, he was beaten up and robbed."

"How's he doing?" she asked.

"He's still out of it but he's getting better," Theo answered.

"Who's the attending surgeon?"

"Runyon. What's all this about, Alex? Why the sudden interest in Dr. Key?"

Ignoring his question, she asked, "How long are you going to be in the hospital?"

Theo's voice was now more measured. "I'm not going anywhere. I have at least a dozen patients to see and maybe a tracheostomy to do. I'll be here for hours."

"Where are you?"

"I'm in the stepdown unit."

Alex stood up and looked around for her purse. "I'll be there in fifteen minutes. Wait there for me. I want to talk to you."

Before heading for the hospital, Alex went upstairs, knocked on Olivia's door, and told her that she'd be gone for an hour or so. As she hurried down the hall, she suddenly stopped and then quietly opened Jessie's door. As she usually did, Jessie had thrown off her comforter and was sleeping on her back with her knees pulled up and her mouth wide open. She was a sound sleeper but Alex still took care to tiptoe into her room. She watched her for a few seconds before straightening out her legs and replacing her blanket. Then she kissed her on the forehead and sneaked out without making a sound.

Calmly, Alex drove down N Street, taking care not to exceed the speed limit. Among a short list of minor vices was her chronic failure to adhere to the posted speed limits. She had a collection of citations to prove it and probably would have had a lot more had it not been for the understanding nature of most of the MPD officers, who let her go with a warning when they learned she was a trauma surgeon at Gillette.

A light drizzle began to polka-dot her windshield. Just as she was about to put on a CD, her cell phone rang. It was Micah.

"I just called you at home. Olivia said you were on your way to the hospital. I thought you were off tonight."

"I am."

"Is David okay?"

"He's doing fine," she answered.

"So why are you going in?" he asked casually, trying not to appear as if he were snooping.

"I want to speak to Theo Hightower about Robert Key and have a look at his chart," she answered.

"I thought you told me he was admitted with a severe head injury. Has he recovered consciousness?"

"Not yet," she answered.

"Then what could you possibly find out?"

"I'm not sure, Micah," she said impatiently. "I just want to have a look at his chart."

"Supposing Key is the physician who met with David. What does it prove? How can you be so sure his mugging had anything to do with his meeting with David?"

"Don't you think it kind of stretches the limits of coincidence to believe that an investigative journalist and a physician meet to discuss mysterious goings-on at a major trauma hospital and then within days they're both victims of unexpected violence and wind up in an intensive care unit?"

Micah was careful to let Alex finish before responding. "Just remember that these 'mysterious goings-on,' as you put it, are alleged."

"Oh, Micah. Do you really—"

"Let me finish, Alex. All we know is that one doctor whom neither of us has ever met made some accusations about Gillette. We have no way of knowing whether they're credible or baseless."

"Look, Micah, I'm not asking you to get behind me on this thing, but at least keep an open mind. If David was attacked by somebody because of his interest in Gillette, I want to know about it."

"I am keeping an open mind, Alex. My concerns are not about Gillette. They're about you," he said with some hesitation.

"I appreciate that."

"It might not seem like it, but I'm trying. Give me a call on your way home and tell me what you found out," he said.

"Okay, if it's not too late . . . and Micah, thanks for calling."

The drizzle ended as quickly as it had started and exactly fifteen minutes after Alex pulled out of her driveway, she drove into the physicians' parking lot at Gillette.

When Simon Lott pulled up to the curb across the street, he saw Alex jump out of her car and go straight into the hospital. A little perplexed as to why she would be racing to the hospital on a night when she wasn't on call, he climbed out of the Hummer and gazed across the street at the bright lights of the emergency receiving area. Pushing his shirt sleeve up past his wrist, he checked the time.

His interest now piqued, he reached into the center console for a cigar. A longtime connoisseur of fine cigars, he lit the handmade Dominican and watched as the white ash burned in a perfectly even manner. A skeptic by nature, Lott was quite certain that Alex Caffey didn't believe for an instant that her brother had attempted suicide.

In fact, his guess was that she had every intention of snooping around until she found out what had really happened. It would be interesting to see just how far Morgan would let her go before putting an end to her nonsense.

# Chapter 26

Alex went directly to the acute care unit on the third floor. It took her only a few seconds to spot Theo, who was examining a teenage girl who had been admitted earlier that evening after coming in second in a knife fight.

One of the younger nurses, appearing awestruck in his presence, stood next to him with captivated eyes. As soon as she saw Alex approaching, she quickly found something else to do. Theo turned and frowned as Alex neared.

"You're killing my love life, Alex."

"I'm confident you'll find the means to resurrect it later."

"My my, we're in a charming mood tonight."

"Bring me up to date on Robert Key," she said.

"He has a pretty bad skull fracture and a bunch of abrasions. He's still out of it but I think he'll come around."

"Is he at least responding to commands?" she asked.

"Not yet."

"Did they catch the guy who mugged him?" she asked.

"Not to my knowledge, but that's not the kind of thing the police generally go out of their way to share with us." By the tone in his voice, Alex knew that Theo was a little baffled by her questions. "If you don't mind me asking again, what's the big interest in Robert Key?"

"He's a fellow faculty member. I'm concerned about him."

"Have you ever met him?" he asked.

"No, but what difference does that make?"

"I see," Theo said with dubious eyes as he pointed across the unit. "His girlfriend's in with him now if you want to say hello."

Alex looked in the direction that Theo had pointed and then back again. "I thought he was still in the ICU."

"George transferred him out this afternoon while I was still in the operating room. We needed the bed for a guy who fell off his roof. Robert's actually quite stable. His breathing's fine and all we're really doing is giving him his tube feedings and waiting for him to wake up. We're sending him to a regular room either tonight or in the morning, depending on how bad the bed crunch gets."

"I'm going to have a look at his chart and then speak to his girlfriend."

Instead of responding, Theo simply nodded politely and then smiled. Without saying another word, Alex turned and headed across the unit. After spending fifteen minutes at the nursing station perusing through Robert's chart, Alex walked over to his room. Peering through the sliding glass door, she observed a young lady wearing embroidered jeans sitting in the chair next to the bed with her legs crossed under her. She had a large book open on her lap and was taking notes. Alex couldn't help but notice that she was left-handed and had a peculiar way of gripping her pen between her third and fourth fingers.

She slid the door open and said, "Hi. My name's Dr. Caffey. I'm one of the trauma surgeons. I just wanted to stop in and see how he was doing."

The young lady closed her book and removed her reading glasses. "Thank you for stopping in. My name's Jamie Dennison," she said in a distinctive southern accent as she stood up to shake Alex's hand.

"How's he doing?" Alex asked, noting that Jamie was exactly her own height.

"He's getting better every day. I've been talking to him ever since the accident but tonight was the first time I think he actually heard me," she said as she leaned over and stroked his hand. "He's a tough guy. I know's he's going to be okay."

"How is his family holding up?" Alex asked as she walked over to the bedside and carefully examined both of his head wounds.

"Rob's parents were killed in a car accident when he was in college."

"I'm sorry to hear that."

"He has a brother but the last we heard from him, he was

living in the south of France chasing his dream to be the next Claude Monet."

"Really?"

She smiled before going on. "Rob has some of Seth's paintings in his house. I'm not an art critic but from what I can see I would guess he's working to support his passion for painting."

"Maybe he's living off his inheritance."

She shook her head. "According to Rob, his parents lived month to month."

"How long have you known him?"

"We started dating last year."

"Are you one of our residents?" Alex asked.

"No," she said with a grin. "I thought about going premed but the thought of taking organic chemistry was just too much for me so I majored in marketing. I finished my master's at American about five years ago and I've been doing consulting work ever since."

"I hope you know that everyone thinks very highly of Robert," Alex said, having no idea whether that was really the case.

"He's certainly passionate about being a doctor. He loves everything about medicine." She stopped for a moment, wiped a few drops of perspiration from his forehead, and went on. "His caseload must have been getting really heavy the last few weeks."

"What makes you say that?" Alex asked.

"He wasn't his usual self. It just seemed like he had something on his mind."

"I think that has happened to all of us at one time or another," Alex said before asking, "Has Robert had a lot of visitors?"

"Some of the radiologists he works with came by and some of his friends from a medical organization he's in stopped in earlier."

"Really? Which one?" Alex asked nonchalantly.

"I think it's some kind of a political group. Rob's been a member since he started medical school. It's a funny name and I can never remember it."

"Was it the Caduceus Project?" Alex asked, trying not to do or say anything that might betray her rising anxiety.

"That's it," Jamie said with a broad smile. "They stayed for a long time. They said such nice things about Rob." Jamie went on to elaborate, but with the realization that Robert Key was a member of the Caduceus Project, Alex's mind was now reeling and processing very little of what she was saying.

Just at that moment, the door slid open and a nurse's aide with a gray stethoscope suspended around his neck stepped in. "Sorry to interrupt, but it's time for Robert's vital signs."

"I was just going," Alex said, extending her hand to shake Jamie's. "I'll try to stop in again soon. It was very nice meeting you. Robert is very lucky to have someone who cares about him as much as you obviously do."

"Thank you."

As soon as Alex stepped out in the hall she spotted Theo on the other side of the unit slipping on a pair of sterile gloves. Staring across the ICU absently, Alex found herself wondering what could have possessed Robert to see David to expose an organization of which he himself was a member? Still stunned by what Jamie had said, Alex didn't even notice when Theo approached.

"How did it go?" he asked.

"Okay. His girlfriend seems nice."

"She's certainly been optimistic. I'll say that for her. We're going to move Dr. Key out to the floor tonight instead of in the morning. We really need his bed."

"Do you think he's ready?"

"He's been rock stable for three days. He's breathing on his own and all we're doing is watching his tube feedings. They can do that on the floor."

"What do you think about those head wounds?" Alex asked.

"What do you mean?"

"Anything about them strike you as peculiar?"

"Not really," Theo answered, wrinkling his brow in thought. "I didn't see anything peculiar about the wounds, but something tells me you did."

"We've both seen an awful lot of people who have been

mugged. Did you ever see any of them come in with two distinct blows to the head like that?" Alex asked.

"Like what?"

"Both clean—one exactly in front, and the other exactly in back? Think about it. Two symmetrical wounds, one in the front, the other in the back," she repeated slowly. "What did the mugger do? Hit him in the front and then run around behind him to hit him again?"

Theo nodded slowly. "Most of the muggings I've seen, the victim has been beaten up so badly you couldn't make heads or tails of the wounds."

"That's exactly my point," she said.

"But the wounds aren't the same," Theo said.

"What do you mean?" she asked.

"The one in the back wasn't so bad. It didn't even cause a skull fracture, but the one in front was so severe that the neurosurgeons almost had to operate on him."

Alex hadn't thought about Theo's theory, but it certainly made sense. For the moment, she didn't want to discuss it any further for fear of further arousing Theo's curiosity regarding her interest in Robert. "I'm going over to the ICU to visit David," she said. "I'll speak to you in the morning."

"Don't forget about teaching rounds. The students are looking forward to it."

"I'll be there," she said with a wave as she turned and started for the exit.

The ICU was relatively quiet. Most of the visitors were gone and for the moment no new patients were being admitted. For the next hour Alex sat with David. She spent a lot of the time reading over his chart, reviewing his most recent blood tests and X-rays while he slept peacefully.

As she thought about her conversation with Jamie and again considered the events of the past few days, she became even more convinced that locked away somewhere in the recesses of both David's and Robert's minds was information that almost got them killed.

# Chapter 27

Simon Lott spotted Alex the moment she walked out of the emergency room. Checking the time, he determined that she'd been in the hospital for an hour and a half.

Walking quickly, she approached her car, hit the keyless entry, and after a few seconds of hesitation climbed in. Simon's window was down and he was only about fifty feet away. He was generally cautious to a fault and perhaps shouldn't have had the window down, but he could have sworn that just before Alex got into her car she looked directly at him. It might have been nothing more than a random glance but it was a little too long for his liking.

Favoring a cautious approach, he changed his mind about following her home. Taking the last few puffs of his cigar, he tossed the butt out the window. He then reached into the center console for his cell phone. Fran Worthington, a radiology technician, answered on the second ring. Rather ordinary in appearance and feeling trapped in a life that was humdrum at best, Fran had recently celebrated her thirty-second birthday by taking herself out to dinner.

"What happened?" he asked.

"Dr. Caffey came into the unit," Fran answered.

"What did she do?"

"She spoke to Dr. Hightower for a few minutes and then went into one of the patients' rooms."

"Really. Which patient?"

"His name's Robert Key. He's a doctor."

Instead of being surprised or taken aback by the news, Simon merely smiled. "Why do you think she did that?" he asked.

"I don't know. I guess because she's a doctor or maybe to speak to his girlfriend."

"Did you hear anything they said?"

"No, I was busy pretending to be setting up an X-ray. I was worried Dr. Caffey saw me follow her up to the unit. I did hear Dr. Hightower mention that they were moving him to a private room tonight."

"Do they usually do that sort of thing at night?" he asked.

"Not usually, but if the patient's doing okay and they really need the bed they will," she answered. "Key is breathing on his own. He's still mostly out of it but he doesn't need to be in a monitored unit anymore."

"How long did they talk for?" Lott asked.

"Not long, maybe ten minutes or so."

"Is that the first time Dr. Caffey has done that?"

"I don't know. It's not like I stake out this unit all day."

"You sound annoyed," Simon said calmly.

"I feel like a snitch. This whole thing is starting to give me the creeps."

"Really? Aren't we paying you enough?"

"I'm not talking about the money. It's the sleazy feeling I get sneaking around spying on people."

"You're helping a private eye do his job. That's what I do for a living. I told you that from the beginning."

"I'm not sure that makes me feel any better."

"Dr. Caffey happens to have a serious boyfriend who's thinking of asking her to marry him. He's suspicious that she's seeing someone else. Supposing the shoe were on the other foot. Wouldn't you want to know if the person you were planning on marrying had a girlfriend on the side?"

"I . . . I guess so," she said with an impatient sigh.

"Of course you would," Simon said. "It's a very common practice today. My firm handles dozens of these types of background checks and surveillances every month."

"It may be just work to you, but that doesn't mean I feel too good about it," she reiterated.

"Are you working tomorrow night?" he asked.

"Yes."

"What time do you get off?" he asked, willing to make the ultimate sacrifice to maintain the best source of information he had inside Gillette.

"At eleven, but I'm tired after work and I'm not going to follow or spy on—"

"Relax, Fran. I wasn't thinking about work. I was going to suggest that you join me for a drink."

"Really?" she asked with a giggle.

"You sound surprised but if you'd rather not, I can—"

"I'd love to have a drink with you," she said, again tittering in an irritating manner.

"Great. I'll pick you up outside the emergency room tomorrow night at about eleven."

"What about my car?" she asked.

"I'll drive you back in the morning," he said. She was still giggling when he flipped the phone closed.

Leaning back against the headrest, he started thinking about Alex Caffey. There was no longer any doubt that either her brother or Kurt Findlay had spoken to her about Robert Key, a reality that Morgan was not going to be very happy about. Lott filled his lungs with the dry night air and then let it escape slowly. Flipping his cell phone open, he tapped in Morgan's number.

"Yes," Morgan answered.

"Dr. Caffey has been a busy girl. She came back to the hospital tonight. I assumed she was coming to see her brother but she went to Dr. Key's room instead."

"That's a little disturbing."

"I was told that she spoke to Key's girlfriend for quite some time."

"Did we get any of the specifics of their conversation?"

"I'm afraid not," Lott said.

"Even so, this puts a different slant on things."

"I think it's obvious that Dr. Caffey has more than a medical interest in Robert Key."

"So it would appear," Morgan said. "Under the circumstances, I think you should take the necessary steps to prevent Dr. Caffey from intruding any further into our affairs."

"Is she to become a patient at Gillette?" he asked directly.

"Absolutely not. Dr. Key and her brother are quite enough to meet our needs for the moment."

"Okay," Lott said, pleased that he had gotten the go-ahead to permanently deal with Alex Caffey.

"What about Key?" Morgan asked.

"They're moving him to a private room tonight. As soon as they do I'll be able to get the number and some information on the floor routines."

"Does that mean you'll be proceeding tonight?"

"Yes," Lott answered as he pulled away from the curb. "It will take me a few hours to make the final arrangements."

"Call me when it's done," Morgan said as Lott blended into traffic behind a dark panel truck. He tossed the phone onto the seat next to him and glanced in the rearview mirror. He was happy to be completing his business with Robert Key tonight, leaving him free to concentrate on Dr. Caffey. There was no question that she was a thorn in his side, but he didn't view her as an immediate threat and cautioned himself against acting impetuously. After tonight, there would be ample time to deal with her.

# Chapter 28

**APRIL 28**

For Myra Shepard, working the graveyard shift was a reality of nursing that had never really bothered her.

She had a breezy personality with no particular affectations and was a conscientious nurse who spent most of her free time writing banal poetry or traveling to the extent that her limited budget would allow. After spending the last half hour catching up on her charting, she grabbed her stethoscope and headed down the hall to begin taking her four A.M. vital signs. When she reached her final room, it was almost four-thirty. Her shift had been a quiet and uneventful one and the last thing she expected to find was one of her patients in full cardiac arrest.

From the doorway, Myra flipped on a small light that dimly illuminated the area around the bed. As she approached, she immediately noticed that the young man was curled up in an awkward position on his side with his arms stretched behind him. When she reached his bedside and saw that his eyes were wide and fixed, she knew he was in trouble. She quickly placed her fingertips on his wrist. His skin was cold and dry and there was no pulse. Reaching over the bed, she flipped on the main lights and then picked up the phone. The operator answered immediately.

"Code blue, Four North, room four twenty-one," she stated clearly and then hung up without waiting for a response. A moment later, the hospital-wide code blue alert came blaring over the paging system.

"Shit," she muttered as she put her stethoscope on his chest. As she suspected, there were no heart sounds. Myra was a seasoned nurse who had spent considerable time in the ICU. She had attended and assisted at dozens of code blues and she knew the difference between a patient who had a chance of being resuscitated and one who did not. She had no idea how long he had been in full cardiac arrest but her instincts told her it had been a lot more than a few minutes.

Patients on Four North were generally stable enough not to be on central cardiac monitoring, so there was no way of knowing when he had run into trouble. Even though she knew it was an exercise in futility, Myra began CPR by pressing her mouth firmly against his and delivering three hard breaths. Moments later, she heard the rising commotion outside the room as various members of the code blue team came charging down the hall.

As soon as the senior resident came through the door, Myra backed off.

"What's the story?" Barry Tolliver asked.

"I found him in full arrest," Myra answered. "He was just transferred to the floor a few hours ago."

"Let's get a monitor on and start bagging him," he said, moving to the bedside and feeling for a pulse. "What can you tell me about him?"

"He's a thirty-one-year-old recovering from a head injury."

"When was the last time you were in here?" Barry asked, pulling a black stethoscope out of his coat.

"About an hour ago to check his tube feedings. His last set of vitals were normal."

"Someone start chest compressions. He must have thrown an embolus. What about his respiratory status?" Barry asked Myra as he began a quick examination.

"He was fine," she said. "Absolutely fine."

Barry stopped for a moment and looked directly at Myra. "He's cold, for God's sake," he said in just above a whisper.

"I know."

Barry looked around for a moment and then said, "He's a young guy. Let's at least get a tube in him and give him a round of drugs." As Barry suspected, the young man did not respond at all to the medications and less than ten minutes after it began, he halted the code, thanked everybody, and waited for the room to clear. "Do you have any idea what happened?" he asked Myra.

"I don't have a clue. His midnight vitals were fine."

"Who do we notify?"

"He has no immediate family but I think he has a girl-friend."

"Do you have her number?" he asked.

"It's at the desk."

When Myra glanced toward the door, she noticed two orderlies standing in the doorway waiting to help her clean up and then transport Robert Key to the morgue. She motioned them in and for the next few minutes the three of them worked in silence, gathering up the empty boxes and long coils of EKG paper that festooned the floor.

Finally they transferred Robert to a special cart with a false top specifically designed for transporting deceased patients to the morgue. Even though she had never cared for the young man before, she was deeply saddened by his death.

She thanked the two young men as they wheeled Robert out of the room. She stepped out into the hall and watched as the stretcher disappeared down the hall—still mystified as to why her patient had died.

# Chapter 29

Olivia Mills was an excellent au pair. Chubby, with mousy brown hair and short legs, she was both plain in appearance and devoid of much flair. She loved Jessie with all of her heart. At age thirty, living in a beautiful Georgetown home with a generous paycheck, she felt that the only thing missing in her life was someone to share it with.

On this day, she packed a picnic lunch, loaded a bunch of Jessie's toys into the four-year-old Ford Explorer Alex had bought for her, and set out for Montrose Park. After parking the SUV, the two of them made their way to Jessie's preferred playground. It was just past noon and the temperature had already climbed to seventy degrees. Olivia was preoccupied and hadn't even noticed the black Hummer that pulled in right after her—the same Hummer that had been following her since she had left Georgetown.

Following a gently curved path, they eventually reached the playground. Olivia spread a large blanket on the ground while Jessie grabbed her pail and shovel and ran for the sandbox to join several other children who were all busy shoveling sand from one place to another. Jessie wasted no time taking up her position in the box and fell right into the business of starting a tunnel. Unpacking the large basket, Olivia glanced up from time to time to check on Jessie, who remained engrossed in the task at hand.

Walking a beautifully groomed two-year-old golden retriever, Simon Lott, wearing dark sunglasses and a Washington Capitols cap, blended inconspicuously with the many joggers and walkers. As soon as the kids saw the retriever coming they all dropped their toys and scurried out of the sandbox. Most of the caretakers were sitting together on nearby benches. Seeing the children running for the dog, they simply smiled and then returned to either chatting or catching up on their reading.

Wagging her tail as the children approached, Gretel, whom Lott had borrowed from a young lady he knew fairly well, immediately began licking their delighted faces as they all petted her at the same time. He used the opportunity to study Olivia's manner and her methods of keeping an eye on the child.

"What's his name?" one little boy asked.

"It's Gretel, and she's a girl," Lott answered, kneeling down with a broad smile as the dog joyfully danced around the kids.

"Does she bite?" he asked.

"Never," Lott said. "She's a nice dog."

"She sure is soft," Jessie said as she stroked the fur on Gretel's back.

"You can pet her anytime you want," Lott told her, again casting a glance in Olivia's direction.

"Is she your dog?" Jessie asked, looking up at him.

"She sure is. I got her when she was just a tiny puppy."

"You talk funny," Jessie said.

"That's because I'm not from around here," he said just as one of the moms joined the group and placed her hands on her son's shoulders.

"She's beautiful," the woman said.

"Thank you," he said, taking note of her trim figure and light-blue eyes. "She really loves kids."

Lott noticed that every minute or so, Olivia cast one eye in Jessie's direction, but by this time she had opened a book and had moved where she was sitting so that the sun would be on her back.

"I wish I had a dog like this," the little boy said, which immediately caused his mom to frown.

"Me too," Jessie piped in.

"Well, maybe someday you will," Lott answered with a smile, making sure to look squarely at Jessie and not the little boy.

With the boy's mom standing right there, he was very careful not to ask any questions that might raise the slightest suspicion that he was anything more than just a guy out for a walk with his dog. She wasn't wearing a wedding band and Lott wondered if she assumed he was parading around the park with this lovable dog for the sole purpose of meeting women.

The kids continued to hover around Gretel for the next few minutes until their caretakers finally waved them back to the sandbox. Lott said good-bye to each of them but made sure to keep his back to Olivia. He then doubled back along the path, which brought him back to the parking lot. He was pleased with how things had gone.

He had learned that Jessie's au pair did not appear to be the compulsive type who kept herself glued to the child every second—a piece of information that might turn out to be critical in dealing with the Alex Caffey dilemma.

# Chapter 30

Jeanette Airoway was the only one in the ICU waiting room when Micah came through the door. Seated in a small club chair, she mindlessly leafed through a magazine.

"Have you seen David yet?" he asked, taking the chair next to her. Looking through her glasses, he noticed the fatigue in her eyes.

Jeanette tossed the magazine aside. "I was just with him. They don't let me stay very long. I'm not a doctor but he certainly looks better to me."

"That seems to be the general word."

"How are you doing, Micah? Alex tells me that she still worries about you."

"Alex worries about everything and everybody. It's her nature."

"You know what I mean, Micah."

"Jeanette, it's been almost five years since Beth died. She

suffered far too much for far too long. When her time finally came, she was ready."

"I guess I felt the same way when I finally lost Jim. He was so proud of both David and Alex."

"With good reason," he said.

"David was always the easy one," she reflected. "Alex has given me my fair share of gray hairs, but I'm just as proud of her. Do you remember when you were seniors and she couldn't decide whether she wanted to be an architect, a vet, or a physician?"

"There are a lot of people out there who are still walking around because she decided to go to medical school. I think she made the right choice."

"I know she's still worried about David, but I'm certain there's something else on her mind. It's almost as if she's being driven by something."

"Maybe you're reading too deep into it," he suggested, doubting that Jeanette would agree.

"I don't think so. I know my daughter, and I know when she's in the doldrums. There's something definitely troubling her." Micah felt Jeanette's probing eyes. Her unspoken request for him to share whatever he might know wasn't as lightly veiled as she had probably hoped, but it didn't matter because he wasn't about to divulge Alex's confidence.

"What are you two talking about?" came a voice from the doorway.

"Your love life," Micah told Alex without hesitating.

"You promised, Mom."

"Micah's just teasing you a little, dear. Actually we were discussing *my* love life."

Alex approached, leaned over, and kissed her on the cheek. "I thought that your love life was a taboo topic."

"Not exactly, but it *is* on a strictly need-to-know basis," Jeanette said.

Micah laughed. "I thought we were going out to dinner," he said.

Jeanette stood up and turned to Alex. "I'm ready. Anything new with David?"

"He's doing great. I'm going to stop back after we eat."

Alex and Micah waited for Jeanette to pick up her purse before starting for the door.

"What are you two in the mood for?" Micah asked as they started down the corridor leading to the elevator.

"I hadn't really thought about it," Jeanette said.

Alex stopped suddenly. "I have to go back to the ICU for a minute. I want to give David's nurse my new pager number in case she needs me. I'll meet you in the lobby."

Alex was just about to go into the ICU when she saw Samantha approaching. "How's David doing today?" she asked as soon as she saw Alex.

"Great," Alex said with a smile.

"Just like you predicted?"

"Listen, Micah and my mother are down in the lobby. We're going out for dinner. How about joining us?"

"That sounds great, but I kind of wanted to spend some time with David."

"It's early. You can come back after we eat. I'll arrange for the nurses to let you spend as much time with him as you want."

"Okay," Sam said.

"Great. I'll meet the three of you downstairs in five minutes. I like your hair."

Sam took a deep breath. "David's going to hate it. They cut it too short."

"It looks great. How's work?"

"It's a pressure cooker," Sam groaned. "I'm learning a lot, but I'm not sure I'm cut out for the cutthroat life of Washington politics. There are some very serious people in this town."

"I'm sure you can handle it," Alex told her.

"I guess we'll find out. The rumor in the office is that they're going to let a few people go to cut overhead."

"It won't be you," Alex assured her.

"I wish I had some of your confidence."

"I'll see you downstairs," Alex said as she tapped the metal plate that opened the doors to the ICU.

Alex headed toward the nursing station to find David's nurse. When she was a few feet away, she saw Victor Runyon come out from one of the patient bays.

"You look busy," she said.

"I am," he answered in a curt tone, walking straight past her and stopping at the nursing station.

Unable to resist the temptation of a second chance to broach the topic of the Caduceus Project, she said, "I spoke with George. I might be interested in attending one of your meetings."

Victor's tie was crooked, his shirt was wrinkled, and he appeared tired and agitated.

"Really? I find that a little surprising," he said without looking up.

"Why's that?" she asked.

He threw the medical chart he'd been carrying down on the desk and said, "C'mon, Alex. Who are you trying to kid? You're a die-hard liberal," he scoffed. "What possible interest, or should I say legitimate interest, could you have in the Caduceus Project? Trying to enlighten physicians like you to the realities of medicine is about as productive as shouting at the rain. And by the way, I don't appreciate your interrogating George about me."

Offended by his tone but not allowing herself to be provoked, Alex took a step back and then looked around. She pointed to an empty patient room and said, "Why don't we continue this conversation in private?"

"I don't have time for this nonsense right now, Alex."

"Make time," she insisted.

With a loud sigh, Victor pushed the chart across the counter toward the rack, shook his head and said, "Fine," and then followed Alex into the room.

# Chapter 31

Alex waited until Victor was in the middle of the room before closing the sliding glass door. "I'm not sure I appreciate your tone, Victor."

"My tone is hardly the issue here and whatever your real agenda is, I'm not the slightest bit interested in hearing about it."

"What the hell's that supposed to mean?" she demanded. "Why are you so angry?"

"Because the Caduceus Project is made up of serious people who don't appreciate outside busybodies and meddlers. To be more specific, I don't believe you have any serious intentions of joining. I think this is nothing more than your inability to control your feminine curiosity."

"Let's leave your archaic views on gender out of this. Maybe it's time you understood that you're not the only physician interested in the political issues facing the practice of medicine."

Victor paused just long enough to unfold his arms. His expression became circumspect. "Medical issues? Okay. I'll be happy to discuss the issues with you. Tell me your position on national health insurance."

"I'm not sure," Alex answered.

"I thought you wanted to have an honest talk," he said. "Everybody in the department know you're a die-hard liberal."

"Fine. For the purpose of this conversation, let's say I'm in favor of it."

"In that case, my response would be that in addition to being naive you've also taken a position that's diametrically opposed to the position of the Caduceus Project."

Alex could feel the muscles in her neck stiffen. She had

been in situations before where she had been intentionally provoked, sometimes as part of the Socratic method of teaching young doctors. She had always prided herself on her self-restraint and ability to stay composed under fire. Victor was not only betraying his intolerance, but he was also judging her. It was a darker side of his personality that she had not seen before.

"I may not be possessed with the wisdom of the ages, as you seem to be," she said, "but my mind remains open regarding national health insurance and any other health care issue. Obviously, that's considerably more than you can say."

Victor let her finish, stared at her with disdain for a few seconds, and then countered, "National health insurance will ruin health care in this country. How many countries have tried it and paid the price for their stupidity, for God's sake? Why do we have to reprove the proven? Do your homework, Alex."

"Our health care costs are nearly double that of any other country in the world. We rank twenty-fourth in the world in infant mortality. Our runaway medical bureaucracy now accounts for over thirty percent of our health care budget. Our system isn't working, Victor, whether you choose to recognize it or not."

"And you think the fix is universal health care? Do you know how many people in Britain and Canada die every year waiting for medical treatment and surgery while patients with money get preferred care?"

"You can say what you want about health care in Canada, but the bottom line is that their life expectancy is two years longer than ours, so I guess they must be doing something right."

With the veins on his forehead bulging, Victor threw his hands up in the air. "This is hopeless. You've obviously been brainwashed by the liberal left. I can't stand listening to your philistine rhetoric."

Alex smiled, determined not to give him the satisfaction of seeing just how angry she was.

"If you're trying to incite me, forget it. In a war of wits, Victor, you're hopelessly unarmed." Before he could rebut, Alex took a step closer, looked him straight in the eyes, and said, "And with respect to George—don't you dare ever tell me again to whom I can and cannot speak."

Victor never blinked, but the fury in his eyes was obvious. Without saying a word, he slowly turned and looked through the glass door directly at David's cubicle.

"Maybe it would be better if you concentrated on your brother's recovery," he said as a cryptic smile crept across his face. "If he should get better, I'm sure we'll have the opportunity to discuss all of this again."

"Do you have any brothers or sisters?" Alex asked, trying to find some reason to explain Victor's heartless attitude.

"No, I'm an only child," he answered, and with that he simply walked away.

Dumbfounded, Alex remained in the middle of the room, unable to erase the image of Victor's spiteful grin and heartless comments from her mind. It was the most deplorable, unfeeling behavior she'd ever seen by a physician. Every ounce of instinct she possessed told her that her suspicions about Victor Runyon were correct and that cloaked beneath the facade of a caring physician beat the heart of a monster.

# Chapter 32

In spite of her unexpected and disturbing encounter with Victor, Alex did everything she could to conceal her outrage and have a pleasant dinner with Micah, Sam, and her mother.

After dropping Sam back at the hospital, Alex and Jeanette arrived home at about nine. Alex tucked Jessie in and then spent the next two hours working in her study. Before calling it quits and heading upstairs, she decided to have a glass of wine and went to the kitchen. The only light in the room was being cast by a very small lamp mounted over a bulletin board. She opened the cabinet door and removed a bottle of Bordeaux.

"How's my son doing?" came a voice from the other side of the room. Even though she recognized it, she was still a little startled.

"He's doing fine, Mom. I just called the ICU. What are you doing up so late?"

"I couldn't sleep. I felt like a glass of wine so I came downstairs. I didn't want to disturb you so I stayed in here."

"I didn't know you were the type who liked sitting in the dark," Alex said as she poured herself a glass of the red wine and walked across the room to join her mother at the kitchen table. "I thought I was the only one who did that."

"Your father said the same thing the first time he found me in our kitchen."

"What did you tell him?" Alex asked, taking the first sip of her wine.

"I told him that I found it relaxing. I remember that he hugged me from behind and never asked me again."

Alex smiled. "That sounds like Dad."

"You've been awful secretive lately."

"Your imagination's acting up again, Mother."

"Please, Alexandra. I know how your mind works and lately it has been spinning like a top. What's going on?"

"I guess I'm just worried about David," she offered.

Jeanette did nothing to disguise the doubt in her face. "That's nonsense, dear. You're the one who keeps telling me he's getting better, so I'm forced to assume that there must be something else bothering you."

Falling silent, Alex placed her wineglass down on the table. Jeanette studied her daughter's eyes, readily sensing her uncertainty at how to proceed. "There's nothing else, Mom. I'm just concerned about David."

Jeanette was disappointed but saw no reason to press the point. She knew that when Alex was ready she'd open up. "If you say so, dear. You look very tired." She leaned over and kissed her daughter's cheek. She wasn't quite sure why Alex was being so coy but she harbored no animosity about it. She knew that David and Alex were completely different in that respect. Once David made the decision to keep something confidential, he was unshakable. Alex could keep problems to herself for a while but eventually shared her concerns. "I'm about ready to head upstairs," she told Alex. "I'll see you in the morning."

Alex walked her mother to the stairs and then returned to her study. Glancing across the room, her eyes focused on an ornately framed painting of a simple colonial church. The unique way the artist had captured the setting sun reflecting off the building always conjured up a peaceful image in her mind. She knew her mother had been terribly affected by David's accident and she couldn't see any reason to upset her more by revealing that his injuries were probably intentionally inflicted and that he still might be in danger.

Weary from a long day and still troubled by her encounter with Victor, Alex finally decided to go upstairs. Before going into her room she walked down the hall to check on Jessie. Her door was ajar and she took a moment to peek across the room before tiptoeing in. The Mickey Mouse nightlight from Disney World that Jessie had begged her for with the persistence of a drill sergeant cast a soft blanket of light across her face.

Jessie was generally a sound sleeper but on this occasion, as Alex reached for the blanket to snug it up, she half opened her eyes. "Hi, Mommy," she murmured.

"Hi, baby."

"Were you at the hospital?" she asked in words that rolled together.

"Uh-huh, but I missed you so much I came right home," she said, sitting down on the side of the bed. She fluffed up one of the pillows and then gently slid it under Jessie's head.

"Did you see Uncle David?"

"I sure did."

"When's he going to be better?"

Alex nudged Jessie over until there was enough room for her to lie down next to her. Jessie turned on her side, facing the wall. Alex reached across her, pulling her in close.

"Uncle David's getting better every day."

"But when can he leave the hospital?" Jessie asked.

Alex sighed and then began stroking her daughter's hair. "I hope soon."

"Is he going to take me bowling when he's better?"

Alex picked up Jessie's stuffed giraffe and handed it to her.

"Of course. He loves going bowling with you. Now, how about getting some sleep?"

"Can I sleep in your bed tonight?" she asked, rolling on her back to watch the reaction in her mom's face.

"I'm not sure."

"Please, Mommy."

"Well, maybe just this once. But that's only because I love you so much."

"I love you more," Jessie said.

Alex pulled Jessie's covers down and said, "Don't forget your giraffe."

Hand in hand, they tiptoed down the hall. Once in her room, Alex helped Jessie climb into bed and then slide under the soft down comforter. As she tucked her in, Alex watched Jessie's eyes start to droop. It didn't take Alex very long to get ready for bed. When she returned, Jessie was already in a heavy sleep.

# Chapter 33

## APRIL 29

Alex had just walked into the lobby of the John Adams Medical School when she spotted the dean, Morton O'Leary, coming toward her. Her eyes focused on the man flanking him, who she recognized immediately.

As soon as O'Leary saw her, he stopped and smiled broadly.

"Are you here for the admissions committee meeting?" he asked.

"Yes I am, but I think I'm a little early."

"Alex, I'd like you to meet somebody. This is Congressman Brice Beckett. Congressman, this is Dr. Alexandra Caffey. She's one of our most outstanding trauma surgeons."

Beckett took a step forward and extended his hand. "It's a pleasure to meet you, Dr. Caffey."

"Thank you, Congressman," she said.

Beckett had an imposing and aloof nature about him. If Jeanette Airoway were to meet him, she would have told Alex that he looked like a matinee idol. Charismatic and a champion of national health insurance, Beckett had, of late, received a significant amount of media attention. Hailing from Maine, he was considered by many savvy political analysts to be the front-runner for his party's presidential nomination.

"Do you happen to know Ted Simmons?" Beckett asked Alex.

"Very well," she answered. "He's an outstanding orthopedic surgeon. We're fortunate to have him on our staff."

Beckett said in a brassy voice, "Ted and I grew up in the same town. We were inseparable. In fact, he was going to be my roommate at Colby College but at the last second decided to go to Northwestern. We still play basketball together every Sunday." He paused for a few seconds and then said, "Gillette's a fine institution. All of us on the hill admire the fine work you and your colleagues are doing there."

"None of it would be possible without the funds you've helped us get."

"We're working hard for health care reform. Hopefully, you'll see a lot of changes after the next election."

"There are a lot of physicians out there who would like to see that."

"Well, I can tell you this: the support of the doctors in this undertaking is going to be of paramount importance. We're not going to be successful in adopting a policy of universal health coverage without rallying the physicians. We learned that lesson under Clinton—as did our opposition. When this debate really starts to heat up you can bet your bottom dollar that both sides are going to go after the doctors with a passion." Beckett paused for a moment, nodded slowly a couple of times, and then said, "In fact, if you wouldn't mind, my staff and I would be very interested in getting your personal insight. Would you mind if we called?"

"Of course not. I'd be happy to help," Alex said, knowing that her neck must have developed her signature blotchy red rash, which came from being either flattered or embarrassed, a curse that she had carried for as long as she could remember.

Beckett glanced over at Dean O'Leary, who was looking down at his watch.

"We better get going," O'Leary told him before turning back to Alex. "It was wonderful seeing you, Alex, and make sure you come talk to me if that old curmudgeon, Owen Goodman, gives you a hard time about anything."

"I'll remember that," she said, going along with the dean's joke as she shook each of their hands.

Still a little awestruck over just meeting the man who could very possibly be the next president of the United States, Alex crossed the lobby and headed down the corridor until she reached the office of admissions.

# Chapter 34

Finding it a perfect place to attend to her administrative responsibilities, Alex frequently used the small conference room directly across from her office.

She had been working for about an hour when Owen poked his head in the door. "How are you doing?" he asked. "My secretary said you were in here working on a research grant."

"I'm trying, but it's going kind of slowly."

"Grant writing is one of the great burdens of academic surgery, but I'm afraid it's a necessary evil," he said, walking over to where Alex was working. A number of tomes, scientific journals, and legal pads practically covered the entire table.

"How long did it take you to finish your grant on the use of antioxidants in severe head trauma?" she asked.

"Over a year, but it took the NIH only three months to turn it down," he said with a sigh. "In spite of their unexcited view of my research, I still think we're on to something very exciting."

"Research dollars are tight. Maybe when things loosen up a little you'll get your funding," she said.

Owen smiled and gave her an encouraging thumbs-up. "Is there anything I can do to help you with your grant?"

"Not at the moment but if I get bogged down, I'll give you a holler," Alex said reaching for a clean legal pad.

"Okay then, I'll be around if you need me."

"How come you canceled the research meeting tonight?" Alex asked.

Owen frowned. "My wife has me going to another one of those black-tie affairs. This time it's the Partnership for a Healthy America."

"Well, at least it's a good cause."

"An excellent one," he said with a nod and then started back toward the door. When he was a few feet from it, he turned and said, "Were you aware that we had a rather tragic event on the service?"

"No, I hadn't heard."

"Robert Key died," Owen answered in a solemn tone.

"My God," she said, feeling her breath catch. Speechless for the moment, she unknowingly pushed down on her pencil until the point suddenly snapped off. The sound forced her to refocus and when she looked up, she saw the queer expression on Owen's face.

"Are you okay, Alex?" he asked.

"I just saw him the other night. He was doing so well."

"His death was totally unexpected."

"Do we know what happened?"

"We suspect a pulmonary embolus," Owen answered.

"A pulmonary embolus . . . but he had a caval filter in."

"Really? I wasn't aware of that. That would certainly make

a pulmonary embolus very unlikely. Maybe it was a cardiac problem."

"A cardiac death in such a young man?"

"It's possible. We'll just have to wait for the autopsy results to clarify the cause of death. The case has been sent to the medical examiner."

Alex was overtaken by anxiety and fear but she maintained the presence of mind not to let on to Owen. "I just can't believe it," she repeated.

"Everyone's devastated by what happened. It's bad enough when one of our patients dies but when he's one of your own—well, it really hits home. Did you know him well?" Owen asked.

"Not really. I spoke with his girlfriend for a few minutes."

"I understand she's pretty broken up."

"She was very optimistic and seemed quite attached to him," Alex said.

"It's a real tragedy," he said, again moving toward the door.

"Will I see you at the radiology conference later this afternoon?"

"I'll be there," Alex answered with her eyes fixed on the opposite wall, still in shock about the news of Robert Key's death.

After a minute or two, she stood up. Leaving all of her materials strewn across the conference table, Alex marched out of the room and headed straight for Micah's office.

# Chapter 35

The moment Alex walked into Micah's outer office, Lisa picked up the phone.

Alex took note of the disapproval in her eyes, but at the

moment she had more important things on her mind than trying to figure out why her mere presence seemed to aggravate Lisa so much.

"Right away," she said as she made a note on the pad in front of her. A few more moments passed and then, without looking up, she said, "Mr. Henry will see you now."

Without waiting for Lisa to escort her, Alex filed into Micah's office and closed the door.

"Hi, Alex."

"I want you to put a security guard on David."

Having started to get up, Micah stopped, took a deep breath, and then slowly sat back down. Narrowing his eyes, the way he always did when he was caught off guard, he said, "I beg your pardon?"

"I want you to put a twenty-four-hour-a-day guard on David immediately."

"Why?"

"Because he's in danger."

There were a few moments of deafening silence before Micah raised his hands, interlocked his fingers behind his head, and said, "Slow down, Alex, and tell me what's going on."

"It's the hospital's responsibility to do everything in their power to make sure nothing happens to a patient."

"I'm well aware of the hospital's commitment to patient safety, Alex, but David's in an intensive care unit under twenty-four-hour-a-day observation. What could possibly happen to him?"

Feeling more frightened and dismayed than angry, Alex struggled to gather herself. "Listen, Micah, I'm very worried that somebody's going to try to hurt David." She paused only long enough to look away. "It wasn't easy for me to come here, especially after our conversation the other day."

"What we discussed in my office wasn't intended to discourage you from talking to me."

"Maybe not, but I didn't get the feeling you were very receptive to my concerns."

"I was concerned about you. This is a hospital and if you start acting like a bull in a china shop . . . well, the wrong people may take notice. I certainly didn't mean to imply I wasn't interested in what you had to say. There aren't too many people more important to me than you and Jessie." Micah hesitated briefly before adding, "Now, tell me what's got you so worked up?"

"I'm sure you've heard about Robert Key?" she asked.

"Yes."

"I don't think he died as a direct result of his injuries," Alex stated with total conviction.

Micah leaned back in his chair. "What makes you think that?"

"I never told you how I knew Robert was the one who met with David."

"I'm well aware of that."

"A man told me," she said.

"What man?"

Alex took a deep breath. Micah tracked her eyes as she looked around the room. He didn't have to be a mind reader to sense her hesitancy to confide in him.

"His name is Kurt," she finally answered. "I was supposed to meet with him the other night but he never showed up."

Understanding how upset she was, Micah was determined to be patient. "Who is this guy?"

"He came to see me here at the hospital. He said he was a very close friend of Robert's but didn't want to speak to me in the hospital. But he did tell me that what happened to David and Robert were no accidents and that the Caduceus Project was involved."

"And that was it?"

"I think he intended to tell me more when we met."

"You think?"

"He never showed up and I haven't heard from him since," Alex said. "Look, Micah. I have major concerns about David's safety. I think both he and Robert Key were attacked by the same people. Robert's now dead. I don't want the same thing to happen to my brother." Micah noticed the desperation in her voice. "I'm asking for your help, Micah."

"I'll have a word with our director of security this afternoon."

"Thank you," she said barely above a whisper.

Micah then gestured toward a small table on the other side

of his office. When they were both seated, he said, "Let's talk about this a little more." Alex seemed more composed and less unsettled. From her expression and the way she kept looking away instead of at him, Micah wondered whether she regretted bringing the entire matter up.

"Tell me why you're so panicked," Micah said.

"Robert Key told David that there have been a series of unexplained deaths at Gillette that had been intentionally covered up . . . and that the Caduceus Project was involved."

"You're talking about murder, Alex," he said outright. "I'm aware that a lot of people regard the Caduceus Project as a bunch of right-wing loonies but we've never had any trouble with them. Do you have any specific information of anything criminal?" he asked.

"No. I found out that Victor Runyon is a bigwig in the organization. I tried to speak with him about it but he completely dodged me."

"Maybe he had his reasons. What kind of relationship do you two have?" Micah asked.

"Let's just say that it has deteriorated of late. I've always found him egotistical and, at times, less than forthcoming."

"At our critical care meeting this morning, Lynn Gordon mentioned to me that you two were in a rather heated discussion the other day in the ICU."

"Really?"

"That's what she said. She's the nurse manager and I'm quoting her verbatim."

Alex said, "Were we disruptive to patient care or did anybody overhear us?"

"Apparently not, but that's not why I asked. This is not a formal inquiry into your professional conduct."

"So what's the problem other than some busybody nurse?"

"Relax, Alex. I'm not the enemy here. Now what happened?" he asked.

"Victor was upset with me for asking around about the Caduceus Project."

"That's it?" he asked with a glimmer of doubt in his eyes.

"In a nutshell, yes. The last time I checked we still had free speech in this country. I think Victor was way out of line."

"Did you and Victor work out your differences?"

*Gary Birken, M.D.*

"Would you believe me if I told you we had?"

"Probably not."

"It's as simple as this, Micah. I'm not prepared to dismiss the possibility that both David and Robert were attacked because they had acquired information that was potentially devastating to the Caduceus Project."

"I don't want to get too graphic, Alex, but if your theory's correct, why didn't these people simply kill David and Robert?"

She shook her head in frustration. "I . . . I don't know. Maybe they just screwed up or have something else in mind that . . . or—"

"And Victor Runyon is the mastermind behind the whole thing?"

"He's a political zealot with an incendiary personality. People who feel as strongly as he does have done some pretty atrocious things in the name of their cause."

"I agree, but on the other hand not every politically active person has the mind of Adolf Hitler. There are a lot of people out there who enthusiastically support their cause without ever stepping over the line."

Alex said, "Maybe he hasn't stepped over it, but he's certainly moved it."

Being as diplomatic as he could, Micah asked, "Were you aware that Victor and Robert Key were pretty good friends?"

Her mouth dropped open a little. "I was unaware of that. How did you know?"

"Alex, everybody at Adams is talking about Dr. Key's death. He was a fairly well-known member of the medical faculty and it was no secret that he and Victor were good friends." With the wind dumped out of her sails and her theory that Victor Runyon was responsible for Robert Key's injuries now appearing less probable, Alex found herself at a loss for words. Micah went on. "Look, Alex. This is obviously important to you and I appreciate your talking to me about it, but this little investigation that you're embarking on could have some serious professional repercussions for you."

"What are you trying to say, Micah?"

"I guess what I'm trying to say is that it could bring your meteoric career crashing back to earth. Just be careful, and try not to step on the wrong toes. I'm telling you this both as the COO of this hospital and as your friend."

"Thanks, Micah," she said politely. He knew at once she wasn't taking his well-intentioned warning very seriously.

"I'm not trying to rain on your parade, Alex. I'm just trying to tell you to use good judgment. You're a doctor, not an FBI agent. If you get yourself between a rock and a hard place, there's just so much I'll be able to do to help you."

Alex stood up. "I'll be careful," she said.

"What I'd like to know is, where do you go from here?"

"I have no idea," she said as she started for the door. "I really don't have too much to go on and for right now I can't prove anything, but if there's someone out there who thinks I'm going to stand idly by and allow them to harm my brother, they're nuts."

# PART
Two

# Chapter 36

Alex pulled up a chair and sat down a few feet from David's bed. Almost lost in the cacophonic buzz of the ICU, the monotonous tone of the cardiac monitor beeped rhythmically.

For the first time since that horrible night when he was brought into the emergency room, she noticed that a hint of color and animation had returned to his face. As she did every time she visited him, Alex held his hand while she sat with him. The good news was that the swelling in his brain had gone down dramatically—a situation that usually heralded a predictable improvement in the patient's neurological status— and, much to Alex's delight, the neurosurgeons had cut way back on the amount of sedation David was receiving.

"How's he doing?" came a robust voice from behind her. Alex recognized it as Tom Calloway's. He was dressed in royal-blue scrubs and a white coat that was too tight across his husky shoulders.

"I think he looks better every time I see him. You guys are doing a great job." Tom's complexion turned a little rosy. "What's the plan?" she asked.

"I think he needs to be in the ICU another couple of days, but after that I don't see why he can't go to the stepdown unit. Apart from that, just the usual supportive measures. I think we'll continue the antibiotics because his chest X-ray's still a little hazy. I was also thinking of putting in a vena caval filter. We still may be looking at an extended period of bed rest."

Alex nodded, well aware that Tom's concern regarding David's increased risk of suffering a pulmonary embolus was a realistic one.

"I assumed a filter was on the horizon," she muttered.

"You don't sound too thrilled about the idea."

"I'd just like to think about it a little bit."

"Well, it's your call. I won't do anything until I speak to you again, but, Alex, I do feel strongly he needs a filter."

"I hear you."

"Good," he said, rolling his wrist to check his watch. "I have to get over to the operating room. Theo and I just saw a guy in the ER with a bad dog bite to his neck. I'll speak with you tomorrow," he said as he started away.

Alex was a little upset that the entire time she was speaking to Tom, David's nurse was at the nursing station. She had been watching her out of the corner of her eye and it didn't seem to Alex that she was doing anything more than gossiping with the unit secretary. Finally, the young lady returned to David's bay. She smiled at Alex.

"Hi, my name's Kate."

"I haven't seen you before."

"I just started. I was over at G.W. for the past five years."

"As an ICU nurse?" Alex asked without returning her smile.

"That's right."

"I'm a surgeon on staff here and this is my brother," Alex told her in a formal voice.

"I'm aware of that, Dr. Caffey."

"I don't want him left alone again, even for a minute. I don't want him out of your sight. Do you understand?"

"I understand, Doctor," Kate said, shifting uneasily and looking past Alex toward the nursing station. "I won't leave him alone again."

Before Alex could respond, a voice from behind her said, "Good morning, Doctor." Alex recognized Theo's voice but was in no mood for his sarcastic formality.

"Good morning, Theo."

Alex walked right past him and out of the bay. Theo followed a few steps behind. When they were far enough away that Kate couldn't hear them he caught up and put his hand on her shoulder. "What the hell was that all about?" he asked.

"What are you talking about?"

"I'm talking about the Dr. Josef Mengele approach with Kate. She's a damn good nurse. In case you haven't heard,

ICU nurses are tough to come by. It would be nice to keep her around for a while."

"I simply asked her not to leave David alone."

He shook his head. "No, I'd say you *commanded* her not to leave David alone. What the hell's going on?"

Alex fell silent. She knew Theo was right. She glanced back at Kate, who quickly looked away.

"I'm just a little worried about David—that's all."

"David's doing fine. You're the one I'm worried about. Try lightening up a little bit. Everybody around here's busting their butts to get him better."

Alex closed her eyes and then filled her lungs with a deep breath. "I know. I guess I'm still a little on edge. I'll go back and say something to Kate."

"Good idea."

"Before you go I have something to ask you. Do you have a sec?" she asked.

"Shoot."

"Were you on call the night Robert Key died?" she asked.

"No, I found out about it on morning rounds."

"What happened?"

"They think he had a pulmonary embolus. That's the second fatal one this month."

"Really? Who was the other one?" she asked.

"Kyle Dolan, the kid who was paraplegic from the football injury."

"I remember him," she said. "Did he have an autopsy?"

"Yeah, which confirmed the cause of death as a pulmonary embolus."

Alex thought for a minute and then asked, "Did he have a caval filter in?" Theo nodded in a way that Alex knew immediately meant that they were both thinking the same thing. "Two healthy young males both with caval filters die unexpectedly of a pulmonary embolus. It's a little unusual, don't you think?" she asked.

"I would say so."

"Do you know the specifics of what happened to Robert?"

"There wasn't a whole lot to it. The nurse found him at about four A.M. Barry Tolliver ran the code but said it was an exercise in futility. They didn't even get a heartbeat."

"It certainly sounds like a massive pulmonary embolus," she said, drifting off in thought briefly. "What about an autopsy?"

"The case was referred to the medical examiner's office," he said. In view of the criminal act that led to Robert Key's admission to Gillette, Alex was hardly surprised to hear that the case had been sent to the District of Columbia medical examiner. Alex assumed that the report of the autopsy would be ready in about a week. "I have an idea for a paper we could publish," Theo said. "I heard you were looking for a topic to write about. Are you interested?"

"I'm an academic surgeon, Theo. I'm always interested in hearing a good idea for a research paper. The rule is still publish or perish. What's your brilliant idea?" she asked.

"Let's look at deaths in young adults, especially as related to pulmonary emboli and failure rates of caval filters. What do you think?"

She nodded her head slowly and then said, "I like it. Why don't you check all the deaths for the last eighteen months?" she suggested. "Let's see if any other patients with filters died from a pulmonary embolus."

"That shouldn't be too hard. I'll get the monthly death and complication records from Dr. Goodman's office." Theo looked down at his beeper. "I gotta go. I'll give you a call later."

Starting back toward David's room to apologize to Kate, Alex thought about the two young people who had died at Gillette with caval filters in place. By themselves, two such events would hardly constitute an epidemic but it was still pretty unusual to see two young patients die of a massive blood clot to the lung, especially if their filters were functioning properly. Alex had put dozens of filters in, had never had a problem with any of them, and was a firm believer that they saved lives.

Normally she would be enthusiastic about tackling an interesting clinical enigma and then writing it up for publication, but in this case, she was clearly more than just academically interested in what Theo might uncover.

# Chapter 37

After leaving Theo, Alex had spent most of the afternoon in her office organizing her upcoming medical student lectures.

She was just about to lock up and head back to the ICU to see David when her phone rang. For an instant she was tempted not to answer it, but after a long sigh she walked back to her desk and reached for the phone.

"This is Dr. Caffey."

"Are you ready for this?" came a familiar voice. "There have been four deaths."

"Are you sure?" she asked Theo.

"If you count Robert Key, in the last eighteen months, four patients with caval filters have died of pulmonary emboli."

Alex's grip on the phone tightened. "What were their ages?" she asked

"They were all young adults."

Her mind was already going off in a dozen directions when she said, "That's unbelievable. Do you think there could be any more?"

"I went through the books pretty carefully. It's possible I could have missed some others, but I doubt it."

"Did you go to medical records and look at their charts?"

"Of course. That's how I know they all had caval filters. I think we may have really stumbled onto something here, Alex. There must be something defective with these filters."

Alex stood up for a few moments and then took a seat on the corner of her desk. "Was there anything in their hospital courses linking them together?" she asked.

"I'm not sure. I didn't have enough time to go through their charts as thoroughly as I would have liked to, but I will."

Alex closed her eyes. Tapping her fingertips on her lips for a few moments, she finally relaxed and said, "Have medical records leave the charts out for us. We'll meet and go over them tomorrow."

"Sounds good, I'll give you a . . . hold it a second," he said as Alex heard the chirping of his pager through the receiver. "Shit, I have a stat page in the ER. I gotta go. Call me in a couple of hours. I should be out of the OR by then."

Alex was already starting to lower the receiver when she suddenly had a thought. "Theo, are you still there?"

"Yeah."

"Did you happen to notice whose service these patients were on?"

"I do remember because it struck me as kind of strange. All four of them were patients of Victor Runyon's. I gotta go. I'll speak to you later."

Even after the line went dead Alex held the receiver pressed to her ear. Slowly, she replaced it. There was no way that four patients with caval filters should have all died from a pulmonary embolus in less than two years. And why, with eight trauma surgeons on staff, would all four patients have been on Victor Runyon's service?

Alex moved away from the desk and again started for the door. Amid a morass of confusion and unanswered questions, she certainly took solace in the fact that David was on Tom Calloway's service and not Victor's. But just as she was stepping out into the hall she remembered that the night David was injured and brought to Gillette, Victor Runyon was on call—not Tom Calloway. Had it not been for a last-minute change in the schedule, David would be on Victor's service right now.

# Chapter 38

Lleyton's first opened for business in the late 1970s and over the years had become a favorite meeting spot for Australians who lived and worked in the D.C. area.

The bar provided live music and the menu boasted the best shepherd's pie and ocean trout east of Brisbane. When Olivia arrived, her friend Caitlin was already seated at a booth sipping a Victoria Bitters from a large mug. Caitlin was from Canberra, was also a nanny, and had recently broken up with her latest in a long line of boyfriends. She was more attractive than Olivia, always dressed provocatively, and was quite at ease around men, a situation that sometimes left Olivia a little envious.

"Where have you been? I had to start without you," Caitlin said, lifting the mug.

"Jessie insisted on being tucked in one more time."

Caitlin grinned. "Have you ever said no to that child?"

Olivia put on a smile of her own, took a deep breath, and said, "I'm afraid not. I love her too much."

"Would you ladies object to a little company?" a man asked as he approached their booth. Dressed in khaki pants and a black sweater vest over a white T-shirt, he smiled as he waited for an answer. Olivia looked at Caitlin, who covered a quick giggle with the rim of her mug and then pointed to the seat next to her.

"That's an Irish accent," Caitlin said as the gentleman slid in next to Olivia instead. "Are you sure you're in the right place?"

Ignoring Caitlin, he turned and looked directly at Olivia. "Any enlightened Irishman will tell you that Australian women are much more sophisticated and beautiful than Irish women." Simon Lott extended his hand in Olivia's direction and added, "My name's James Harkins. What's yours?"

"Olivia," she answered, shaking his hand.

"May I buy you a drink, Olivia?" he asked.

"I'll have a Bailey's on the rocks."

"I could use another," Caitlin said with a miffed look, waving her empty mug in the air. When James failed to respond, she said, "Excuse me for a moment. I have to make a call. You two look like you could use some private time."

James smiled at Olivia as she smothered another chuckle by pressing her lips tightly together. He had moved in closer and she found the subtle scent of his cologne pleasant enough. He was more attractive than most of the men who frequented Lleyton's and with her love life in an uncontrolled free fall, Olivia was determined to give this unexpected opportunity her best shot.

"Are you a tourist or do you live in Washington?" he asked.

"I've lived here for the last several years," she answered, turning toward him and tilting her head.

"Are you a student?"

"Actually, I'm a nanny. I take care of the daughter of a very busy doctor."

"That's a shame," he said.

"And why's that?"

"Because that means you don't have your own place." Olivia was tickled by his boldness. Afraid his answer had made her blush, she looked away. The waitress returned with her drink and set it in front of her. "I'll have another whiskey," he said with an easy smile. "When I was looking at you from across the bar, I had a feeling you worked with children."

Olivia recoiled a little. "Really? And how did you know that?"

Without moving back he told her, "You can just tell. Some women have a certain aura about them. Maybe it's the softness in your face."

"That's kind of you to say," she said, taking the first sip of her drink.

Lott glanced across the bar. "I hope your friend has a number of very long calls to make," he said, placing his hand over hers.

"I'll go check on her," she said.

Lott slid out and allowed Olivia to get up. He checked his watch. It had been less than ten minutes since he had sat down. He barely had time to finish his drink before she returned.

"Caitlin just remembered she was supposed to meet her boyfriend in Foggy Bottom."

"Have you ever spent any time with them?"

"With Caitlin and her boyfriend?"

"Yeah," he answered.

"Sure."

"Then why's he still with her and not you?" he asked.

Olivia turned her head to hide a smile. "Are you always this bold with women?"

"I guess that depends on the woman."

Olivia knew she was being hustled but it made little difference to her. "So, James, let me see if I've got this right. You just happened to be in the bar, saw Caitlin and me over here, and decided to come over. Is that it?"

"Who's Caitlin?" he said, raising his glass and touching hers.

In spite of his determined come-on, Olivia was completely taken by his good looks and irresistible allure. It was at that moment that she decided that if James Harkins was moving in the same direction that most men do, she was not going to need a lot of courting.

"What do you do when you're not talking to Australian women?" she asked.

"I'm an importer."

"Of what?" she asked.

"Anything I can make a lot of money on."

"Do you live in D.C.?"

"I spend about half of my time in Washington and the other half in Europe."

She regarded him carefully and then smiled. "Are you rich?"

"Bloody loaded," he said as he gently began making small

circles on the back of her hand. "And very generous to all those I become close with."

They spent the next several hours drinking and talking about a number of different things, most of which ended in either a sexual metaphor or some risqué double entendre. At the end of the evening, when he invited her back to his apartment to share his bed, she couldn't conceive of a single good reason to refuse.

The tryst turned out to be everything Olivia had hoped for. It was four A.M. when she finally arrived back in Georgetown. As long as Alex was in the house and not on call, Olivia had no curfew. The only thing that was expected of her was that she be home in time to help Jessie with breakfast.

It had always been a source of comfort to Olivia that she and Alex had more than just an employer-employee relationship, which allowed her to feel comfortable sharing many aspects of her personal life with Alex. After a hot shower, Olivia climbed into bed. She thought about James, admitting to herself that he wasn't the best lover she'd ever had but he was more accommodating than most. It certainly came as a pleasant surprise to her when just before she left his apartment, he asked for her phone number.

Olivia cautioned herself against getting her hopes up, but if James did call, she'd certainly agree to see him again. She considered herself a pretty good judge of character, and in spite of his brash outward nature, she was convinced that it was nothing more than a facade.

Her last thought before drifting off to sleep was that James Harkins was actually a very kind and gentle man, but perhaps sleep wouldn't have come quite so easily if she had seen through Simon Lott's manipulative exterior and questioned what his real agenda was.

# Chapter 39

Alex looked down at David. His eyes were open but instead of the same distant stare she had become accustomed to, there was a renewed clarity in his gaze and perhaps even an attempt to focus on his surroundings.

Even though he was speechless, she felt as though he sensed her presence.

"David?" she whispered, taking his hand. "Can you hear me?" After a few moments she said, "Squeeze my hand if you can hear me."

Alex waited for at least a minute or two, but if David did try to squeeze her hand she was unable to feel it. Undaunted, she continued to talk to him for the next fifteen minutes or so about everything under the sun. Finally, she slid her hand away, leaned over, and kissed him on the forehead. In her heart she knew he was starting to come around.

As much as she wanted to stay, she was scheduled to meet with the new third-year medical students as part of their orientation to the trauma service. She particularly enjoyed working with the junior students because they were still mystified and excited by everything they saw—a distinct departure from many of the fourth-year students, who were already seasoned veterans in their own minds and more concerned about where they would be doing their internship and residency than concentrating on their rotations.

At eleven-thirty Alex finished her presentation. A little hungry because she had skipped breakfast, she decided on an early lunch and headed over to the cafeteria. Just as she was about to pay for her chef salad, she spotted Sue Johnson waving at her. Sue was one of the ICU nurses who had spent many shifts taking care of David. Alex waved back, paid the cashier, and then walked over and sat down. Alex and Sue were of similar age, were both single parents, and had shared some interesting conversations about their lives.

"How have you been?" Alex asked.

"I could use a six-month vacation," Sue answered, taking the first bite of her sandwich.

"I was just thinking the same thing this morning," Alex lamented.

"I'm not assigned to David today but I checked in on him. He seems to be doing great. Just before I came down they were setting up to put his caval filter in."

Alex instantly stopped mixing the dressing into her salad and looked up.

"It must have been another patient. I spoke with Tom Calloway. I told him not to put a filter in yet because I wasn't sure whether I wanted David to have one."

Sue shook her head a couple of times and said, "I guess I could be wrong but I'm pretty sure it was David. And it wasn't Dr. Calloway, it was Dr. Runyon."

"Now I know you're wrong. David's on Calloway's service."

"I know, but Dr. Calloway had a family emergency and had to go out of town. His parents' house caught on fire. They were both pretty badly injured. He signed out to Dr. Runyon and—"

"What time was that?"

"Early this morning."

"I was with David early this morning," she stated as she looked around the cafeteria briefly. Before Sue could respond, she stood up and in a raised tone of voice added, "Nobody said anything to me. The charge nurse should have told me that Calloway went out of town. It's her responsibility."

"Take it easy, Alex. David's fine. I was just up there," Sue said, trying to calm her down as she would any overwrought family member of one of her patients.

"It's her responsibility to tell me," Alex repeated. As her panic crescendoed, she pressed her palms tightly together. Forgetting that Sue was there, Alex's eyes darted to the other side of the cafeteria, where two doctors' phones hung on the wall. Unfortunately, they were both in use, which only served to further bank the fires of her frenzy.

"Are you okay?" Sue asked. Without answering, Alex pushed in her chair and dashed out of the cafeteria.

# Chapter 40

Yanking open the heavy metal door that accessed the stair-well, Alex bolted up the stairs. Breathless from terror more than the climb, she charged out of the stairwell and into the ICU.

The moment she reached the nursing station, she could see a procedure in progress in the fluoroscopy room. Feeling the tightness in her throat, she marched across the ICU and stopped in front of David's room. It was empty. Her eyes flashed back to the fluoroscopy room. At the very last moment and on the brink of losing control, she collected herself enough to approach the room.

Wearing a sterile surgical gown and standing over David with a syringe in his hand, Victor Runyon slowly lowered the needle.

"What's going on?" Alex asked, perhaps with a little more misgiving in her voice than she would have liked but relieved in the knowledge that she had arrived in time. Victor's hand stopped and he looked up. In spite of his mask, the confusion in his eyes was apparent. His two assistants, also gowned and gloved, looked up at the same time.

"We're placing a filter in David. Tom left me a message and said the two of you had discussed it and that I should go ahead." As much as she wanted to take a few steps closer, she remained well away from the sterile surgical field.

"Tom and I did discuss the possibility of a filter, but I told him that I would like to hold off for the time being."

"Well, that's not the message I got," Victor said as he tossed the syringe on a small supply table. "As a family member, I didn't expect to see you here," he added with raised eyebrows as he glanced at the other members of the surgical team.

"Perhaps we should discuss this in the conference room," Alex said, having no difficulty in sensing his disapproval.

"Fine." Victor took a step back, removed his gloves, pulled his mask off, and tossed them both on the ground. The contempt in his manner only incensed Alex more. She had no way of knowing whether he was telling her the truth about Tom's message, but with all eyes on her, it was hardly the time or place for an unpleasant scene between two attending surgeons. If word of such a display were to reach Owen, it would surely meet with his displeasure. Without waiting for Victor, Alex walked into the small consultation room that adjoined the family waiting area. Fortunately, it was empty.

She took a seat on one of the two couches that faced each other and waited for Victor. With each passing minute, the anger and frustration continued to well up inside her. Just as she was about to get up and see what was delaying him, the door swung open. Victor walked directly over, but instead of sitting down he stood directly over her.

"What's with you lately?" he demanded. "Your behavior is extremely unprofessional."

She stood up. "When it comes to the medical treatment of my brother, I'm a family member, not one of your colleagues."

"Then stop acting like a child, for God's sake," he said in a contemptuous voice.

"My brother's in a coma and I'm entitled to a voice in his treatment. If that's a source of frustration for you, I don't give a shit."

Victor raised his hand, pointing his finger at her as he spoke. "Look, I know you're under a lot of stress, Alex, but—"

Before he could continue she raised her own hand. "Spare me the psychological drivel and condescending bedside manner."

"If you won't listen to me then perhaps you should consider getting some professional help."

"This isn't about me. This is about my brother. So why don't we confine the conversation to his care?"

"Fine. Tom's message was clear. He told me to place a caval filter in David."

"I'm sorry. I don't see how that's possible. There was no room for confusion in our conversation," she insisted.

"I guess that's between you and Tom," Victor stated.

"Right now, my decision is to hold off on the placement of a filter. Do we understand each other?"

"It's pointless to discuss anything with you lately. I don't agree with your decision, Alex, but I'll respect your wishes, so just let me know if you reconsider. Your brother needs a filter and you know it. I'm going to Boston at the end of the week for a meeting. I'd prefer to put it in before I leave."

"I'll let you know," she said, tempted to inform him that she was fully aware of his recent track record with caval filters. She would have loved to see his reaction, but there was no way she was going to tip her hand just yet. Even if she did decide that David needed a filter, he'd be the last person she'd allow to put it in.

"The ball's in your court, Alex." Without waiting for her reaction, he turned and left the room.

From her conversation with George, she assumed the meeting he was referring to in Boston involved the Caduceus Project. After a few minutes, Alex left the consultation room hoping that Victor was no longer in the ICU. Unfortunately she noticed him sitting at the nursing station making a note on a chart. He must have sensed her eyes on him, because he looked up, glanced over at her, and then shot her a mocking smile.

Alex was careful to maintain the outward appearance of composure but on the inside she was seething. If Tom Calloway weren't in the middle of such a horrible family crisis, she would be on the phone with him right now to find out whether he had really left Victor a message to proceed with the filter.

"Is everything okay?" came a voice from behind Alex. "You flew out of the cafeteria without even touching your salad," Sue said.

"You were right. They were about to put a filter in David."

Sue looked concerned. "I was just speaking to some of the girls. They said you looked pretty upset."

"I'm okay. I'll go over in a minute and say something to them."

"We had to break down that whole sterile setup, but at least they didn't take the filter out of its package. Those things are so expensive and it's the last Medivasc we have," Sue said.

"Medivasc? I've never even heard of them. I thought the only filters we carried were manufactured by American Health Technologies."

"We have two suppliers," Sue said. "Medivasc is a small company in the Midwest. They mostly make vascular devices."

"Who else uses the filters besides Dr. Runyon?" Alex asked.

"No one, and if we don't have any in stock when he wants to put one in, he has a hissy fit and insists one be shipped by overnight air."

"Why does he like Medivasc so much?" Alex asked.

"I have no idea."

"Is he like that with other devices and equipment?"

Sue thought for a moment. "Not that I'm aware of." She looked across the unit and waved to one of the other nurses. "How well do you know Dr. Runyon?" she asked in just above a whisper.

"About as well as I want to," Alex answered.

Sue scanned the immediate area before going on. "After his divorce, Allyson Coleridge from the night shift dated him for a while. She told me that his ex got a restraining order against him."

"Why?" Alex asked.

"Let's just say he had a little problem with anger management."

"Are you saying he beat her up?"

Sue's smile was a coy one. "I'm not saying anything, but I don't see why Allyson would make something like that up," she said, waving to a nurse across the unit who was trying to get her attention. "I've got to get going. I'll see you later."

Alex walked slowly back to David's room, taking care not to look in Victor's direction. It had never occurred to her that he might have been using a different type of filter than the rest of the surgeons. Perhaps there was a fundamental defect in the Medivasc design that accounted for its high failure rate. But if that was the case, why wasn't he aware of it, and why hadn't he reported it to the FDA? Alex didn't have an answer, but she did know that it would be an easy enough matter to check with the FDA and find out.

Victor may not have been the most conscientious surgeon Alex had ever worked with, but he was adequate, making it hard for her to believe that he could have unintentionally overlooked four deaths in less than two years.

# Chapter 41

Theo was already seated at a round conference table toward the back of the medical records department when Alex walked in.

She was surprised to see him dressed in a shirt and tie as opposed to his usual scrubs.

"What's with the fancy attire?" she asked.

"I'm almost done with my training. I have to start acting like an attending."

"I see," Alex said, remembering having the same type of thoughts when she was finishing up her fellowship. "Are you sure all of these patients were on Dr. Runyon's service?"

Theo spread the four charts out in front of Alex. "Have a look for yourself. Even though we don't have the autopsy report yet, I pulled Robert Key's chart too."

"How come we don't have it yet?"

"I told you. It's a medical examiner's case and they operate at their own pace. I'll give them a call in a day or two to see if the report's available yet."

"Fine, let's look at the other cases in the meantime," Alex said.

Theo grabbed the closest chart and flipped it open. "Okay, the first one's a thirty-four-year-old schoolteacher by the name of Nancy Olander from Rockville. She was admitted last spring with a bad pelvic fracture."

"How did it happen?" Alex asked.

"She fell down her basement steps. When she first got here, she had quite a bit of bleeding but they were able to get it under control."

"Any other significant injuries?"

"No. Five days later she was doing fine and a caval filter was placed without any apparent complications." Alex continued to read with Theo as he moved through the doctor's daily progress note section.

"It sounds like she was out of the woods," Alex said. "I wonder what happened."

"Well, it looks like rehab services had already seen her and made some recommendations." Theo flipped to the next page. "Everything seemed to be going okay until the morning of March nineteenth, when she had a sudden cardiac arrest."

"Was she still in the ICU?" Alex asked.

"No, she was in a private room."

"What time did it happen?"

Theo turned to the nursing notes. "It looks like at about two A.M."

"Is there a code blue note?" Alex asked.

Theo again thumbed through the chart until he located the note that chronicled the emergency efforts to resuscitate Nancy Olander. They both read silently for a few minutes, after which Theo looked up and said, "It doesn't look like they were ever able to establish any kind of cardiac rhythm. She was pronounced at two-forty-five A.M."

"What about an autopsy?"

"They did one. The pathologist reported the cause of death to be a direct result of a pulmonary embolus."

"Any mention of the filter?" Alex asked.

"No."

Theo closed the chart and cast a glance at Alex, who was

sitting forward in her chair with her arms folded. "Let's see the next one." she said.

"That would be Graham Pierce, a forty-year-old physician from Omaha who was struck by a car. According to the first note, the only injuries noted at the time of admission were a broken leg, a thigh laceration, and a sprained wrist."

"What about a head injury?" Alex asked.

"No, he was wide awake and alert in the emergency room."

"So why would a patient like that wind up with a caval filter?" she asked.

"I asked myself the same question and then I found an addendum to one of the radiology reports that indicated a missed pelvic fracture. From the description it was a pretty bad one."

"That makes a little more sense," Alex said. "I guess with a broken leg and a bad pelvic fracture it was probably reasonable to put a filter in." Alex reached over and pulled the chart a little closer, read the report, and shook her head.

"What?" Theo asked.

"It's kind of unusual to miss a pelvic fracture of this magnitude. Don't you think?"

"We're a big hospital, Alex. Shit happens."

Alex remained unconvinced. "Flip ahead in the progress notes. I want to see how he got into trouble."

"He was out of the ICU and doing fine. The filter had been in for about a week. Let's see," Theo said, running his finger down the page as he read. "It says that he was still on bed rest. He got acutely short of breath and lost consciousness. Before the resident could get there he was in full cardiac arrest. It looks like they got him back for a few minutes but then he arrested again. He was pronounced just after three A.M."

"How about an autopsy?"

"The medical examiner passed but we did one at the family's request."

"What did they put on the death certificate as the cause of death?"

"Pulmonary embolism." Theo glanced up at a clock mounted over the door and said, "I gotta get going. I told Brown I'd scrub with him on a laparoscopic appendectomy."

He picked up the other two charts, stacked them with the

others, and put them in front of Alex. "The other two patients you already know—Kyle Dolan and Robert Key. Doctor Key's case has been referred to the medical examiner's office."

"Stay on top of the ME. I want to see that autopsy report as soon as it's available."

"I'll call them every couple of days," he said. "If you want, we can go over these other charts later, but I've already studied them in detail."

"I'll have a look at them myself and then give you a call."

Theo asked. "Do you think there's enough here to write up?" he asked.

"Absolutely," she said, far less interested in the scientific merit of what Theo had uncovered than figuring out what was the common thread linking all four of these patients together, and why all four just happened to be on Victor's service."

Alex gathered up the four charts, tucked them under her arm, and walked over to a secretary who was intently studying her monitor.

"Excuse me."

The young lady, who had a pug nose, bright red lipstick, and a congenial expression, answered, "Yes, Dr. Caffey."

"I'm not quite finished with these charts yet. Would you please send them up to my office? I should have them back to you in a few days."

"No problem," she said reaching out and taking the charts from Alex. "I'll have them signed out to you and have one of the volunteers run them up to your office."

"Thank you," she said and then closed the door behind her.

# Chapter 42

Micah was just about to call it a day when Lisa buzzed him and told him that Carson Gillette was on the phone. It was close to six P.M., and had the call not been from one of the university trustees, he would have certainly dodged it.

Micah was fairly well acquainted with the man waiting to speak to him. As a member of the Gillette family, Carson had cleverly maneuvered his way onto the board. An entrepreneur in every sense of the word, Gillette was as polished and shrewd as they come. His fellow board members held him in high esteem, viewing him as a man with the type of diplomatic skills it took to deal with the most ticklish of situations.

"Thanks, Lisa," he said. "I'll see you tomorrow." Micah then tapped the flashing light and connected the call. "Hello."

"Micah. It's Carson Gillette. How's everything?"

"Very well, thank you."

"I'm pleased to hear that. You should be proud to know that there are a lot of people who feel that Gillette has become the flagship hospital in the Adams health care system."

"That's very flattering. Hopefully, when the university approves the funds for our expansion program, we can increase our services even more."

"I admire your optimism, Micah, and we're working on it, but thirty million dollars is a considerable sum of money for a private institution to raise."

"I understand," he said.

"Micah, the reason for my call is that the board's a little concerned about the activities of one of your physicians."

Micah had a fairly good suspicion whom Gillette was talking about but decided to remain aloof. "Really? Who would that be?"

"Dr. Alexandra Caffey. We understand her twin brother was recently injured and is a patient in the ICU."

"That's correct."

"How's he doing?"

"He was pretty badly hurt but he seems to be making slow progress."

"That's good to hear," Gillette said. "How's Dr. Caffey handling all this?"

Micah had a pretty good idea where he was going with all this and was mindful not to divulge anymore than he had to. "I would say that she's doing reasonably well. Is there a problem?" he asked.

"Well, to be honest with you, Micah, there seems to be some concern that Dr. Caffey's not handling the stress very well."

"Who specifically is concerned?" Micah asked.

"We are," came Gillette's direct and immediate response. "For some reason, she's been asking a lot of questions, which is making some people uncomfortable. I also understand she made quite a scene in the ICU recently. Victor Runyon was quite incensed. Is it true that she's pursuing some kind of conspiracy theory?"

Micah responded, "My understanding is that she has some questions about how her brother and Dr. Key were injured."

"That may be so, but we hired her to practice trauma surgery. Perhaps you could discreetly remind Dr. Caffey that Washington, D.C., and John Adams University are well represented with people to look into any reasonable concerns that she might have."

"I'll certainly do that," Micah said.

"Do you think she'll be receptive to your advice?"

Glad that Gillette was on the phone and not sitting across his desk, Micah shook his head in guarded optimism. "I think she will be," he finally said, making sure to sound sincere.

"Good. Will I see you at the annual fund-raiser next week?" he asked.

"Of course."

As soon as Micah hung up, he was tempted to call Alex.

Grumbling to himself, he was just about to dial her number when he suddenly thought better of the idea, deciding it would be better to give the matter some further thought so that he might figure out the best way to appeal to her good judgment.

# Chapter 43

At exactly 1 P.M. Simon Lott received a call from Morgan to make himself available for a meeting in one hour.

Fifty minutes later he found himself seated under a red umbrella at a small outdoor café on Connecticut Avenue. It was unseasonably cool but still pleasant enough to sit outdoors and watch the throng of shoppers pass by with their arms laden with packages.

The pleasant surroundings were made even more refreshing by an extremely attractive young lady who walked up and sat down about three tables away. She glowed in appearance with seductive eyes and a Roman nose; her straight auburn hair plummeted gracefully over her shoulders. When she looked up and caught him smiling at her, she merely looked away. This was not the response he was hoping for and he wondered whether she was the type of woman who was spoiled by her own beauty.

When ten after two came, Lott was still seated alone. He signaled the waiter and ordered another iced tea. He watched overhead as a news helicopter made several passes and then hovered over an area about a mile away. When he lowered his eyes, Morgan was taking the seat directly across from him.

"Our concerns regarding Dr. Caffey are escalating," he said.

"As I recall, we've already had this conversation," Lott reminded him as a lanky waiter placed his drink in front of him.

"Which raises the question, why is she still around and still meddling into our affairs?"

Lott's patience for Morgan's pompous nature was drawing thin.

"I'm not a rank amateur, Morgan. Patience is not only an asset in my work, it's a prerequisite for staying alive. When the right opportunity presents itself, I will deal with Dr. Caffey."

"I thought you were the type of man who created his own opportunities. In case I was unclear the last time we spoke, Alex Caffey is your number one priority." On that note, Morgan stood up and started down Connecticut Avenue. Lott watched him for a few seconds and then with a smirk picked up his drink and finished it.

Most of the tables that had been empty when he had arrived were now occupied. Lott glanced over at the young lady whom he had admired earlier. She was reading the paper and sipping a cappuccino. He suspected that she knew his eyes were on her but she didn't look up. He had always been intrigued by aloof women, and since the day had so far been a complete waste of his time, he stood up and walked over to her table.

"I was just thinking what a beautiful day it was and that I had no one to share it with," he said.

The young lady removed her reading glasses and replaced them with a pair of lightly tinted rose-colored sunglasses.

"How devastating that must be for you," she said in an accent very close to his own.

"Tragic, actually," he said as he sat down without being invited. "Where in Ireland are you from?"

"I was raised in Limerick."

"That can be a rough city," he said. "Dublin's considerably more civilized. What brings you to the States?"

"I live here. You, on the other hand, strike me as a visitor."

Lott grinned, noticing that apart from a rather expensive gold watch with a diamond bezel, she wore no jewelry. "My work requires that I travel quite a bit," he said.

"Really. Have you considered finding something else?"

"I'm kind of set in my ways but it's always nice to meet

someone from home, especially someone so beautiful. My name's James Harkins."

"Kerry," she said, without extending her hand.

The young lady didn't respond in word or expression to his compliment but she didn't get up and leave. The conversation flowed easily and Lott found her refreshingly bright and insightful. Finally, she reached into her purse and pulled out a pen. She signaled the waiter, who brought over her check. Lott covered it with his hand and said, "I insist."

Kerry reached for the check with her other hand, turned it over, and wrote something on the back and then left it for him. After a tempting smile, she pushed her hair back, got up, and walked away. Simon watched as she disappeared down Connecticut Avenue. Her youthful and perfectly proportioned figure was a welcome relief from Olivia's frumpy body. Lott wasn't usually taken so by a woman, but he found Kerry's flair and elegance almost arresting.

When he glanced down at the check, a broad smile came to his face as he read her note. He reached for his pen and copied her name and phone number onto a napkin.

"Kerry Nealon, now that's a beautiful name," he whispered as he got up. He then tucked the napkin into his pocket, fully intending to take her up on her invitation to meet at ten P.M. at the Four Seasons Hotel in Georgetown for a drink.

# Chapter 44

It was ten minutes past nine when Alex and Micah pulled into the parking lot at the National Zoo. Located along Rock Creek, the zoo stretched over a hundred and sixty acres and boasted one of the most eclectic and interesting collections of animal exhibits in the country.

A cold front had moved in overnight and it was a blustery, gray day. Alex, wearing a Georgetown University sweatshirt, was the first one out of the car. She opened the back door for the kids and the moment they flew out she grabbed each of them by the hand and then knelt down beside them. Trying to avoid the usual bickering about which exhibit they'd see first, she said, "I have an idea. Why don't we start with the great apes and then figure out what to do from there?"

Hands on hips, Jessie's eyes flashed. "But I want—"

"I know what you want, honey, but let's try it my way this time." Jessie puffed up her cheeks and leered at her mother in much the same way Alex used to do at hers under similar circumstances. Gabe, being a far more reserved child, stood silently with an agreeable expression. Unusually thoughtful for a six-year-old, he had a strong attachment to both Alex and Jessie and became much more relaxed and animated when he was around them. With his front two teeth missing and sporting a freckled nose and crested cheek bones, he was a source of extreme pride of Micah.

"Is everyone ready?" Micah asked, joining them on their side of the car.

Without responding, Jessie and Gabe ran out in front but then waited impatiently for Alex and Micah at the main entrance. Once inside, they followed Olmsted Walk past a large concession stand that was framed by multicolored balloons and an eclectic collection of stuffed animals. A young woman carrying a large textbook and a legal pad fell in behind them.

"What's been going on?" Micah asked. "You've hardly said a word since I picked you up. Is everything okay with David?"

"He's fine. I saw him early this morning."

"So what's all the gloom and doom then?" he asked just as they entered the great ape house. She watched as the kids pushed their way closer to get a better view of the latest addition, a very animated lowland gorilla. Gabe and Jessie particularly liked this exhibit and Alex figured they would be occupied for at least fifteen minutes. She pointed to a bench next to the central arboretum, Micah nodded, and they sat down.

Neither of them particularly noticed the young lady with the textbook who followed them in. After walking past them, she sat down on the next bench over. She stared at the apes for a few seconds before setting the legal pad atop the book and pulling out a pen. This particular pen, which had been given to her by Simon Lott, was rather distinctive. Although it was not very effective as a writing instrument, it was an extremely sensitive infrared audio surveillance device.

On this day, Simon Lott had also decided to visit the zoo and was, at that very moment, comfortably seated on a bench about a hundred yards away sipping a diet soda. The earpiece he wore was hardly noticeable. The woman who was pretending to study the apes' behavior had been sent to him by Morgan a couple of days earlier. As a rule, Lott didn't like working with people he couldn't personally vouch for, but he was assured by Morgan that she was entirely capable.

"So why don't you tell me what's on your mind?" Micah asked.

Alex moved a little forward on the bench. "I thought we had a policy that we don't talk about hospital business when we're out with the kids."

"That's true, but I'm prepared to overlook that rule today. So go ahead, tell me what's going on," he said, crossing one leg over the other. When a few seconds passed and she didn't respond, he added, "Go ahead—even if it's about Robert Key and the Caduceus Project."

"Are you sure?" she asked.

"Absolutely, go for it."

"I was thinking," Alex began cautiously. "What if Robert came across some information about the Caduceus Project that he found morally and ethically repulsive?"

"Are you saying that he had an attack of conscience and felt compelled to go public?" Micah inquired.

"Why else would somebody go see an investigative reporter?" she asked, waving at Jessie, who had turned around and was now jumping up and down, mimicking the apes.

"The fact still remains that Victor and Robert were not only good friends but were also in the same medical organization. Political differences aside, I'm still unclear why Victor would resort to such extreme means even if Robert suddenly decided to completely reject the Caduceus Project."

"I can't explain that right now," Alex said, "but that doesn't mean I've dismissed the possibility." She paused for a moment to consider whether she should disclose what she had found out about the four patients who had died of a pulmonary embolus. To this point, Micah had been, at a minimum, polite and perhaps even receptive to her concerns. He could have just as easily rejected her theories as the ranting of a grief-stricken sister. Alex remained unsure of how to proceed, but her instinct told her that it was premature to mention anything about the caval filters.

"I hope you're being discreet in your inquiries. Just remember what I told you about being too visible. You have your career to think of."

Alex smiled. "Are you saying that you might not be able to gallop up astride a white horse, dressed in your armor, and rescue me from the tower?"

"I'm glad you find this amusing. Just try to remember that some of the more powerful and influential people at Gillette are a little old-fashioned in their ways and might not understand your inquisitive nature."

When she realized he wasn't amused by her teasing, she said, "I know you're concerned about me and I appreciate it." Micah was a little red-faced and looked away. Alex feared she had embarrassed him, so she took the opportunity to look over at the kids, who were weaving their way through the other observers trying to get a better view of the apes. Every few seconds they stopped, grabbed hands, and laughed uncontrollably.

"I don't know who's worse, you or your mother," he muttered.

Alex couldn't help but giggle. "I can't help you with that one."

"You don't even know what I'm going to say."

"I think I have an inkling," she assured him.

"She's very direct, Alex."

"You're a big boy. Tell her to cool it."

"I'm not so sure that's such a good idea," he pointed out.

"First Maxine and now my mother. Do you have a problem confronting women?"

At the moment, he was asking himself the same question. "I got a call from someone on the board of Trustees—Carson Gillette. He had some concerns."

"Really? About what?"

"About you, Alex." Before she could jump in, Micah raised his hand. "Let me finish. We had a very short conversation."

"What's he so upset about?" she asked.

"I didn't say he was upset. I said he was concerned."

"About what?"

"Evidently, word has reached the board of your not-so-discreet inquiries and your run-in with Victor. He asked that I have a word with you to remind you that the board expects you to behave in a professional manner and confine your activities to the practice of trauma surgery."

"Were you asked to have the same word with Victor?"

"No."

Nodding as Micah spoke, Alex looked around for a few seconds before responding. "I appreciate the advice. You can tell Mr. Gillette for me that we've spoken and that I completely understand."

"Does that mean you'll comply?"

"It means I understand."

"You're playing with fire here, Alex. If I were you . . ."

Micah paused to rub his chin and before he could say anything further, Gabe and Jessie came running over.

"We're hungry," Jessie announced.

Micah squatted down like a catcher, looked at Gabe, and said, "We ate right before we picked up Jessie. Are you really hungry?" Gabe looked over at Jessie, who gave him a grim stare. After thinking things over for a few seconds, he just shrugged. Micah then placed his hands on Jessie's shoulders. "I think you've got a lot of your mother in you," he told her.

"That's okay with me," she answered. Micah's head dropped as Alex laughed out loud.

The four of them exited the great ape house. "I have an idea," Micah said. "Let's go over to *How Do You Zoo?* and when we're done there, we can get something to eat."

Gabe and Jessie exchanged a quick look and then nodded eagerly. Alex particularly liked this interactive exhibit because it offered the kids the opportunity of putting on zookeeper uniforms and pretending to be veterinarians.

"Let's get going," Alex said. "Do you guys know the way?"

"It's that way," Gabe said, pointing with total conviction.

"Okay, we'll be right behind you. No running," she said as the kids started off shoulder to shoulder in a fast walk.

While the kids enjoyed the exhibit, Micah updated Alex on his relationship with Maxine. It wasn't a very encouraging picture and for the first time she sensed something more than frustration in his voice. By the end of the day, Alex's intuition told her that Micah was giving serious consideration to breaking his engagement to Maxine, a possibility that didn't sadden her one little bit.

# Chapter 45

Standing on the sidewalk across the street from Alex Caffey's house, Simon Lott savored one of his favorite Cuban cigars while he stared up at the second story. When the light went out, he gave Gretel's leash a gentle tug and started back down the block to where he had parked his Hummer.

"She spent the day at the zoo with Micah Henry and their kids," he told Morgan, pressing his cell phone a little harder against his ear because of the poor reception. "After they left they had dinner in Foggy Bottom. She's home now."

"Were you able to hear any of their conversation?"

"They were moving around a lot but I think we got most of it."

"And?" Morgan asked impatiently.

"They didn't say anything that you're not already aware of. She knows her brother didn't jump from his balcony and has no intention of stopping until she figures out what really happened to him."

"Specifics, Mr. Lott. I'm interested in specifics, not your opinion." Lott spent the next five minutes filling Morgan in on Alex's conversation with Micah. Morgan had several questions, all of which tested Lott's patience, but he decided to answer them without becoming antagonistic. Finally Morgan said, "Are you ready?"

"It will be done within the next day or so."

"I assume you have every detail worked out and there will be no unexpected surprises this time." Ignoring the condescending remark, Lott chuckled to himself and then hung up without saying another word.

It was still fairly early and Lott figured he had more than adequate time to go back to his apartment before meeting Kerry, the young lady he'd met at the outdoor café. The night before, they spent over two hours together at the bar at the Four Seasons Hotel, enjoying a very expensive bottle of Beaujolais and talking about a host of topics.

It was almost one in the morning when the bellman opened the cab door for her. Lott kissed her once on each cheek and waited until the taxi disappeared. Before it reached her apartment, he had already called Kerry and suggested that they meet again tonight. He knew the chemistry was there and was hardly surprised when she accepted immediately.

Turning down New Hampshire Avenue, Lott reached over and petted Gretel on the head. Fantasizing about Kerry, he wondered whether there might be some middle ground between inconsequential sex and unconditional commitment. Perhaps Kerry Nealon was the woman who could fit that bill.

# Chapter 46

**MAY 4**

On the nights she was on call, it had become Alex's custom to stay at the hospital until about eleven o'clock before heading home. If she tried to leave any earlier, it was inevitable she got called back in. To pass the time between trips to the emergency room, she would work in her office, catching up on her administrative responsibilities.

It was about ten P.M. when Alex stepped off the elevator on the sixth floor of the medical office building. The large modernistic building, which also contained the research center, had been erected directly adjacent to the trauma center and was attached to it by a series of connecting halls and walkways. Once inside her office, she closed the door and sat down at her desk to have a more careful look at the charts of the patients who had died of a pulmonary embolus.

She had been looking over the charts for about ten minutes when she was startled by a sudden crash from somewhere out in the hall. Assuming it was one of the custodial staff, she took a deep breath and chided herself for being too jittery, taking an extra moment to remind herself that she had worked alone at night in her office dozens of times and had never had a problem.

When she heard nothing further, she again turned her attention to the charts. Sue Johnson's information regarding Runyon and the Medivasc filters had been right on the money. All four of the patients who had died did so with a Medivasc filter in place. Curious about how many total filters had been put in, Alex picked up her phone and dialed central supply.

"Central, this is Nick," answered the night supervisor in his southern drawl.

"Hi, Nick. It's Dr. Caffey. I was hoping you could help me with a problem."

"Sure, Dr. Caffey," he said. "How can I help you?"

"I'm interested in the Medivasc vena caval filters. Do we have any in stock?"

"Let me check," he said. "Hold on. It might take a sec. I have to pull up the right screen. Let's see, let's see. Here it is. We have two."

"Do your records show a history of usage?"

"Sure. What do you want to know?" he asked.

"How many have been used in the last . . . oh, say eighteen months?"

"Let's see. We've sent out a total of five and they've all gone to the ICU. We got one back the other day, so I assume four have been put in."

"Can you read me the names of the patients?" she asked. As Nick read them off, Alex confirmed that she had each of their charts in front of her. "Thanks, Nick. I appreciate the info," she said, finding it hard to believe that every single patient who had undergone placement of a Medivasc filter had died.

"Any time, Dr. Caffey. Hey, before you hang up, did anyone ever tell you that you look like that actress Ashley Judd?"

"Uh, no, Nick. I don't think so."

"Well, you do. Are you sure nobody's ever told you that?"

The answer was yes, but Alex answered, "I think you're the first."

The next forty-five minutes passed quickly. When Alex looked up and realized it was eleven o'clock, she decided to call it a night. Apart from their ages and the fact that all of the patients were on Victor Runyon's service and died with Medivasc filters in place, she couldn't find anything else linking them except that they had all been transferred to private rooms from the ICU.

She was just about to give up and call it a night, when something suddenly occurred to her. She quickly opened each of the charts again and turned to the nursing notes to see what time each of the patients had died. Her hunch had been right, causing her to shake her head in bewilderment at how she could have missed the fact that all of the patients died between two and five in the morning. She leaned back in her chair, wondering whether it was nothing more than just a strange coincidence. Worn out and more confused than ever, she decided to call it a night.

When she stepped out into the hall, she immediately noticed a white-haired man in dark-green coveralls at the opposite end of the hall slowly turning a mop in a metal pail. Alex started down the hall, watching him with each step. By the awkward way he was handling the mop, she assumed that it must have been he who knocked the bucket over earlier and caused all of that racket.

With his shoulders hunched, he finally took the mop out of the pail and slapped it on the floor. But when she watched him make purposeless movements with the mop as if it were the first time he'd ever held one in his hands, her sense of uneasiness mounted. Her pace slowed and with each step the muscles in her forearms tightened from the fists she had unknowingly made. When she was about thirty feet away the man stopped for a moment and cast a quick glance over his shoulder. He smiled, nodded at her, and then returned to his work.

Acting instinctively and without any further thought, she immediately stopped and announced in a scatterbrained voice, "Oh shoot, my keys." Turning as she spoke, she walked quickly back to her office. Standing in the middle of the room, she found herself tempted to call security. But not wanting to appear hysterical, she waited a couple of minutes and then peeked out in the hallway again. The man was still mopping in the exact same place.

Not interested in either admitting to herself that her imagination was running wild or proving how brave she was, Alex slipped out of her office and started down the hall in the opposite direction. Her plan was to take the elevated walkway over to the adjoining research facility and then ride the back elevators down to the ground floor. Moving quietly, she strolled past several offices until she reached the walkway. When she was about halfway across and starting to feel a little more secure, she heard the first footsteps.

Barely audible at first, they quickly became fast-paced and louder. Without looking back, she reacted to the adrenaline by breaking into a run. With her arms extended and locked, she slammed into the handle of the double doors at full speed. Crashing through them, she crossed over into the main hallway of the research facility. There were several laboratories between her and the back elevator. She strained to see the end of the hall but it was a long way away and the only light came from a series of dim bulbs that marked the emergency lights mounted high on the walls.

She was certain that it was the maintenance man who was pursuing her and that the chances of her making it to the elevator and getting away before he caught her were zero. Alex had ridden the back elevator a number of times. It was small and slow as an intern struggling through her first appendix. Terrified and needing time to think, she prayed she wouldn't hear the sound of the double doors opening for several more seconds.

Gasping for each breath and having no idea what to do, she stopped and pinned her back against the wall. Feeling her heart galloping as if it were about to burst out of her chest, she heard the slam of the doors. With no other choice, she stretched out her arm, desperately exploring for the door handle. The pulsations of the arteries in her temples pounded harder with each passing second. Finally, when she was on the verge of giving up and making a desperate run for the eleva-

tor, her fingertips found the doorknob. Opening the door just
far enough to squeeze through, she gently pulled it closed.

The laboratory was one of the bigger ones and consisted of
two long parallel research benches that ran from the front of
the lab all the way to the back. An extensive bank of highly
sophisticated scientific instruments lined the entire length of
both side walls. Apart from the small amount of light cast by
the multicolored digital readouts, there was no other light.
Alex knew that there must be at least one phone in the lab, but
in the dim light she knew it would be a miracle if she found
one.

Without taking her eyes off the door, she moved silently
toward the back. Looking around, she quickly realized her options for concealing herself were limited. Making her way to
the end of the lab bench, she knelt down behind it. Fortunately, she could see the front of the lab by poking her head
out on either side of the bench and looking down the aisles.

Well aware of the effects of breathing too fast, Alex forced
herself to slow down while at the same time struggling to
keep her wits about her. Several seconds passed and she heard
nothing. Finally, she peered out from her hiding place.

As far as she could see, no one was there but when she noticed the crack in the door with a sliver of light filtering
through, her heart practically stopped. She turned as silently
as she was able and peered down the opposite aisle. This time
she could definitely make out the silhouette of a man standing
not more than twenty feet from her.

Pulling her head back behind the bench, she again felt her
breathing racing out of control. Her first thought was to wait
until he walked past her and then crawl out on the opposite
side. She might be able to make it to the door undetected but
she knew as soon as she opened it, he'd see the light and come
after her. Even if she ran for the back elevator, he'd surely
catch her before she could get away.

Just at that moment, her eyes drifted across the aisle to the
opposite bench. Underneath it, not more than five feet away,
was a small metal fire extinguisher. Since the man was moving down the opposite aisle, Alex reasoned that she had a
fairly good shot of getting the extinguisher without him seeing her. Leaning out, she slowly stretched her arm across the

aisle. Straining for every inch she could get, she finally managed to curl her fingers around the top of the fire extinguisher. When she was positive her grip was secure, she carefully pulled it in.

After taking a deep breath, Alex again assumed a kneeling position. She heard two footsteps and then nothing. After a few more seconds of silence—another two steps. The same pattern of starting and stopping continued with the same precision as a metronome. Afraid of being seen if she looked out in the aisle again, Alex could do nothing more than concentrate on the sound of the approaching footsteps.

When she sensed he was only a few feet away, she cocked the fire extinguisher behind her shoulder. Alex could smell the fruity scent of his cologne, and from the sound of his next steps she knew he was no more than a few feet away. Her fear paled in comparison to the rage and self-preservation that now consumed her. As tempted as she was to swing the extinguisher blindly out into the aisle, she held back for fear of missing him. Just another couple of steps was all she needed to bring him to the end of the bench and into striking range. There was plenty of weight to the extinguisher and Alex was fairly confident that if she timed the blow right she would bring him down.

With each second that passed, Alex's muscles quivered and ached as her arms tired from the weight of the extinguisher. A sudden wave of frenzy jolted her when she wondered whether he had figured out where she was hiding. But just then, the man took the two steps forward that she had been praying for. Now his right leg was no more than a couple of feet from her.

As if a steam-powered catapult were assisting her, Alex whirled the fire extinguisher around from behind her shoulder, catching the man squarely on his shin. His wail shattered the silence as he came crashing down on his back.

Alex was tempted to slide out on his side and hit him again but she dropped the extinguisher and rolled the other way. But before she could pull her legs out and scramble to her feet, she felt his powerful grip lock around her ankle. Gasping for each breath, she rolled on her back and began kicking him wildly with both legs. In spite of her relentless efforts, he was able to maintain his grip and drag her toward him. As another burst of adrenaline entered her bloodstream, she twisted her torso wildly while flailing her hands in all directions.

Alex knew she had only seconds before she was completely within his grasp. He was now coming to his knees and she could feel his grip tightening. As she writhed and kicked, her hands fell on the fire extinguisher. Grasping it by the handle and with her arms fully extended over her head, Alex whirled it around, this time striking the man on the point of his chin. The blow was square and sent him sailing backward.

Free from his grip, Alex pushed herself backward and jumped to her feet. When she looked down at him, he was rolling slowly from side to side and moaning softly. Fearing that he'd come around in a matter of seconds, she raced for the door. Once she was out in the hallway, she sprinted back across the walkway and into the medical office building.

When Alex finally reached the elevators, she immediately began pounding the down button. She was so out of breath, she feared she would pass out. She glanced to her right and saw the man's bucket and mop exactly where he'd been using them. Still uncertain just how much damage she had inflicted on him, she fixed her eyes and ears on the far end of the hall.

When the doors finally rumbled open, she charged on to the elevator. The half minute it took to reach the first floor seemed like an eternity. As soon as the doors began to open, Alex forced her way past them and ran for the first phone she could find.

# Chapter 47

By twelve-thirty in the morning, Simon Lott had returned to his apartment and was sitting in his living room with his leg elevated on a small ottoman.

It had taken every bit of strength and ingenuity he could manage to limp out of Gillette's research facility before the police arrived. He was fairly certain that Alex Caffey had failed to break his leg, and the laceration under his chin would heal but not without leaving a noticeable scar, which was hardly an asset in his business.

As the two Percodans he had taken about thirty minutes earlier started to ease the throbbing, he thought about what he'd tell Morgan regarding the events of the evening. He certainly had no interest in being truthful regarding how she had managed to slip through his fingers. Although his instructions were to provide a permanent solution, Lott felt comfortable that he'd be able to persuade Morgan that terrorizing Dr. Caffey was a much smarter way to go than killing her.

When the doorbell rang, he groaned and then twisted his head around and stared at the door for a few seconds. When it rang for the second time, he swung his leg down, struggled to his feet, and then slowly made his way to the front door.

"I was a little surprised by your call. I thought we were going to meet at Clyde's. Why the sudden change of plans?" Kerry Nealon asked.

Lott had seen quite a bit of Kerry since they had first met in the café. In addition to their two late-night dates, he had seen her once for lunch and had spent several hours on the phone with her. Such an investment of time and effort was something he was unaccustomed to when it came to women.

What perplexed him was that she didn't strike him as a woman who required a lot of courting when she was attracted to a man, but so far she had managed to derail any and all of his amorous advances.

Lott started back toward the couch. "I had a slight accident. We can have a drink here."

"No problem," Kerry said, studying him as he hobbled slowly back across the room. "For goodness' sakes, what the hell happened to you?" she asked, taking his arm and then helping him back into his chair.

"I had an accident," he repeated, reaching for an ice pack and placing it squarely on his shin. Lott reached for a crystal brandy snifter and then cradled it between his fingers. He had been injured before but never by a woman, and at the moment his ego was as bruised as his face and leg.

Kerry looked at the large dressing on his chin and asked, "What exactly happened to you?"

"I tripped over the sidewalk getting out of my car. I had to go to the hospital and have a few stitches put in." Lott had actually been to an ex–Marine Corps medic who charged amply and had no interest in keeping medical records or remembering names.

"Is your leg broken?"

"No, it's just bruised a little."

She moved in closer, knelt in front of him, gently removed the ice pack, and touched his leg gently.

"That's quite a bit of swelling and soft tissue injury. Did you have it X-rayed?"

"Soft tissue injury. You sound like a doctor."

"Not exactly," she answered, replacing the pack. "I have a degree in nursing. I just never liked it very much so I stopped practicing."

"Really. I could use the special attention of a private-duty nurse tonight. Why don't you stay over?"

Kerry smiled as she sat down on the floor in front of him.

"In the first place, you're hardly in any condition for what you have in mind, and in the second, I have to get up early tomorrow."

"Make an exception this one time," he said. "I really could use a very caring angel of mercy right about now."

"I don't think so," she said in a way that he knew she wasn't going to waver from her decision. "Why don't we just have that drink and then I'll help you into bed?"

"Okay," he groaned, "but you're taking this hard-to-get routine to a new level."

She looked up at him and smiled. "Where can I get a glass of wine?"

"There's a bottle of a nice dry white in the fridge."

"I'll be right back."

When they had finished their drinks, she helped him into his bedroom, kissed him goodnight, and quietly left. In spite of the narcotics and alcohol, his sleep was restless and at five in the morning he found himself staring at the fan over his bed as it slowly rotated. His shin throbbed and he reached for another couple of Percodans, swallowing them without any water.

Instead of calming down about Alex Caffey, his rage reached a crescendo. The matter between the two of them was no longer just business—it was very personal. He had been made a fool of by a bumbling, meddlesome woman who had spent too many hours with her head crammed in a medical book. He would exercise patience but at the same time look forward with great pleasure to settling the score with her. Killing her would be easy but before she drew her final breath he would make sure to inflict a degree of emotional pain on Dr. Alexandra Caffey that would far exceed anything she could imagine.

# Chapter 48

After a long day at the hospital, Alex locked up her office and rode the elevator down to the lobby.

The only thing on her mind was to get home, spend some time with Jessie, and go to bed early. It had been a difficult five days since she had been attacked. The only good thing was that David continued to recover rapidly. He was still unresponsive but he was showing more and more signs of coming around.

The night she was attacked, the Metropolitan Police Department had responded immediately to Gillette's call for help and quickly searched the fifth floor of the research building. When the man wasn't found, the search was expanded and a canine team was brought in to check the other floors of the building as well. Unfortunately, they didn't come up with anything.

The officers spent a long time taking Alex's statement that night, and afterward she felt confident that they had believed her story. Beginning the next morning, an MPD officer had called daily to update her, but much to Alex's dismay, they didn't have a single viable lead and informed her that it was unlikely they'd be able to find the man who had assaulted her. When she broached the topic of a possible link between her attack and that of her brother, it was promptly dismissed as highly unlikely.

At Owen's insistence, Alex went to see one of John Adams's psychologists, who, after spending two hours with her, was satisfied that she was handling the emotional trauma of the event reasonably well. She did, however, insist that Alex take a few days off and return for another appointment before returning to work. In reality, the fear for her own personal safety, which consumed her for the first day, had been largely replaced by an intense visceral anger and an unshakable resolve to expose whoever was trying to harm her and David. She had no way of proving that the people who were responsible were somehow linked to the Caduceus Project but she was, nevertheless, sure that was the case.

More than ever, she was convinced that Victor Runyon was the mastermind behind everything that was going on and that he was nothing more than an unprincipled thug. If he believed, even for a minute, that he had dissuaded her from continuing to search for the truth about what had happened to David, he was sadly mistaken. In spite of what he obviously wanted, the last thing she was going to do was act like a deer in the headlights.

As Alex strolled past the information desk she heard a voice call out, "Alex, is that you?"

She stopped, turned, and immediately recognized the young lady coming toward her as Robert Key's girlfriend, Jamie Dennison.

"It's nice to see you again, Miss Dennison."

"Please call me Jamie. I was just on my way up to the ICU to thank the staff for the wonderful care they gave Rob."

"That's very thoughtful of you. I'm sure they'll appreciate that very much. I've been meaning to call you myself to express my personal condolences. We're all very sorry about Robert's death. He was an excellent radiologist. How are you holding up?"

"I'm okay, I guess. It gets a little easier every day. I don't know if I mentioned it the first time we spoke, but Rob's entire family consists of one brother who is somewhere in Europe, so I've been pretty much the only one tying up his affairs."

Alex noticed a subtle hesitancy in her voice, prompting her to wonder whether she could use the opportunity to find out a little more about Robert. "Is there anything I can do to help you?"

"I don't think so, but it's very nice of you to offer. Unfortunately, Rob viewed himself as immortal and never had a will prepared. He has an awful lot of possessions and it's keeping me pretty busy trying to figure out what to do with them all."

"Robert and I worked at different hospitals, so I only knew him by reputation. Where did he live?" Alex asked.

"Actually, he has two homes. One's in McLean and overlooks the Potomac. The other's in Snowmass, Colorado." Alex wasn't exactly familiar with the property values in these areas, but was well enough informed to know that they attracted mainly the affluent.

"I've been to Snowmass. It's a beautiful spot."

"His home out there is beautiful. It's huge and right on the mountain. He just bought it a few months ago."

"So I assume he was a skier," Alex said.

"He loved it. Besides medicine, his two major passions in life were skiing and cars."

"Cars?" Alex asked casting a curious grin in Jamie's direction.

"He had four," she said with an affectionate sigh. "And every few months he'd trade one of them in on something new. When it came to cars, he was like a little kid in a toy store." Jamie paused just briefly enough to glance across the lobby. "Hopefully I'll be able to get all of his personal affairs sorted out in the next couple of months."

Alex said, "Well, as I mentioned, if there's anything at all I can do to help, please call me."

"Thanks again, Dr. Caffey, and please tell everyone how much I appreciate the great care they gave Rob," she said, taking a peek at her watch. "It was nice seeing you again."

"It was nice seeing you too," Alex said, and then watched as Jamie turned and headed toward the elevators.

It was true that Alex didn't know much more about Robert Key other than the fact that he was a second-year radiology attending. But she was familiar with the salaries that John Adams Medical School paid its junior teaching faculty, and as a second-year attending, there was no way he could have made the kind of money it would take to own four cars and have homes in both McLean and Snowmass.

As Alex started across the lobby, she was suddenly reminded of her first conversation with Jamie in the stepdown unit. She slowed her pace, wondering whether her recollection regarding a comment Jamie had made was accurate. After a few moments of further thought, she was sure, distinctly remembering that Jamie had told her that Robert had come from modest means. If that was the case, then where in the world did he get the money to support such a privileged lifestyle?

# Chapter 49

Lott arrived at the Fairmont Hotel exactly on time for his meeting with Morgan.

When he went out into the courtyard, a double-tiered terrace with beautiful greenery interwoven between meticulously arranged flowers, Lott was surprised to see that Morgan was already seated. He walked across the courtyard, pulled out the white metal chair across from him, and sat down.

Morgan set his glass of red wine down and then leaned in and studied Lott's face. "How's that nasty cut of yours healing?"

Lott stroked his chin. "I'll live," he answered.

"That's good to hear. That Dr. Caffey must have some leopard in her."

Lott's expression never changed. "If you're finished, perhaps we can discuss why you asked me here today."

"I'd just like to know what the hell went wrong—and don't give me any of that nonsense about deciding at the last moment to frighten her instead of doing what you were supposed to do."

"Nothing went wrong," Lott insisted. "Your problem is solved. Dr. Caffey's far too terrified to be meddling in our affairs any longer."

"In the first place, they're not your affairs, they're ours, and in the second, my understanding was that you were going to get rid of her."

"I used an appropriate and proportional amount of force to handle things," Lott stated.

"You sound like a police officer," Morgan said with a droll grin. "We seem to have a problem communicating. As I recall our earlier conversation, it was your suggestion to deal with Dr. Caffey permanently."

Lott wasn't surprised that Morgan wasn't buying into his explanation of what happened in the research center, but there was no way he was going to admit that Alex Caffey had gotten the best of him. "Your recollection of our conversation is correct. But when I rethought the problem, I decided that it made no sense to employ such extreme means. Why eliminate her and possibly bring all that heat down on us when the same goal could be accomplished much less drastically?"

"So you're sticking to that fairy tale? I fear that you've overlooked one minor detail. We don't pay you to think. We pay you to carry out our orders."

Resting his arms on the handles of the chair, Lott steepled his fingers in front of his abdomen, resolute not to show any emotion. "I was under the impression that I had some authority to act independently, but obviously, I was mistaken. But if you feel that strongly about Dr. Caffey, it shouldn't be a problem to find another opportunity to—"

"I don't think so," Morgan interrupted with a raised hand, remaining silent for the moment as an elderly couple approached. While they walked past, Lott reached into his pocket, pulled out a paper clip, and began untwisting it under the table. "I'm afraid we've lost confidence in you and to be perfectly candid, we're starting to get nervous regarding the security of the entire project."

"Really," Lott said, feeling the rage mounting inside him.

"In fact, we've decided that we'd like you to stop any further efforts on our behalf."

"For how long?"

"Forever," Morgan answered with an incendiary grin.

"What about Dr. Caffey?"

"That's no longer your problem."

"And if I don't see it that way?" Lott asked.

"I don't know how to make this any clearer for you. We want you to stay away from her. Your services are no longer required."

"You can't be serious."

Morgan laughed. "Oh, I assure you, Mr. Lott, we are deadly serious."

"You understand that I've never been terminated before."

"Frankly, I find that a little hard to believe," Morgan scoffed. He then stood up, reached into the inside pocket of his double-breasted black blazer, and tossed an envelope on the table.

"You'll regret this decision," Lott said calmly.

"We're prepared to take that risk," he responded in a dismissive tone. Staring down at him as if he were a child, Morgan then made a cursory gesture toward the envelope. "That should square things between us. I've been instructed to thank you for your services. We'll call if we need anything further."

Lott picked up the envelope. "This is absurd, you know."

"Perhaps, but then again, if you had been a little more efficient in your work perhaps you wouldn't be sitting there receiving your final payment." Morgan then started away, but he hadn't taken more than a few steps when he stopped and turned. "There's one other thing. Don't do anything rash or stupid. This is business. We've already tolerated enough of your ineptitude. Take your money and disappear."

Now it was Lott's turn to smile. "That sounds very much like a threat."

"Why don't you just consider it some good advice?"

Lott realized there was nothing to be gained by either losing his cool or making any threats of his own. In spite of what Morgan had just said, he probably didn't have the first clue that he had just sealed his own fate. Lott tucked the envelope in his pocket, stood up, and approached Morgan.

"I'm afraid you've misjudged me. I never get emotional about money or work. Perhaps we'll cross paths again another day." He extended his hand; after a few moments Morgan shook it with a limp wrist, and then without even a backward glance left Lott standing there in the courtyard.

Lott waited a few minutes and then made his way back through the lobby and out onto Twenty-fourth Street. When he thought about what an uninspired fop Morgan was, it helped him understand why he had acted the way he had. Could he really be that obtuse to think that he was the type of man to walk away from Alex Caffey, forgiving and forgetting that she had made a complete fool of him and cost him his assignment?

Walking back to his Hummer, he knew he had a bit of tidying up to do in Washington before returning to Dublin. If he never saw the United States again it would be too soon, but he was not going anywhere until his business with Alex Caffey and her brother was completed. Morgan's optimistic contention that David Airoway would never remember a thing about the night he was attacked was not good enough. He had no intention of spending the rest of his life looking over his shoulder.

As for Alexandra Caffey, the best advice he could give her was to grow a pair of eyes behind her head because whether he was in the employ of Morgan or not, she was a dead woman.

Walking the two blocks to his car, Morgan decided that his meeting with Lott had gone pretty much as he expected. He reached into the inside pocket of his tweed sports coat and slid out his cell phone.

"That didn't take very long," the man said without even saying hello.

"You told me not to beat around the bush," Morgan answered.

"How did Mr. Lott take it?"

"He may be a bungler but he's a professional. I don't think we'll have any trouble with him."

"I wish I could say that I share your optimism."

"Do you want me to locate a replacement?" Morgan asked.

"I would move slowly. Make some subtle inquiries. Find out who might be available but don't go forward with anything without talking to me first."

"I understand."

"And keep an eye on Lott. I want to know what he's up to."

"I have a feeling that he'll be on his way back to Europe

within the next few days," Morgan responded, having no intention of spending his entire next few days keeping tabs on Lott.

"I hope you're right," came the response. "Meet me later at the usual spot. Let's say at around four."

"I'll be there," Morgan said.

Climbing into his car, Morgan again wondered whether Lott would be a problem. Pulling away from the curb and blending into traffic on Twenty-fifth Street, he continued to ponder the possibility, but after some further thought, his gut feeling was that Simon Lott wouldn't be that stupid.

# PART
Three

# Chapter 50

It was seven A.M. when Alex pulled into the doctors' parking lot. The moment she stepped out of her car, she saw Detective Maura Kenton approaching.

Alex looked down to conceal a subtle groan.

"Good morning, Dr. Caffey," Maura said, extending her hand. "I wanted to catch you before your day started. How's your brother doing?"

"He's improving every day."

"That's great," she said, smiling at Alex.

After an uncomfortable silence, Alex said, "Detective, I don't mean to appear rude but I have kind of a busy day. Was there something specific you wanted to talk to me about?"

"I kind of heard about your little ordeal the other night. I just wanted to touch base with you to make sure you were doing okay and maybe get your take on things."

"Ordeal? That's an interesting way of putting it."

Maura asked, "Do you have any idea who was responsible?"

"According to MPD, I was just the random target of some lunatic who stalks the halls of Gillette looking for poor defenseless trauma surgeons to prey on."

Maura didn't appear irritated by Alex's sarcasm and rancor. "It sounds like you don't agree with our findings."

"I don't know. I guess I believe in coincidence as much as the next person, but I'm not naive."

"What do you mean?" Maura asked.

"C'mon, Detective. What are the chances that both my brother and I were attacked within days of each other?"

"You're assuming that your brother was attacked."

"That's right—I am, and I also believe that the same people who attacked my brother came after me," Alex said, lowering her voice as two nurses hurried by.

"Assuming you're right, why would the people who attacked your brother have a gripe with you?"

"Maybe I've been asking too many questions and haven't been as discreet as I should have been." Maura nodded politely, being careful not to interrupt. "I get the feeling you find me a tad paranoid," Alex said.

Maura boosted her purse a little higher on her shoulder. "Paranoia is a very relative thing in my business. You mentioned something about making some inquiries. Do you feel like sharing any of that with me?" Maura asked directly, hoping Alex's level of comfort with her might be increasing.

"If I thought that anything I'd have to say would change your decision about what happened to David or MPD's decision not to investigate the matter further, I'd be happy to."

"Unless you tell me what you know, there's certainly nothing I can do to help you." Maura was sincere in her offer and did harbor some concerns that MPD was missing the boat on this one.

"Look, Detective. I appreciate your taking the time to come speak with me—I really do—but I'm not quite sure I'm ready to discuss this right now."

"If you are right about things and someone is intentionally targeting you and your brother, what about your personal safety?"

Alex took a step closer and then stated emphatically, "I don't give a damn about my personal safety. I know I'm right about what happened to my brother. Whoever these people are, they want David dead."

Maura took a breath before answering. "Do you still have my card?"

"Yes. It's at home."

"Here's another. Keep it in your purse. Call me when you're ready to talk. I can't guarantee I can do anything on an official level, but I can at least listen."

Maura extended her hand. Alex shook it and then stood silently as she started away. She had taken only a few steps when Alex said, "Look, Maura. You've been really nice and I appreciate your trying to help me. I'm not always this much of a bitch."

"That makes us even, because I'm not always this nice," Maura said as she started away.

Alex didn't go into the hospital immediately. Instead, she leaned against her own car, staring vacuously across the parking lot. She considered herself a good judge of people and was sure that Maura was sincerely trying to offer her support. After a long sigh, Alex started toward the hospital. Just before she reached the emergency room entrance, her pager went off. It was the ICU. Reaching into her purse, she pulled out her cell phone and dialed the number.

"This is Dr. Caffey."

"Hold for Sue, please," the unit secretary told her. A few seconds later, Alex heard her familiar voice.

"Alex, where are you?"

"I'm in the parking lot. I was just on my way in. What's going on?"

"Then I recommend you come straight up to the ICU," Sue said.

Alex was a little confused because there was no sense of urgency in Sue's voice. In fact, she sounded elated.

"What's going on?" Alex asked.

Sue's answer was preceded by a joyful laugh. "Just get your buns up here. David's awake."

# Chapter 51

As she bounded up the stairs, Alex cautioned herself not to be overly optimistic regarding David's condition.

She was elated by Sue's news, but she was also painfully aware that it could be months before David made any kind of meaningful recovery. Alex had taken care of enough trauma patients with severe head injuries to know that they tended to wake up in many different ways.

When she came through the doors, the ICU was already bustling with activity. The nursing shift had just changed and several small groups of physicians and students were in the middle of their morning rounds. As Alex approached David's cubicle, Sue turned. Her jubilant smile spoke volumes.

"What took you so long?" she asked as Alex made her way to the head of the bed.

Expressionless but with clear eyes, David was sitting up with a pillow propped behind him, gazing straight ahead. Before saying a word, Alex hugged him around his shoulders. When she let go, he was still staring straight ahead with the same blank look.

"David? Can you hear me? It's Alex." When he didn't answer, she looked over at Sue.

"He hasn't said anything intelligible yet, but I think he's trying," Sue said.

His eyes began blinking rapidly. Alex renewed her question. "Do you know who I am, David? You're in the hospital. You had an accident but everything's going to be okay now." David turned his head slightly. The flickering in his eyes slowed.

"We may be rushing him a little," Sue suggested in a soft voice.

Alex nodded in agreement, sat down next to him, and reached for his hand. His palm was moist but his fingers were cool and dry. He made no effort to close his hand in hers. Feeling the disappointment mounting and as if she were grasping at straws, she asked Sue, "Is he responding to commands?"

She shook her head. "Not yet."

Alex turned back to David and squeezed his hand a little tighter. She never took her eyes off his face. At first she wasn't quite sure whether her eyes were deceiving her, but when she leaned in closer she was sure he was slowly parting his lips. Moving her mouth close to his ear, she whispered, "Try to say something." She was so intent on listening for a response that she hardly noticed when his fingers curled ever so slightly around hers. She immediately looked at his hand. While she was studying it, she heard a soft voice say, "Alex."

Astonished, she immediately pulled away and stood up. Hovering over him, she gasped. As she covered her mouth, her teardrops tumbled to his pillow. She saw an almost imperceptible and fleeting smile come to his face but before she could say anything, he closed his eyes and began to breathe deeply.

"I can't believe it," Sue said in a cracked voice.

Still shocked, but trying to control her joy, Alex said, "I'm going to let him sleep for a while. Please call me when he wakes up again."

"Of course," Sue said, "and Dr. Caffey, congratulations."

When Alex turned to leave, there were already a half dozen ICU personnel with beaming smiles standing outside David's cubicle. She thanked everyone and then walked by them. She hadn't gone more than a few steps when she heard the sudden burst of elated applause from the group. Having never heard such an outburst in the ICU, she turned back around. Speechless at first, she did manage a teary thank-you before heading for the exit.

With a bounce in her step that had been conspicuously absent for the last week or so, Alex stopped for a moment at the nursing station and picked up one of the phones. Her mother was just getting ready to go out for her morning walk when the phone rang.

"Where are you off to?" Alex asked.

"I thought I'd head toward Dupont Circle," she answered.

"Enjoy your walk. I'll be home in a couple of hours to get you."

"Why so early?" Jeanette asked.

"Because your son is awake and I thought you'd like to see him."

# Chapter 52

It was only at the end of a very long day when Alex finally found the time to go over to the pathology department at Adams's main teaching hospital.

It had been almost a day and a half since David had regained consciousness and he was becoming more alert and communicative with each passing hour. She had spent most of the afternoon with him observing one of the more dramatic neurological recoveries she had ever seen, but instead of being delirious with joy she remained cautiously optimistic. She was already starting to wonder when the best time would be to find out what he remembered about the days surrounding his assault.

When Alex came through the doors of the pathology department, she didn't see a soul and her first thought was that everyone had left for the day. She was just about to head home herself when she noticed one of the secretaries pop her head up from behind a large steel desk.

"Hi," Alex said to the frazzled-appearing woman, who was trying to yank her purse out of the bottom drawer. "I'm Dr. Caffey. Would you happen to know if any of the pathologists are still around?"

"I doubt it," she stated without looking up as she continued to tug away at her bag. "I think they're all over at the medical school at a conference." Exasperated, she stopped briefly and motioned down the hall. "You might want to check the chief resident's office. Dr. Everly may still be here."

Alex looked down the corridor and then glanced back to say, "Thanks, I think I will."

When Alex reached Tess Everly's office, the door was

open and she could see her hunched over a microscope. Two months shy of finishing her residency, Tess had already lined up a job in Santa Barbara and was lame-ducking it until she moved to California. At times opinionated but always diplomatic, Tess had completed her four-year residency without a significant stumble. She was slight in stature with curly blond hair and faint gray eyes, and most considered her an eye-catcher.

As soon as Alex approached, she looked up. "Hi, Dr. Caffey. What brings you to my world?"

"You're almost an attending, Tess. Call me Alex."

Tess flicked the microscope light off and then spun around on her tall wooden stool. "Thanks."

"I need some information about some autopsies."

"Sure thing."

Alex pulled out a piece of notepaper from the pocket of her white coat and handed it to Tess. "I'm interested in these three patients. Do you think we could go over their posts and maybe have a look at the photos?"

"I don't see why not," Tess said, holding the list out at arm's length.

Alex smiled. "Have you thought about getting a pair of reading glasses?"

"I have a pair around here somewhere but I can never find them. Let's see, Kyle Dolan, Nancy Olander, and Graham Pierce. Did they all die within the last two years?"

"Yes."

Tess jumped off the stool. "What's your interest in these cases?" she asked.

"I'm working on a paper," Alex said.

"I see. Sounds like you're climbing the academic ladder."

"You know what they say: publish or perish."

Tess raised her eyebrows. "If I help, do I get my name on the paper?"

"Absolutely."

"C'mon, let's go back into the main office."

When they arrived, Tess strolled over to a long line of file cabinets. While she hummed a Broadway tune and moved from one file to the next, Alex sat down and gazed across the room at a collection of serigraphs of famous Asian landmarks, which had been hung on the wall without much regard for symmetry.

After a couple of minutes Tess rolled the last drawer shut and returned with the reports of the autopsies and two manila files that contained the photos. "I couldn't find a file on Pierce," she said.

"I know he had an autopsy. I read the report myself. Dr. Silver did it."

"I'm not saying he didn't have one. It just means it's not here. Somebody must have pulled it for some reason. I'll check with the secretaries tomorrow. They'll find it. Now, before we start, let me just take a quick look at these." For the next couple of minutes, Alex listened to Tess's humming as she read through the reports. When she was finished, she looked up and said, "These seem to be pretty straightforward. Both of these patients died of a massive pulmonary embolus."

"Nothing peculiar about them at all?" Alex asked.

"Not that I can see from the reports, but let's have a look at the photos," Tess said, setting the files down and then removing the color prints from the folders. Holding them up to the light, she studied them for a minute or two, shrugged her shoulders, and said, "There's nothing out of the ordinary here. Have a look for yourself at the pulmonary arteries. These blood clots were big enough to kill a horse. Nobody could have survived this."

Alex took the photos and studied each of them in turn. Tess was right. The blood clots were large and completely blocked the main arteries leading to the lungs. Alex took one last look and couldn't help but feeling as if she'd hit a dead end.

"You seem bothered," Tess said. "We're a big hospital. People die of pulmonary emboli all the time."

"I would agree except for the fact that all of these patients had caval filters in when they died," Alex told her as she replaced the photos in the folders. "Why was that fact barely mentioned? The only reference was that there wasn't a great deal of clot stuck in them, which means that the filters had to have been defective and allowed major clots to pass through them and travel to the lungs."

"That sounds logical."

Alex then asked, "If a patient died of a pulmonary embolus and the pathologist knew he or she had a filter in, shouldn't the filter have been removed and examined for defects and some pictures taken?"

Tess paused for a moment before answering. "We autopsy people with all kinds of medical devices in them. We don't necessarily remove them and test them for failures. The other possibility was that it was simply overlooked."

"What do you mean?" Alex asked.

"I didn't make the connection; maybe the other pathologists didn't either."

"I could understand that if we were discussing a patient whose death had nothing to do with the device, but that's not the case here. We're talking about three patients who died of the exact same complication—a complication that people with caval filters aren't supposed to get." Alex stood up. "You would think that fact would trigger some intellectual curiosity in the individual doing the autopsy," Alex said, realizing immediately that her tone betrayed her frustration and the fact that she was overreacting.

If Tess noticed, she didn't let on. "I'm not disagreeing with you, but you have to consider that these particular autopsies were done several months apart by three different pathologists, none of whom thought it was necessary to remove the filters and examine them."

"I don't remember. Who did the autopsies on Nancy Olander and Kyle Dolan?" Alex asked.

"One was done by Patrick Whitman and the other by Dr. Boyette."

Fearing that she may have carelessly impugned three of Tess's professors, Alex decided it was time to retreat. She was well aware that Hayden Boyette was the vice chief of the department of pathology and a highly respected member of the John Adams Medical School faculty. "I'll tell you what," Alex said. "There's no reason why you should be in the middle of this thing. Why don't I just speak to Whitman and Boyette myself?"

The relief on Tess's face couldn't have been more obvious. "I think that's a great idea."

Alex knew Patrick Whitman and Ann Silver and liked them both. They were affable and accommodating; Alex had served on committees with each of them and had always found them reasonable and easy to work with. Dr. Boyette, on the other hand, was a bit of a prima donna and often unapproachable. It was no secret in the hospital that the residents didn't care for him very much because of his laissez-faire attitude toward his teaching responsibilities. Although it was a mystery to her why, the administration of Gillette thought highly of Boyette, clearly valued his opinion, and considered him a member of the inner circle.

Alex and Tess continued to talk for a few minutes, mostly about Tess's future, before Alex wished her good luck in California and promised to stay in touch. As she started back toward the exit, Tess called out to her. "I'll take another look at the autopsies and see if I can find Pierce's file. If I come up with anything I'll give you a call."

"You're busy, Tess. Don't worry about it. I've already taken up too much of your time," Alex said with a wave, trying her best to let Tess off the hook.

"I don't mind . . . anyway, something tells me your interest in these cases goes beyond academic."

Alex smiled and shook her head. "I'll see you soon."

Once she was out of the building and on her way to the parking lot, Alex pondered whether she should approach the pathologists about their autopsy findings. She felt comfortable with Whitman, but Boyette was another story. The last thing she wanted to do was offend a faculty member of another department, especially one who clearly outranked her, by questioning his competency. If Boyette took her inquiries the wrong way, he just might give Owen Goodman a call to complain about her. Depending on Owen's response, the repercussions could be quite unpleasant for her.

As Alex made her way down a vine-covered canopied walkway, she could understand how Drs. Silver and Whitman could have overlooked the issue of the filters. They were both junior faculty and still relatively inexperienced, but Boyette was a seasoned pathologist who should have paid more attention to an obviously defective caval filter by removing it and then referring the problem to Medivasc's quality-control department and perhaps even the FDA.

By the time she reached her car, Alex realized she could

conjecture about Boyette's oversight for the next six months—but if she really wanted to find out what happened, there was only one real way, and that was to confront him.

# Chapter 53

## MAY 12

When Alex finally decided to take a day off, it gave her the perfect opportunity to spend some quality time with Jessie.

Candy Cane Park in Rock Creek Park was one of Jessie's favorite places. On the spur of the moment, Alex decided to give Olivia the day off and surprise Jessie. They were just about to leave when the phone rang. Alex smiled when she saw it was Micah calling.

"What are you guys doing?" he asked.

"Actually, we were just going out the door. We thought we'd go to Candy Cane Park. I didn't know you took the day off."

"We had an all-day seminar that got canceled at the last minute. I couldn't resist the opportunity to disappear for the day."

Jessie began tugging at Alex's arm. "Is that Gabe and Micah?" Alex nodded and mouthed yes. "Tell them to come," Jessie screeched.

"What are you two doing?" Alex asked.

"Nothing, just hanging out." After a few seconds of awkward silence, he went on. "Gabe wanted to talk to Jessie . . . but if you guys are getting ready to—"

"Why don't you just meet us out there?" Alex suggested.

"We don't want to intrude if—"

"No, we'd love to have you. We'll see you out there in twenty minutes."

"Okay," he said, "if you're sure it'll be okay."

"I'm sure. We'll see you in a little while. Bye."

Watching the kids chase each other around the playground, Micah and Alex sat comfortably on a bench. It didn't take her long to realize that Micah was in a bit of a funk. Maxine had been unexpectedly delayed in Chicago and informed him that she wouldn't be back in D.C. for at least another couple of days. Alex tried to make Micah feel better by excusing the unforeseen delay as something that was nothing more than an unexpected business problem, but in spite of her best effort, it appeared to Alex that Micah had his doubts and that any further conversation on the topic wouldn't help matters.

"I was thinking about going up to Boston," Alex said nonchalantly.

"What's going on in Boston?" he asked, giving Gabe the thumbs-up for his swinging prowess.

"The Caduceus Project is having a meeting."

"I didn't know you had joined," he mentioned, making every effort to tread softly and not appear disapproving.

"I think you already know that I wouldn't be going as a member. I'm interested in seeing who'll be there."

"What are you going to say when you run into Runyon and he asks you what the hell you're doing there?"

Alex cleared her throat, hesitated a moment and then explained, "Actually, I was going to do my best to avoid Runyon and anybody else who might recognize me."

"So you're going to go up there incognito?"

Alex stretched her legs out, crossing them at the ankles. "I called the hotel. It's a pretty big place with a lot of meetings going on. They're expecting about a hundred members of the Caduceus Project. There can't be more than a handful of people who would recognize me. If I keep my head down, I should be okay."

"I see. Now, what happens if you're wrong? What's plan B?"

"At the same time the Caduceus Project is having their meeting, there's a patient safety seminar for hospital administrators. I can say I'm attending it."

"Except for the fact that you're not a hospital administrator," he reminded her as they both nodded to a young mother who strolled by with her toddler.

Alex said, "Well, I've always talked about getting a master's in hospital administration."

Micah rubbed his chin. "Do you think anyone is really going to believe that?"

"Whether they believe it or not is irrelevant. If I do run into somebody, that's what I'm going to say."

At that moment, Jessie and Gabe ran over and began chasing each other around the bench.

"C'mon, you guys," Micah said. "Someone's going to get hurt."

They both stopped running but couldn't stop giggling and swatting at each other. Out of breath, Jessie said, "We're hungry."

Alex glanced down at her watch. "It's a little early for lunch. Go play for a little while longer and then we'll go get something to eat."

"But, Mom," she whined.

Alex raised her eyebrows and waited for Jessie to look right at her. "Go play for a little while and then we'll eat," she said calmly. After studying her mother for a few seconds, Jessie pushed Gabe and dashed off with him in quick pursuit.

"Are you going to try to sit in on any of their meetings?" Micah asked.

"Only if I can do it without being recognized."

"Didn't you tell me that you were suspicious that certain members of the Caduceus Project may have been behind what happened to you in the research center?"

"That's right," she said.

"Wouldn't it follow then that you might be putting yourself at risk to suddenly appear at one of their meetings?" Micah waited patiently for Alex's answer but all he got was a half shrug. "I'm not sure I like any of this, Alex. Have you thought about contacting the police again?" he asked.

"I just spoke with them a couple of days ago. They're not interested in reopening the investigation. So, the way I see it, I'm on my own."

"That may be but that doesn't mean going up to Boston is such a great idea."

"Why?"

"Because I think there's an excellent chance that you're going to stir up one hell of a hornet's nest and do more damage than good. Maybe we should talk about this again before you make a final decision," he said, putting his arm around her. He then gave her shoulder a quick but definitely platonic squeeze. "Now what do you say we get these kids something to eat?"

"Sure," she said, admitting to herself that Micah was right and that going up to Boston to sneak around some hotel was probably a pretty dumb idea.

As soon as the kids saw Micah and Alex on their feet, they raced over. Micah hoisted Jessie up on his shoulders, Alex took Gabe's hand and together, the four of them marched off.

# Chapter 54

**MAY 15**

The weekend passed uneventfully. Alex hadn't been on call, which allowed her to spend a considerable amount of time with David.

On Saturday, she had been able to meet with both Dr. Silver and Dr. Whitman regarding Graham Pierce's and Nancy Olander's autopsies. They were both extremely cordial and cooperative, but unfortunately had no specific recollection of either case. Her frustration mounting, she decided to go see Hayden Boyette.

Boyette was a politically crafty man who, after considerable lobbying and arm twisting, had persuaded the hospital board to name him to the position of vice chairman of the department of pathology. Alex knew him more by reputation than anything else. She had met him once briefly, and the only thing she could really remember about him was that he had a deadpan voice and the personality to match.

It was only after considerable deliberation that she decided to see him regarding Kyle Dolan's autopsy. On this particular afternoon she found him in his office organizing several dozen microscope slides. As she stood in his doorway, he seemed to sense her presence and looked up. He was clearly unattractive; his spotty gray hair did little to cover his leathery scalp. Alex also noticed that the collar of his powder-blue dress shirt was too large for his scrawny neck.

"Dr. Boyette?" she asked in a polite voice from the doorway.

"Yes," he answered with an impatient look on his face after casting a flash glance in her direction.

"My name is Alex Caffey. I'm on the trauma service."

"Resident or student?"

"I appreciate the compliment but I'm an attending."

He rubbed his eyes, replaced his wire-rim glasses, and said, "I think Owen Goodman has mentioned your name."

Tired of waiting for an invitation, she entered his office. "I left a couple of messages for you but I guess you didn't get them."

"I probably did but I've been attending at three different hospitals and I no longer have the time to get to all of my messages."

*Probably only the important ones,* she thought to herself. Alex stared at the chair that was a few feet from him but instead of a gesture to sit down all she got was a curious stare.

"If you have a moment I'd like to talk to you about an autopsy you did."

Boyette stole a peek at his watch, looked past Alex, and said, "I have to warn you that I did over a hundred and fifty postmortem examinations in the last twelve months. It's incredibly difficult to remember the details of individual cases."

"I understand. You might remember this one because the case was a little unusual. It involved a young man who became paraplegic from a football accident who eventually died of a massive pulmonary embolus."

Boyette tucked his glasses into his shirt pocket and leaned back in his chair. "That doesn't sound that unusual to me."

"I would agree with you under normal circumstances, but this young man had a vena caval filter in. His name was Kyle Dolan."

Boyette took a deep breath and then drummed his lips as he was thinking. Finally he let out every drop of air in his lungs and said, "I'm sorry. The name doesn't ring a bell. What's your particular interest in the case?"

"I'm working on a paper. I'm interested in caval filters, specifically the reasons they fail."

Without stopping to give the matter any thought at all, Boyette said, "I'm sorry, young lady. The patient's name is not familiar to me and I have absolutely no recollection of the case."

A little miffed by his abrupt manner, she asked, "Are you quite sure?"

"I beg your pardon?" he said in an indignant tone.

Without the slightest hesitation, she restated her question. "I asked if you were sure."

"Yes, I'm quite sure."

"That's too bad," Alex lamented. "Do you think you could go over your report with me and perhaps have a look at the photos?" she asked.

Seeming even more pained by her request, he answered, "I can't right now, but if it's absolutely necessary, I'll try to find some time in the future. Why don't you call my secretary and set up a meeting?" he suggested as he reached for a new tray of slides.

"Okay. By the way, do you generally remove caval filters and inspect them when you do a post?" Alex asked.

"Not generally."

"Supposing the cause of death was a pulmonary embolus?" she asked.

"I don't know. As I mentioned before, I don't recall such a case."

"The reason I asked was because you didn't," she said.

"I didn't what?" he asked.

"You didn't remove the filter and examine it in this case."

"Now listen, young lady, I already told you—"

"It's Doctor. My name is Dr. Alexandra Caffey. I'm an attending trauma surgeon, not one of your students."

Red-faced, he said, "You're also quite impertinent."

"I'm sorry. That wasn't my intention. I was just trying to get some help with this case."

"And as I said, I don't have time right now. Have your secretary arrange a meeting. I'll be speaking with Owen Goodman later today. If you'd like I can discuss this matter with him. Now if there's nothing else."

Not intimidated by his rudeness and pomposity, Alex forced a conciliatory smile. "I'll see if you're available toward the end of next week."

He shook his head. "I'll be out of town." Without saying another word and acting as if she had already left, Boyette placed a slide on his microscope and fitted his eyes on the instrument.

Alex marched out of his office and was still seething when she reached the street. She hadn't had the displeasure of being around anybody like Boyette in a very long time. It was one thing not to exude warmth, but to be downright rude and patently chauvinistic was quite another. Alex approached the curb to see whether she could spot an approaching cab but then decided to walk back to Gillette instead. It was a long way, but a straight shot down Connecticut Avenue, and she hoped the exercise would help calm her down.

As she crossed the Taft Bridge, she just couldn't understand how Boyette could have done the autopsy on Kyle Dolan and have absolutely no recollection of it. Maybe pathologists were different from surgeons, but it had always been her experience that irrespective of the total number of cases a surgeon did, the interesting ones became a permanent part of his or her memory.

Intrigued by the mention of his trip to Boston, Alex began to conjecture about Boyette's political convictions. It would certainly be interesting to know whether he was a member of the Caduceus Project and, perhaps, even a pal of Victor Runyon's. If that were the case, then it was obvious he was headed to Boston for the same reason that Victor was.

Alex suddenly slowed her pace and then came to a complete stop. Several people walked quickly past her as she stood in the middle of the sidewalk plagued by the obvious question. If Boyette was a part of the elite hierarchy of the Caduceus Project, was it possible that he had knowledge of what had really happened to David?

# Chapter 55

It was still early and Alex was eager to get up to the ICU and spend some time with David.

Although he had regained consciousness only a few days earlier, the amount of progress that he had made was truly remarkable. His speech and long-term memory were steadily recovering, but he still had absolutely no recollection of anything that happened to him for the last couple of weeks. Alex had taken care of enough recovering head trauma patients to know that they could be very impatient and easily frustrated, which left her reticent to discuss his injuries in detail for fear of upsetting him. In any case, the issue didn't seem pressing at the moment because she was fairly certain that he would have no recollection of his meeting with Robert Key.

"How are you doing?" Alex asked him as soon as she walked into his room.

"I feel better," he answered as she kissed his cheek. His speech was improving but it was apparent that he was still struggling with word retrieval.

"Well, you look great." Alex turned to Christine Adams, the nurse taking care of him, and asked, "Doesn't he look great?"

"A lot better than most people who have been through what he has," she said.

"How's he eating?" Alex asked.

Christine held up her hand and then wavered it. "So-so."

"The more you eat, the sooner you'll be out of here," Alex told him. She knew she must have sounded as if she were talking to one of her pediatric patients and cautioned herself to be more careful.

"What happened to me?"

Alex sat down on the side of his bed, taking a moment to gather her thoughts. "Well, we're not exactly sure. Our best guess is that you fell."

"Fell?" he asked.

"The paramedics found you behind your apartment."

He shook his head. "I don't remember."

From the strained look on his face, Alex could sense he was having trouble expressing himself. It was as if the harder he flogged his memory, the less likely it was to respond.

"Mom wanted to come back tonight, but I persuaded her to wait until tomorrow. I figured you could use the rest."

"Thanks," he said, appearing to her as if his mind had already moved on. "When can I go home?"

"Well, that kind of depends on a few things."

"What?" he asked.

Her answer was measured. "Well, for one, how quickly you progress in rehab, and other things that are mostly medical—infection, nutrition, things like that."

"Am I going to be here a long time?" he asked.

"It's hard to say, David. Let's just take it one day at a time." Christine walked over, handed him a pill and a small cup of water, and then walked away. "I know this is hard for you to understand but the progress you've made has been incredible. Try to stay positive." As he swallowed the pill, Alex used the opportunity to shift gears and talk to him about things other than his injuries and expected recovery. She kept the mood upbeat. He continued to speak mostly in short phrases and in a voice that lacked much animation or emotion. When his eyelids began to droop, she said, "I have to go do some stuff in the hospital. I'll come back and see you later."

"Okay," he muttered. She watched him for a moment. His breathing slowed, and shortly he was asleep.

"Everybody's so happy about his progress," Christine said softly as she pulled his covers up to his neck. "I know he's frustrated, but it'll get better."

"I don't know how I'll ever be able to thank all you guys."

Alex kissed David on the forehead, thanked Christine again, and was just starting toward the exit when she saw Samantha coming toward her. She waved and immediately caught Sam's eye; Sam smiled and picked up her pace.

"How's he doing?" she asked.

"He's doing great. He just fell asleep," Alex told her.

"I was here earlier. Maybe I shouldn't bother him."

"Did you get a chance to talk with him?" Alex asked.

"Only for a few minutes, but I can't believe how much better he's doing. Will he continue to improve this rapidly?"

"I wish I could say yes but it's impossible to tell," Alex said.

"Did you talk about the night he was hurt?"

"No. I think it's too soon."

Sam asked, "What are the chances that he'll eventually remember?"

Alex shook her head. "I don't have the first clue."

"I wonder if it really matters." Alex shrugged and Sam looked over her shoulder into David's cubicle. "I think I'll come back tomorrow. He looks like he's out for the night."

"Do you have any dinner plans?" Alex asked. "I could use some adult conversation."

"I thought you had Micah for that," Sam teased.

"I see you've been talking to my mother," Alex moaned. "I don't know who's worse, she or David. They're both obsessed with finding me the perfect soul mate."

"I guess they both really like Micah," she answered as the two of them headed across the ICU.

"They both seem to be overlooking the fact that Micah's spoken for—he's off the market."

"That's not what I heard," Sam said, raising her finger and then giggling.

"Why don't we save the topic of my love life until dinner," Alex suggested.

"How's your mom doing?" Sam asked.

"She's been like a new person since David woke up."

"That's great. I was worried about her." As they exited the hospital, their conversation shifted. "The word on the hill is that you have a celebrity in your hospital."

"Really?" Alex asked. "I wasn't aware of it. Who was injured?"

"Brice Beckett. He twisted his knee playing basketball yesterday. They were going to take him to Walter Reed or Bethesda but he insisted on coming here."

"I just met him a few weeks ago," Alex said with a chuckle.

"What's so funny?"

"I was just thinking that if we admitted every sprained knee in Washington, we'd have no room for the real traumas."

"Well, he won't be here for long. He's supposed to be discharged tomorrow. He's having some kind of procedure today."

"Probably an arthroscopy," Alex said.

Suddenly seeing an intriguing opportunity in the congressman's unfortunate athletic mishap, Alex wondered whether she could get in to see him before he was discharged and somehow pick his brain about the Caduceus Project.

# Chapter 56

Hank Dumont had worked for Medivasc for the past five years as their regional sales representative covering the D.C. area. He enjoyed the business and was a talented salesman who had a special gift for closing the big deal.

Arriving outside Alex's office with about ten minutes to spare before their meeting, he decided to stroll back down the hall. Stopping at the far end, he gazed out over northern Georgetown through a large bay window. Hank considered himself a savvy and persuasive sales rep but one who understood the realities of the business, and one of those stark truths of trying to sell medical devices to doctors was that it was very difficult to get an appointment with them, so when

Dr. Caffey's secretary called him to arrange a meeting, he was elated.

Well-dressed in a dark pinstripe suit, Hank rolled his wrist and checked the time. He walked back down the hall and into Alex's outer office. Her secretary, Joyce, had just returned from lunch and was putting her purse away when he appeared.

"May I help you?" she asked.

"My name is Hank Dumont. I have an appointment with Dr. Caffey."

"You're right on time. She's expecting you," Joyce said, walking over to her desk and picking up the phone. "Mr. Dumont is here." She replaced the receiver and pointed toward the door leading into Alex's office. "You can go in."

Alex was already out from behind her desk when Hank came through the door. She extended her hand. Her eyes were drawn to his walruslike mustache, his chubby face, and the fact that he was in dire need of a haircut.

She said, "It's nice to finally meet you. I've heard a lot of nice things about you."

"That's kind of you to say." He shook her hand and set his briefcase down. He was a little surprised by her courteous welcome, being far more accustomed to the *I've only got five minutes* greeting.

She pointed to a chair and waited while he lowered himself in. She then moved back behind her desk and sat down. Normally she didn't set meetings with medical products salesmen, but in the case of the Medivasc caval filter she was willing to make an exception. She was well aware that she might be getting herself into a rather prickly situation but she was willing to take that chance. One thing she was convinced of was that the kind of information she was looking for wouldn't be found on the company's Web site.

"I'm quite interested in your caval filter. What can you tell me about it?"

Hank sat up tall and with his warmest smile covering his face. "It's one of our best products. I just got back from our national sales meeting in Des Moines. The company announced that it's our fastest-growing product."

"That's very interesting," Alex said. "What about its safety record?"

"According to our quality-control department, there haven't been any significant problems with respect to either its design or function reported to either us or the FDA."

"So you haven't had any failures at all?" Alex asked, even though she had already called the FDA herself and knew that Hank was correct in his information.

"None that I'm aware of, but that doesn't mean there couldn't have been a few that were never reported," he confessed.

"I've never used your filter, but Dr. Runyon tells me he's quite pleased with it. I don't think he uses any other type."

Gaining in both comfort and enthusiasm, he responded, "Dr. Runyon's a big fan of our product. He's visited several hospitals across the country for us to familiarize other surgeons with its use." Hank stopped for a moment and added in a voice she perceived to have just a hint of disapproval, "He's well compensated for his efforts, of course."

Alex could only assume that Dumont felt compelled to imply that Medivasc would be happy to make a similar arrangement with her if she were so inclined.

"I'm certainly interested in giving your filter a chance," she said.

"Have you had trouble with the device you're presently using?"

Alex grinned. "I hate to knock your competition. Let's just say that I'm interested in trying an alternative product."

"That's great. We keep a few filters in stock for Dr. Runyon but I could add a few more just in case you want to try it."

"Fine. By the way, I've noticed that Medivasc has sponsored some educational dinners in the past."

"It's the policy of our company to support the physicians that support us. If you're interested we would be happy to arrange and sponsor an educational meeting. If you're personally interested in helping us take our products to other physicians, I'm sure an arrangement could be made."

Alex again got the distinct impression that Dumont was saying what he was supposed to but was unhappy about it.

"I'll pass," she said. "You'll have to excuse me but I'm a die-hard liberal. Nothing against your company but I don't approve of these financial relationships that seem to be more and more common between medical products companies and physicians."

Dumont looked over his shoulder at the closed door. "You're preaching to the converted. I was raised in Massachusetts and lived outside Boston for most of my life. I never met a conservative until I accepted the job at Medivasc."

"I guess that explains it," she said.

"I beg your pardon?"

"Why your company's so enamored with Dr. Runyon." She smiled as if she had just made a new best friend. "It sounds like politically they're both just to the right of Genghis Khan."

Dumont laughed. "I guess the sad truth is that there will always be a connection between business and politics. Medivasc is no exception. I guess the rules regarding the relationship between business ethics and medical ethics are still kind of nebulous."

She smiled. "We're definitely both on the same page but I can tell you that Dr. Runyon feels a lot differently."

"Dr. Runyon's been a major supporter of our product, and I guess the powers that be feel it's good business to show appreciation in any way possible."

"In any way possible?"

"As long as it's legal. At Medivasc, moving the line and stepping over it are two different things."

"I lost you," she said, wanting to make Dumont feel as if this would be his opportunity to enlighten her.

"It's a reality of the business environment we live in. In Dr. Runyon's case, he's very much committed to a certain political agenda that closely mirrors that of Medivasc."

"Are you talking about the Caduceus Project?"

He nodded.

"I wasn't aware that medical products companies took a financial interest in political groups," she said.

Hank again looked around and then leaned in. "Let's just say that the board members of Medivasc aren't averse to lending their financial support to certain select groups of influential and responsible medical organizations that share their political philosophies regarding the future of health care in this country."

"I have to stop living in a dream world," she said.

Alex was quite surprised by what she had just heard. Although she would have liked to press the subject, she didn't want to make Hank suspicious of her real agenda for today's meeting. She shifted gears and allowed him to complete his pitch on the complete line of Medivasc products. It was quite a dog-and-pony show and when he was finally finished, she stood up and said, "That's a very impressive group of products. I'm certainly looking forward to giving one of your filters a try."

He shook her hand vigorously. "I'll check with central supply on my way out just to make sure there are a few extra in stock."

"Sounds great."

Hank picked up his briefcase and with a broad smile walked out of her office. Alex closed the door the instant he was out in the hall. She returned to her desk, picked up the remote from her CD player, and put on a collection of Broadway hits.

She thought about her meeting with Hank and wondered just how much money Medivasc had donated to the Caduceus Project. She then could only speculate how much money it would take to tempt Victor to disregard every ethical standard of medicine and turn a blind eye to a product that he knew was both defective and dangerous.

# Chapter 57

"The congressman's had a lot of well-wishers today, Doctor. Let me check if he's sleeping before you go in. What did you say your last name was again?"

The very serious young man sitting outside Brice Beckett's room, who looked more like a lumberjack than a congressional aide, remained straight-faced as he reached for the door handle.

"Caffey," she said.

"I'll be right back," he promised. Alex had been wrestling with the idea of trying to get in to see Beckett for the better part of the morning. Finally she decided that it was unlikely that she'd ever have another opportunity like this one. If she did get in to see him, she would have to play it by ear because it was certainly a possibility that he would have no interest in discussing politics. If she broached the topic and he was unenthusiastic, she'd try to see him at a later date. Before she could lose any of her conviction, the congressman's aide returned. "He'd be happy to see you," he said.

When Alex came through the door, Beckett was sitting in a wheelchair with his right leg propped up. The knee immobilizer he wore was as elaborate a model as she had ever seen.

"Dr. Caffey," he began. "It's nice to see you again. Please excuse me for not getting up."

Alex crossed the room and extended her hand. "I was on the floor and just wanted to stop in and extend my best wishes."

"That's very kind of you. Dean O'Leary certainly had a lot of nice things to say about you. I think he views you as Gillette's latest rising star."

"Coming from the dean that's quite a compliment." She

pointed to his knee. "So do you think this will end your basketball career?"

"Not a chance. Six months from now I'll be back out on the court."

"When do you think you'll feel up to going back to work?"

"I guess in a day or two." He paused for a moment. An introspective look came to his face. "I hope you won't be offended if I mention that you look like somebody who has more on her mind than just wishing me a speedy recovery."

"Guilty," she said with a grin, welcoming the entrée into her real reason for being there.

He pointed to one of three leather club chairs arranged in a semicircle. "Seeing as how I'm a captive audience—why don't you go for it?"

Relieved, Alex said, "You mentioned when we met that you were interested in the physician point of view on national health insurance."

"Well, since that's the topic I'm most passionate about and seeing how this is the most bored I've been in months, why don't you have a seat?" While he waited for Alex to pull up a chair, Beckett added, "How politically active are you?"

"Like most physicians, I recognize there's a problem but my time is limited."

"Well, that's a start," Beckett said. "What do you think is the biggest obstacle to rallying the support of the physicians behind universal health care?"

"Getting them to slow down long enough to listen to the issues."

"Anything else?" he asked.

"Dealing with medical organizations that oppose universal health care—like the Caduceus Project," she said.

"The Caduceus Project," he said with a frown.

"Are you familiar with the organization?"

"Are you kidding? You're looking at the guy who's number one on their ten most hated list."

"I think I've heard something about that," Alex said. "I'm a strong advocate for universal health coverage and many physicians feel as strongly about the issue as I do, but our efforts to convince our colleagues who are sitting on the fence that this country needs a policy of national health insurance are stymied by organizations like the Caduceus Project."

"There were many reasons why national health insurance never became a reality in spite of President Clinton's efforts. One that experts continually cite was Clinton's inability to rally enough physician support."

"So how do we accomplish that when we're up against organizations like the Caduceus Project?"

He answered, "I've learned one important lesson since coming to Washington. No matter how righteous you think your cause is, there will be those who passionately disagree."

"So what do you do?"

"Play by the rules and try to figure them out, and then stay one step ahead of them. In that way you at least have a fighting chance of diminishing their influence. With respect to the Caduceus Project, there's no question that they're a tough group and a formidable opponent. They're highly organized, well funded, and aggressive."

"Have they ever crossed the line?" Alex asked, hoping she wasn't pushing her point too far.

"It's hard to say. We've had our suspicions and looked at things like money falling into the wrong hands and dirty tricks, but we've never been able to get enough information to go public."

"I see," Alex said, a little disappointed.

Before she could say anything further, there was a knock at the door. Beckett hollered, "Come in."

Escorted by the congressman's aide, two physical therapists came into the room. One of them, a young lady with long strawberry-blond hair, said, "We need to give you some discharge instructions and set up an outpatient schedule of rehab for you, congressman."

Alex stood up and said, "I'll be going."

Beckett extended his hand. "If there's any way I can help you, give my office a call. I'm betting my whole political future on the fact that we can convince the American people that national health insurance is a must."

Alex was escorted to the door by the congressman's aide. Heading back to the operating room, she wondered whether Beckett had been intentionally cautious about his comments about the Caduceus Project. It seemed as if his impression wasn't too much different than hers except for the fact that she was more convinced that they were quite capable of stepping over the line.

# Chapter 58

Simon Lott stood outside the ICU.

He unhooked his latest Gillette Trauma Center identification badge, which read *Ian Abbington,* from his shirt pocket and scrutinized it again. He then took one final glance at it before fastening it back to his uniform. Grasping the handles of the wheelchair that he had commandeered from the admitting department, he strolled into the ICU as if he had done the same thing a hundred times before.

His plan was brilliant in its simplicity. Once he had David Airoway out of the ICU and supposedly on his way to physical therapy, he would take him directly to the old blood bank, which was now closed and slated for renovation beginning next month. Using the monofilament line that was neatly coiled in his pocket, he figured it would take him less than two minutes to make sure that David Airoway would never remember anything about the night he attacked him. In reality, Lott doubted that Airoway would ever remember a thing, but why take the chance and why lose the perfect opportunity to emotionally devastate Alex Caffey?

Lott moved inconspicuously across the ICU, stopping when he reached David's cubicle.

"Is he ready?" Lott asked with a smile.

"Where are we going?" Carrie Melfi, his nurse, asked.

"Physical therapy."

"He was already there this morning."

"His physical therapist called us a little while ago and said they had a cancellation. They thought he might benefit from another session. She said they checked it out with his doctor and he said okay."

Carrie placed her hands on her hips and then glanced over at David. "It must have been one of the residents. I wonder why he didn't call me."

Lott shrugged. "I couldn't tell ya that. All I do is move 'em from point A to point B. If you want, I can come back later."

Lott watched as the skepticism on Carrie's face vanished. "No, I guess it'll be okay. Let me help you get him into the wheelchair." Carrie walked over to the bed and tapped David gently on the shoulder. He opened his eyes slowly. "How about another dance in physical therapy?" she asked.

"Again?" he moaned. "Why?"

"Orders from your doctor, I'm afraid."

"My doctor? I bet it was my sister," he grumbled.

"No comment."

"This place is worse than Parris Island." He then took a deep breath and added, "I thought you told me that I needed to get plenty of rest."

"That's true, but you don't want to overdo a good thing."

"Now you're starting to sound like my sister. You two have an answer for everything," he complained.

"That comes from having three older brothers," Carrie said.

With Lott's assistance, it wasn't very difficult to move David into the wheelchair. "Thanks very much. I'll have him back to you in an hour," Lott promised.

"I'll be here," she said.

Nobody raised an eyebrow as Lott wheeled David out of the ICU. Carrie didn't even notice when he failed to stop at the nursing station to make a note on the patient signout sheet.

The old blood bank was on the third floor at the far end of the south wing—the same floor the ICU was on. Pushing the chair slowly down the corridor, Lott passed several hospital employees, all of whom were too busy or preoccupied to even notice him. He glanced down at David and smiled when he saw he had nodded off.

No other departments were located in that area of the hospital so it didn't surprise him that when he arrived outside the doors, there was nobody in sight. Lott quickly rotated the wheelchair around and pushed the swinging door open by backing through it.

The lights were on but all of the phones, computers, and other equipment had already been removed. There was a faint but definite musty odor in the air. Three rows of long black benches, which once supported sophisticated scientific instruments, were now bare and collecting dust. Staying directly behind the wheelchair, Lott reached into his pocket, slipped out the line, and began to pass it around David's neck.

"The blood bank's closed," came a woman's voice. From the distant sound of it, he realized that she had to be on the other side of the room. "It's been temporarily moved to the second floor."

Without turning, Lott moved his hands together, pushing the line into his right palm. He then grabbed the handles of the wheelchair, concealing the line between his palm and the handle. By the time he turned around the woman had crossed the room and was standing just a few feet from him.

"From the looks of things I figured that, but nobody told me," he said as he turned the chair back around. "I just started work here." He looked around, sighed, and then asked, "Do you think there's a phone in here so I can get some help?"

"They've all been disconnected."

"What are you doing here?" he asked.

"I work for the general contractor doing the renovations. I've been here for a couple of hours and you're the third person who's accidentally come in here." The young lady, who was of Asian descent, sneaked a peek at David. His chin was squarely on his chest, his breathing slow and rhythmic. "It looks like your rider's out for the count."

"He's heavily medicated," Lott whispered. "I better get going."

Lott pushed the door open and maneuvered the wheelchair back out into the hall. Having only one option, he headed back toward the ICU. When he arrived back at David's cubicle, Carrie looked at him quizzically.

"What happened?" she asked.

"Physical therapy suddenly got jammed up, so they sent us back."

"I'm kind of glad to hear that," Carrie said. "He was pretty tired."

Lott assisted Carrie as she helped David back into bed. He awakened only long enough to be moved and then went straight back to sleep. Lott realized that there were some holes in his story but with all of the students, residents, and doctors involved in Airoway's care, it was unlikely Carrie would ever give his aborted trip to physical therapy another thought.

"I gotta get back," Lott said.

Carrie was busy attending to David and didn't even look up when she told him thanks.

Thirty minutes after he left the hospital, Lott had already destroyed the identification badge and dumped the uniform. He sat in his lounge chair with his legs propped up on an ottoman. He had only about an hour before meeting Kerry for dinner.

He may have been disappointed with the events of the day, but he quickly dismissed his failure as nothing more than bad luck. Of much greater importance was that his resolve to kill David Airoway had in no way been shaken.

# Chapter 59

## MAY 16

Although David remained amnesic of the events that caused his injuries, his language skills were rapidly returning, making it much easier for him to communicate and process information.

"We couldn't have picked a better morning for a stroll," Alex told David as she pushed his wheelchair out the rear entrance of the hospital.

"I would say that one of us is strolling and the other is riding," he said.

"Your day will come. I'm sure as I get old and doting you'll have your chance to push me around in one of these things."

"I'll look forward to it," he said, turning around and smiling at her.

Alex had given a considerable amount of thought to the best time to broach the topic of what had happened to him. She had discussed the matter with the neurosurgeons, who felt there would be no harm in trying to jog his memory a little. She had even bounced the question off Sam Tanner, one of the psychiatrists on staff at John Adams, who saw no reason not to discuss it with David.

"Do you remember anything about the night you were injured?" she asked.

"Not really," he answered in a plain enough voice, giving Alex no reason to believe that he was uncomfortable discussing his accident.

"I was just getting off call when they brought you in," she said as she slowly guided the wheelchair down a long ramp leading to a large park behind the hospital.

"I must have been some sight."

"Actually, I didn't recognize you at first, but then I noticed your watch."

"That's amazing," he said.

"Do you remember anything about the days before you were hurt?"

David shook his head and then added, "Not really, but the neurosurgery resident told me a lot of people with bad head injuries never remember what happened."

"Do you want to hear something funny? The police think you tried to kill yourself."

David hesitated for a few moments and then asked, "And you want to know if that's possible?"

"Of course not. I know you'd never do a thing like that," she assured him.

"I may not remember what happened, but I sure as hell didn't try to kill myself, Alex. Why would anybody think such a preposterous thing?"

"You have to remember that the police don't know you."

"So?"

"There was no evidence that you were attacked, so they wondered if perhaps there was something terrible going on in your personal life that pushed you over the edge."

"Well, I hate to second-guess the police but as far as I remember my life was going along pretty well. Didn't you tell them that?"

"Of course I did, but they have no way of knowing if the information I gave them was accurate."

"I guess it would be nice to remember what happened," David said.

Alex pushed the wheelchair slowly along the sidewalk that gently encircled the park.

"I wouldn't worry about it too much. In spite of what the neurosurgery resident told you, I bet everything comes back to you."

Alex stopped in front of a bench. Before sitting down, she placed her hands on David's shoulders and gave them a quick squeeze. It was at that moment that she realized that it was probably better if David never remembered a thing about his awful ordeal.

For the next half hour or so they talked about many different things. David was the most alert Alex had seen him, but she watched him carefully for signs of fatigue.

"What time is Mom coming over?" he asked.

"Not until this afternoon. You know, there's a little girl who has been driving me crazy about seeing her Uncle David."

"Well, if I ever get out of this place, maybe I'll be able to see her."

"Actually, I think I have enough pull around here to have her come visit you. How does tomorrow sound?"

David couldn't contain his smile. "That would be great."

"Good," Alex said as she stood up. "I hate to be the one to spoil the moment but if we don't head back pretty soon, they'll send a search party out for us."

As Alex began pushing David back along the path, she saw Sam approaching and waved at her.

"Hi, you guys," Sam said, leaning over to kiss David.

"How did you know we were out here?" Alex asked.

"Dave's nurse ratted you out. How are you feeling?" she asked him. He raised his eyebrows and looked at her amorously. Sam winked at Alex. "I guess he's starting to feel better."

"Don't be flattered," Alex said. "That's the first bodily function that returns in all men."

With the two of them pushing, they started back down the sidewalk. Sam tried to quietly ask Alex how David was doing.

"Hey, what are you two mumbling about back there?" he asked.

Alex tapped Sam on the shoulder and then raised her finger to her lips.

"We're talking about you," Sam told him.

"There must be something more interesting to talk about than that," he said.

Sam and Alex shifted gears and made a conscious effort to include David in the conversation, which continued nonstop until they arrived back in the ICU.

# Chapter 60

The hospital's weekly surgical conference had been considerably more boring than usual.

As soon as it was over, Alex avoided the usual social gathering of surgeons outside the auditorium and headed back across the street to see David again. It was a few minutes before nine in the morning.

When she reached his bay, she noticed that David's nurse, Caroline, was packing his personal things up and loading them onto a cart.

"What's going on?" Alex asked, assuming that perhaps they were moving him to a different ICU bed.

"Dr. Runyon called in this morning from Boston. When we updated him on David's condition, he said it would be okay to transfer him out of the ICU to a regular room."

"I beg your pardon?" Alex said in an indignant tone of voice. Since she had dismissed the idea of going to Boston, mainly because of Micah's advice, she had forgotten about the meeting.

"Dr. Runyon said that David was well enough to go to a regular room and ordered him transferred out of the ICU."

"Well, I disagree," Alex insisted, crossing her arms in front of her. "My brother is staying right here. I've already discussed this matter with Mr. Henry. David is not to be transferred out of the ICU."

Caroline was an experienced nurse, but it was apparent from her sudden silence that she was uncomfortable and unsure of how to handle the situation. Finally she suggested, "Maybe you should discuss this with Bette. She's in charge today."

"I'd be happy to."

David had turned in his wheelchair and had been listening to the entire conversation.

"What's going on, Alex?"

"Nothing, I'd just be more comfortable if you stayed here."

David looked around. "I'm not a doctor but I think I feel well enough to go to a regular room."

"You're right," she said. "You're not a doctor."

"You're doing it again, Alex."

"Doing what?"

"Being a control freak. I have a doctor. Why don't you let him make the decisions?"

Before Alex could respond, Caroline returned with Bette, a short nurse with blond hair and an accommodating nature. She and Alex had spent many a long night together taking care of terribly injured patients.

"Hi," she said. "Caroline was just filling me in on the problem."

"There is no problem. My brother's staying right where he is."

"I'm sorry, Alex, but we have an order from his attending

physician to transfer him out of the ICU, so until I hear otherwise I really have no choice."

Alex took a breath, held it for a few seconds, and then let it escape. "Bette, I'm also an attending in this hospital. Do you have any way of reaching Dr. Runyon?" she asked, making sure it sounded as calm as she was able.

Bette turned to Caroline, who said, "I have his beeper number. It's a national pager."

"Why don't you beep him," Bette suggested. "When he calls back, come and get me." Caroline nodded, turned her shoulders, and carefully slid past Alex.

Alex sat down next to David and again assured him that he was better off remaining in the ICU. Fortunately, he didn't ask too many questions because if he had, Alex would have been hard-pressed to share her reasons with him. She did feel badly about placing the nurses in the awkward situation of trying to accommodate two physicians, especially when one was a family member. Alex knew that it was probably only out of courtesy and their good relationship that Bette did not point out to her that technically she was not one of David's attending doctors and therefore could not give the nurses orders in his care.

Alex was filling David in on Jessie's latest accomplishments when Bette returned. She motioned to Alex and they stepped outside.

"Did he call back?" Alex asked, taking care not to sound abrupt.

"Yes, he did."

"And?"

"He wants David to go to a private room. He thinks it will help him regain his normal sleep patterns and free up an ICU bed for a patient who really needs it."

"I see. Did you mention to Dr. Runyon that I wanted to talk to him?"

Bette looked away. "Yes, I did. He said he was very busy and couldn't talk to you at the moment. He told me that he'll be back in town late this afternoon and if you or any other family member has any concerns, they can call him at that time. He also asked that I remind you that you're not supposed to be giving any medical orders on David."

Alex shook her head and then took a couple of steps away. "This is my brother and I'll do whatever I think—"

"Don't shoot the messenger, Alex, but maybe you should think about what he's saying." Bette took a step closer and whispered, "Just because he's a pompous jerk doesn't mean he's not right."

Trying to gather herself, Alex took a deep breath and told Bette in a quiet tone, "I'm not trying to take any of this out on you."

"I know that, Alex."

"I'm going down to see Mr. Henry. Please don't move my brother until I get back to you."

Bette moved closer to Alex and put her hand on her arm. "Alex, we all have a pretty good idea of what you're going through. I have a twin sister myself. Don't worry. I'm not going to move David until I hear from you."

"Supposing Runyon calls back?"

"He won't but if he does, I'll handle it."

A wave of relief consumed Alex. "Thanks, Bette."

Alex went back inside to tell David that she would be back later, but he had already fallen asleep. She grabbed her purse and headed across the ICU. If Runyon thought for one second she was going to give him another shot at her brother, he was sadly mistaken.

# Chapter 61

Alex stood in front of Micah's smirking secretary, calling on every particle of self-restraint she could summon.

"As I told you, Dr. Caffey, Mr. Henry is out of town."

"Do you know when he'll be back?" Alex asked, now remembering that Micah had mentioned that he'd be out of town for a couple of days.

"Mr. Henry doesn't like me discussing his personal schedule with just anybody who walks into his office."

"I see," Alex acknowledged, trying to overlook her petulant jealousy. "It's rather important. I'm quite sure Mr. Henry wouldn't mind."

She looked carefully at Alex for a few seconds before finally caving in. "I think he'll be back this evening," she said, pausing for a moment to shake her hair. "Perhaps there's something I could help you with?"

"It's rather personal. Are you expecting Mr. Henry to call in?"

"He generally calls me quite often when he's out of town."

Alex knew that Micah hated pagers and refused to own one. He carried his cell phone but for some reason never turned it on unless he wanted to make a call.

"Do you have his cell phone number?" Lisa asked.

"I do."

"Why don't you leave him a message?"

"Thank you," Alex said. "If you'll just tell him I was here and ask him to either page me or call me on my cell phone as soon as possible."

"Does he know your pager number?"

"By heart," Alex said as she forced an obsequious smile.

Still steaming at Runyon, Alex marched out of Micah's office. Feeling helpless for the moment, she stopped in the hall to gather herself. Rather than return to the ICU, she decided to go up to her office and wait for Micah's call before getting back to Bette.

Still angry regarding Victor's arrogance and disregard for her wishes, she sat at her desk trying without much success to concentrate on her latest *Journal of Trauma*. She was just about to reread the same paragraph for the third time when her private line rang.

"What's going on?" Micah asked. "My secretary said you were pretty upset."

"Runyon's trying to have David moved out of the ICU."

"Did you speak with him about it?" he asked.

"His imperial majesty was too busy to talk with me. He's in Boston at a Caduceus Project meeting and I guess the demands of his political life exceed that of his patient care responsibilities."

"Take it easy, Alex. Why does Runyon want him moved out?"

"Because he doesn't think David needs to be in ICU any longer."

"Is that true?" Micah asked.

"It doesn't matter. I want him to stay there," she insisted.

"Do we need the bed for another patient?"

"Not at the moment," she answered. "But if things get tight and we get into a bed crunch, we can always move him then and I'll arrange for a private-duty nurse—one that's about six foot four and an ex–Green Beret."

"Who's the charge nurse today?" Micah asked.

"Bette. I've already spoken to her. She said she'd stall the transfer until I had a chance to talk to you."

"I'll have one of the administrators give her a call. It's no big deal. David can stay in the ICU."

"Thank you, Micah. What about Runyon?"

"Let me worry about him, but please don't call him, and if he calls you, I'd appreciate it if you wouldn't start World War Three over this."

"I promise," she said.

"Obviously, you and Victor still have issues. I didn't mention this to you but I got another call from Carson Gillette."

"Great."

"Take it easy. He just wanted to know how things were going and whether you had taken my advice about not prying into areas that didn't concern you."

"What did you tell him?"

"I tap-danced a lot but I think he was satisfied," Micah said.

"So you lied your ass off."

"In a manner of speaking. Look, I'll be back in town later. Why don't we have dinner? I'd like to talk about this whole thing again."

"I think that can be arranged," she answered, hoping Micah's interest wasn't purely business.

"I'll come by and get you around seven-thirty. I'll leave my phone on. Call me if there are any other problems."

"Thanks, Micah," she said.

Still consumed by a sense of relief, a smile spread across her face as she thought about how much Micah's friendship meant to her. Nobody else could lighten her mood and put her at ease as easily as he could. More than anything, he was someone she could always depend on.

# Chapter 62

Alex had just arrived home and was downstairs with Jessie in her playroom when Olivia summoned her with a holler from the top of the basement stairs.

"I'll be right up," Alex said, closing the book she'd been reading to Jessie.

"Can I watch TV until you come back?" she asked.

"Not until seven-thirty. You know the rules." Without her usual pout, Jessie picked up another book and opened it. "I'll be right back, baby," Alex said, kissing her on top of her head.

When she reached the top of the steps, she saw Olivia standing there with a peculiar expression on her face. She didn't say a word but pointed in the direction of the front door. Alex took the last couple of steps and then stepped into the hall. The moment she did, she saw Victor Runyon standing in her entrance hall. The first thing she noticed was that his eyes were transfixed on her and he appeared angry. She wasn't in the least intimidated as she walked down the hall to meet him.

"I must have missed your call that you were coming over, Victor. Is there something I can do for you?"

"I just came from the hospital and David was still in the ICU. The nurse told me that you called Micah Henry and had my orders countermanded. Is that true?"

"Yes, it is."

"Would you mind telling me why?"

"For the obvious reason that I'm not comfortable with my brother being sent out of the ICU just yet. If you had taken the time to speak with me, I'm sure we could have resolved the problem without getting administration involved."

"So because I was tied up and not available to speak to you at the exact moment you wanted, that gives you the right to get administration involved?"

"You left me no choice," she said.

"That's ridiculous, Alex. I asked the nurse to convey my reasons to you. You knew I'd be back late this afternoon. It's my call, not yours, and by acting the way you did, you've confirmed my suspicions that you're too personally involved with David to be objective about his medical care."

"I guess you're entitled to your opinion," she said.

"I'm not the only one who holds that opinion. I checked with Owen. He told me that he made it clear to you that you were not to act as a treating physician and you were supposed to leave the day-to-day management of David's care to us. I'm telling you again. Your actions today were neither rational nor professional."

"I think the COO of the hospital would disagree with you."

Victor's smile was a nasty one. "I'm not sure he's being totally objective."

"What the hell is that supposed to mean?" she demanded.

"Nothing, but in case you haven't heard, Micah Henry's engaged to be married."

Alex took a step forward and crossed her arms. She was just about to respond to Victor's barb when she heard the basement door open. A moment later Jessie appeared and stared down the hall at them with a wary expression. Before Alex could say anything, Olivia appeared from the kitchen and whisked her away. The few seconds that passed were insufficient for Alex to quell her rising anger.

"You're hardly in a position to sling arrows, Victor, and I would suspect that the only thing you know less about than rational behavior is professional behavior."

"What?"

"I'm not an idiot, Victor, and I think you know exactly what I'm talking about."

Victor waited a few seconds before again turning to look

at her. His manner was controlled. "I hate to disappoint you but I don't have the first clue what the hell you're talking about and furthermore, I don't give a damn. What I do know is that your behavior of late has been extremely questionable. We've all bent over backward to indulge you because of the obvious stress you've been under but you are beginning to test the limits of my patience. You're forcing me into a corner, Alex."

"Are you threatening me? You've already been to the board of trustees."

"I'm merely voicing my outrage at your unethical behavior."

"This isn't over, Victor. I'll go to the authorities if I have to."

"Authorities? What in God's name are you talking about? I think you've gone mad, Alex. You need help immediately." Just as he started to turn and reach for the door, the bell rang. He stopped, stepped aside, and allowed Alex to answer it.

When she opened the door, Micah was standing there. The moment he walked in, he saw Victor. After surveying the situation for a few seconds, he cast a suspect look at Alex. Ignoring the obvious tension in the air and trying to defuse an uncomfortable situation, he said in an upbeat voice, "Has everyone already eaten? Because if you haven't, I'm buying."

At the pinnacle of his frustration, Victor threw his hands up in the air, gave Micah a disdainful look, and stormed past him.

Micah craned his head and watched as he walked down the path and got into his car.

"Well, so much for diplomacy," he said. "How did you wind up with two dates in the same night?"

"I'm not in the mood, Micah."

"Are we still going to dinner?"

"Absolutely. I'm not going to let that deceitful, egotistical jackass ruin my dinner. I'll just go say good-bye to Jessie."

Alex disappeared into the kitchen, but moments later Jessie came flying down the hall. Micah caught her under the arms and lifted her high over his head.

"Hi, Micah," she screeched. "Is Gabe here?"

"It's a little late for Gabe," he said swinging her back and forth. "Maybe we'll all do something this weekend."

"Where are you and Mommy going?"

"Out to dinner. Have you already eaten?" he asked her, to which she nodded. "What a shame," he cried, putting her down next to Alex.

"I'll come kiss you goodnight when I get home," Alex told her.

"But I'll be asleep."

"That's when I love you the most."

Jessie smiled and then giggled. "Have a good time with your *boyfriend*."

"Olivia," Alex yelled down the hall. "Come get Jessie before I do something I'll regret in the morning." She turned to Micah, who was doing everything he could to remain expressionless. "Don't say a word," she told him as she shooed him outside and closed the door behind them.


# Chapter 63


"Where would you like to eat?" Micah asked Alex as they walked down her path. He looked up, took her by the arm, and pointed toward N Street. It was a clement, star-filled night.

"Anywhere as long as I don't have to drive. I'm planning on having quite a bit of wine with dinner."

"In that case, let's go to La Perla. It's a perfect night for a walk."

They had walked two blocks east on N Street when she finally asked, "When are you going to say something already?"

"The only thing I'm going to tell you is that you have to think with your head, not your heart. Victor's not without influence. He could very easily go to the board of trustees and make another complaint about you."

"Let him. Maybe the board should be more concerned about his criminal activities than my overbearing nature."

"I'm not sure the board's prepared to accept on your word alone that one of their trauma surgeons is a criminal. You just might be putting your entire career on the line."

"I appreciate your concern," she said in a businesslike manner. Micah didn't pursue his point.

For the next fifteen minutes, Micah found several things to talk about, all of which had nothing to do with David, Victor, or the Caduceus Project. He anticipated that she might want to discuss things more at dinner, which he would be happy to do, but he decided if they were going to talk, he'd allow her to initiate the conversation.

After a ten-minute wait at the restaurant's bar, they were seated in front of a large bay window with a view of Pennsylvania Avenue by a hearty-appearing host with a sparse mustache. A minute later the server, a young lady whom Alex assumed was a student doing some moonlighting, appeared at the table. After perusing the wine list for a minute or so, Micah ordered a bottle of Corvo.

They had just finished their second glass when the young lady returned to the table. Micah ordered the scelta di risotti, one of the house specialties, and Alex decided on trout stuffed with spinach and crabmeat.

"You're very conflicted," she said to him casually.

He looked at her curiously, wondering what in the world was on her mind and how much the Corvo had to do with it.

"That was kind of out of the blue. What do you mean?"

"A part of you is trying very hard to be an understanding friend, but your logical and pragmatic side is screaming out to you that Alex Caffey is out of her mind." She set her glass back on the table before going on. "I'm going to help you out of this mess. For now, just be my friend." She raised her hands. "See? Now there's no more conflict."

"I am trying to be your friend, but I'm worried that you don't see it that way."

"You're doing fine," she assured him.

"So what are you going to do next?"

"I'm not exactly sure but I think it's time to talk to Owen."

"Officially?"

"Is there any other way?" she inquired.

"I'm not so sure that's such a good—"

"Micah, before you get rolling, I have an idea. Why don't we talk about something else?"

"I was only going to say that—"

"We've both had a long day. Let's just enjoy dinner. Okay?"

"Done. Sometimes I forget that you're wise beyond your years," he said, letting out a deep breath and sensing that retreat was his best course of action.

By the time their main courses arrived, they had finished the bottle of Corvo. Alex ordered a second, to which Micah nodded in approval.

"Let's talk about you for a change. What's going on with Max?" she asked.

Micah picked up his fork and then cleared his throat. "Well, I didn't think we were going to get into this tonight, but we finally had a heart-to-heart. It was a very productive and honest talk."

"You make it sound like a meeting of the executive committee. What did Max say?"

"It seems that she can't cope with the pressures of getting married and the demands of a high-powered job at the same time."

After an uncomfortable silence, Alex asked, "So what does that mean exactly?"

"She suggested that we put our relationship on hold for a while. I then suggested that we break our engagement. She sounded relieved and told me that she would have my ring returned by courier within a day or two."

"I see," Alex said, not at all saddened by the news. "Are you guys still going to see each other?"

"I don't think so. I think I've played the chump long enough."

"What do you mean?"

"I had second thoughts about breaking our engagement this morning, so I called her office. Her assistant told me that she and her boss had gone out of town on business and they wouldn't be back for three days."

"They've gone on business trips before together. You've never gotten that bent out of shape about it."

"I guess her assistant felt sorry for me because she casually shared with me that it was only a one-day meeting."

"Ouch."

"I guess you were right about Max. I should have listened to you," he lamented with a painful grin as he reached for his wine. "It looks like the Alexandra Caffey perfect first-kiss theory is for real. I don't think Max was ever really in love with me."

"I'm sorry, Micah, but maybe it's better that you found out now. You'll just have to get back into circulation again. You'll find somebody who interests you in no time."

Micah felt a surge of anxiety, which, after a deep breath, found its way smack to the hollow of his stomach. He felt as if an enormous door of opportunity had just opened wide. Alex's statement was either quite innocuous or her way of broaching a very delicate topic.

Gathering enough courage to answer her was definitely bolstered by the wine. "Maybe this is all for the best," he began. "I guess I've kind of been distracted by someone else for quite some time," he confessed, lifting his eyes and gazing across the table at her as nonchalantly as he could. In his heart, he was hoping Alex would say something and put an end to this cat-and-mouse game, but to his dismay, she remained silent, averting her eyes and looking right past him and out onto Pennsylvania Avenue.

After an awkward few seconds, Micah suddenly regretted his overture and was afraid that maybe the door that had flung open was the wrong one. If she smiled at him politely and then told him that she was deeply flattered by his feelings but could never think of him romantically, he would crawl under the table. The only thing worse could be if she gave him the ego-flattening speech about how much she valued their friendship and how he was just like a second brother to her— the thought of that was too embarrassing to even consider. With panic building inside him, Micah went to a preemptive strike and asked, "When do you think David will be getting out of the hospital?"

"Hopefully in the next few weeks," she answered with just

the slightest strain in her voice. He would be kidding himself if he didn't say she looked quite relieved that he had moved on to a new topic.

Determined not to demonstrate any hint of disappointment or appear flustered, Micah smiled and said, "That's terrific news." Wallowing in remorse, he wondered how he could have been so stupid as to think that Alex had any romantic interest in him at all. The only redeeming thing was that he hadn't stuck his foot any farther into his mouth. He cleared his throat and repeated, "That's really great news about David getting out of the hospital so soon."

"It will be the end of a horrible nightmare," she told him.

Plying himself with more Corvo, it didn't take Micah long to regroup. Alex, too, relaxed again and seemed to have forgotten his awkward overture at romance.

By the end of the meal, they had finished the second bottle of wine, leaving both of them feeling no pain. Returning to Alex's house in a cab, Micah couldn't remember spending any evening with Max that he had enjoyed more than the one he had just spent with Alex.

# Chapter 64

**MAY 17**

Alex had a fairly good notion that she'd find Owen in his office working, just as he always did every Wednesday morning.

Standing in front of his door, she took two slow breaths before gathering the last dram of courage she needed to knock.

"Come in," came the response.

"Excuse me, Owen. Do you have a minute?" she asked, poking her head in. "If this isn't a good time I can—"

"Nonsense," he said, motioning her forward and then directing her to a large chair in front of his desk. "Sit down. How's David doing?"

"David's doing great," she said with several slow nods.

"How's the medical student lecture series shaping up for next year?"

"I just finished it. I think it came out pretty well." From the watchful look in Owen's eyes, Alex suspected she was wearing her emotions on her sleeve.

"So what's on your mind?" he asked.

"I think we have a problem on the service."

"Really?" he answered. "What kind of problem?"

"It's a little difficult to talk about because it involves one of the faculty members," she explained while Owen sat back in his chair.

"Well, if there's a problem, you have to give me the details. I can't administrate a myth."

"I realize that," she said before adding, "It's Victor."

"Victor? I'm a little surprised to hear that. What's the problem?"

"I think he's become so consumed with the Caduceus Project that he's lost sight of his professional ethics."

Owen didn't move; his expression remained impassive. "That's quite an accusation, Alex."

"I'm well aware of that, and I want you to understand that coming to see you was not a capricious decision. I've been wrestling with it for days."

"Have you discussed any of this with Victor?"

"No."

"What specifically is the problem?" he asked, his manner direct.

"Victor uses the Medivasc caval filter exclusively. It was brought to my attention that the company is extremely supportive of the Caduceus Project."

"Supportive in what way?"

"Financially."

"Go on."

"Four patients in the last eighteen months with Medivasc caval filters have died—all from pulmonary emboli."

"Are you sure?" he asked. "That sounds awfully high."

"It's more than high. It's off the wall compared to other filters. The problem is that I think Victor is well aware that there's a problem with these filters and he's intentionally overlooking it."

"Why would he do that?"

"For fear of possibly jeopardizing his relationship with Medivasc and losing their financial support."

"That's a pretty serious allegation, Alex. What you're suggesting goes way beyond unethical."

"I'm well aware of that but I wouldn't be in your office if I didn't have strong reasons to believe that I'm correct. I've reviewed our service statistics and looked at the autopsy reports. Victor never reported any of the cases. I even met with the sales rep from Medivasc, who told me that Victor's in bed with the upper echelon of the company. I've also spoken to their quality-assurance department. They have received no reports from anybody at Gillette regarding defective filters."

"Did you check with the FDA?" Owen asked.

"I did. They have nothing on file that would suggest that there's a problem with the Medivasc filter."

"That doesn't make sense, Alex. If there's something wrong with the device, how come other institutions haven't had a problem?"

"I don't know, but Medivasc is a fairly recent entry into the caval filter market. At the present time their market penetration isn't very high but they're aggressive and pressing hard to become a major player."

"Are you suggesting that they're deliberately withholding quality issues from the FDA?"

"Maybe, or perhaps other institutions haven't put enough of the filters in or they just haven't realized that there's a potential problem and haven't reported it to Medivasc."

"You said there were four patients."

"That's right. I reviewed three of the charts. Robert Key's case was referred to the medical examiner and I still don't have the report of the autopsy but I'm fairly certain the cause of death will be determined to be a pulmonary embolus."

Owen stood up, came out from behind his desk, and walked over to his window.

"I'd like to have a look at those charts, the autopsy reports, and your reviews. Can you get them to me?"

"I'll bring everything to your office."

"That would be fine. Now, there's one other thing. Until I look at the material in detail, I feel obligated to give Victor the benefit of the doubt. We're talking about a very sensitive issue here. If what you suspect about his relationship with the Caduceus Project is true and it becomes public, well, the impact on Gillette could be catastrophic."

"I understand that, Owen."

"So until I've had a chance to complete my review of this matter, I am asking you not to discuss it with anyone." Owen paused for a moment and then added, "I assume I'm the only person you have talked to about all this?"

"Micah knows some of what's going on."

Owen tried to quell a knowing smile. "In that case, I'll speak with him about it."

"I told Micah that I would be talking to you."

Owen stood up and, in silence, escorted Alex to the door. She was a little surprised when he turned and walked back into his office without closing the door. She watched him stroll over to a large window. As he gazed out, he crossed his arms and shook his head. She knew that Owen loved being chief of the department of surgery and selflessly gave the position every ounce of energy he had.

He was a fairly flexible and open-minded leader but was absolutely unwavering on the importance of professional ethics and conduct. Alex's heart went out to him because at the moment, he looked like a man with the weight of the world on his shoulders.

# Chapter 65

It wasn't often that Owen summoned Alex in the middle of the day, so when she got the call from his secretary that he wanted to see her, she quickly finished her monthly medical student evaluations and went directly to his office.

The moment he caught sight of her in his doorway, Owen stood up and came out from behind his desk. His sports coat was hanging on the back of his chair and he was wearing his signature striped bow tie.

"Have a seat, Alex. I'll only keep you a few minutes," he said and then closed the door. "Since you were the one who brought the Medivasc matter to my attention, I thought I'd bring you up to speed on what's going on." Owen settled back into his chair before continuing. "I didn't want to appear impetuous on such an important issue so I did my homework. The information you gave me was quite accurate. We have had four patients with Medivasc filters who have died over the last year or so, and as you pointed out that goes way beyond the expected failure rate of the device, especially since we've only placed a total of seven of them in the last eighteen months. That makes our failure rate better than fifty percent, which is of course totally unacceptable."

"I agree," Alex said, intentionally keeping her answer brief to hide her elation.

Owen leaned forward and placed his palms flat on his desk. "As I know you are aware, all the patients who died were on Victor's service. Now, while I think, to a certain extent, all of us dropped the ball on this one, Victor had the ultimate responsibility of bringing this matter to my attention." Owen cleared his throat and then went on. "As of this morning I have ordered that no further Medivasc filters be placed. I have also notified the FDA. They have assured me they will begin an immediate investigation, recall all the filters, and advise Medivasc not to ship any further filters until this matter is resolved."

"I think that's very reasonable," Alex agreed.

"Now, that leaves the matter of Victor."

"I don't really think that concerns me, Owen. Perhaps it would be better—"

Owen raised his hand and waited for Alex to stop speaking. "I want you to hear this. We have strong evidence pointing to an improper relationship between Victor and Medivasc. While we are well aware of the custom and permit drug companies to support our educational efforts, the custom of these companies supporting political groups is a little more prickly. In this particular case, the amount of money involved was so excessive, it has to raise the concern that Victor's judgment was, at the least, extremely poor."

"I assume you're referring to the fact that he intentionally didn't notify you?"

"Exactly." More grim-faced than she'd ever seen him, Owen looked away before continuing. "In any event, until this matter can be more fully investigated, Victor will be summarily suspended from the medical staff. All of his administrative responsibilities with respect to the medical school will be reassigned to other faculty members. While Victor will be given every opportunity to defend himself in this matter, we unfortunately find ourselves in the very unpleasant situation of possibly having to refer this matter to the local authorities." Owen stopped as abruptly as he'd begun, his eyes finding the floor. Alex could see that he was visibly shaken.

"I'm sorry, Owen. I know how much this must be upsetting you. Unfortunately, I still have my suspicions that you may be just scratching the surface with respect to some of the activities of the Caduceus Project."

"I'm aware of that," he assured her. "I may be nothing more than an old pain in the ass but I won't turn a blind eye. I assure you that the Caduceus Project is going to be examined under a microscope."

"I think you'll find that they're not exactly a Partnership

for a Healthy America. I hope none of this becomes public and reflects poorly on the medical school," she offered.

"I stopped predicting long ago what the media considers newsworthy," he responded as he stood up and walked out from behind the desk. The conversation was obviously over; Alex took her cue and stood up as well. He escorted her slowly across the room. Just before he reached the door, he paused for a moment and said, "I spoke to Victor about an hour ago. We're not ready to make any of this public, so I'd appreciate it if you would keep our little conversation confidential."

"Does Victor know that you and I talked?" she asked.

"Certainly not, which brings me to my next point. I would also ask you to refrain from speaking to Victor about this matter until the university trustees have made their final decision. I know you still have issues with him but it might be better for the hospital and everyone involved if you kept a low profile."

"I understand completely," she said.

"I assume I'll see you later at the M and M conference," he said, opening the door.

"I'll be there."

Alex felt badly for Owen. She knew how difficult this entire matter with Victor Runyon was for him. She was pleased he had no intention of sweeping it under the carpet to avoid dealing with a very dicey and potentially embarrassing problem.

# Chapter 66

A young couple wearing sunglasses rollerbladed past Alex as she sat on the edge of the huge marble fountain that sat directly in the center of Dupont Circle. Mesmerized by its pure and simple beauty and the fact that it never attracted many tourists, she loved the fountain.

On this particular day, she had been there only about twenty minutes when her cell phone rang. Miffed by the intrusion, she reached into her purse and pulled out the phone.

"Hello."

"Alex. It's Theo. I'm calling to fill you in on Robert Key's autopsy. Remember he was sent to the medical examiner's office for the post?"

"I remember. What did the autopsy show?"

"Well, it seems that there was a bit of a screwup. Instead of sending Robert's body out there, our brilliant staff sent a John Doe who died in our ER. Robert was tagged as an indigent for the county to take care of."

"Are you saying they accidentally switched the bodies?" Alex asked.

"That's exactly what I'm saying."

"So what happened to Robert Key?"

"He was cremated and his ashes disposed of at the county's expense."

"Are you kidding me?" Alex asked.

"I wish I were. I spoke to the assistant medical examiner about it. He told me the police are not very happy about the whole thing."

"This is unbelievable," Alex said. "So we'll never find out Robert Key's true cause of death."

"Technically speaking, no, but what else could have killed him? It had to have been a pulmonary embolus."

"I agree," she said, "but I would have liked to see it confirmed by autopsy."

"Well, I'm afraid that's not going to happen. I gotta run. I'll speak to you later."

Alex had just replaced her phone in her purse and was thinking about what Theo had just told her when she glanced up to see Victor Runyon approaching. He was only a few yards away and any chance of slipping away unnoticed seemed improbable.

"Your secretary told me I could find you here."

Alex neither stood up nor answered him at first. At the moment he was not an imposing figure, and she felt no fear for her personal safety. She would have to say that his expression was more reminiscent of desperation than anger.

"What can I do for you, Victor?" she asked with a cold affect.

Without being invited, he sat down next to her, leaned forward with clasped hands, and rested his forearms on his thighs.

After a few seconds of uneasy silence he said, "I thought you should be the first to know. I've been officially suspended pending an investigation into my unprofessional conduct as it pertains to the Medivasc Corporation." He looked overhead for a moment, and then reached back, swept a handful of water toward the middle of the fountain and then added, "But somehow I think you already know that." When Alex only shrugged, Victor pulled his hand from the water and laughed nervously. "Did you know that this fountain was designed by the same artist who designed the Lincoln Memorial?"

Alex took a deep breath. "No, I didn't know that."

"It's true."

She made no effort to conceal her disdain. "I'll have to remember that the next time I'm here with my brother."

"Do you want to tell me what's going on here, Alex? What the hell have I done to make you hate me so much?"

Alex was having a hard time believing Victor's demeanor. He couldn't possibly believe that she was naive enough to be taken in by his feeble attempt to portray himself as the innocent victim.

Her answer was brief. "You'll have your day in court. I don't think we should be discussing any of this."

"Why the hell not? What's the difference? You already have me tried, convicted, and drummed out of medicine. Is it really asking too much for an explanation?"

"You really astound me," she said. "Where do you get your nerve? What did you think I was going to do? Just stand by and watch your organization kill my brother?"

Victor stood up. "What in God's name are you talking about?"

"Nothing. It just seems like it gets a little dangerous if anyone starts asking questions about the Caduceus Project."

"What does any of that have to do with your brother? We had an argument, Alex. Can't you put it behind you?"

Alex realized that she had already said too much and good judgment would dictate that she keep her mouth shut, but it was difficult to ignore the overwhelming urge to tell Victor what she thought of him, irrespective of her promise to Owen.

"How do you explain the problem with the Medivasc filters? You had four patients die with their device in place and never brought it to anyone's attention. How do you account for that minor oversight, especially when it turns out that Medivasc is one of your biggest contributors to the Caduceus Project?"

Victor didn't answer immediately. He covered his lips with his fingertips and just stared out across Dupont Circle. "I have no explanation," he finally offered in just above a whisper.

"The deaths occurred to your patients. The responsibility was yours. Anybody can make a mistake but I still don't understand how it escaped your attention that there might be something wrong with those filters."

"I'm human, Alex. I guess I just screwed up."

"That's a mild understatement," she said.

"I'm starting to believe that your anger toward me doesn't have as much to do with vena caval filters as you're trying to make me believe."

"You're wrong," she stated categorically.

"Are you telling me that all of this has nothing to do with

our political differences? I mean . . . you seem almost emotional about the project. Whether you believe in our philosophy or not, it's still a free country and you should be tolerant of our right to pursue the political goals we believe in."

"Don't wave that flag at me. I may not be a card-carrying member of the ACLU but I'm a fairly liberal person and I certainly have no problem with any individual's right to support any law-abiding organization they so choose."

Victor sat back down. "I guess coming here was a bad idea."

"No comment," she said.

Victor paused for a few moments before adding, "None of this makes sense to me, Alex. We disagreed about a couple of things and the next thing I know you're calling me a criminal and coming after me with a vengeance. I don't get it."

"Think about it. Maybe it will come to you," Alex said.

Without saying another word, Victor got up and headed toward Massachusetts Avenue. When he reached it, he turned around, and for several minutes just stood there, staring directly at Alex.

# Chapter 67

**MAY 20**

"Are you going to eat that cereal or just play with it?" Alex asked Jessie, who immediately looked up and scowled at the inquiry.

"I *am* eating it," she insisted. "Micah told me and Gabe that when he was in the navy—"

"Never mind what Micah told you," Alex said, wondering what crazy navy story Micah had told the kids this time. Before Jessie could continue her plea, the phone rang. Alex gestured to Olivia that she'd get it and reached for the phone.

"Hello."

"Is this the residence of Dr. Alexandra Caffey?" asked a man in a very polite voice.

"Who's calling, please?" she asked.

"My name is Ned Villamar. I'm a patient relations representative at Memorial Hospital in Hollywood, Florida." His somber tone and the location of the hospital left little doubt in Alex's mind what the nature of the call was. "Your mother was brought in by rescue to our emergency room about an hour ago. I'm afraid she's had a rather serious stroke. We're admitting her to our neuro-intensive care unit."

Consumed by fear and the dread of hearing any further horrible news, Alex looked over at Jessie's smiling face as she nibbled away at her English muffin.

"How serious is her condition?" Alex finally managed in just above a whisper.

"Dr. James Hope is our emergency room physician. I'm afraid he's listing her condition as critical."

"My God," Alex muttered before clearing her throat. "My mother was just here in D.C. She's only been back in Florida for a few days. There were no signs of . . . may I speak with Dr. Hope, please?"

"He's in the middle of an emergency procedure right now, but he suggests that you come down here as soon as possible. Dr. Lindsay Margate is the neurologist admitting her."

"May I speak with her?"

"She's on her way in and I have no way of reaching her right now but the moment I see her, I'll give her your number."

Alex's mind was suddenly consumed with lurid visions of her mother being left in an incapacitated state, a neurological cripple to languish away in some nursing home—a state of degradation her mother had expressly instructed Alex never to allow. After what she had just gone through with David, she doubted that she had the strength to endure another ordeal right now.

"I'll check the airline schedule and get there as soon as I can," Alex told Villamar. She slowly replaced the receiver and caught Olivia's eyes as she pulled her head out of the refrigerator.

"You're white as a ghost. What's wrong?" she asked, walking over to Alex.

"My mother's had a stroke. I have to go to Florida right away," she said, struggling not to cry.

"My God," Olivia whispered. "Is she . . . ?"

"She's alive but I'm not sure how bad she is."

Not wanting Jessie to hear or see her crying, Alex walked quickly out of the kitchen and into her study. It took her only a few minutes to call the airlines and book a ticket to Fort Lauderdale. She didn't feel in any condition to drive, so she called a cab and then ran upstairs to pack a few things and grab the extra set of keys she had to her mother's home before returning to the kitchen.

Drying her eyes with her fingertips, she knelt down next to Jessie. "Did I tell you that I was going to visit Grandma today?"

"Can I go too?" she begged, with an intensity in her face that made Alex smile.

"Not this time, honey. Grandma needs my help with something and we're going to be real busy."

"But I can help too," she pleaded.

"I know you can, but this is grown-up-type work."

Puffing up her cheeks in a major pout, she asked, "When are you coming back?"

"I'm not sure. In a day or two, I think, but I'll call you later," she promised, stroking Jessie's hair. "Hey, I know. Maybe Olivia will take you to the zoo."

Jessie's eyes widened as she quickly turned and looked over her shoulder at her nanny.

"Of course we can go," Olivia said, looking at Alex with encouraging eyes.

Grabbing her carry-on, Alex kissed Jessie twice on top of her head and then gave her a fierce hug. "I'll call you later," she told her and then turned for the door. Holding up crossed fingers, Olivia walked her out and then took her by the hands and gave them a gentle squeeze.

The traffic was lighter than Alex expected and she made the trip to National in thirty-five minutes, which left her ample time to catch her nine o'clock flight. As soon as she reached her gate, she called Owen's office and left him a message that she would be out of town for a couple of days because of a family emergency.

Waiting for her flight, Alex gazed out onto the tarmac and watched as a twin-engine commuter taxied out. More numb than anything else, she wondered why she had never really given serious thought to the way she'd feel when her mother eventually became ill. Without David for support, the prospect of dealing with the situation seemed daunting. Being a physician didn't seem to help stem her rising level of anxiety even in spite of her self-warnings to remain calm until she had all the facts regarding her mother's condition. When her flight was called, she picked up her carry-on, stood up, and fell into line.

About fifty feet away, dressed in a T-shirt and wearing sunglasses, Simon Lott stood at a public phone with the receiver pressed to his ear watching every move Alex made. When he saw her disappear down the jetway, he hung up the phone and started back down the concourse. Passing the ticket counter, he exited the terminal and went directly to the cab stand. A young man, absent a smile, waved the next cab forward and opened the door for him.

For Lott, the ride back to his apartment was lost in thought as he carefully considered the final steps of his plan to permanently deal with Alex Caffey.

# Chapter 68

Alex's flight pulled up to the gate right on schedule at the Hollywood–Fort Lauderdale Airport.

As her cab cruised south on I-95, her thoughts were momentarily diverted from her mother's condition when she gazed across the interstate at a huge wooden roller coaster. The towering structure immediately reminded her of her childhood and the many times a loving and vital*Jeanette Airoway had shared in the excitement by riding along with her and David.

Ten minutes later, the driver pulled up to the emergency room entrance of Memorial Hospital. Alex went straight to the registration desk, where a pregnant woman in a wheelchair, clutching her husband's hand, was being attended to. An elderly man dressed in a short red coat, who was serving as a volunteer, appeared and quickly whisked the two of them away.

Alex stepped forward and the woman behind the desk greeted her with a pleasant smile. "May I help you?" she asked, lifting her oversized glasses that hung around her neck and then placing them squarely on the bridge of her nose.

"My name is Alexandra Caffey. My mother, Jeanette Airoway, was admitted this morning to the neuro-intensive care unit."

"I'm so sorry. Let me just check for you," said the woman, whose name tag read *Lydia Torres*. Alex noticed that she was looking at her carry-on. "Did you just get in from out of town?"

"My plane landed about half an hour ago."

Lydia turned toward her computer screen, tapped away for a few seconds, and then, with a slightly confused expression, asked, "I'm sorry, what was that name again?"

"Airoway, Jeanette Airoway," Alex said plainly and then spelled the name.

Lydia nodded and again returned to her keyboard. Her eyes shifted back and forth across the computer screen until finally she looked up and asked, "Could it possibly be under another name?"

"I don't think so."

"That's strange. I don't show her in our data bank at all. You mentioned that you just flew in this morning. Does that mean you don't live in this area?"

"I live in Washington, D.C."

"Are you sure you have the right hospital? We have two others in our system."

"My mother's lived in Hollywood for several years. I'm a physician myself and am quite familiar with your hospital. I was called earlier this morning by Mr. Villamar, one of your patient care representatives, who told me that my mother was being admitted here."

Lydia removed her glasses and let them fall against her chest. "Dr. Caffey, I've been a supervisor in this area for fifteen years. I'm sorry, but we don't have anybody by the name of Villamar working in patient relations."

Instinctively Alex asked, "May I use your phone, please?"

"By all means," Lydia said, turning it in Alex's direction and then sliding it closer to her. "Just dial eight for an outside line."

"Thank you," she answered, reaching for the phone and then dialing her mother's number. Over the last ten years, Alex had seen almost every conceivable foul-up and blunder a hospital could commit, but she never imagined that she or anyone in her family would be the victim of such an unfortunate mistake. Perhaps she should have had the sense to call her mother before leaving Washington, but the thought never crossed her mind. The most obvious explanation was that Lydia Torres was correct and that her mother was at a different hospital.

"Hello," came a familiar voice, causing Alex to spin around and close her eyes. Whatever confusion she might have felt at that moment paled in comparison with the pure joy of knowing that her mother was okay.

"Mom? Is that you?"

"Of course it's me, dear," she answered. "I'm the only one who lives here, or have you forgotten that? You sound terrible. What's wrong? Oh, my God, did something happen to David?"

"No, Mom. David's fine. Actually, I'm here in Hollywood. I'm over at the hospital."

"Why didn't you tell me you were coming down? What are you doing here?"

Just as she was about to explain to her mother what had happened, she thought better of the idea and decided to take a simpler way out. "I just found out that Memorial was hosting an interesting trauma conference. I decided to come at the last minute, go to the meeting, and then surprise you. I was going to call you later this afternoon but the meeting's kind of boring, so how about the two of us girls going out to lunch like we used to?"

"I would enjoy that."

"I'll grab a cab to your house and then we can go."

"When are you going back?" her mother asked.

Alex was stumped for the moment, seeing as how she had booked the return for later in the week. "I'm going back late this afternoon."

"My little girl's become quite the jet-setter."

"I'll see you in twenty minutes, Mom," Alex said, feeling more relief than she had in a very long time.

Alex hung up the phone and then glanced down at Lydia. From her expression, it was obvious that she had heard the entire conversation.

"Is everything okay?" she asked.

"I guess it was just a mistake," Alex offered. "Thank you for your help."

It wasn't until Alex was outside that she started to reflect on the strange events of the day. It was inconceivable that the phone call she had received only hours earlier was some bizarre hospital debacle, which left only one possibility. The question was, what kind of a sick, twisted individual would do something like this and why? Was it possible that Victor was so upset regarding their recent argument at Dupont Circle that he could have done such an atrocious thing merely in the name of spite?

Alex spotted a cab across the street, hailed it, and then started across. With each step she became more and more convinced that Victor was somehow involved in this warped act. Perhaps he was sending her some kind of warning. If that was the case, he had wasted the phone call.

Alex climbed into the backseat. More angry than intimidated, she removed her cell phone from her purse and called the airlines. She considered calling her mother and telling her that she had decided to return to Washington immediately, but didn't want to disappoint her. As soon as she had made a reservation to fly home, she called Olivia and told her about the mix-up and that she'd be on the five P.M. flight home.

# Chapter 69

From his Hummer, Simon Lott watched as Olivia pulled into the driveway.

As soon as he confirmed that Alex's plane had departed National, he returned to Georgetown and took up a position just down the street from her house. When Jessie and Olivia left for the zoo, he followed them. He glanced down at his watch. It was twelve forty-five. He knew they hadn't eaten lunch yet.

Olivia opened the back door for Jessie, who jumped out and immediately streaked across the yard. It took Olivia only a few seconds to gather up her things and join Jessie at the front door. After a quick look around, Lott pushed open the door and started across the street. It was a pleasant enough day with a clement wind. Walking up the short red brick path, he paused for a moment to check the sidewalk before ringing the bell. As he had hoped, it was Olivia who answered the door.

"What are you doing here?" she asked with a bashful smile, looking behind her to see if Jessie's usual inquisitiveness had brought her flying to the door.

"I thought I'd take you to lunch. Have you eaten yet?"

"No," she said with a giggle that he found even more irritating than usual. "I'm working. You just can't show up here and take me to lunch. I have a little girl to take care of."

"What's the problem? I assume your boss is at the hospital. I don't mind if you want to bring the child along."

"That's a very kind offer, but actually my boss is out of town and I don't know if she'd approve."

Lott put on his best befuddled look, reached forward, and gently stroked her wrist. "I thought you told me that she trusted you implicitly."

"Naturally she does, but that's not—"

"Well, does she or doesn't she?" he asked calmly.

"Of course . . . it's just that—"

"It's broad daylight and I'm not exactly an ax murderer. C'mon, I'll have the two of you back in an hour."

Olivia looked over her shoulder toward the basement door. "I guess it'll be okay, but let me ask Jessie. She's down in her playroom. I don't want her telling her mother that I made her go."

"I understand. Would you like me to wait here?"

"Don't be silly," she answered, pulling him forward by his sleeve.

"Is there anybody else home?" he asked, running his hand under the back of her blouse, causing her to cackle in a staccato fashion.

"It's just the two of us," she replied, stepping back and slapping him playfully on the chest.

Lott could see that the door to the basement was slightly ajar. Moving forward, he embraced Olivia and began kissing her.

"Stop it," she warned in a whisper. "I could lose my job."

"Why should I stop? You just said that your boss is out of town and the child is downstairs," he said, moving his lips down her neck. Olivia's head fell back a little to ease his way. "Maybe we can have dinner too?" he suggested.

"I don't think so."

"Why not?" he asked.

"Because she's coming back tonight."

"What time?"

"Her flight gets in around seven-thirty."

"What's the problem then? I'm sure I could have you back here with plenty of time to spare before she gets home."

"I don't think so," she protested, wiggling free and then using her outstretched arms to keep him at a safe distance. "You better cut it out," she warned again. "Jessie might come upstairs."

With a painfully disappointed look, he moved forward and placed his hand on her chin and began gently stroking her lips with his fingertips. As he thought she might, Olivia closed her eyes. He took another quick peek down the hall.

From stillness, Lott's right hand suddenly thrust forward to grab Olivia's hair with incredible force. Using his opposite hand to cover her mouth and use it as a pivot, he spun her around like a top until her back was pressing into his chest. The lethal stranglehold was completed as he jammed his forearm under her chin with more than sufficient force to crush her windpipe. Ignoring her frenzied contortions, he thrust her head downward and toward her left shoulder. He knew the precision and execution had been perfect by the characteristic crack of Olivia's neck bones as they snapped like a pencil. Without ever uttering an audible sound, Olivia was dead within seconds.

Lott allowed her lifeless body to slide easily to the wood floor. He glanced at the basement door and then into the kitchen. He assumed that if Jessie decided to come upstairs, he would hear her footsteps. Grabbing Olivia by her ankles, he walked backward, dragging her along the floor until he reached the kitchen.

The door to a large pantry next to the laundry room was open. After taking a moment to catch his breath, he yanked her across the kitchen and into the storage closet. Before leaving, he rolled her body to the back of the pantry, shoved her under the lowest shelf, and left her wedged there.

Lott stepped back into the kitchen and stared at her body. Fancying himself quite the expert in the art of chokes, he was quite pleased with how easily he had taken Olivia down. He closed the pantry door. Knowing how responsible she was, he took only a minute to find the list of emergency phone numbers that were posted on the refrigerator door under a magnet. Alex's cell phone was clearly marked.

Sliding the piece of paper out, he folded it once and slid it into his pocket, and then, with a macabre intensity in his eyes, he slowly approached the basement door.

# Chapter 70

When Lott reached the bottom of the steps, Jessie's eyes were already on him. The playroom was brightly lit and quite spacious with red and blue polka-dot wallpaper. A widescreen TV in a floor-to-ceiling wall unit sat angled into the corner.

He yelled up the stairs, "I found her, Olivia. She's down here in her playroom."

Jessie's face betrayed a state of confusion, not fear. Lott smiled and walked slowly across the room. When he was just a few feet in front of her, he stopped and knelt.

But before he could say anything, Jessie's eyes became wide and she said gleefully, "Did you bring your dog?"

"You mean Gretel?"

"Uh-huh," she said, nodding her head like a bobble toy.

"You have a terrific memory."

Jessie renewed her question. "Did you bring her? Did you bring Gretel?"

"Of course I did," he assured her, relieved that the child hadn't displayed one iota of apprehension toward him.

"Do you know my mommy?"

"Of course I do. We're great friends. Olivia too. In fact, your mom just got back into town and wants to meet all of us at the park for a picnic lunch."

"Okay," she said, jumping to her feet. "Can we bring Gretel?"

"What would you say if I told you that she's in my car right now waiting to see you?"

"Let's go!" she thundered. The smile that covered her face was as broad and ebullient as Lott had ever seen. He was amused by it, but hardly touched or remorseful to the point of being dissuaded from his purpose. Hand in hand, the two of them walked up the stairs. "Where's Olivia?"

"She went to get your mom. She's going to meet us there."

Lott, proceeding with complete impunity, walked side by side with Jessie out the front door. "That's the car right over there. The black one. Can you see Gretel in the backseat?"

"How come Olivia's car is here?" Jessie asked, shading her eyes from the sun with one hand and pointing with the other.

"Oh, it's broken. She had to take a cab," Lott explained. "We'll see her as soon as we get to the park." As promised, when Jessie jumped into the backseat of the Hummer her face was covered with a barrage of very excited kisses from Gretel. Jessie immediately grabbed her around the neck, hugging her and petting her soft fur.

"I wish my mom would get me a dog like Gretel," she lamented.

"She sure looks happy to see you," Lott said as he started the engine and slowly pulled away from the curb. "Do you like soda?"

"Yeah, but I'm not allowed to have any until dinner."

Simon reached into a small cooler he had on the passenger-side floorboard and handed Jessie a can of soda. "Your mom said it would be okay. Try this," he said, passing it back to her.

"When will I see my mom?" she asked, still completely consumed with Gretel.

"In your dreams," he whispered, sneaking a peek in the rearview mirror as Jessie took a long swallow.

Ten minutes later, with Gretel lying next to her, Jessie had fallen into a heavy drug-induced sleep.

# Chapter 71

Lott pulled into the parking lot of his apartment building and quickly pulled into his assigned space.

He turned off the engine and then looked over his shoulder at Jessie, who was now under the maximal effect of the chloral hydrate that he had given her. Before climbing out, he opened the glove compartment and took out a child's silver party hat.

Exiting the Hummer quickly, he moved to the back door and opened it. Wagging her tail madly, Gretel jumped to the front seat.

"Hang on, girl. I'll be back for you in a few minutes and then it's back to your mom's house," he told her as he leaned over and gave her a couple of pats on the head. Leaning in, he propped Jessie up a little, placed the hat on her head, and then snugged the elastic band under her chin. He then easily scooped her up in a fireman's carry, slid her out of the backseat, and started across the parking lot toward the back entrance of the building.

Lott nodded at an impatient soccer mom as she herded her two kids into a white minivan, belted them in, and then slammed the door. She saw Lott coming and said, "That must have been some party." Her sympathetic smile was obviously from someone who had played out the same scene herself.

"A world-class affair," Lott announced without breaking stride. "Thank God it's over."

Arriving at the back entrance, he tapped in his code on the touchpad and pushed the door open with his hip. When he was just a few feet from the elevator, the doors rumbled open and a squatty man wearing a dark-green maintenance uniform stepped off.

Lott grinned and then shrugged his shoulders.

"I have two of my own," the man whispered.

"My other daughter's with her mom. I'm just getting used to the single-parent life," Lott said.

"I haven't seen you around. Did you just move in?"

"Uh-huh. One day the ex threw everything I owned in about a dozen boxes and showed me the door."

The man laughed but then sighed. "You're lucky. Mine just tossed all of my stuff on the front lawn."

"Ouch," Lott said with a quick laugh. He then turned sideways, walked past the man, and stepped onto the elevator. "I'll see you," he said.

Fortunately, the elevator went directly to his floor. By design, Lott had always avoided his neighbors. If he did encounter any of them in the hall or lobby, he merely smiled politely and continued on his way. He quickly made his way down the short corridor to his apartment. Without putting Jessie down, he managed to unlock the door and step inside.

After using his foot to slam the door closed, he went straight to the guest bedroom and dropped Jessie on the bed. The room was sparsely decorated and consisted of nothing more than a queen-size bed, a small night table, and a chest of drawers. The walls were painted a dull shade of gray and a simple ceiling-mounted fixture was the only source of light.

Reaching into the top drawer of the night table, Lott removed a roll of duct tape. He studied the little girl, regarding her as nothing more than an extension of the woman he held in such contempt. Jessie was completely limp when he rolled her onto her side. Pulling her hands behind her, he bound her wrists with the tape. When he finished, he secured her ankles.

He considered not gagging her, but a moment later thought better of the momentary weakness and taped her mouth as well. It was just as he was putting the second piece of tape across her mouth when she whimpered and tried to open her eyes, but her efforts were futile and her eyes rolled back in her head. Lott assumed now that he had finished fussing with her, she'd fall back into a deep sleep for several more hours.

With the last piece of tape in place, Lott moved away from the bed, turned out the light, and closed the door behind him. He checked his watch. There were still some things he needed to do before his showdown with Dr. Caffey. He was well aware that Jessie was the key to drawing her mother out, but once his business with the good doctor was completed, the child would become a heavy liability.

He certainly knew people in Europe who knew people who would pay handsomely for her. He was in no way personally averse to such a prospect, but he was well aware that getting involved in enterprises that involved the salacious use of children entailed a certain amount of risk. To chance something like that might not be worth it and in view of the fact that she could identify him, it might be simpler and cleaner just to get rid of her.

Lott checked Jessie one more time before leaving his apartment to get Gretel. As he waited for the elevator, he considered how the remainder of the day might play out. He looked forward to watching Dr. Caffey's face and listening to her pleas as her world came crashing down around her. Perhaps she might even try to persuade him to spare her daughter in some rather imaginative and unconventional ways. The thought of such an erotic experience between them caused him to snicker.

As he waited, one fantasy led to the next, but the final one he conjured up was clear and would become a reality. The last thing he wanted to see just before killing her was Alexandra Caffey on her knees, begging for her daughter's life.

# Chapter 72

Two hours after her abduction, Jessie Caffey began to emerge from the hypnotic effects of the chloral hydrate and Ativan.

She had no idea where she was, reminding her of the time she had gone to the hospital to have her tonsils out. She tried to rub her eyes but her hands were stuck behind her and wouldn't move. She didn't know why but it hurt her wrists every time she tried to pull her hands out.

Lott reached down, grabbed the corner of the tape, and stripped it from her mouth, causing her to cry out in pain. She tried to open her eyes but the bright light burned. After a bit of a struggle, kind of like when she and her mom came out of a movie, she was able to see the large man who owned Gretel standing over her.

"Where's my mom?"

His laugh was loud and scared her. "She's sleeping."

"I want to see my mom."

"You'll see your mom when I say so, you little shit."

Before she could make another plea, she felt something dry and soft being pushed into her mouth. For a few seconds it pinched her lips because they were pressed against her teeth. The harder she pulled her hands to free them, the more her wrists hurt. She couldn't understand what sort of stupid game he was playing but she hoped that in a few seconds, when she could see better, her mom would be standing there and Gretel would be wagging her tail and kissing her face.

But the only thing Jessie felt was a mosquito bite on her thigh. But this one hurt a lot more than the others she could remember from when her mom took her camping. She wanted to ask her mom for some of that medicine she always put on the bites to make the stinging go away but she couldn't move her lips to speak. Suddenly, the whole room started to twirl and light up like Space Mountain. Her eyes were so heavy that she couldn't even begin to keep them open. She stuck her legs straight out, hoping that Gretel might be curled up at her feet, but she felt nothing.

Then everything went dark. She could hear hard footsteps clip-clopping on the wooden floor for a few seconds, a slam of a door, and then there was nothing.

# Chapter 73

With the information that Olivia had provided, it wasn't difficult for Lott to figure out what flight Alex would be on.

Pushing past a busload of German-speaking tourists who were busy gathering their luggage, Lott entered the terminal and went directly to the area where the arriving passengers exited the concourse. Selecting an inconspicuous spot against the wall, he had an excellent view of the exit.

Confident that the large dose of drugs he'd given Jessie would keep her in a deep sleep for several more hours, Lott never gave the little girl another thought. If everything unfolded the way he had planned, his business with Alex Caffey would be finished in a few hours and he would be safely out of the country by this time tomorrow. His new passport and other documents had been exquisitely prepared by a masterful but very discreet forger with whom he had done business several times in the past. He had paid handsomely for the documents, but they were worth every penny.

As a rule, Lott would never conduct business in such a cavalier manner, but he had already decided that he would never again set foot on U.S. soil. He looked overhead. According to the monitor, he still had a few minutes before Alex's flight was parked at the ramp. The thrill of the game hadn't peaked yet, but it was quickly gaining in intensity. A few minutes passed and when he looked up at the monitor again, it indicated that Alex's flight had landed.

The more minutes passed. He was momentarily distracted from watching the steady stream of passengers flowing through the exit by a frustrated young mother who was herding her three toddlers toward the baggage claim area. Had he not looked back at that exact moment, he might have missed

Alex among the hordes. She was walking along at a fairly quick pace.

He immediately left where he was standing and fell in about twenty feet behind her. When he was sure he wasn't going to lose her, he pulled out his phone. He dialed her number and watched carefully. On the third ring, he saw her look down at her purse. Without breaking stride, she reached down and pulled out her phone.

"Hello."

"Dr. Caffey, I'm afraid I have some bad news for you," he said.

"Who is this?" she inquired, without yet looking around.

"I've never placed much importance on names. Why don't you just think of me as your daughter Jessie's new babysitter?"

"I beg your pardon?" Alex said, stopping dead in her tracks and looking around with a desperate look on her face. It was easy for Lott to blend in with the people around him, many of whom were also talking on their phones.

"Look, I've had a bad day, so if this is some kind of a sick joke, I'll—"

"Dr. Caffey, I am a serious man. I have better things to do with my time than play ridiculous practical jokes on people. I sent you to Florida today for a very specific reason, so let me assure you this is no hoax. I have your daughter. If you'd like her back, then I suggest you do exactly as I say."

Alex leaned back against the wall and used her position to carefully look around. Consumed with panic, she had every reason to believe that the man she was talking to was telling her the truth. As he walked by her, not more than fifteen feet away, Lott hit the mute button, smiled broadly, and then laughed as he babbled away into the dead phone. He never looked back.

Shivering in fear and overtaken by desperation, she finally asked, "What do you want? I have money. I can get you all the money you want."

Lott laughed and then hit the mute button again so she could hear him. "Money? Do you think this is about money? You're as shallow as you are stupid."

"Then what do you want?" she snapped.

"I want you to meet me so we can talk."

Alex tried to speak but her breath caught. She stopped, filled her lungs with a deep breath, and then asked, "How do I know you really have my daughter?"

"That's a fair question. Why don't you try calling her babysitter? I assure you that you'll get no answer. If that's not enough to satisfy you, Jessie's wearing jean overalls with a cute little bear logo and red sneakers. Her playroom in the basement has two large bookcases and a—"

"Is she alive?" Alex asked, barely able to think. "Please tell me the truth."

"She's very much alive."

"Have you touched . . . I mean, have you—?"

"Come now, Dr. Caffey. I'm a professional, not a pedophile."

She spoke in a monotone. "Just tell me what to do."

"As I told you, I just want to talk to you."

"When?"

"Now you're being sensible," Lott said in a patronizing tone. "I'm sure you're familiar with the Georgetown Library on R Street."

"Yes, I know it."

"Good. I'll meet you out front in an hour."

"One hour," she repeated.

"That's what I said. And by the way, Dr. Caffey, I'm not working alone. If you contact the authorities or I even get the hint that you're not alone, you'll never see me or your daughter again. We'll be watching you. We dealt with your brother and we're quite prepared to do the same with you and your daughter."

"What about Olivia?"

"Who?" he asked, seeing no reason to alert Alex to the fact that he knew her.

"My au pair."

"She's been detained. If after we've had our little talk, I'm satisfied that we've come to an understanding, you'll find her in the kitchen tomorrow."

"Even if I do cooperate, how do I know you won't just kill us all anyway?"

"Because if that were the case, you'd already be dead. As

I said, we just want to talk to you about coming to a reasonable understanding. We're even prepared to make it worth your while."

"I just want my daughter back," Alex said, feeling her first glimmer of optimism that she might get Jessie back.

"That's entirely up to you," Lott said.

"None of this has anything to do with her. Why did you have to take her?"

"C'mon, Dr. Caffey. We're merely strengthening our negotiating position. I doubt seriously that you'd be agreeing to meet with me tonight without some added incentive."

Having no wiggle room and seeing no other alternative, she again agreed to his demand. "I'll be there in one hour."

"Remember, Dr. Caffey. Come alone and don't tell a soul about this call, especially Micah Henry. You're a smart woman. Keep your wits about you. Your daughter's life depends on it."

Desperate and looking for any shred of information that might help her, she said, "You can tell Victor Runyon for me that I give up. He wins."

Alex waited for his response but after a few seconds it was obvious the line was dead. She remained frozen against the wall for a time before gathering herself enough to call Olivia. Her hands trembling, she fumbled the phone as she first dialed her home number and then Olivia's cell phone number. Neither answered. Alex left voice messages on each but was pessimistic about the chance of receiving a call back.

As she made her way toward the exit, every man around her with a cell phone pushed against his ear looked suspicious. She struggled to stay focused, carefully considering her options. The only thing she was sure of was that she was not going to call the police. When she reached the baggage claim area, she decided to stop for a moment to look around. If she was being watched, the pure chaos of the area was more than enough to hide it from her untrained eye.

Alex took one final look around. Seeing nothing, she ran for the terminal exit. In quiet desperation she suddenly felt quite stupid for allowing herself to be duped into going to Florida on a wild-goose chase. Crossing the street to get to the parking garage, Alex Caffey found herself praying for divine intervention and prepared to make any sacrifice to ensure the safe return of Jessie.

# Chapter 74

The ride home seemed like an eternity. In spite of the caller's explicit warning, Alex was tempted to call Micah, but each time she considered the idea, she thought better of it.

Alex pulled into her driveway and headed for the front door. She and Jessie had spent many hours in the Georgetown Library on R Street and she knew it was no more than a five-minute ride from her house. Although she suspected it was hopeless, a small part of her prayed that when she went inside, she'd find Olivia sitting with Jessie in the study playing Candy Land.

Alex opened the door and stepped across the threshold but stood in the foyer. Except for one dim light in the kitchen, the downstairs was dark. Alex knew that if Olivia and Jessie were home the house would be lit up like a Christmas tree. While her pulse sprinted, the muscles in the back of her neck began to spasm. The annoying cramps quickly intensified, rolled upward, and soon became a dull headache. Out of the near darkness, she yelled, "I'm home. Olivia? Jess? I'm home."

When there was no answer, she headed cautiously for the kitchen. She hadn't noticed when she first came in, but the door to the basement was just slightly cracked, allowing a spear of light to break into the hallway. Alex opened the door, stared down the steps for several seconds, and then started down the spiral steps in silence, taking one step at a time. Stopping when she reached the landing, she looked down into Jessie's play area. The TV was on and there were a number of books in the middle of the floor.

Alex covered her mouth and closed her eyes as the stark

truth now seemed incontrovertible. Olivia and Jessie both knew how she felt about leaving the TV on when nobody was watching it. It was a rule of her father's that had always stuck with her. Alex also knew that Olivia would never leave the basement in such disarray. She didn't bother going downstairs. She had seen enough.

Frightened but unwilling to cave in to the fear, she spent the next few minutes walking around the house. She knew there would be nobody in the house but she still decided to do a cursory check of each room. As she suspected, one empty room led to the next, draining her of what little hope she still clung to. Finally, she went into her study and fell into a high-backed chair.

The impulse to call the police again flashed into her mind, but as she had already done five times in the last forty-five minutes, she rejected the idea. She gazed over at an antique clock that sat on her bookcase. She still had twenty minutes before she was to meet with the man who had abducted Jessie. If there was ever a doubt in her mind whether she would have the courage to kill someone, it no longer existed. Alex didn't move for the next ten minutes. When she again checked the clock, it was time to leave. As she regained her composure, her resolve mounted and by the time she reached the front door, she was determined to do whatever it took to get Jessie back.

Deep in thought and already halfway to her car, she barely noticed the familiar face coming up the walkway.

"Your secretary said you were out of town. You must have just gotten back," Maura Kenton said.

Alex stopped, waited for her, and then forced a smile. Knowing she only had a few minutes to get rid of her, Alex cautioned herself to do it without arousing the suspicion of this very savvy woman.

"My mother was ill. I went to Florida."

"I'm sorry to hear that. How is she?"

"Actually, it turned out to be a false alarm. She's fine," Alex explained.

"I'm glad to hear that. My mom's always crying wolf about her health, so it's tough to know when it's the real thing." Maura looked toward the house and then back at Alex. "When did you leave?"

"I left this morning. When I found out she was okay, I took an early flight back. It was a good thing because I have a lot of sick patients in the hospital. As a matter of fact, I'm on my way there now."

"I'm sure glad I'm not a doctor," Maura said.

"Is there something I can—"

"It wasn't anything in particular. I was just on my way home and thought maybe you had gotten back. I haven't spoken to you in a while and just wanted to see how you were doing. Hey, I heard your brother's doing great."

"He's improving slowly."

Maura's eyes never left Alex's. "Is there anything you'd like to talk about?"

Still smiling, Alex shook her head and said, "Nope."

"You seem to have lost some of your enthusiasm since the last time we spoke."

"Time has passed and David looks like he's going to make a full recovery so I guess I'm getting more practical about things—and calming down."

Alex could see the doubt in Maura's face. "I see," she finally said.

Alex looked down at her watch. "I don't mean to appear rude but I really have to get—"

"Sure, I understand."

"Thanks for stopping over," Alex said as she headed back toward the driveway.

"Dr. Caffey?"

"Yes."

"If you were in trouble, you'd tell me—right? Because if you were . . . in trouble, I mean. I'd want to help you."

"Of course," she said without breaking stride.

Maura never moved. There was no question there was a difference in Dr. Caffey's manner. She was clearly more laid back but it just didn't seem genuine to her. Watching as the car disappeared down the street, Maura could only hope that Alex Caffey was being honest with her and that she hadn't somehow gotten herself into trouble.

# Chapter 75

As soon as Alex turned onto R Street, she spotted the Georgetown Public Library.

She eased off the accelerator, driving past the building slowly. There was nobody out front. She continued down the street until she spotted a parking place. She pulled in and turned off the engine but before getting out, she took a good look around. There was nobody in sight and the traffic was limited to an occasional car. Finally, she stepped out of the car, crossed the street, and walked the short distance to the front of the library.

The first person she saw was a man approaching from across the street. At first she thought he was going to walk by, but then, without breaking stride, he took her gently by the arm and said, "Let's walk." Alex couldn't move. His grip tightened. He smiled and shook his head. "You're hardly in a position to be uncooperative." With that, Lott gave her a firm nudge and they started down the sidewalk.

After just a few paces, he stopped and pointed across the street. They waited for one car to pass and then crossed. Alex expected to keep walking but Lott stopped in front of a house that was set well back from the street and almost entirely concealed by dense foliage. The entrance to the driveway was flanked by two stone pillars with colonial-style lanterns mounted atop them. One of the pillars had a FOR SALE sign posted on it.

"Let's go," he said.

"Where's my daughter?" Alex insisted.

"They'll be plenty of time for questions later. Now move."

"You're Irish," she said.

"Really? How did I give myself away?"

Understanding the risks, but seeing no alternative, Alex escorted Lott down the driveway. A crescent moon cast a shallow light on an eight-foot stone wall that separated the driveway from the property next door. They walked about fifty yards before encountering paired wooden gates that stood across the driveway. As if he'd been there before, Lott gave one of the gates a sufficient push to make it swing open smoothly.

The driveway, which initially had been inclined upward, now turned downward, allowing Alex to see a brick two-car garage. "Let's go," Lott said, moving a few steps forward before closing the gate. To her left, Alex could now clearly see the large Federalist-style house.

Staring down the driveway, Alex noticed there were no cars parked in front of the garage. The light, which mostly came from the floods of the house next door, was enough to allow her to see fairly well. Just at that moment, a rogue wisp of cool wind blew through the overhanging trees. When they were about ten feet from the garage, Lott brought them to a stop.

"Where the hell's my daughter?" Alex demanded. Lott moved forward, cutting the distance between them in half. Alex stood her ground. "I'm not making any deals until I see her."

Lott chuckled for a few seconds before his expression and demeanor became deadly ardent.

"Are you really that arrogant to think that you're in a position to dictate anything to me?"

Alex's voice was clear. "Give me my daughter back and I'll leave Washington. You'll never see or hear from me again."

Lott reached inside his sports coat and casually removed a handgun. "That's a very generous offer, but I'm afraid you're a little late."

"I don't understand. I assumed that's what you wanted," she said.

"You assumed wrong," he said in a nonchalant voice.

From the sadistic look in the man's eyes, Alex knew she was in trouble. Amid the confusion and uncertainties of the moment, one thing suddenly became patently clear—the man standing in front of her had no interest in negotiating for Jessie's release.

"You son of a bitch," Alex said.

Lott said nothing. Instead he lifted his chin and pointed to the jagged laceration. "Does this remind you of anything?" he demanded. At first she didn't make the connection, but then the clear image of slamming her attacker in the face with the fire extinguisher crystallized in her mind.

"I don't know what you're talking about," she stated, realizing almost before the words were out of her mouth that it was an unconvincing effort.

"Really?" he said, studying her eyes with a slight tilt to his head. "I'm afraid I don't believe you. In fact, I think you know exactly who I am. You disfigured me, made a bloody fool of me, and seriously complicated my life." Lott paused for a moment to rub his chin. "You got away from me once. That's not going to happen again."

Alex felt each breath as it filled her lungs. Consumed by desperation regarding Jessie and resigned to the fact that she was within minutes of being killed, the only thing that now mattered was to find out what his intentions were concerning Jessie.

Trying to buy as much time as possible, she said, "You got me here. That's obviously what you wanted. Why harm my daughter? She's not involved in any of this."

Lott gestured at her with his gun as he spoke. "What would you have me do now that our business is almost over? Adopt the child? You cost me a lot of money, Dr. Caffey. As far as your daughter's concerned, it may interest you to know that not everybody on this planet lives in your pristine world."

"Just what the hell's that supposed to mean?"

"It means that your daughter has a certain monetary value."

Alex instinctively jumped forward, prompting Lott to jam the working end of his semiautomatic flush against her neck. For the first time he was close enough for her to see the brutality in his face.

"What kind of a twisted psychopath are you?" she demanded. "She's only a child, for God's sake."

"Your daughter's age is a matter of complete indifference

to me," he said, stepping back. "She's nothing more to me than a commodity. You're going to die tonight, Dr. Caffey, wondering what unspeakable things await your precious daughter." He smirked briefly. Alex watched as his eyes tracked upward toward the house. His intention to get her inside couldn't have been more obvious. Lott leveled the gun at Alex's chest. "Why don't we continue our meeting inside?"

"I'm not moving," she said.

"So you really want to die out here and lose your one last chance to persuade me to spare your daughter? Think about it. It's your only chance—or should I say, her only chance. Persuade me to spare her and I'll put her on a plane to your mother tomorrow. For all you know, Jessie's in that house right now crying crocodile tears to see her mother."

His manner was persuasive but Alex knew he was lying. Jessie wasn't in that house and there was nothing she would be able to do to change his mind bout killing her. Knowing full well what he was capable of, she stood fast. There were only two truths she was aware of: she wasn't going into that house and she wasn't going to stand there and be shot without doing anything.

Unfortunately, Lott must have sensed her intent. He laughed. "You can't be serious," he said. "Surely you can't believe that you can disarm me and then use my own gun to kill me?" he asked. "You Americans watch too many John Wayne movies." He shrugged and then sighed theatrically. "Have it your own way," he said with a laugh as he directed the gun sight between her eyes. "Make your move, Doctor."

Before Alex could respond, she heard two distinct but muted thumps that appeared to come from down the driveway. The self-satisfied look on Lott's face gradually turned to one of disbelief. Hollow-eyed, he arched his back slightly and the gun dropped from his hand. Then, as if it had been choreographed and rehearsed a dozen times, he fell forward and came to rest on his knees. Kneeling in front of her in apparent confusion, he looked down at his shirt and then gently rubbed his hand across his chest. He looked up at her for a moment before his eyes rolled up, and then, as if someone had given him a shove, he toppled forward.

His forehead took the brunt of the fall, but then he rolled

onto his side two feet in front of her. Before it clicked in Alex's mind what had happened, she heard footsteps. Looking down the driveway, she saw the silhouette of a woman approaching. Her first thought was that Maura Kenton hadn't believed a word she had said and had thankfully followed her.

The woman, acting as if Alex weren't even there, never took her eye off Lott's fallen body as she moved forward. Holding her gun in her left hand, she kept it pointed directly at him until she was close enough to kick his gun away. Waiting a few more seconds, she then gave him a hard nudge with her heel, sending him onto his back.

From the side of his head, a steady stream of blood slowly drained onto the driveway. Alex didn't try to examine him but was sure he was dead. When she looked up, she realized that the woman standing in front of her was not Maura Kenton.

"Are you okay?" Kerry Nealon asked in her distinct Irish accent.

"I—I think so." Somewhere between shocked and relieved, Alex asked, "How did you know I was here? I didn't call the police."

Kerry grinned. "I have nothing against the police but I don't think it's the career for me."

"Who are you, then?"

"I guess you can call me an independent contractor."

Not knowing why, Alex asked, "Are you going to kill me?"

"Good heavens, no. I have no arrangement that involves you."

"Who is he?" Alex asked.

"His name's Simon Lott. He's a rather nefarious man, I'm afraid."

As her chin fell to her chest, Alex again closed her eyes. "You should have let him kill me."

Kerry replaced her handgun in a leather purse that hung from her shoulder.

"For heaven's sake. Why would you say that?"

"He kidnapped my daughter. With him dead, I have no chance of finding her."

"Do you know when he took her?"

"Earlier today," Alex said.

"Reach into his pocket," Kerry said. Alex heard her suggestion but didn't move. "Go ahead."

Alex approached the body but before taking Kerry up on her suggestion, she asked, "What am I looking for?"

"His keys," Kerry stated. "Don't bother looking for a wallet. There won't be one."

Alex kneeled down and reached into Lott's right front pocket. There was nothing.

"Try the other pocket," Kerry said.

Wondering whether Lott would suddenly lurch forward like the final scene from a Hollywood thriller, Alex reached gingerly across his body and then slid her hand into his opposite pocket. This time she felt his key ring and pulled it out. There were only three keys on it. Two looked like they were for his car and the third, she guessed, was for his house or apartment.

"What good do these do me?" she asked. "I don't know where he lives."

"But I do."

Alex clenched the keys tightly in her fist, fixing Kerry with her eyes. "Where?"

"In an apartment just off Connecticut Avenue," Kerry said, before giving Alex the exact address.

"He said he was working with someone and that if I contacted the police he'd kill my daughter."

"He may be telling the truth but my guess is that's he lying. Men like this one generally work alone. Kidnapping is probably not his expertise. Calling the authorities is definitely an option . . . or you might go over to his apartment yourself. You have the key. There's a chance that you'll find your daughter there alone. If you do, then you won't have to answer a bunch of very tough questions about what happened here tonight. If your daughter's not in his apartment, you can always call the police then."

"I don't know whether to thank you or—"

"Why don't you ask me?" Kerry inquired.

Alex backed away from Lott's body. "Ask you what?"

"I just shot a man. You must be asking yourself why I would leave a witness behind who might identify me." Alex stood there in silence, plain-faced. Kerry went on. "I saved your life and maybe even helped you get your daughter back. I have no personal quarrel with you and I assume you feel the same way about me. If you are questioned by the police about tonight, I'm going to hope that you'll tell them you never saw the person who fired the shots. When we leave here tonight, that's the last time we'll ever see each other." Kerry took one final look at Lott, again told Alex his exact address, and then extended her hand. "Good luck, Dr. Caffey."

Alex took it and noticed that she had a small blood clot under her thumbnail, probably from some trivial accident. After a quick smile, the woman withdrew her hand and then, as quickly as she had appeared, she vanished into the night.

Alex had no interest in remaining but she decided to wait a minute or so before starting down the driveway. When she reached the end, she stopped to watch the approach of a slow-moving vehicle with its bright lights on.

The white van passed without slowing and Alex took a quick look around before starting across the street. Just as she reached the other side, it occurred to her that she had never asked the woman how she knew her name.

# Chapter 76

Fumbling for her keys, Alex prayed that the woman who had just killed Simon Lott was right about where she might find Jessie.

Even though she was overtaken with confusion, Alex still had the presence of mind to realize that charging headlong over to Lott's apartment to rescue Jessie could easily end in disaster. Seeing no other alternative, she reached into her purse, pulled out her cell phone, and hit number three on her speed dial. Before she had left for Florida, Alex had called

Micah to tell him about her mother. When she discovered that she had not suffered a stroke, she called him again.

"Jessie's gone," she told Micah between rapid breaths.

"What do you mean gone? Where's Olivia?"

"I don't know," she sobbed, finally breaking down from the sheer terror of what was happening. "They took my baby," she screamed.

"Calm down, Alex. Tell me where you are."

"It's that bastard Runyon," she continued to rave. "He did this. He's trying to get even."

"Alex. Where are you? Just slow down and tell me where you are. I'll come get you."

"I think I may know where Jessie is," she said, clutching the steering wheel. "I'm going over there now to get her."

"Listen to me carefully. You're in no state of mind to do anything right now. Are you in your car?"

"Yes."

"How far are you from your house?" he asked.

"Just a few blocks," she said, no longer shouting and trying to make herself understood above her crying.

"I'm leaving for your house right now. I want you to meet me there. Do you understand me?"

"I can't, Micah. I have to—"

"I'll be there in ten minutes. Ten minutes isn't going to change anything. We'll go get Jessie together."

As dazed as she was desperate, Alex looked out the side window, trying to decide what to do. She was just about to answer Micah when her eyes were suddenly snapped back to the road by the blast of a horn. Seeing the oncoming lights of a speeding vehicle closing rapidly, Alex yanked the wheel to the right, which sent her swerving back across the median line and into her own lane. Alex opened her eyes only when she knew she had averted the crash. Numb from the near miss, she consciously loosened her grip on the wheel, slowed down her breathing, and fought to concentrate on the road.

"I'm leaving my house now, Alex. I'll see you in ten minutes."

"Okay," she finally said.

Turning down Reservoir Road, Alex realized that if she was to get Jessie back she'd have to regain her composure.

The only way she could see to do that was to force herself not to think about the worst possible scenario.

Arriving home exactly five minutes after she hung up with Micah, Alex sat in her car for a few minutes gazing through the windshield. When she finally got out, she decided to wait for him on the front steps. By the time he pulled into her driveway she had managed to calm down considerably. For the moment, panic was replaced by pure fatigue, both physical and mental.

"What happened?" Micah asked calmly, sitting down next to her. "Start from the beginning and take your time."

Glassy-eyed, she gazed straight ahead and spoke in a flat-toned voice. "When I was on my way out of the airport, I got a call from a man. He told me that he had Jessie and Olivia and that unless I met with him tonight I'd never see either of them again. He told me exactly what Jessie was wearing and what her playroom looked like. I tried calling Olivia but she didn't answer. When I got home the house was empty. Jessie's playroom was a mess and lit up like a Christmas tree. Olivia would never leave it like that."

"Did you call the police?" he asked.

"The man told me he was working with someone and that if I contacted the police, they would kill Jessie. He told me he just wanted to talk to me about staying out of their affairs. He promised that if I cooperated with them, they'd return Jessie to me."

"By their affairs, I assume he was referring to David and the Caduceus Project?"

"Yes."

"So you decided not to call the police and meet him," Micah said.

"Yes, but when I got there, he made it clear that he had no intention of returning Jessie and that his only interest was in getting even with me."

"Getting even with you for what?"

"He was the man who attacked me in the research building. I guess I hurt him pretty badly when I hit him with the fire extinguisher. He also mentioned that the people he worked for were concerned about my interest in the Caduceus Project."

Micah was speechless. He wanted to believe Alex, but he

found himself wondering whether she had come unglued
under the stress of David's ordeal and was imagining all of
this.

"I don't understand. If this man was so hell-bent on killing
you, why did he let you go?"

Alex turned and looked over the tops of her shrubbery to
the house next door. Without looking back at Micah, she said,
"I never said he let me go."

Ever cautious not to sound unbelieving, Micah said, "Then
how did you get away?"

"I didn't. Somebody shot him."

Micah rubbed the back of his neck, took a slow breath, and
asked, "It wasn't you . . . I mean, you weren't the one
who . . ."

"Shot him? Of course not."

Relieved but uncertain of how to proceed, Micah stood up
and took a few steps down the path to gather his thoughts. His
four years as a midshipman at the naval academy had honed
his ability to handle the most difficult of situations, but at the
moment he felt as if he had run smack into a brick wall. The
last thing he wanted to do was say the wrong thing and lead
Alex to believe that he doubted her.

After a few more moments, Micah walked back down the
path and again sat down. "You said on the phone that you
might know where Jessie is."

"The man who tried to kill me has an apartment just off
Connecticut Avenue. I think Jessie may be there."

"Did you ever see this man before he attacked you?" he
asked.

She shook her head. "Never."

"Why did he tell you where he lives?" Micah asked.

"He didn't."

"Then how do you know?"

Alex's uneasy expression and the way she hung her head
made it plain to Micah that she had no interest in answering
the question. Seeing no reason to press the point, he asked
gingerly, "Do you think going over to this man's apartment
without the police is really the best way to handle the situation?"

"If you had asked me that twenty minutes ago, I would have said yes but now, I'm not sure."

"Well, if just the two of us go over there and Jessie's not alone, we might not get her out at all."

"I . . . I don't know. You might be right, but if he was lying about working with someone and Jessie's alone in his apartment right now . . . well, I thought if we went over there together, maybe we could—"

Micah reached for Alex's hands and held them both between his. "Listen to me. We have to call the police. If we have any hope of getting Jessie back, we have to call the police. Do you understand what I'm telling you, Alex?"

Alex didn't answer at first. But after a few seconds she slowly removed her hands from Micah's. She then opened her purse and took out her cell phone.

Maura Kenton's card was sitting in plain sight. She picked it up, dialed the number, and after a very brief conversation, she flipped the phone closed.

"Maura Kenton's on her way over," she said.

# Chapter 77

Waiting for Maura to arrive, Alex found herself both physically and mentally drained.

As they sat together in silence, Micah put his arm around her. Alex barely noticed when a midsized sedan followed by a police cruiser pulled up in front of the house.

When she didn't react, Micah squeezed her shoulder gently and said, "The police are here."

As if he had snapped his fingers and awakened her from a hypnotic trance, Alex stood up. With two uniformed officers at her side, Maura Kenton walked quickly up the path.

Formal introductions were brief and at Maura's behest

Alex began to recount the events of the day. Put at ease by her patience and professionalism, Alex found herself more composed than she thought she'd be, and was able to give the police an accurate accounting of what had happened. When Maura had finished her interview, she motioned the two officers to join her on the driveway and then told Micah and Alex that she'd be right back.

Maura looked back at Alex for a moment before speaking. "Call central and have them send a unit to check out this house on R," she instructed Mike Flushing, the more senior of the two officers. "I want to be called as soon as they've had a look around. In the meantime, let's secure the doctor's house."

Mike's eyes drifted up. He looked unconvinced. "C'mon, Maura. This woman's a certifiable fruitcake. They're not going to find anything over there. It's a waste of time."

Maura had worked with Mike for years, respected him, and knew that in spite of his occasional cynicism, he was a damn good cop.

"You may be right. But it's not our time we're wasting." She paused for a moment and then added, "I've got a feeling about this one."

Mike let a deep breath out. "Okay, but ten bucks says we don't find a thing."

"Give me two to one and you've got a bet."

"Done," Mike said with a smile.

Maura walked back up the path and found Micah and Alex just where she had left them. She took a moment to review her notes. "I just want to check a couple of things. You said the name of the man who was shot was Simon Lott?"

"That's right," Alex answered.

"Just so I understand this, Dr. Caffey. You're sure you didn't see anything and you don't have any idea who might have shot this guy?"

She nodded.

"And this is his name and address?" she asked, showing Alex her notepad.

"Yes."

"Which you got from a dry-cleaning ticket you found in his pocket?"

Alex looked past Maura and again nodded.

"But he didn't have a wallet and you don't remember what you did with the ticket?"

"I guess I must have dropped it in all the chaos," she said.

"I understand. It must have been a very frightening few minutes. It's a good thing you were able to remember the address," Maura said. The suspicion in her voice was clear, prompting Alex to steal a glance at her face. The dubious look in her eyes was hardly subtle. Maura closed the notebook and put it back in her purse. "I'd like to go inside now and have a look around."

"But I've already done that," Alex protested. "We're wasting time. We should be going over to his apartment."

"We just can't go storming into this guy's apartment," Maura explained. "We have to speak to the manager, the doorman, and maybe even some of his neighbors. If the building has video surveillance, we may even want to look at today's tapes. If Jessie is in there, we want to do everything we can to get her out safely, and in order to do that we—"

"I still don't understand why you just don't—"

"Listen to me, Alex. Before we do anything, we need to find out as much about this guy as we can. It's not a waste of time. It's crucial."

Maura knew that she would have an answer from the unit dispatched to R Street within a few minutes. Mike's warning had not fallen on deaf ears and until Maura had a report from the dispatched unit, there was no way she was going to initiate a major police operation based on information from an individual who might be on the brink of cracking from emotional stress.

"Let's do what Detective Kenton suggests," Micah said. A little to his surprise, Alex no longer protested. Instead, she turned, walked up the steps, and unlocked the door.

"Where would you like to start?" she asked Maura.

"Jessie's playroom."

With Micah at her shoulder, Alex led Maura and the two officers down the hall. She opened the basement door and the three officers descended the stairs with Alex and Micah behind them.

Maura started in the middle of the room and spent about

five minutes looking around. From the landing, Alex said, "Olivia would never leave the playroom like this."

"Did you touch anything?" Maura asked.

"I don't think so," she answered.

"Let's go back upstairs," Maura suggested, taking a final look around.

After going through the upstairs, the living room, and Alex's study, they went into the kitchen. At Maura's suggestion, Mike and his partner went outside to have a look around the yard.

Standing in the kitchen, Maura pointed across the room and asked, "Where does that door go?"

"It's a pantry," Alex said.

Maura crossed the room and opened the door. Alex trailed behind her.

"Where's the light?" she asked.

"It's right here," Alex said, reaching for the switch.

The moment she flipped it on, Alex saw Olivia's twisted body wedged under the lower shelf. Her knees were flattened against her chest while her back was pushing flush against the wall. Alex gasped, pushing her fist hard against her mouth. Maura moved first, but Alex was only a second behind. Together, they knelt at Olivia's side.

Hearing Alex's gasp, Micah raced across the kitchen but stopped in the doorway when he saw Olivia's body. Working together, Maura and Alex gently moved Olivia out from under the shelf and then rolled her onto her back. Alex's fingers had already found the main muscles of Olivia's neck and were feverishly palpating between them for a carotid artery pulse. Her skin was cool and dry and it was quickly apparent that there was no pulse.

Alex moved back a foot or so to observe Olivia's chest. It was motionless. Knowing it was almost certainly an act of futility, Alex moved her other hand around the back of her neck for support, pinched her nose, and blew three large breaths into her mouth. It was then, when she was holding her neck, that she easily felt the disconnected and shattered bones of her cervical spine. In spite of her obviously fatal injury, Alex began giving Olivia mouth-to-mouth resuscitation and told Maura to initiate chest compressions.

After about a minute of feverish CPR, Alex suddenly stopped. She looked at Maura and shook her head. "We should stop," she said, falling back into a seated position.

"Don't touch anything," Maura warned as she stood up. "I have to use the phone."

Micah stepped back from the entry, allowing Maura to pass. Alex slid forward, raised Olivia's head from the ground, and gently lowered it into her lap. Micah stepped into the pantry and whispered, "I'm so sorry, Alex."

Dazed, Alex stroked Olivia's hair. "They're going to kill my baby, Micah."

Micah knelt down behind her. "Don't say that. We're going to get her back. I promise."

Micah continued to try to comfort Alex while Maura called for assistance. She requested a crime scene investigation team and two detectives from the homicide division. Fortunately Kevin Armbruster was on duty, a solid detective with whom she had worked many times before.

After briefing him, she gave him the address of Lott's apartment and told him to get hold of the manager. She also asked him to check to see whether Lott had any prior arrests or outstanding warrants. The last thing she told Kevin was to have an additional unit meet her at the apartment. She was just about to return to the kitchen when Mike and his partner returned.

Mike took off his hat and then ran the back of his hand across his forehead. He cleared his throat and said, "I just heard from the unit that went over to R Street." He paused for a moment, averted his eyes, and added, "They found a victim—a male with two rounds in his back."

"I don't suppose he had a wallet on him?" she asked, having no interest in reminding Mike about their bet.

"No," he answered, "but they did find a semiautomatic."

"Near the body in the middle of the driveway?" Maura asked.

"Yeah."

"Just like Dr. Caffey said."

Mike put his hat back on before going on. "Maybe she's the one who shot him."

"I doubt it. Is homicide and an investigation team on their way out there?" Maura inquired.

"The place should be swarming in about five minutes."

Maura pushed her hair back off her forehead and then shook her head. "This is developing into quite an interesting evening."

"Do you want us to go with you over to the apartment?" he asked.

"Yeah, as soon as our backup arrives we'll head over there. I've already called for another unit to meet us. We'll need some intel before we go in."

Mike watched as Maura walked down the hall toward the kitchen. "Hey, Detective," he said. "Nice going."

When Maura reached the kitchen, she stopped for a moment and gazed through the doorway at Micah and Alex, who were now seated at the table. She replaced her phone in her purse, walked in, and sat down across from a bleary-eyed Alex Caffey.

"I just spoke with my office. We're going to go over to Lott's apartment."

"I'm going with you," Alex said. "Maybe I can help when you speak to the manager."

Maura considered Alex's suggestion for a few moments before telling her, "Okay, as long as you understand that's as far as you go."

"Agreed," she said.

The moment the homicide detectives arrived, Maura, Alex, and Micah headed for the front door. Very little was said as they made the ten-minute ride over to Lott's building. Maura spent most of the time wondering what, if anything, they would find. On the one hand she prayed that Jessie would be there, but on the other she was terrified that she might be dead.

Maura's final thought as she pulled up to the brick four-story building was to notify emergency medical services to have the paramedics on hand well before her team went into the apartment.

# Chapter 78

Austin Carlen was a petty man whose crowning achievement in life was holding his present job as the manager of the Greenway Apartments for the past three years.

Sitting behind his desk impatiently drumming the blotter, he was obviously annoyed to have been dragged back to his office by the police without the courtesy of an explanation.

"As I just told you, Detective, Mr. Lott occupies apartment 4F. He's been here over a year. I've already answered all of these questions."

"What kind of tenant is he?" Maura asked in a pleasant tone, again taking note of his slight build, small jaw, and pockmarked skin.

"He pays his rent on time and seems to go about his business without disturbing anybody." Carlen narrowed his eyes, leaned forward, and asked in just above a whisper, "What's he done?"

Ignoring Carlen's inquiry, Maura went on. "Does he live alone?"

"Nobody else is registered in the apartment, if that's what you mean, but we don't exactly conduct nightly bed checks," Carlen said, picking up Lott's file.

"Do you employ a doorman?"

"No, we do not."

"Were you around all day today?" she asked.

"I was in and out."

"Did you see Mr. Lott at any time?"

"No."

"I noticed you have video surveillance," Maura said.

"When it's working," Carlen answered, covering a yawn with the palm of his hand. "At the moment it's on the fritz."

"Thanks," she told him before getting up from her chair

and crossing the room to speak to Mike. "Were you able to get a hold of any of his neighbors?"

"We spoke with the woman who lives across the hall and a married couple who occupies the apartment at the far end of the hall."

"And?"

"They all said the same thing. They barely know the guy. He never speaks to anyone."

"Did any of them hear or see anything out of the ordinary today?"

"They both said no."

Maura thought for a moment and then walked back across the room. "Mr. Carlen, I'd like you to call Mr. Lott's apartment. If someone answers, just tell them that there might be a problem with the hot water tomorrow. Can you do that?" she asked him.

He shrugged and then reached for the phone. After about ten rings he hung up. "No answer," he said.

"I want to thank you for your help, Mr. Carlen. Before we leave, is there anything else you can tell me about this man?"

"For instance?"

"Anything that might have struck you as peculiar."

"As I've already told you, Detective. He just kind of blends in with everybody else."

"Yeah, just your everyday Joe," she told him. "I'll need a key to his apartment." She then looked at Mike and said, "Let's make sure we have all the exits covered. Okay, let's have another look at the floor plan and head upstairs."

# Chapter 79

Standing outside Lott's apartment with her service revolver drawn, Maura signaled Mike and the officers flanking her with a single nod.

Standing flush against the wall, she again signaled Mike, who moved forward and slid the key that Carlen had provided them into the lock. Maura could hear the bolt slide across easily. She gave him a second nod. He then turned the knob and gave the door a quick shove. With both hands now on a readied weapon, Maura moved forward into the entrance hall of Lott's apartment. She took a few steps forward and waited for the other three officers to move in behind her.

The apartment was well lit but absolutely silent. The distinct smell of a recently cooked meal was in the air. Using the barrel of her Smith & Wesson as a pointer, she motioned toward the living room. Mike and one of the officers moved in front of her and entered the room. After a few seconds, Mike shook his head and the two of them returned to the hallway.

As they moved down the corridor, the first room they reached was the master bedroom. The door was open. Maura reached along the wall, found the light switch, and flipped it on. Slowly, she edged her way toward the center of the room while Mike checked out the closet and bathroom. The bedspread and pillows had been arranged with precision. Waiting for Mike, Maura couldn't help but notice that the bedroom was immaculate. If this guy was a kidnapper, he was the most meticulous one she'd ever been up against.

Slipping back into the hall, the four of them continued on to the second bedroom. From beneath the closed door, a stream of light filtered out and fanned out across the floor. Although it was barely audible, she was sure she heard music coming from the other side of the door. Maura found Mike's eyes and then pointed to the door. He nodded, looked at the other two officers, and then with one fleet motion grabbed the doorknob, lowered his shoulder, and went through it as if it were made of papier-mâché. Maura was right behind him as he crashed into the middle of the room.

Back to back with him, she leveled her weapon and scanned the room. The closet door was open but there was absolutely nothing inside.

"Nothing this way," Mike said.

When Maura was convinced the room was empty, she lowered her weapon and let out a deep breath. When she glanced over at the bed, a foreboding feeling of doom overcame her. The thin woolen blanket was rumpled and pulled out from under the far side of the mattress. She approached the bed. Sitting atop the nightstand was a roll of duct tape and an empty medicine bottle. Without touching it, she leaned over and read the label: VERSED. Maura recognized the drug from a case she had worked on a couple of years ago. She couldn't recall a lot of the specifics but did remember that it was in the Valium family. On the opposite nightstand she saw the small radio.

Whatever doubts still lingered in her mind about whether Alex Caffey's daughter had really been kidnapped vanished.

"Check out the rest of the apartment," she told Mike, who then motioned the two other officers to join him. Maura returned her weapon to her purse and then removed her cell phone to call for an investigation unit to start going over the scene. By the time she finished her call, Mike and the two officers returned and told her the apartment was secure. "Take another look around and then meet me downstairs," she told Mike. "Make sure these guys wait here until the investigation team arrives. I'm going back down to Carlen's office. I'll meet you down there in a few minutes."

Riding down on the elevator, Maura prayed that the fate of Jessie Caffey hadn't already been sealed. Unfortunately, she was a trained police officer who understood the brutal realities of a kidnapping. Disappointed and fearing the worst, Maura struggled with the best way to break the bad news to Alex.

As the doors rumbled open, her cell phone rang. The detective calling informed her that the house on R Street had been thoroughly searched and nothing of substance had been uncovered. He had also contacted the real estate agent, who told him that the owners had moved out and that the house had been vacant for the past three months.

Walking through the lobby on her way to Carlen's office, she dreaded the prospect of facing Alex.

# Chapter 80

The moment Alex saw Maura come through the door, she and Micah jumped to their feet.

Alex's eyes darted back and forth. When she didn't see Jessie, she craned her neck and looked past Maura. Her face quickly changed from one of guarded optimism to one of total despair. After a few moments, when it was finally clear that Maura had returned without Jessie, Alex fell back on the couch and began to cry.

Maura walked across the office and sat down next to her. "I'm sorry," she said. "Jessie wasn't there."

"Did you find anything at all?" Micah asked.

Maura looked at Alex, who had now buried her face in her hands, and said, "I don't think there's any question that Jessie was there."

Alex dropped her hands and then closed her eyes. "No," she insisted, shaking her head repeatedly. "This can't be happening." No longer able to conceive of any mind games to help her deny the obvious, Alex's head was suddenly filled with all of the unspeakable things that might have already happened to her child. Nobody in the room spoke. Finally, Alex opened her bloodshot eyes. Breathing in short bursts and speaking in a staccato voice, she looked straight at Maura and said, "If Jessie wasn't there, that means Lott was telling the truth about working with somebody. We'll never get her back. I know it."

"We're going to get Jessie back," Micah told Alex, sitting down on the arm of the couch. "I promise you," he said to Alex but looking straight at Maura.

"We've barely started into this thing, Alex. You can't give up hope yet," Maura added.

"She could already be dead . . . or worse," Alex whispered.

"We're not going to make that assumption," Maura told her with complete conviction.

Alex knew that Maura's words of encouragement were nothing more than lip service but it hardly seemed important. She reached into her pocket for a tissue and felt Lott's keys. She shook her head, wondering how she could have completely forgotten about them.

She pulled them out. "I just remembered something. As I told you, Lott didn't have a wallet but I did find these on him," she added, handing the keys to Maura.

Maura studied the pewter key ring and noticed when she flipped it over that it had the Hummer insignia on it. She continued to examine it until she finally signaled Mike.

"I want you to follow me over to the house on R Street. I'll take Mr. Henry and Dr. Caffey with me. I want one additional unit for backup."

"What's going on?" he asked.

"It's just a hunch. I'll fill you in later." Maura walked back over to the couch. "I want you to come with me," she told Alex.

"I don't understand," Alex said.

"I just want to check something out," Maura explained. "Maybe your original impression was right. Maybe Lott was working alone."

"I don't follow," Micah said.

"If my guess is right, the last thing Lott expected when he went to meet Alex was that somebody was going to shoot him."

# Chapter 81

To Alex's surprise, when they reached the house on R Street, Maura drove straight past it, circled the block, and then proceeded to Avon Place, where she turned right.

About halfway down the block, parked behind a Lincoln Town Car, she found what she was after. Maura continued past the black Hummer to the end of the street, where she pulled over. Mike was right behind her.

"I want your word of honor that you'll stay right here," Maura said to Alex.

Before she could answer, Micah said, "Of course we will."

Mike got out of his car and joined Maura. Together, they started down the street.

"Did you see that Hummer in the middle of the block?" she asked him.

"Sure."

"I want to check it out."

"Let's go," he said.

The two of them then made their way down the street. The traffic was sparse but several joggers and walkers were enjoying the perfect spring night. As they approached the Hummer from the rear, Maura noticed that the windows were heavily tinted. They were now about fifteen feet away. Mike removed his flashlight. The streetlamps provided some light, as did a large colonial lamppost located on the front lawn of the house that the Hummer was parked in front of.

Shoulder to shoulder, Mike and Maura moved slowly around the vehicle. As they did, Mike shined the light into each window. Even with the help of the flashlight, Maura could make out very little. After a shared glance, they stepped back from the vehicle.

"I can't see too much," she said to Mike, pulling out the

key ring. "Let's hope this is the son of a bitch's car." Maura hit the open button of the keyless entry system. The SUV responded with two quick beeps and the characteristic snap of the locks disengaging. She hit it again and the remainder of the locks opened. Mike cast her a cautious smile and a thumbs-up. He unsnapped the guard on his holster and covered his revolver.

When he was ready he gave her a nod. Maura decided to enter the vehicle through the back door on the driver's side. Reaching for the handle, she opened the door and then waited a few moments before leaning her head into the backseat. Using Mike's flashlight to illuminate both the front and back seats, she saw nothing suspicious. Maura then decided to climb in to have a better look. Unfortunately, she found nothing that might provide her with any clue as to Jessie Caffey's whereabouts.

Disappointed, she turned to examine the rear cargo area, which was partially covered by a canvas tarpaulin, something she hadn't noticed when she had inspected the Hummer from the outside. Leaning over the backseat, Maura reached for the tarpaulin, running her hand along the top of it to find a crease to grab on to. As she did so, her hand struck a solid object that was both cupped and angular. She knew instantly what it was.

Praying she wasn't too late, she tore the tarpaulin back. It snagged on the first attempt but with a second tug it flew back, exposing Jessie Caffey. Her body was crimped to one side, angled against the sidewall of the cargo area. Her knees were pulled tightly against her chest, which was exactly what Maura had felt before she ripped the tarpaulin back.

Jessie's mouth was gagged with duct tape, as were her ankles and hands. Her forehead was speckled with droplets of sweat. Maura reached for the tape across her mouth and gently removed it. As she did, Jessie straightened her legs and then whimpered.

"My God," Maura whispered as she jumped out of the car and moved around to the back.

"I got her, Mike," she yelled, even though he was only about five feet away. Maura flipped open the rear doors. Jessie's eyes were half open but there was no fear in them. Maura scooped her up and yelled to Mike, "Call the paramedics." To Maura's delight, Jessie was pink and breathing easily. She lay comfortably in Maura's arms, making no effort to pull away. She seemed drugged but in no apparent danger.

"I want to see my mommy," Jessie said in a sleepy voice.

"That's where we're going right now, honey. She really wants to see you too." As much as Maura fought it, she found herself thinking about her own daughter, and at least for the moment, her emotional side took over, leaving her feeling more like a mother than a police officer.

With the rest of the tape off and Jessie comfortably cradled in her arms and Mike flanking her, Maura started back down R Street. When they were about a hundred feet from where they had parked, she saw Alex standing in the middle of the street. Maura stopped. With a few cautious steps, Alex started toward them. Clutching Jessie's giraffe, she gradually broke into a run. When she reached Maura, she was gasping for each breath. Before taking Jessie into her arms, she swept a few moist strands of stubborn hair from her child's forehead. Alex's swollen eyes found Maura's. "Thank you," she whispered as Maura carefully transferred Jessie to her open arms.

Cheek to cheek, Alex pressed Jessie's body tightly against her own. She fell to her knees, clutching her little girl as she rocked her from side to side. Micah stood right behind them. Not wanting anyone to see the flood of tears in her eyes, Maura looked down for a moment. When she did, she spotted Jessie's giraffe. She slowly bent over and picked it up and then spent a few seconds brushing the dirt off of it.

Two MPD units rolled up with their lights flashing. An ambulance was only a few seconds behind. Still clinging to Jessie, Alex looked at Maura. "I don't know what to say," she said.

Maura couldn't do much more than just nod, but then after a few seconds she took a few steps forward and gave both mother and daughter a firm hug. "I'm going to send some officers over to keep an eye on your house tonight. They'll be there when you get home and when you wake up . and Alex, you don't have to worry about getting our attention any longer. I give you my personal guarantee that there will be a full investigation. I'll be over in the morning to speak with you about it."

It was at this point that two paramedics arrived.

"Are we going home now, Mommy?" Jessie asked.

"We sure are, but first we have to stop at the hospital for a few minutes."

"Are we going to see Uncle David?"

"Maybe not tonight, but real soon. I promise." Alex then turned to the two paramedics and said, "I'll carry her." With Jessie's legs locked around her waist, Alex boosted her up a little higher.

By this time, a large group of curious onlookers had gathered on either sidewalk. Out of a steady murmuring, one of the bystanders started to applaud in a slow and rhythmic pattern. The expression of joy was immediately contagious and seconds later both groups broke out into a spontaneous burst of cheering and clapping that filled the night with pure jubilation.

# PART
## Four

# Chapter 82

Alex's day had been made long by endless meetings and three cases in the operating room.

She had been in her office for about ten minutes when she looked up and saw Micah standing in her doorway. "What's it like having things relatively back to normal?" he asked as he came in and sat down.

"It's been fun. This new group of residents and students seem to be pretty enthusiastic."

"Have you heard from the police?" he asked.

"Maura Kenton called the day before yesterday. We had a fairly long talk."

"And?"

"With Simon Lott dead, there's not too much they can do."

"Why?"

"Evidently this guy didn't exist. According to Maura, it was as if he were never born."

"You heard about Victor?" he asked, reaching for one of the hard candies in a small crystal dish that sat on her desk.

"What do you mean?"

"He confessed."

"To attacking Robert and David?" she asked.

"No, nothing like that. I guess after some extensive soul searching, he admitted that he looked the other way about the filters because of the money Medivasc was giving to the project. He also poured his heart out about all kinds of shifty and unprofessional activities the Caduceus Project was involved in."

"Like what?" Alex asked.

"Oh, things like questionable fund-raising techniques, discrediting physicians professionally if they were opposed to the Caduceus Project's political agenda, planting false stories in the press. The list went on and on."

"All unscrupulous but nothing illegal," she pointed out. "What's going to happen to him?"

"That's hard to say at this point, but he has made it clear that he won't fight any decision the board of trustees makes about his future at Gillette."

"What's going to happen to the Caduceus Project?" she asked.

"I think we're hearing its death rattle. All of this will probably make the national news. There's no physician in his right mind who'd stay affiliated with such a tarnished organization."

"You really don't think when push comes to shove, Victor's going to defend himself?"

"Apparently not," Micah said. "His hospital privileges have already been suspended and the word is that the medical board's going to pull his license."

"For how long?" she asked.

"Who knows? But it's possible that his career as a physician is over."

"What about criminal charges?" she asked, not knowing quite how she felt about the thought of Victor having to face prosecution.

Micah leaned back. "I've heard nothing about criminal charges, but I don't think he'll ever practice medicine again."

"Don't bet on it. After a year or so, people and medical boards tend to forget. I'm sure Victor will wind up someplace where they really need a doctor. Some board will turn a blind eye and give him a license."

"I hope you're wrong," he said. He watched her for a few seconds and then asked, "So how does it feel to be vindicated?" Micah was expecting a smile but Alex remained straight-faced.

"Vindicated? I'm not sure that's how I feel."

"What do you mean? David's out of harm's way. You exposed Victor and the Caduceus Project and you're no longer viewed as the hospital heretic. What more could you ask for?"

Still a little unsettled about how things had turned out, she said, "I guess I'll feel better when David's home."

She was just about to go on when there was a knock at her door.

"I'm sorry to disturb you, but are you Dr. Caffey?"

Micah turned in his chair and Alex looked up from her desk at a lightly complected young man with shoulder-length blond hair, large hazel eyes, and a pleasant enough smile.

"Yes I am. How can I help you?" she asked.

"My name is Seth Key," he said, taking a few steps forward. "I'm Robert's brother."

Alex stood up, reached across her desk, and shook Seth's hand. "Please have a seat. This is Micah Henry."

Micah came to his feet, shook the young man's hand, and said, "It's a pleasure." He pointed at his watch. "I should get going. Gabe's waiting for me. I'll speak with you later. It was nice meeting you, Seth."

Seth was toting a tattered brown backpack, which he removed and placed next to his chair. After an awkward pause he cleared his throat and said, "I just arrived from Europe yesterday. I recently received the news of my brother's death from his attorney. Robert's wishes were quite specific. He asked me to return to the United States and contact a man named David Airoway here in Washington. When I couldn't locate him, I called Robert's attorney. It took him a couple of days but he eventually found out that Mr. Airoway had also been injured."

Seth edged toward the front of his chair, pausing for a few moments as he glanced around the room. Alex, easily sensing his uneasiness, considered trying to say something that might make him more comfortable but then decided it would be better just to keep it simple.

"I'm not sure how I can help you," she said, intrigued by the fact that Robert Key must have realized he was at risk for bodily harm and had taken painstaking measures to prepare for it.

"I decided to come to the hospital to see if I could speak with your brother. But when I arrived he was asleep and the nurse asked me not to disturb him. She told me that you were his sister and that you might be able to help me."

"I'm sorry, Seth, but I still don't understand—"

"My understanding is that my brother was robbed and

beaten unmercifully, and then died of unexpected complications in the hospital."

"That's right," Alex said, finding herself a little perplexed how to proceed. There were questions she clearly wanted to ask Seth, but without being candid and direct herself it was unlikely that she would get very far. Although he hadn't said so in words, it was obvious that he questioned the circumstances surrounding Robert's death.

"Robert left me a great deal of money. I have no idea how he acquired such an enormous sum. I was hoping your brother would have the answer."

Fearing that she would lose a golden opportunity to learn more about Robert, she decided to move forward cautiously. "Perhaps it was the remainder of a trust fund."

"Trust fund? Dr. Caffey, my brother and I didn't exactly grow up in Beverly Hills. We come from modest means. I assure you, neither of us was fortunate enough to be the recipient of a trust fund. When my parents died there was barely enough money to settle their affairs and pay the funeral expenses."

"Perhaps your brother was involved in a successful business enterprise."

"I imagine anything's possible, but if he was that fortunate, I think I would have known about it."

"Have you had a chance to speak with his girlfriend?"

Seth smiled. "Girlfriend? I don't think so, Dr. Caffey. If my brother had a relationship with a woman, I assure you it was purely platonic."

"How can you be so sure? You said you hardly spoke with Robert."

"That may be true, but when we did talk, we were quite candid with each other. Robert was gay, Dr. Caffey."

"That's certainly not the impression I got from talking to the young lady who he was dating. Maybe . . . I mean perhaps Robert was—"

"Bisexual? Not in a million years. He was a confirmed gay with absolutely no romantic interest in women."

"How can you be so sure?" Alex asked.

"Because he was my brother, and *I'm* gay. I know for a fact that he never came out. He was a very private person, especially when it came to his personal life." Seth stopped for a moment and gazed around the room, his eyes coming to rest on Alex's diplomas. With a smile, he said, "I can tell you this, he was passionate about being a physician."

Just at that moment, Alex's phone rang. She glanced at it but decided to ignore it. "I'm afraid I don't have the answers you're looking for. I didn't know Robert but I can assure you he was very highly thought of."

With pursed lips, Seth first nodded at Alex and then stood up. "I better get going, Dr. Calley. Thank you for taking the time to talk with me. I'm sure we'll speak again."

Alex stood up and shook Seth's hand. "What are your plans?"

"I'm going to spend a few days in Washington before going back to France. I have another meeting with Robert's lawyer tomorrow."

"If there's anything I can do to help, please give me a call. Is there some way I can get hold of you?" she asked.

"I have a cell phone," he said, grabbing his backpack and hoisting it into place. He waited for Alex to find a notepad and then recited the number while she wrote it down.

Alex walked Seth to the elevator and then returned to her office. Although their meeting was brief, he struck her as a reflective person who embraced a true affection for his brother. Alex was astounded to learn of Robert's homosexuality. As far as she was concerned, there was no doubt that Jamie had represented her relationship with Robert to be a romantic one. The question was, why would she have intentionally done that?

As much as she hated to admit it, the answer was staring her right in the face.

# Chapter 83

Even though Seth had been gone for almost an hour, Alex was still sitting in her office thinking about their meeting. Her mind was focused on how to best approach Jamie.

When her phone rang, she reached across her desk and picked it up.

"Alex, it's Tess Everly."

"Hi, Tess."

"Boy, you're one tough lady to get hold of. I've left three messages for you."

"I'm sorry. I got your messages but it's been a hell of a few days."

"I've been there," she said, having no real idea of what Alex had just been through. "Look, there's something I'd like to show you. Can you come over to the path department?"

"Do you mean right now?"

"Yeah, if you can. I think I've come across something that you might find intriguing."

Alex glanced over at the small clock on her desk. It was already past six. She thought about trying to put Tess off until tomorrow, but then decided she'd stop by the pathology department on her way home. "Give me half an hour," she told Tess.

"I'll wait for you."

Alex grabbed her purse, locked up the office, and went directly to the faculty parking lot. It was a short drive to Adams's main teaching hospital, where the administrative offices of the pathology department were located.

Alex walked up the two flights of stairs and then down a long gray hall. When she arrived at the entrance to the pathology department, she found the large glass doors open and went inside. She looked around for a few seconds before spotting Tess behind a computer in one of the offices. She walked across the hall, tapped on the open door, and walked in.

"Hi. You sounded funny on the phone. What's going on?"

"I wanted to show you something regarding those cases you asked me to have a look at." Tess stood up, took off her white coat, and hung it on the back of her door. "By the way, Boyette knew you were here. He hauled me into his office and wanted to know why you were so interested in those autopsies."

"What did you tell him?" Alex asked, following Tess out of the office.

"I told him that you were working on a paper."

"What did he say?"

"He asked me a bunch of questions, all of which I dodged."

"And that was the end of it?"

"He did tell me to inform him at once if you showed any further interest in those cases."

"He really said that?" Alex asked.

"You bet."

"Look, Tess. I'm not trying to get anybody in trouble here, so maybe it's better if we just drop this whole thing right now."

"Not a chance. Boyette's a selfish jerk. Since the first day of my internship, he hasn't given me the right time of the day. Anything I've managed to learn over the last four years has been in spite of him."

"Supposing he finds out I was here again?"

"He's in Cincinnati at some meeting. Plus the secretary who ratted you out left an hour ago." She shrugged and added, "Even if he does find out, I'll deal with it."

Alex followed Tess toward the back of the department and into a conference room. Atop a wooden racetrack-shaped table, Tess had laid out all of the photos from Nancy Olander's and Kyle Dolan's autopsies.

"I thought we already looked at these," Alex said as she took a seat. She leaned forward, picked up the photos, and began shuffling through them.

"I decided to check them out again," Tess said with an impish grin. "I guess I was curious to know why Boyette had such a bug up his butt about your interest in these cases."

"You really don't like that man very much," Alex said with

a giggle, thoroughly amused by Tess's feisty nature. She then set the pictures back on the table exactly the way she had found them and said, "Listen, Tess, I'm not a pathologist. You're going to have to help me out here a little."

Tess moved from behind Alex, pulled out a chair, and sat down next to her. She scanned the dozen or so photos and then selected two from each autopsy. Pulling them forward, she lined them up next to each other.

"Look at these carefully," Tess said, tapping the table as if she were sending Morse code. "I can't believe I missed it the first time around."

Alex shook her head and looked again. "I don't see anything."

"Look right here," she said, pointing with the eraser end of her pencil. "The magnification's different and so's the angle, but I'd bet a year's salary that all four of these pictures came from the same autopsy."

Alex looked over at Tess as if she were speaking a foreign language. "I don't understand what you're saying. How's that possible? These are two separate autopsies."

"Maybe so, but these photos all came from the same one."

"Which one? Nancy's or Kyle's?"

Tess leaned back in her chair and crossed her arms with that same silly grin. "That's just it. Neither," she said flatly.

"You've lost me again," Alex complained.

"I don't think these pictures came from either autopsy. Do you see it now?"

"Tess, all I see are two large pulmonary emboli."

"Forget the pulmonary emboli. You're focusing on the wrong thing. Look right here," Tess said, using the pencil again. "In both pictures you can see quite a bit of surrounding lung tissue. Now, even though the angles are different, look at this area right here. There's quite a bit of carbon deposits, which means that if we are dealing with two distinct autopsies, both of the people were relatively heavy smokers."

"So what? A lot of people smoke."

"I realize that, Alex. I grew up in New York City, not the foothills of North Dakota. I took the liberty of having a peek at Nancy Olander's hospital chart. She was a nonsmoker and Kyle Dolan was seventeen years old."

"Maybe all the carbon deposits were environmental," Alex suggested.

"I don't think so, and I'll tell you why," Tess said with total conviction. "Look over here, just above the pulmonary artery. It's kind of small but that's definitely a pulmonary hamartoma. Do you see it?"

"I see it, but I still don't understand what—"

"The photo is marked as Nancy Olander's. Now look over here," Tess said, referring to the second photo. "Right there. It's the exact same hamartoma and it's in the identical location, but this photo came from the Dolan autopsy. Now, as I'm sure you're aware, pulmonary hamartomas are benign lung tumors that are extremely rare. So I ask you, what are the chances that two patients who were heavy smokers both die of a pulmonary embolus and both just happen to have the same rare tumor in the exact same location in their lung?"

Alex didn't have to ponder Tess's question very long to calculate that the chances of such an occurrence would approach zero. Baffled for the moment, Alex tried to arrive at a logical explanation for Tess's discovery. "Did you ever stop to consider that maybe this whole thing is just some secretarial screwup?"

"You mean that maybe the wrong photos got placed in the wrong charts?" Tess asked.

"Exactly."

"As a matter of fact, that did occur to me. So I went back in our files for the last three years and pulled every autopsy where a major pulmonary embolus was found."

"And?"

"I found it."

"Found what?" Alex asked with conelike eyes.

"The real autopsy where these photographs came from. It was an elderly lady who had a fifty-five-year pack-a-day history. She underwent removal of a large pelvic tumor and died two weeks later while still in the hospital." She paused for a moment. "The family requested an autopsy—and guess what it showed?"

"She died of a massive pulmonary embolus," Alex said.

"Bingo."

"Did she have a caval filter in?" Alex asked.

"Nope."

"But the dictations of Kyle Dolan's and Nancy Olander's autopsies clearly identified huge pulmonary emboli, and it was mentioned in both of the reports that photos were taken."

"I'm well aware of that."

"So where the hell are the real pictures?" Alex asked.

"I don't have any idea," Tess stated. "Maybe somebody got rid of them."

Alex took a deep breath and then asked, "Have you told anybody about this?"

"Nope."

Alex paced up and down for a few moments before asking, "Would you mind keeping this under your hat for a few days until I can come up with some explanation for all this?"

"Not a problem."

"Thanks," Alex said. "What about the autopsy on Graham Pierce?"

Tess shook her head. "I was just about to mention that. I couldn't find it in our computer system so I checked the log book for that date."

"And?"

"There's no record of it," Tess said.

"How's that possible?"

"Anything's possible with our out-of-date computer system, but the staff's pretty compulsive about hand-entering every autopsy we do into the log . . . and there's something else."

Alex groaned. "I'm almost afraid to ask."

"I checked the files. There are no slides or lab reports for this guy."

"Maybe you had the wrong date," Alex suggested.

"I checked the entire month. As far as I can tell, we never did an autopsy on a Graham Pierce."

"But I saw the dictated report," Alex insisted.

"Well, in that case, I'd hold on to it because the original's no longer in the system and all the slides are missing. So for all intents and purposes, the autopsy never happened."

Alex could sense that Tess was very curious about just what the hell was going on. She was sure that Tess was waiting for an explanation, but at the moment Alex neither had the time nor the inclination to share anything with her.

"I bet in the end we'll discover that all of this is just some administrative screwup."

Tess nodded at Alex skeptically but didn't say a word. She didn't have to. Her silence spoke volumes.

On her way home, Alex tried to remain calm and go over things slowly to see whether she could put the pieces together. But no matter in what direction her thoughts took her, she kept coming up with the same conclusion—and that was that the autopsies of Nancy Olander, Kyle Dolan, and Graham Pierce had been either falsely dictated or altered after the fact. But if that were the case and these three patients hadn't died of a pulmonary embolus, then her whole theory about Victor Runyon's sinister intentions now had more holes in it than a ten-year-old pincushion.

# Chapter 84

When Alex came through the front door, her mother was there to greet her.

As soon as Jeanette had heard about what had happened to Olivia and Jessie, she insisted on coming to Washington to help out until Alex could locate a new au pair. When Jessie asked about Olivia, she decided to tell her simply that she suddenly became ill and had to return to Australia right away.

"Jessie hasn't eaten. She insisted on waiting for you," Jeanette said.

"How's she doing?"

"I'm not an expert but she seems to be fine. Did you get a chance to speak with anyone at the children's hospital?"

"Actually, I spoke to one of the psychologists. He said that if the abduction wasn't physically traumatic and she received a drug with a strong amnesic effect then—"

"Speak English, dear."

"Sorry, a drug that causes amnesia. If that was the case, then it's quite conceivable that a child, especially one of Jessie's age, would remember little or nothing of what happened."

"That's wonderful news. Were there any problems with the arrangements for Olivia?"

"No, her body arrived in Brisbane today. Her parents called. They were very nice. The service is tomorrow."

"Well, it was wonderful of you to take care of all that. Why don't you put your things down in your study? I'll go get Jessie and we'll meet you in the kitchen."

"Okay."

Jessie was already at the table when Alex came in.

"Hi, Mommy."

"I smell something great," Alex said, rubbing her hands together and sitting down next to Jessie.

"Grandma made fried chicken," she said.

"Your favorite," Alex said. Jessie picked up her fork and shook her head up and down vigorously.

For the next hour, Alex enjoyed a wonderful meal with her mother and daughter. Her pager didn't go off a single time and there were no phone calls. When Jessie was done with her peach cobbler, she insisted on being put to bed by both her mother and grandmother. When all the antics and stalling were finally over, Alex came downstairs, shared a cup of coffee with Jeanette, and then went into her study.

She was still unsure of how to proceed with the information that Tess Everly had given her. She knew that if she spoke with the pathologists at Adams who had done the autopsies on Kyle Dolan and Nancy Olander, Dr. Boyette was certain to find out, an eventuality that Alex didn't relish. Things were finally starting to calm down at the hospital and the last thing she needed was Boyette calling Owen to complain about her.

It was when she first began to consider an alternative to the Adams pathologists that the idea popped into her head. Nicholas Sacco was a first-rate pathologist whom she had worked with and gotten to know pretty well while she was in Miami. He had moved to Virginia about five years ago and was now working at Fairfax Hospital, which was no more than a half hour drive from Georgetown. She had run into him a few times and they occasionally spoke on the phone.

Alex opened the middle drawer of her rolltop desk, pulled out her phone book, and found his home number.

"Nick, it's Alex Caffey. How have you been?"

"If I weren't spending every waking moment of my life at that godforsaken hospital I'd probably be a lot better. We could use at least two more pathologists."

"Don't get any ideas about stealing any of ours. Adams is just as shorthanded. I have a favor to ask you."

"For a fellow Miami grad, anything. Ask away."

"I'm working on a paper that examines failure rates in caval filters. I have a few autopsy reports I'd like you to have a look at."

"I'd be happy to. What am I looking for?"

"Nothing specific. I'd just like you to review them and tell me what you think."

"What's wrong with those highfalutin' academic pathologists over at Adams?" he asked.

"Well, they're the ones who did the autopsies. I want an objective opinion," she stated simply.

"Okay, let me give you my fax number."

"Hold on a sec." Alex grabbed a pad and jotted down the number. "Thanks a lot, Nick. I'll have my secretary fax over the patient files to you first thing tomorrow."

"I'll have a look at them when I get in and give you a call some time tomorrow. How's that?"

"Perfect. Thanks again. I owe you one."

"In that case, how about having dinner with me next week?"

"I thought you were married," she said.

"I'm between wives at the moment. Are you interested?"

"In dinner or marrying you?"

"Take your choice," he said.

Alex laughed. "Maybe you've forgotten, but I've seen you in action."

"What's your point?" he asked.

"My point is that being the next feather in your cap is not exactly my idea of a meaningful relationship."

"I think you'll find that I've really matured since Miami and besides, think of all the fun you could have."

"Sounds great but I'll pass."

"You're a cold woman, Alex Caffey."

"Don't forget to call me tomorrow after you've had a chance to review the cases."

After getting off the phone, Alex spent another few minutes in her study looking through her most recent *Journal of Trauma* before heading upstairs. As soon as she opened the door to her room, she saw a familiar bulge under her comforter. Too tired to fight the inevitable, and actually a little pleased that Jessie had sneaked into her room, Alex quietly got ready for bed, climbed in, and curled up next to Jessie.

# Chapter 85

**MAY 25**

The spa at the Ritz-Carlton in Georgetown was one of the few places that Morgan could completely unwind. Over the past couple of months, his weekly Swedish massage had become an inviolate part of his schedule.

As he made his way through the lobby, he felt a lot better than he had an hour earlier. In spite of maintaining an outward demeanor that was controlled and businesslike, the events of the last several days had weighed heavily on him. He was being paid an obscene amount of money to keep his employers happy, and before the Simon Lott debacle, he would have said that he was highly regarded by them, but now he was worried that he was losing their confidence.

At least the matter of Mr. Lott had now been dealt with without any apparent repercussions. The only thing he regretted was not recognizing the man's ineptitude sooner. Alex Caffey, on the other hand, remained a riddle wrapped in an enigma. She was still a problem and he realized that new arrangements would have to be made to deal with her. He could only hope in the meantime that she would continue to hit one dead end and roadblock after another.

One problem that continued to plague him, however, was that he had no way of knowing just how much Key had told Airoway. Morgan was encouraged by the information from his sources in Gillette, who felt it was highly unlikely that Airoway would ever remember anything, but Morgan was nobody's fool and would of course continue to monitor Airoway's recovery. As long as he remembered nothing, he posed no threat to the project.

Morgan stepped out of the hotel lobby and took a deep breath. He waited as an overdressed and petty woman finished admonishing the doorman for his careless handling of her priceless luggage. When she finally finished, the young man, who recognized Morgan, signaled the first cab in line to move up. Morgan exchanged a sympathetic smile with him, slipped him a ten, and climbed into the backseat. Still feeling relaxed from the massage, he fell asleep for most of the cab ride home.

The beautiful Regency-style home that he had rented in Alexandria was secluded and more expansive than he required, but he preferred it that way and actually enjoyed the added space and privacy. Except for a lackadaisical maid who came for three hours every other day, Morgan allowed no one else in the house.

Climbing the winding oak staircase to the second floor, he ambled through his bedroom and into the bathroom. Even though he always showered at the spa, it was his custom to repeat the ritual when he arrived home. He undressed, stepped into the shower, and languished under the hot pulsations of water for nearly half an hour. When he finished he cracked the shower door and reached for a large bath towel, drying his face as he stepped out.

Deciding whether he'd shave now or before dinner would prove to be the last decision of his life. Still rubbing the water from his face, he never imagined that standing five feet behind him was a man with a semiautomatic handgun leveled at the back of his head. The man had no interest in turning the situation into a showdown and simply squeezed off a single round.

Morgan heard nothing as the hollow-point round struck him squarely in the head, splaying out as it bored through his skull, sending bloodied fragments of bone and brain splashing against the mirror. Even with the ample force of the forty-four-caliber round, Morgan wasn't driven forward; instead, he simply crumpled to the floor right where he had been standing.

The man lowered the gun from his quivering hand and considered approaching the body, but did not. There was no need to. He knew Morgan was dead. Having done what he had come to do, he turned and walked back into the bedroom. As he crossed the spacious room, he noticed Morgan's cell phone sitting on the dresser being charged. He stopped for a moment, considered his options, and then quickly walked over and picked it up.

Scrolling down the list of Morgan's recent phone calls, he glanced at each one briefly. When he reached the fifth one, his eyes suddenly widened in astonishment. He swallowed hard and checked the phone number again. When he realized there was no mistake, he briefly closed his eyes and allowed his chin to fall.

Grasping the cell phone tightly in his hand, he left Morgan's bedroom and then descended the spiral oak staircase one cautious step at a time, and with each of those steps, he wondered what in the world had made him believe that killing Morgan would be the solution to his problems. He had gone to such painstaking measures to eliminate Morgan, had pulled it off without a hitch, only to find out two minutes later that his efforts would prove about as productive as shouting at the rain. The irony of the whole thing was almost frightening.

As he entered the large foyer, he stopped for a moment and looked back toward the staircase. It was at that precise moment that he realized that there was only one way out of his horrible nightmare.

# Chapter 86

Alex had just gotten back from the morning radiology conference and was about to give Nick Sacco a call when her secretary buzzed in.

"Dr. Sacco's on line one," she told her.

"Thanks, Joyce," Alex said, reaching for the phone. "Hi, Nick."

"I had a look at those cases you sent me. They seem pretty straightforward but I'm still not sure what I'm supposed to be looking for."

Not surprised by Nick's response, Alex leaned back in her chair, pinning the phone between her shoulder and ear.

"I was trying to find out if you noticed anything unusual about the cases."

"Did you speak to the pathologist who did the autopsies?" Nick asked.

"Actually it was three different ones."

"Impossible," Nick said.

"How can you be so sure?" Alex listened closely as Nick shared his reasons with her. In total disbelief of what he was telling her, she finally interrupted and asked, "Are you positive about all this?"

"Of course I am," he answered.

"Listen, Nick, I'm leaving the hospital right now. I'll be in your office in thirty minutes."

"But, Alex, I have a million things—"

"If you're busy when I get there, I'll wait. I'll wait all night if I have to, but I want you to show me exactly what you're talking about."

Alex said a quick good-bye, hung up the phone, and

grabbed her purse. As she flew past Joyce, she said, "I'll be out of the hospital for at least an hour. Don't page me unless it's urgent."

# Chapter 87

As soon as she arrived, Alex was shown into Nick's office by his secretary.

His office was measurably larger than hers and more elegantly decorated. At a time when her mind was filled with many more important things, she found herself just a little envious. Nick was on the other side of the room thumbing through a stack of medical journals when she walked in.

"You sounded a little frazzled on the phone," he said, replacing the journals on the lower shelf of his bookcase. He sat down at his desk and motioned her to have a seat across from him.

"That's because I was completely dumbfounded by what you told me."

"All I said was that all of the autopsies were performed and dictated by the same pathologist."

"How could you possibly know that? I crossed out the names of the patients and the pathologist of record from the reports before I had them faxed to you."

"Because I have an M.D. and a Ph.D."

"I'm very impressed with the depth of your education but I don't think that either answers my question or certifies you as omniscient."

"My Ph.D.'s in English. I taught at the University of Georgia for five years before I decided to go to med school. I've read enough student papers to tell you that all of these autopsy reports were dictated by the same pathologist—and, I might add, not a particularly learned one. In fact, he or she sounds more like a pathology intern than an attending."

Alex was trying to appear patient but she was still having a difficult time understanding.

"I hate to keep dwelling on the same point but without listening to the tapes or seeing the names on the reports, how could you possibly know whether those cases were dictated by one, two, or three different pathologists?"

Nick grinned. "People write and dictate in a very individual and distinctive way."

"For instance."

"Their vocabulary, syntax, sentence construction, dangling participles, misplaced modifiers. I could go on forever. It comes from having graded hundreds and hundreds of term papers. Suffice it to say that the way people write or, in this case, dictate, gives them away faster than their fingerprints."

Alex still had her doubts. "Show me."

"Sure," he said.

Nick reached forward, picked up the autopsy reports, and got up. He walked around to Alex's side of the desk and sat down next to her. He then showed her line by line exactly what he was talking about. Alex hadn't been an English major in college, but she could definitely appreciate much of what Nick was talking about.

"What difference does all this make anyway?" he asked her.

Looking into his puzzled eyes, she answered, "It would take me all day to explain it to you. Let's just say that I'm extremely happy that you agreed to take a look at these reports."

"You know, when I first read them, I thought you were just using me as a guinea pig."

"What do you mean?" she inquired.

"I assumed you were the one who had dictated them as part of a textbook or some kind of medical student study aid and were just trying to see how believable they were. I figured that these were fictitious patients and you were just trying to find out whether the reports were accurate and believable enough."

"Well, I can assure you that's not the case."

"Then you must have the most disorganized transcription department of any hospital in the world."

Intrigued by his comment, she asked, "What makes you say that?"

Nick explained, "One of the patients was a seventeen-year-old boy. He went to surgery to have a large abscess drained from his thigh. I read the surgeon's dictation of the operation and that's when I knew all of these autopsy reports were just the figment of somebody's imagination."

"You lost me again."

"It's not that complicated, Alex. All three autopsy reports and the operative summary were dictated by the same person and I would say that the individual was a surgeon."

"Why do you think that?"

"Because the operative note was the only one that sounded like it had been dictated by an experienced physician who knew what the hell he or she was talking about."

By the look on Nick's face, Alex knew he was waiting for an explanation of just what the devil she had gotten herself into.

"Thanks for everything," she said, having no interest in confiding in Nick. "I have to get going."

"How about lunch sometime?" he asked just as she reached the door.

"I'll think about it," she answered without turning around.

Driving back to the hospital, Alex thought about what Nick had said regarding the hospital's transcription system. She wasn't an expert on the dictating network but she did recall one of the medical records assistants mentioning to her that the tapes of the physician dictations were kept for only about ten days before they were erased and recirculated, which precluded the possibility of her listening to the original dictations.

It now seemed clear that she had made a mistake and that the Medivasc caval filters were not defective and that Nancy Olander, Kyle Dolan, and Graham Pierce had not died of a blood clot to their lungs. Unfortunately, the revelation left Alex with one troublesome question—why would Victor Runyon go to such extreme lengths to make it appear that three of his patients had died of a pulmonary embolus?

All of a sudden, Alex felt a wave of panic grip her. What if she was wrong about Victor? What if she had made a horrible mistake about him, and as a result of her actions his career came crashing down around him? Shuddering at the mere thought of having made such a terrible error, she closed her eyes and realized that she would have to find out for sure. She would have to somehow persuade him to speak with her again.

But this time she'd have to stay open-minded and give him a legitimate opportunity to explain himself. She was confident that if she remained objective and calm, she would know whether he was lying to her. If it turned out that he had been honest and aboveboard with her all along, she wondered whether she'd ever be able to forgive herself.

# Chapter 88

Victor Runyon's house in Bethesda was both grand and gracious. Set on an expansive corner lot of a tranquil tree-shaded street, it had been his home since he had remarried five years earlier.

Walking up the path to the two-story house, Alex still had misgivings and wondered whether she was doing the right thing. After a few seconds of deliberation, she went ahead and rang the bell.

When a little girl with pigtails and freckles appeared at the door, Alex smiled. "Is your dad here?" she asked, guessing her age to be about eight.

The child whirled around and screamed, "Daddy, there's somebody here to see you." Turning back around, she stared up at Alex with faint blue eyes but didn't say a word.

"What's your name?" Alex asked.

"Mandy."

"I'm Alex," she said, extending her hand. "I work with your daddy at the hospital. I have a daughter who's a little younger than you are."

When Alex looked up, she saw Victor coming down the

hall. When he recognized her, his expression suddenly became dismayed.

"Alex," he said, placing his hands on Mandy's shoulders. "You're the last person I expected to see."

"I thought we could talk," she said.

Victor looked down at his daughter. "Go ahead back to the family room, honey. I'll be right back." He waited until Mandy disappeared down the hall.

Instead of inviting Alex in, Victor stepped outside and pulled the door closed behind him.

"No offense, Alex, but I've seen you in action and I don't think that's the type of behavior I'd like my daughter to see."

It hardly surprised her that he was belligerent toward her, but she had decided on the drive over that she would not become incensed if he felt the need to vent.

"There's a few things that I'd like to discuss with you and I was hoping we might be able to put our differences aside for a few minutes."

Guarding his silence for a few moments, Victor studied Alex's face. He then pointed down the flagstone path.

"Let's take a walk."

They walked past two bicycles lying on their sides and an assortment of athletic equipment.

"Why were you so intent on putting a filter in David?" she asked.

"Because I agreed with Tom that he needed one."

"But I never authorized it."

"Nobody shared that information with me. The message I got was to put one in."

"That's not exactly what you told me in the ICU."

"I was trying to avoid a scene. There were a lot of people around and in spite of your efforts to conceal it, you were pretty upset. I didn't think getting into an argument with a colleague, especially one whose judgment was being influenced by emotional factors, would have been a very bright move. I think by your . . ." Victor suddenly stopped and simply kept walking in silence.

"Go ahead. What were you going to say?" she asked.

"It's not important."

"I'd like to hear it, anyway," she urged.

"I was going to add that you act as if I could have no possible idea of what you're going through."

Alex simply nodded. The tone in Victor's voice struck her as sincere.

"I finally got hold of Tom in New Jersey," she said. "I'll admit he was pretty upset the morning he left but he doesn't recall talking to you about putting a filter in David."

"That's because he didn't."

"But you just said that—"

"I said that I got a message. The actual call came from his secretary, who obviously screwed things up." Victor reached into his back pocket, pulled out his cell phone, and tapped in a number. After following two more prompts, he quickly handed the phone to Alex.

*"Dr. Runyon, this is Gina, Dr. Calloway's secretary, calling. He wants you to know that he discussed putting a caval filter in David Airoway with Dr. Caffey and that he would appreciate it if you would go ahead and put it in at your earliest convenience."*

The voice mail was clear enough, but it seemed the most likely explanation was that Tom's secretary had dropped the ball when she conveyed the message to Victor.

"What about your relationship with Robert?" she asked.

Victor looked at Alex askew as they turned and started down the sidewalk. "We were casual friends."

"Did you know he was in the Caduceus Project?"

"Of course I knew. It wasn't a secret," he responded. When they reached the end of the block, Victor pointed across the street and they kept walking. "Do you really think I would intentionally let four people die?" When his question was met with a blank stare and silence, he stopped dead in his tracks and waited for Alex to do the same. He studied her intently, shook his head in disgust, and said, "No, it's worse, isn't it? You still think I had something to do with Robert's death and your brother's accident. That's why you've been acting the way you have. This is insane," Victor added as he threw his arms up in the air and walked off.

Alex watched him for a few seconds, unsure of what to do, but then decided to go after him. Catching up and walking shoulder to shoulder with him at a rapid pace, she said, "Just tell me that you haven't crossed the line."

"What's that supposed to mean?"

"You know what I'm talking about, Victor."

"Look, Alex, I'll admit that I wasn't totally honest with you the day we talked at Dupont Circle. I've done some pretty dumb things in the name of advancing the political goals of the Caduceus Project. They were stupid mistakes and I'm prepared to take responsibility for them, but I've never done anything illegal either as a physician or as a member of the project. I'm guilty of getting caught up in a political battle and using bad judgment, but that's where it ends."

"Where do you stand with the hospital?" she asked.

"I assume I'm going to be thrown off the medical staff. According to Owen, a special committee has been assembled to look into the entire Medivasc matter. Until a final decision is reached, I'm prohibited from setting foot on university property." He shoved his hands deep into the back pockets of his pants. In a much calmer voice, he added, "Owen did suggest that I might want to start exploring other options."

"What type of other options?" she asked.

Victor forced a laugh, looked at Alex as if she were acting just a little too dumb, and then said, "He wasn't specific, but I don't think working as a physician was one of them."

"And the Caduceus Project?"

"He strongly advised that I distance myself as soon as possible. Anyway, there won't be a Caduceus Project for much longer. We're a physician organization. When all of this becomes public, I assume our office will be flooded with resignations."

Alex had listened to every word Victor had uttered. Deciding whether he was telling the truth was much easier than she had anticipated. Normally, she might feel uncomfortable relying solely on her instinct, but at the moment that was not the case. She was convinced she had made a mistake and that Victor Runyon was telling the absolute truth.

"Supposing I told you I think you were framed," Alex said.

"By whom?"

"I'm . . . I'm not sure who, but—"

"Alex, haven't you been listening to me?" he asked in an exasperated voice. "I'm not the victim here. I knowingly allowed myself to become involved in a series of unethical activities. I also should have realized that there was something wrong with those filters and reported it to both Owen and the FDA."

"That's what I'm trying to say," she said, just as they arrived back in front of his house. "I don't think that the filters are defective."

He didn't answer at first, choosing to stare in the direction of his front door. He heaved a breath of impatience and asked, "What in God's name are you talking about now?"

"I have reason to believe that there's a lot more in play here than either of us fully appreciates. If you'll just give me the chance to explain, I think—"

Victor held up his hand for a second and then pushed his palms together. When it appeared to Alex as if he had gathered his thoughts, he said, "With all due respect, Alex, I've heard your outlandish conspiracy theories. They're the talk of the hospital."

"I assure you they are not outlandish and—"

"The last thing I need at this point is for the people who hold my future in their hands to think I've joined forces with some irrational, grief-stricken physician on a wild-goose chase."

"Supposing you could clear your name?"

Victor shook his head in submission as if he had just spent the last fifteen minutes preaching to deaf ears. "The only way I'm going to clear my name is to take full responsibility for my indiscretions, cooperate with the medical board, and act professionally—and then, maybe someday, this nightmare will come to an end."

"I'm not sure you—"

"Why did you come over here today?"

"I just thought I could—"

"Help me? I don't think so. I think you needed to unload all that guilt you're carrying around for the unthinkable way you've treated me. If you are here to help, then you've made a long trip for no reason." He paused briefly, took a breath, and then said quietly, "Now, if you don't mind, I'd like to get back to my family."

Without another word, Victor walked up the path and went back into his house.

Alex waited for a few minutes, staring down the street, be-

fore she finally walked over to her car and got in. Sitting behind the wheel, she was at a complete loss for what to do next.
A week ago she had been sure that Victor was an immoral
physician and a cold-hearted maniac. Now she was convinced
she had made a grave error and that she had caused this man
irreparable damage.

Worst of all, there was no way she could think of to undo
her blunder.

# Chapter 89

Trying to take her mind off her sobering conversation with
Victor, Alex had spent the last hour reviewing the latest resi-
dency evaluations. She barely looked up when she heard
Joyce's characteristic knock.

"I'm going to that administrative meeting now. Do you
need me to do anything before I go?"

"No, go ahead. I'll see you later," Alex told her.

Still trying to busy her mind, she reached for the stack of
patient files that she had faxed Nick Sacco. She had already
been through them several times before, and was barely paying attention as she thumbed through them. Still in a
quandary, she recalled the advice that one of her surgery professors had given her on more than one occasion. She whispered to herself, "When the solution to a difficult problem
eludes you, reconsider your assumptions."

With her professor's words in mind, Alex found the three
autopsy reports. Remembering what Nick Sacco had told her
about Kyle's operation, she flipped through the papers until
she located Dolan's operative report that spelled out the details of the procedure. She read through it, found nothing out
of the ordinary, and was just about to return it to the pile when
her eyes tracked down to the very bottom of the second page.

"This can't be," she muttered in complete disbelief. "I thought Runyon did the surgery." Pulling the operative report a little closer, Alex checked the name of the surgeon over and over again, waiting for some obvious explanation to suddenly pop into her head, but none did.

With the irrefutable truth staring her right in the face, Alex's anger mounted. Her grip tightened on the arms of her chair, becoming so intense that the blood from her fingers emptied like water spiraling down a drain, leaving them white as chalk. Sitting in the silence, she wondered how she could have been so blind.

Alex tossed the report back on her desk and stood up. Seeing no reason to put off the inevitable, she walked out of her office and started down the hall.

# Chapter 90

When Alex walked into Owen Goodman's office she found him slouched in his chair staring aimlessly across the room.

Directly in front of him, surrounded by several scattered stacks of journals, files, and patient records, stood a bottle of vodka flanked by two small glasses.

For a time he seemed oblivious to her presence, but finally he turned and looked in her direction.

"Alex. I've been expecting you," he said, his words just a little garbled. "I'm sure you must have many questions for me."

Alex crossed the room slowly, studying his face as she approached the desk. His hair was disheveled and the skin beneath his filmy eyes was billowy. A thin stubble layered his chin and cheeks.

Filled with contempt, she said, "Do you really think drinking yourself into oblivion's the answer?"

"I'm an alcoholic," he said, picking up one of the glasses in a mock toast. "That's what we do."

"That's nonsense. I've never even seen you have a glass of wine."

He shrugged. "Let's just say that after thirty-five years or so, I've fallen off the wagon."

Alex took another step closer. "I know about the autopsy reports," she said, placing her hands on the back of the small club chair that faced his desk.

He said nothing as he brought the glass to his lips.

"You dictated at least three fake reports and then substituted them for the real ones, and somehow made the legitimate ones disappear from the hospital's permanent medical records."

Placing the glass down after a short swallow, Owen extended his hands as if he were awaiting handcuffs.

"You're right," he stated and then added with a pathetic laugh, "I confess. There's no reason to try to fool you any longer."

Alex sat down. "I also know you're hell-bent on drumming Victor out of medicine and that you used me to try to frame him. You led me down the primrose path and I was stupid enough to follow you every step of the way."

"I've always liked you, Alex, so at this juncture I would offer you the following advice: Life isn't that much different from surgery. Things aren't always what they appear."

"Owen, listen to me. Victor Runyon is a colleague of mine and you used me to crucify him."

Owen began to cough violently. Alex stood up but he waved her away. The coughing stopped as abruptly as it had started and Owen gasped for a few deep breaths. Finally he cleared his throat, got up, and walked unsteadily across the room.

Owen asked, "Did you ever stop to consider that there are just as many people in this country passionately committed to seeing the adoption of national health insurance as the Caduceus Project is to preventing it?"

Alex watched as he reached out and picked up one of his trophies off a long granite-topped credenza. After turning it in his hand several times, he reached into his pocket, pulled out a handkerchief, and lightly buffed the silver cup.

"For God's sake, Owen. What have you gotten yourself involved in?"

He half-smiled, set the award back down, and then carefully made his way back to his desk. "I'm afraid you're looking at an old fool," he said. "I was weak and conducted myself as a man without character—something I've been teaching young surgeons to avoid at all costs for my entire academic career."

Alex stood up, reached across the desk, and gently pried the glass from his quivering fingers. He never looked up. Instead, his eyes tracked over to an eight-by-ten photograph of his grandchildren.

"What happened?" she asked.

"Terrible, unspeakable things that I lacked the strength to prevent."

Alex paused, again noticing that his eyes remained glued to the picture.

"Are you saying that somebody is blackmailing you? Tell me what this is all about and I'll try to help you."

Alex assumed her plea was in vain, but after a few moments he said softly, "Over a year ago, a man named Morgan came to see me. He made some rather unusual requests of me that I flatly refused. When I did, he advised me that I might want to reconsider because he was in possession of certain information regarding my early career that could prove very embarrassing for me. As soon as he said it, I knew exactly what he was talking about."

"What do you mean, unusual requests? What did he want you to do?"

"It was pretty much as you said. He wanted me to disgrace Victor Runyon and make it appear as if the Caduceus Project's political objectives were more important to him than his own patients' safety."

"Why would he want you to do that?" she asked.

"He didn't elaborate but it seemed obvious to me that he had political reasons for wanting to discredit both Victor and the Caduceus Project. At first I thought he represented some opposing political group, but he claimed he was working alone."

Alex said, "You mentioned that he had certain information about you."

Owen's eyes fell closed for a moment as he cleared his throat. He tried to speak but found himself fumbling for the words. He stopped, for a few seconds, taking the time to gather himself. He leaned back in his chair.

"It happened a long time ago. I was about two years out of my residency and drinking way too much. I was working as a general surgeon in a small town in Iowa. One night I received an emergency call to see a twelve-year-old boy who had gotten pinned under a tractor. He was bleeding internally and in shock and needed to go to the operating room. I had been drinking. Usually I could cover things up . . . and get through the operations, but . . ."

"Not this time," Alex said.

"I was too drunk and the boy's injuries were too complicated."

"What happened?"

"I couldn't stop the bleeding. The boy . . . he . . . he bled to death on the table. Afterward, I didn't have the courage to face the parents so I left the hospital without talking to them. The charge nurse in the OR called the police and they picked me up about two miles from the hospital. I was charged with DUI and involuntary manslaughter."

"My God, Owen. I . . . I can't believe—"

He continued to speak in barely above a hush. "My father helped me. His lawyers were able to quietly settle things with the boy's parents. I managed to avoid going to jail and two years later, after doing quite a bit of community service, I got my license to practice medicine back. I changed my name and moved. I was even able to get back into academic medicine. I never revealed anything about my past to anyone."

"How's that possible?" Alex asked. "Everything's in the National Practitioner Data Bank. Any hospital that you applied to for privileges would have known immediately."

"Actually, the data bank's only about fifteen years old. The way hospitals credentialed doctors in the seventies was by rubber stamp. It was assumed that all physicians were above reproach and the most virtuous members of society. Very little of what they submitted in their applications to get on a medical staff was ever checked." He took a deep breath and then added, "Things have certainly changed."

"You complied with your punishment. Why did you have to lie about it?" she asked.

"C'mon, Alex. Do you really think I ever would have been able to get a meaningful university position if I had been honest about what I had done? I would have been lucky to get the graveyard shift in some no-name emergency room. My wife doesn't even know, for God's sake."

"So how did this man, Morgan, find all this out about you?"

"He wouldn't tell me, but he had all the documents to prove he knew what he was talking about. He also made it patently clear that if I didn't cooperate, he'd go public with the information. When I weighed ruining my career and disgracing my family against drumming Victor out of medicine . . . Well, I guess I lost sight of right and wrong."

In disbelief, she said, "People . . . our patients were murdered, Owen."

"I had no part in that," he insisted as his head dropped and his voice returned to a monotone. "All Morgan wanted me to do was fake a few autopsy reports and make Victor look bad. Later, when you got involved, I was supposed to make it look like you were the one who discovered Victor's professional indiscretions. I never appreciated what kind of a man Morgan was or what he was capable of. When I finally realized what was happening, it was simply too late."

"Too late? How can you say that? You could have gone to the authorities instead of sitting idly by and doing nothing."

"You're not listening to me," he insisted. "By the time I figured it out, there was nothing I could do. I really believed that all Morgan wanted was to get rid of Victor. I had no idea what his real agenda was."

"What do you mean, his real agenda?"

"I'm afraid medicine as I once knew it is gone. Our art is now no different than any other commercial enterprise."

"I still don't understand what—"

"Power and money, Alex. It's all about the politics and the business of medicine. Betrayal can come in many forms. When you can reach out and touch the one . . . well, that's the cruelest. I should have seen it sooner," he muttered.

"Who are—?"

He held up his hand. "The specifics don't matter."

"And Jessie's kidnapping?"

He suddenly looked up, searching her face for even a hint of sympathy. "I had nothing to do with that," he insisted. "Surely you must know that."

Alex said nothing.

He slumped forward in his chair, rubbed his eyes, and whispered, "But I guess you have no reason to believe me. Leave me now, Alex. You have what you came for. Leave me in peace, for God's sake."

"Not until you tell me where I can find Morgan."

"Morgan's dead."

"How do you know?" she asked.

"Because I killed him. I thought it would put an end to this nightmare, but it only made things worse. I should have known better."

"So now what do you do?"

"Finish what I started. It's the only way I know of redeeming myself."

"Don't you think it would be better to let—"

Owen raised a tightly clenched fist. "Can't you please just leave me alone now?"

"Let me help you," she said, ignoring his request and hoping that if she gained his confidence, she'd be able to reason with him and persuade him to let the authorities get involved.

"I don't want your help. I know what I have to do. Now, please, just walk out of here now and forget this conversation ever happened. If you stop now, you and David will be safe. I promise."

Standing there, bearing witness to this dismal and beaten man whom she had once revered, was almost too much for her. Owen's hollow eyes gazed right past her. It was as if he didn't even know she was still there.

In the next moment, he reached forward and flicked the glass of vodka. It fell to his desk, spilling its contents over everything. Alex turned and left his office, closing the door silently behind her.

Walking down the corridor, she had already dismissed Owen's advice about abandoning her efforts to find out what had really happened to David. She knew she couldn't give up until she was sure that no further harm would come to him.

# Chapter 91

"I didn't hear from you yesterday," Micah complained to Alex as they walked along Thirty-seventh Street before arriving at the Georgetown University entrance.

Alex had been in love with the campus since the first time she had seen it. It had become another one of her preferred places to take a walk and relax. She liked being among the students and gazing at the various architectural styles of the buildings.

"Did you get my message?" Micah asked.

"I did, but it was too late to call you back."

"How's Jessie doing?"

"She's fine," Alex answered, without going into a lot of detail. At the moment she had no interest in discussing her personal life. What she wanted was to talk to Micah about her conversations with Owen and Victor. "I had a rather interesting day."

"Something tells me I'm going to regret asking what was so interesting about it."

"I went over to Victor's house."

"You're kidding," he said, slowing his pace. "Why did you do that?"

"To apologize."

"Apologize? For what?"

Alex looked off in the distance at a group of students heading up the steps to the student union. "You were right. I made a mistake about him."

"A mistake? The man behaved in a completely unprofessional and unethical manner."

"I'm not excusing his unethical behavior. I'm just saying that there's a big difference between being misguided and being a criminal."

Micah shook his head. "A week ago you saw him as a man

with bloodstains on his hands and now you're feeling sorry for him."

"I was hasty and judgmental. I learned my lesson and told him I was sorry. I met his little girl. He's got a big house and I assume big bills."

"What does that have to do with anything?"

"Nothing, except that my blunder may result in a huge financial problem for him."

"I wouldn't worry about that too much if I were you," Micah said.

"What do you mean?"

"He's pretty close with his brother and from what I understand he's loaded."

"His brother?" she asked, as a wave of dismay spread through her. "I wasn't aware he had a brother."

"I met him last year. He was visiting Victor from somewhere in the Midwest."

"Where did you meet him?"

"I ran into them in a restaurant. They were waiting for a table and I was waiting for Max, so we had a drink together."

Still filled with cautious trepidation, Alex asked, "Are you sure it was his brother?"

"Positive."

"Is he a physician?"

"As I recall, he's in the telecommunications business."

"How do you know he's so wealthy?"

Micah smile was a dry one. "Some people enjoy talking about their good fortune whether they know you well or not."

"Do you happen to remember his first name?"

Micah looked at Alex with a baffled look in his eyes. "What's with the big interest in Victor's brother?"

Not having the time or inclination to explain herself at the moment, Alex simply said, "Because I want to send him a Christmas card. Do you remember his first name or not?"

Micah grinned and then laughed. "I think it was . . . John."

With Owen's words regarding the business of medicine and betrayal echoing in her mind, Alex continued her walk with Micah in silence. She had no way of knowing specifically what Owen had been referring to but she suspected it had a lot to do with the mess he had become entangled in.

"When you called, you said you wanted to talk to me about something," Micah said.

With Alex's mind going off in a million different directions, she barely heard his question. When it finally registered, she answered, "It was nothing. We can talk about it some other time."

"Are you sure?"

"I'm sure." Alex looked at her watch. "Actually, I just realized I have to get back to the hospital."

Alex took hold of his arm. Micah didn't say anything, but she could surmise from his expression and body language that he was confused by her behavior. Setting the pace a little faster, Alex led Micah past the Jesuit cemetery and then Copley Hall, one of the larger residence halls.

"Micah," she began with a note of caution, "if I wanted to find out everything there is to know about the business of national health insurance, who would I speak to?"

"That's easy. Eugene French. He's a professor in the School of Health Policy. He's an expert on the subject. I've heard him speak on a number of occasions. I serve on the university's foundation board with him. I can give him a call if you'd like."

"No, I'll call him, but do you mind if I drop your name here and there?"

"Of course not. Why the sudden interest in the business of universal health care?"

"Do you realize that you ask more questions than the kids?"

"Do you really think so?" he asked with a smirk.

"I have an idea," she said. "Let's talk about you for a change. Have you spoken to Max?"

"Nope."

"Are you going to?"

"Nope."

"Why the sudden hard line?"

"Because I played it straight with her and she made a rather large chump out of me."

"Are you dating anybody new?"

"Are you kidding? I'm still trying to regroup from Max," he answered. "I'm going to wait a little while before trying again, but I can tell you this—next time, I'll be a little more careful."

"Don't get too discouraged," she said with a smile. "You're not totally repulsive to women."

"That's reassuring."

"C'mon," she said, tugging on his arm. "You're walking like an old man. I have something I have to do."

As they approached the entrance to the campus, Alex's mind was suddenly filled by one of her father's favorite expressions. On more than one occasion she could remember him speaking to her about being played for a fool. He would always end the conversation by telling her, "Fool me once, shame on you; fool me twice, shame on me."

# Chapter 92

It was nearing five o'clock when Owen found himself on Fifteenth Street standing in front of the *Washington Post* building. Before going in he pulled out his cell phone and tapped in a number.

Alex was sitting in her office thinking about her conversation with Owen when the phone rang.

"Dr. Caffey," she said.

"Alex, it's Owen. In the next couple of days somebody's going to contact you. It's important that you speak with him."

"Contact me about what?"

"He'll explain everything to you. I have to go now."

"What are you going to do?" she asked.

"I'm going to rely on the fact that somebody has gravely misjudged me."

"I don't understand," she said.

"It's not important that you do. Take care, Alex," he said.

Owen replaced the cell phone in his pocket and again

looked up at the *Washington Post* building. For the first time in months his mind filled with a sense of purpose. With a rekindled sense of dignity and self-respect, he felt as if he had finally found the strength to do the honorable thing. Clutching a large manila envelope in his hand, he felt no reluctance as he walked through the front door and into the lobby.

Sitting behind the information desk, Lucille Marks was waiting impatiently for her lunch relief.

"Excuse me. I wonder if I could leave this envelope for one of your reporters?" Owen asked.

Lucille, a grandmother of eight and a faithful employee of the *Post* for twenty-two years, reached across the desk and accepted the bulky envelope. "It'll have to go through security," she said with a kindly smile.

"That's fine," Owen answered. "I've written the reporter's name on both sides."

"William Sutter," she said, flipping the envelope over. "He's one of our best."

"I know," Owen said. "It's very important that he gets it."

Lucille looked up, her heart going out to the disheartened-looking man standing across from her. "I'll see to it personally," she assured him.

Owen took a couple of steps back and then said, "Thank you. You're very kind."

"Wait a minute," Lucille said. "How can Mr. Sutter get hold of you? There's no return address on the envelope."

Owen looked at her in a manner that made Lucille suspect that her question struck him as inconsequential.

"Everything he needs to know is right there," he said with little feeling in his voice, and then, after a quick nod, he turned and started for the exit.

# Chapter 93

At eight P.M., Owen unlocked the door to his office.

Making his way slowly across the room, he sat down behind his desk. He slid open the bottom drawer, pulled out a small leather toiletry bag, unzipped it, and placed the contents in front of him. After examining them, he rolled up the sleeve of his white dress shirt to just above his elbow.

Stopping for a moment, he gazed over to his large collection of awards and trophies for his roses. With hardly any emotion, he picked up a long rubber tourniquet and wrapped it around his biceps. Placing one end of the tourniquet in his mouth, he looped it around itself and then pulled it into a tight knot. Methodically pumping his fist, he watched as a large tortuous vein on his forearm became engorged with blood.

He reached for a ten-cc plastic syringe and filled it with the contents of a small bottle. As if he had rehearsed the scene a thousand times before, Owen gently slid the needle into his vein. As he drew gently back on the handle, a flash of dark blood entered the syringe. He glanced up for a few moments, scanning the wall where his diplomas, awards, and recognitions hung. As he breathed deeply, his eyes shifted to a picture of his wife.

"I'm sorry," he whispered, and then with one quick tug he pulled off the tourniquet. With his thumb squarely on the syringe, he pushed down and injected himself with Pavulon, a drug used by anesthesiologists to stop patients from breathing on their own during an operation.

For the next few seconds he breathed easily, but then, as if someone were choking him, the intense feeling of suffocation consumed him. With his diaphragm and other breathing muscles now paralyzed by the drug, he was unable to draw any oxygen into his lungs. His eyesight blurred for several seconds, and with his last breath he found himself staring into an endless black abyss.

Instead of crashing to the desk, his head simply tipped forward, his chin coming to rest softly on his chest as if he were taking a short nap before returning to his responsibilities. His lips quivered briefly but soon became a pale blue. Gradually his pupils dilated, becoming fixed and having the appearance of two plain saucers.

In the solitude of his own office and at age sixty-two, Dr. Owen Goodman brought his illustrious career as an academic trauma surgeon to an inauspicious and tragic end.

# Chapter 94

**MAY 27**

The door to Alex's office was wide open.

"I got a message that you wanted to speak with me," Victor said from the doorway.

Alex looked up from her desk. "Your secretary told me you'd stop by this afternoon."

Victor looked at her with a degree of hesitancy. "Now would be better for me."

"Fine," she said. "Have a seat."

He didn't move. "Why don't we talk in my office?"

"What's the difference?"

He stepped forward, looked around, and said, "Let's just say that I'd be more comfortable in my own office."

"Fine," she said, getting up from behind her desk. She followed Victor through her outer office. Joyce stole a peek at her as she walked by and Alex gave her a subtle nod.

They walked in silence down the corridor until they reached Victor's office. He followed Alex in and directed her to have a seat on his couch. The bookcases were almost empty and the floor was filled with half-packed cartons.

"I heard that the university made their final decision," she said.

Victor walked over to a stack of books and began placing them in a carton.

"That's right. Is that what you wanted to see me about? To gloat?"

"When will the board of medicine make their final disposition?"

"At the end of the month, but my lawyer's already told me that I should expect to have my license revoked."

"The board's made up of a group of pretty bright and intuitive people."

"That's very kind of you to say, Alex."

"How's your brother?" she asked.

"My brother?"

"Yeah, your brother."

Victor hesitated and then, with a degree of caution in his voice that Alex was not accustomed to, said, "Well, if you must know, he's fine."

"It's a funny thing," she said as she stood up and walked over toward the bookcase. "I seem to recall a rather heated discussion we had in the ICU a few weeks ago when you clearly told me that you had no brothers or sister."

Victor shrugged in disinterest. "You must have misunderstood me, but if my family tree is a matter of great interest to you, then, yes, I do have a brother."

"Where does he live?" Alex asked.

"Look, Alex. I appreciate your trying to do some fence mending here, but I'm not exactly in the mood for the let's-bury-the-hatchet-and-be-friends routine. At the moment, I'm a little preoccupied trying to figure out how I'm going to support my family."

"I hardly think money's going to be your problem."

This time, Victor stopped what he was doing, placed his hands on his hips, and said in an indignant tone, "Excuse me?"

"Boy, you're really a master at playing the victim. After our talk the other day at your house, you really had me believing that you were just a well-intentioned guy who suffered from poor judgment."

"What's wrong with that assessment?" he asked.

"I went to see Eugene French yesterday," she said.

With renewed interest, Victor asked, "From the School of Health Policy?"

"The very same," she said. "I asked him about the nuts and bolts of how national health insurance would work. As I recall, that's an area that you have a very special interest in."

"As do you, obviously."

"I've learned quite a bit from him. Did you know that if national health insurance became law, the federal government wouldn't administer the program itself? It would be far too enormous an undertaking, so it would contract with a select few private companies that had the resources and expertise to manage the whole thing. They'd be responsible for billing, collecting, monitoring services, patient eligibility, fraud. The list goes on and on."

Victor continued to pack his things. He never looked up. Alex didn't expect him to say anything, so she continued. "Of course, whichever company was lucky enough to be selected would have to have the computer technology and infrastructure to handle the job."

"The term is *fiscal agent*," Victor said. "It's already a common practice."

"Do you have any idea of the amount of money that would be paid by the federal government as compensation to those companies?" she asked.

"I imagine it would be appreciable," Victor stated.

"Appreciable? C'mon, Victor, I think we're talking staggering here. We both know it would be worth millions, maybe billions."

"Now that you're an expert on the subject, what do you plan to do, give up medicine and become a fiscal agent?"

"If I thought it were an original idea, I might, but I think you've already beaten me to it," she said.

"Really?"

"Tell me about Tenucom Industries."

"Why don't you tell me, because I get the feeling there's nothing I could tell you that you don't already know."

"They're an ambitious young telecommunications company."

By this point, Victor had moved closer to his desk. His arms were crossed.

"You've obviously been a busy girl. It appears that you're quite knowledgeable in certain areas that some might consider rather sensitive."

"Is that why you showed up early and we came to your office?"

He smiled. "You're a clever woman. A man in my position has to take every precaution. God only knows what kind of electrical devices you might have installed in anticipation of our meeting this afternoon."

"For that matter, I could be wearing a bug right now."

He looked at her dressed in rumpled green scrubs. "Somehow I don't think so."

"So does this mean that you're prepared to have a frank conversation?" she asked.

"I think we should." He paused for a moment, smiled, and added, "Your life could depend on it."

Ignoring his anything but veiled threat, she said, "I've been doing quite a bit of reading about Tenucom. I know the CEO's a man by the name of John Raymond Runyon. Does the name ring a bell?"

"He's my brother. What's your interest in him?"

"Because I couldn't find any connection between you and any corporate entity."

"That's because I don't have any."

"Of course not. You're too smart for that. That's when I had the idea of checking out your brother. That's where I came up with his link to Tenucom. He was on three different search engines."

Victor remained icy, his stare impassive. "I'm impressed."

"You should be very proud of him. He's quite well known. Not only do they have a nice bio about him on the company's Web site, but there have been a couple of very flattering articles in the St. Louis newspapers."

"My brother's a real publicity hound. He loves to see his name in the paper."

Alex invited Victor to sit down by pointing to the chair behind his desk. As soon as he did, she retook her seat on the couch.

"I was very interested to read that your brother went to Colby College in Maine and was a communications major."

"So?"

"Colby's a pretty small school. When I was a senior in high school, I was thinking about going there so I visited the campus. It's the strangest thing, but somebody else recently mentioned to me that he, too, had graduated from Colby."

"And who might that be?"

"Brice Beckett, you know—the congressman."

"I know who Brice Beckett is," Victor assured her.

"What's even more interesting is that your brother and Beckett graduated the same year and they both played varsity basketball. That's quite a coincidence, don't you think? Your brother and quite likely the next president of the United States, going to the same small college together and playing on the same basketball team—that's the kind of experience that could solidify a lifelong friendship."

Victor rocked back in his chair and then swiveled a quarter-turn to his right. "Do you mind telling me where you're going with all this?"

She smiled. "If I were you, I'd be more worried about where you're going."

Victor clasped his hands and leaned forward across his desk. His callous expression spoke volumes and Alex suspected that the cat-and-mouse game was about to come to an end.

"I applaud your investigational skills. It's your judgment that I question."

She said nothing.

Victor then asked calmly, "Do you have any idea of who you are fucking with?"

With a stony look of her own, she said, "I have an excellent idea of who I'm fucking with. And in case you're interested, I'm not the slightest bit afraid of or intimidated by you."

Pausing for a few seconds to reflect, Victor suddenly laughed.

"Okay, Alex," he began, with an obvious change in his tactics. "You've obviously come here for a reason, so why don't you just tell me what you think you know."

"Over the past couple of years Tenucom has been buying up small telecommunications companies. I'm guessing you and your brother are doing that to increase the organization's computer and other information technology infrastructure."

Victor responded, "If you're implying that Tenucom is preparing to become a fiscal agent, you seem to be overlooking the fact that the company is not in the health care industry."

"You're right, and that had me stumped at first. But then I found out that most fiscal agents have no direct connection to the health care industry. They're usually huge banks or massive companies—and there are even some in the telecommunications industry."

Victor shrugged and then tapped his fingertips together.

"But even if this country should adopt a policy of national health insurance," he said, "there must be hundreds of companies out there who are already fiscal agents and a lot bigger than Tenucom. Wouldn't they have the inside track?"

"That's true, assuming the playing field were level, but supposing a corporation like Tenucom had a CEO who just happened to have a long-standing personal relationship with the man who was very likely to be elected the next president of the United States?"

"I assume you're referring to Brice Beckett and my brother again."

"You're damn right I am, and I'll tell you this: if I were a major player in a company whose CEO was buddy-buddy with Brice Beckett, I'd do everything I could to make sure that universal health care became a reality."

"This is all very interesting and it makes for great theater," he said with an annoying grin, "but I'm afraid it's pure speculation on your part. Maybe instead of being here in my office, you should be out in Hollywood trying to sell it to the movies."

"You're a very cunning and persuasive man, Victor. You almost had me believing that bedtime story about how sorry you were about your unethical actions on behalf of the Caduceus Project."

"Perhaps you're giving me too much credit," he said.

"I hardly think so. You knew how important physician support would be if national health insurance were ever to be enacted. What better way to help ensure its passage than to destroy the most influential physician organization opposed to its adoption?"

"Do you think one person could accomplish such a thing?"

"You're damn right I do. The only reason you became involved with the Caduceus Project and clawed your way to the top was so that you would be in a position to wreck it from the inside."

Victor said, "In spite of how good you're feeling about yourself at the moment, the only thing you've done here today is write your own death sentence. You are right about one thing: left unchecked, the Caduceus Project could be instrumental in defeating Beckett's plan of national health insurance. That's an eventuality that we can't allow to happen."

"Your brother's quite the mastermind," she said.

"My brother's an effective CEO with a fair mind for business, but he's a lamb, not a lion, and not the type to grab control of his own destiny by putting everything on the line."

"But you are?"

"I think we both know the answer to that."

"Why did you have to resort to such extreme means? Wasn't your brother's relationship with Brice Beckett enough? Most people believe he'll be elected president and this country will have universal health coverage."

"That's what they said about Clinton. I wasn't about to leave anything to chance. My brother's relationship with Beckett means nothing if national health insurance doesn't become a reality. The destruction of the Caduceus Project is critical."

"Does Beckett have any idea of what's going on?"

"Of course not. All we need from Mr. Beckett is that when the time comes, he remembers who his old friends are."

"What about Owen?" she asked. "He told me about Morgan. Was Morgan working for you?"

He looked at her with indifference. "Since we agreed to have a frank conversation, I'll answer you. Yes, he was."

"And Owen?"

"Owen Goodman's a hopeless buffoon. He came to see me after he killed Morgan. I was astonished that the old fool actually had the nerve and ingenuity to get into Morgan's house and shoot him."

"How did he make the connection between you and Morgan?" she asked.

"He scrolled down the recent phone calls on Morgan's cell phone and saw my number. He threatened to go to the police, but when I reminded him about how that might affect the health of his grandchildren, he thought better of the idea. He did me a favor by killing himself and saving us the job."

"How did you find out about his past?" Alex asked.

"The paper trail was there and not very difficult to find. My investigator had all the information forty hours after he began looking into Owen's past. Don't get me wrong. I think Owen would have gone along anyway . . . I mean if I had only used his family as leverage, but when I found out about his unfortunate past, well, that was a real stroke of luck and really brought him into the fold. I guess what they say is true. When you have a man by the balls, his mind will soon follow."

"Why Owen?" she asked.

"I thought about using others, but Owen turned out to be the best choice—for obvious reasons."

"So with Owen's help, you implicate yourself in a series of deplorable and unethical acts as the leader of the Caduceus Project. The hospital and the medical board respond by throwing you out of medicine. You then disappear in disgrace and the project is dealt a fatal blow. All that's left is for you to sit back, wait for the election, and then start collecting millions."

Victor simply smiled. "Brilliant in its simplicity, don't you think?"

"Not that it matters, but how did you kill those patients?"

He sighed with impatience. "Does it really matter?"

"If my guess is right, they were injected with a large amount of air directly into the heart."

"You have done your homework," he answered.

"Why David?"

"Because he's a rising star in the field of journalistic exposés with an impeccable reputation and considerable credibility, especially in the area of health care."

"Did you know he was my brother?" she asked.

"As a matter of fact, I didn't. When Morgan found out, he told me."

"So when your little plan didn't work out and David was in a coma, you figured you'd use me instead."

"It seemed like the only sensible thing to do."

"What was Robert Key's role in this whole thing?" she asked.

"Robert was a member of the project. We needed someone to go to your brother to entice him into doing a damaging exposé on the Caduceus Project, specifically implicating me as its corrupt and unconscionable leader. Robert was no fool. He agreed to do it as long as he was generously compensated for his participation. So we quickly came to a financial arrangement, which was more than generous on our part. But pretty soon his demands for money increased and he became a liability."

With Alex's suspicions now confirmed regarding how Robert Key seemed to be living a lifestyle far beyond the means of a hospital-based radiologist, she asked, "So what did you do when he stopped being so cooperative?"

"I still thought he might go along with the plan. But just to make sure, we had him under surveillance when he went to see your brother. Robert was only supposed to tell David that a few patients at Gillette had died because of an unethical physician by the name of Victor Runyon. And that I had hesitated to report a defective medical device to the FDA because the manufacturer of that device was a large contributor to my favorite political organization."

"But he told my brother much more," Alex said.

"I'm afraid so. But we were aware of everything he said, so we weren't left with a whole lot of choices of how to deal with the situation."

"How did Theo get involved?"

"Owen always valued my opinion regarding the progress of the residents. I told him that I didn't think Theo had demonstrated sufficient academic achievement and that he should work on a research project that would lead to a scientific publication."

"Let me guess the rest. You told Owen that I would be the perfect mentor for Theo."

"Exactly."

"And that's when I became David's replacement as the person to expose you."

"I left just enough clues to convince you that I was a deplorable disgrace to medicine who needed to be expunged from the profession. You took the bait and brought the matter to Owen's attention, who immediately acted on it. Unfortunately, I never dreamed you'd be able to figure out the whole thing."

"I'm sorry to have disappointed you."

"Nonsense, I have to give you credit, Alex. Discovering that those patients had been, shall we say, sacrificed, and their autopsy reports forged was quite ingenious on your part."

"So you came to my house that night just to make sure I was really pissed off."

"It was essential that I made you suspicious and angry at first. Later, after I had confessed my unsavory behavior to Owen and turned into the most repentant man on the planet, it was my hope that you would forgive me and back off. Up until about five minutes ago, I thought it had worked."

Alex just sat there in silence, her anger mounting.

Victor then added, "The irony of this whole thing is that if Robert Key had done only what he was supposed to, no harm would have ever come to David. But when he told your brother about the murders, they both became an immediate liability."

Alex then asked, "What about the mysterious screwup with Robert Key's body?"

"That was easily enough arranged. You would think it would be a big deal to switch bodies in a morgue, but it's not."

"Assuming you got away with this, didn't the thought of never practicing medicine again bother you?"

"I couldn't care less if I ever set foot in Gillette or any other hospital again. I never had any interest in being a doctor. I was pushed into it by a couple of very overbearing parents."

"So this entire thing was about money and greed, and had nothing to do with politics."

An arcane smile grew on Victor's face. "Come now, Alex. Would you really expect me to live the rest of my life on a lousy two hundred thousand dollars a year?"

She found his question easy to answer, "No, I guess not."

Victor clapped his hands once and then rubbed his palms together as if one matter had been resolved and now it was time to move onto the next.

"Okay, Alex. You're obviously a resourceful and intelligent woman. So where do we go from here?"

"I know exactly what I'm going to do."

"Don't be hasty," he warned. "Now that we've both laid our cards on the table, you have an important decision to make."

"Really?"

"I'm sure I could find a place for you at Tenucom for considerably more money than you're making now. Just think of it. The finest home, the very best education for Jessie. It's not a bad way out of this mess when you consider the unpleasant alternative."

"Thanks, but I'll pass," she said without an instant's hesitation.

He shrugged. "It's your funeral. Don't say I didn't offer."

"What's to stop me from going to the police?" she asked.

"How about we start with good judgment. I think you have a pretty good idea of what I'm capable of. You have a lovely mother and daughter. Their well-being must be of paramount importance to you. You're far too intelligent to do anything that might place them at risk."

She sighed. "Do you have any conscience at all?" she asked.

"Not when it comes to self-preservation."

Victor walked over to a small refrigerator and took out a can of fruit juice.

"What about David?" she asked.

"David poses no risk to us. He'll never remember a thing of his meeting with Robert Key and I know you're too bright to ever try to refresh his memory." Victor took two short swallows of his juice. "Now, since you've obviously made your decision and I have a lot of packing to do—"

"Right after I heard about Owen's suicide, I received a letter from him. He figured with my help, we could stop you before you could harm anybody else."

"Well, I'm afraid even from the grave, he has made a serious miscalculation," Victor said.

"Maybe not. About an hour ago, I got a call from a reporter at the *Washington Post*. He told me that he had received a rather interesting packet of information from a Dr. Owen Goodman. It was a very meticulous accounting of a series of murders at one of Washington's most prestigious hospitals. It specifically instructed him to contact me."

"You're bluffing," he said, with some of the usual arrogance and conviction missing from his voice. "And even if it were, there's nothing to link me directly to any of this."

"Maybe, but my best guess is that several government agencies are going to have to look into Owen's allegations."

"So?"

"I bet the first thing they'll do is talk to your brother. Based on what you've told me about him, it sounds like he'll probably cave in like a house of cards and pull you right down with him."

Victor turned in his chair, thought for a moment, and then said, "If that happens, I'll simply deny everything he says. It would be his word against mine. There's nothing linking me to his company."

"Maybe, but how are you going to deny that your phone number just happened to be listed in Morgan's cell phone directory?"

"You think you're pretty—"

"There's also the fact that all of the patients who mysteriously died just happened to be on your service. You can count on the authorities exhuming their bodies." Alex studied his face for a few moments before continuing. "But you're probably right, Victor," she added. "There's absolutely nothing specifically linking you to all these murders and you can just simply deny everything."

The color in Victor's face suddenly siphoned, leaving him with a pallid expression of pure panic.

"You're lying," he insisted. "That old man wouldn't have the nerve to go to the papers and neither would you." With the veins in his neck popping out, he slammed his fist down on the desk and yelled, "Just because Lott screwed up with your daughter doesn't mean I'll do the same. You've made a fatal mistake coming here today, Alex. You've just orphaned your only child." He reached for the phone. "Whatever happens to me, you're a dead woman."

"If you're thinking of calling your brother, forget it. He probably already used his one phone call to speak to his attorney." Alex stood up, turned her back to him, and started for the door.

"We're not finished here, Alex," he screamed. "You bitch. Don't you walk out on me."

Alex stopped, waited a few seconds, and then glanced back over her shoulder. She rolled up the sleeve of her shirt and showed Victor the tiny microphone.

"You're one sick man, Victor. I hope you rot in hell."

Having no interest in seeing any more, Alex strolled calmly out of Victor Runyon's office. She simply nodded when she passed Maura Kenton and the two uniformed officers who were waiting in the hall.

# Chapter 95

**MAY 28**

Alex had visited the Albert Einstein Memorial located on the grounds of the National Academy of Sciences numerous times since moving to Washington.

Although it stood in close proximity to some of the city's most popular tourist attractions, it seldom drew much attention. Were it not for some young mothers with energetic toddlers who enjoyed climbing on the massive bronze statue of the renowned physicist, the monument might have gone completely unnoticed.

When Alex approached the memorial, Jamie was already seated around the far side.

"Hi," Alex said. "Thanks for meeting me."

"It was nice to hear from you," she said, moving over a little to make room for Alex to sit down.

"The last time we spoke you said you'd probably be leaving town soon. I just wanted to see how you were doing and say good-bye. Have you decided where you're going yet?"

"I'm moving back to the Pacific Northwest," Jamie answered. "I think I've had enough of big-city life for a while."

"I spent the summer of my sophomore year in medical school working in a clinic about fifty miles outside of Boise. It was probably the prettiest place I've ever seen," Alex said, thinking for the moment that Jamie reminded her of someone, but the image was faint at best and the notion quickly slipped from her mind.

"With Rob gone, there's nothing for me in D.C. except bad memories."

"Did his brother, Seth, ever get hold of you? I gave him your cell phone number."

"His brother?" Jamie asked.

"I'm sorry. I thought for sure he'd call you. He stopped by my office the other day. He's still living in Europe but came home when he learned of Robert's death."

"He hasn't called me, but I'd love to speak with him," Jamie said.

A tennis ball rolled up to Jamie's feet. As she reached for it, a boy of about ten came running around the statue and toward them. Jamie picked up the ball with her left hand and tossed it back to the boy who dashed off to the other side of the monument.

"When I mentioned your name to Seth, he didn't know who you were."

"That doesn't surprise me. He and Rob spoke so infrequently and I don't think they were very close."

"It's just when I spoke to you in the hospital, you mentioned that you and Robert had talked about getting married. You would think he would have mentioned something like that to his only living relative."

Jamie turned away. "I think a lot of couples talk about getting married, but we never really considered it seriously."

"That's another strange thing," Alex said.

Jamie laughed. "Not all couples wind up married, Dr. Caffey."

"That's not what I mean. Seth told me that Robert was gay."

Jamie turned to face Alex. "That's ridiculous. Rob was completely straight. I think I was in a position to attest to that. Why in the world would his brother say something like that?"

Alex stood up and looked directly at Jamie. "I don't know. I was just about to ask you the same question."

Alex was surprised by the look on Jamie's face. It wasn't a bewildered one as she would have expected, but more reminiscent of someone who knew she was in a chess game.

"This is all very disturbing, Dr. Caffey," she finally said. "I think I'd like to speak to Seth personally. Do you think you could give me his phone number?"

"I don't see why not." Alex reached into her purse and pulled out the piece of paper on which she had written Seth's phone number. "Here you go."

Jamie reached for the number and as Alex handed it to her, she noticed that Jamie's right thumbnail was cracked and had a large black blood clot under it. She took Jamie's hand, looked more carefully at her injury, and smiled. "How did that happen?"

"I slammed it in the car door," Jamie said. "It was careless of me. I was lucky I didn't break my thumb."

"You were very lucky. Most people who slam their finger in the car door do break it." Alex paused for a few seconds to wait for a silver-haired nanny pushing a double stroller to walk by. Alex smiled and then shook her head. "How did you manage it?"

"I don't remember exactly. I just slammed it in the car door," Jamie answered.

"That's not what I meant. I'm talking about the southern accent. How did you manage to make it so perfect?"

"I beg your pardon?" Jamie said.

Alex took another look at Jamie's poker face. "What I'm saying is that I think your accent is put on, and if I'm right, I should be complimenting you on your very convincing southern accent." Jamie held silent, so Alex went on. "I noticed that you're left-handed. The night you shot Lott, you held the gun in your left hand."

"With all due respect, Dr. Caffey, thirteen percent of the population is left-handed. Just because I'm one of them doesn't mean I shot somebody."

Alex pointed at Jamie's hand. "The woman who shot Simon Lott had the identical injury to her thumb." Alex stopped. A little surprised by the poise in Jamie's manner, she then asked, "I wonder what percentage of the population both are left-handed and have a large hematoma under their right thumbnail?"

Jamie grinned. "I don't know the answer to that, but you're very observant."

"You did a masterful job at changing your appearance, but your height's identical to mine. I also noticed that the night of the shooting."

Jamie nodded in thought, scanned the area, and this time spoke in her native Irish accent. "It's really not that difficult. Enough bronzing powder and shading easily changes the contour of your face. Different clothing styles, eye shadow, wigs, contact lenses, and a few other things and you're a new person. Part of what I do for a living is becoming the person I need to be. How's your daughter?" she asked.

"She's fine. I got her back that same night just as you said I might. I thought about you a great deal afterward. Until a day or so ago, I never imagined I'd have the opportunity to thank you."

"I'm very happy that things turned out so well." Jamie stood up and took a second careful look around.

Alex reached up and touched her wrist. "I know you don't have to tell me anything but I have a lot of questions," she said.

Jamie exchanged a sympathetic glance with Alex and sat back down. "Go ahead. I'll answer what I can."

"Who hired you to kill Lott?"

"I'm not a contract killer, Alex."

"But the night in Georgetown . . . you told me—"

"I'd just shot a man. I had to tell you something."

"Then who . . . ?"

"If it will put your mind at ease, I'm not one of the bad guys. I'm more what you might call an independent contractor. I make myself available to certain of your governmental agencies for special assignments."

"How did you . . . I mean where did you get involved . . . ?"

"Sometimes your government prefers to use noncitizens as operatives. I can't go into a lot of detail, but let's just say I have the type of military and educational background and training that qualifies me to get involved in these types of projects."

"Why was the government interested in all of this?"

"There was an anonymous whistle-blower at Tenucom. She was a fairly new employee in middle management but very bright. She had only an inkling but she spoke to the right people and as a result the government has taken a particular interest in fiscal agents, especially as relates to irregular or illegal practices."

"So you knew what I was doing."

"That's right."

"Are you saying that you were using me as a decoy?" Alex asked.

"Let's just say that we were aware that you had stumbled into certain delicate areas. Rather than have you removed, we felt that you might be able to get to places and people that we couldn't without blowing almost a year of very intensive investigation and surveillance."

"That's why you just happened to be there the night I met Lott." Jamie nodded and then craned her neck to look toward Constitution Avenue.

"Why did you have to change your appearance?" Alex asked.

"It was the only way I could get closer to Lott. I knew he had come to the hospital a few times and I was afraid he might recognize me as Jamie when I was visiting Dr. Key."

"Why did you care if Lott knew you as Jamie?"

"Well, if you're interested in a man for professional reason, then the best way to get close to him is to allow him to believe that he's drawn you in romantically. Simon Lott was extremely shrewd but he did have an Achilles' heel—women."

"So it was your intention to kill him the entire time?"

"Let's just say that the night he was about to kill you, he left me no choice."

"What brought you to Robert Key?"

"We knew about his relationship with Runyon. I had been

keeping loose tabs on him from afar for months. When he was hospitalized it offered me the perfect opportunity to gather more information. I had learned that he was a loner, so it was a simple enough matter to tell everyone that I was his girl-friend."

"In the hospital that night, why did you tell me about Robert's involvement in the Caduceus Project?" Alex asked.

"I thought you might know something I didn't. Under-standing what makes people tick, figuring out what they're thinking and then knowing what calculated risks to take . . . well, that's the heart of my business." Alex had no response, so she simply shook her head. A waggish grin quickly covered Jamie's face. "It's what I do, Alex . . . and just for the record I also have a little girl who's just about Jessie's age." Jamie stood up and extended her hand. "I'll be going now. I've al-ready said more than I should have. I'm assuming that when I leave here today, Jamie and Kerry no longer exist and you and I never met."

"You have my word."

"Give Jessie a hug for me."

Alex didn't say another word but watched as Jamie strolled away and then started down Constitution Avenue. She had gone only a few steps when a plain white sedan with darkly tinted windows pulled up next to her and slowly rolled to a stop. The back door opened and she climbed in.

Alex found herself smiling as she watched the car pull away. Although she didn't quite understand why, it pained her a little to know that she would never again see the woman who had saved both her life and Jessie's.

# Epilogue

When Alex pulled into her driveway the first thing she noticed was Jessie and Gabe screaming like banshees as they chased each other around Micah's car.

As soon as she was parked, Micah walked over and opened the door for her.

"It's nice to see you have the kids under control," she said, stepping out.

He looked over at them for a moment, shrugged, and said, "Kids need freedom to express themselves."

"I think that's what all single dads say who can't control their children."

Alex moved to the back door, opened it, and helped David out.

"You don't look too shabby," Micah told him, helping Alex steady him.

David looked around, took a couple of deep breaths, and then said, "I'd prefer it if Jessie saw me walking under my own power, so if you two mother hens would back off a step or two, I'd really appreciate it."

Alex smiled and Micah raised his hands high in capitulation, and the two of them stood back.

Alex said, "Apparently that clunk on your head didn't make you any less obstinate."

It was just at that moment when Jessie caught sight of David and came flying toward him.

"Mom says you're going to move in with us," she said, hugging him around the waist.

"For a little while," he answered, returning the hug.

"Grandma's here too," she said.

David raised his eyebrows and looked over at Alex.

"It's a big house," she said. "We have plenty of room."

"Is Micah moving in too?" David asked, mimicking Jessie's enthusiasm. But when a red blotchy rash suddenly appeared on Alex's neck, he knew his teasing had embarrassed her. He instantly knew why and did everything he could to conceal an intuitive grin.

"You look wonderful," Jeanette said, walking up to David. "We have everything you'll need. Alex has made all of the arrangements."

David took a few cautious steps, put his arm around Alex's shoulder, and gave her a quick squeeze.

"I knew she would," he said.

"Let's go in the house," Jeanette told David before turning to Micah and saying, "You are staying for lunch, I hope."

"I wouldn't miss it," he told her.

Alex said, "Mom, Micah and I will get the rest of David's things out of the car. You guys go ahead in. Take the kids, why don't you?"

With Gabe and Jessie running out in front, David and Jeanette started slowly toward the house. David stopped for a moment to steal a glance over his shoulder. Alex had seen that same juvenile smirk a million times before, knew exactly what he was thinking, and gave him her most loving death stare.

"What the heck's going on back there?" David asked Jeanette.

"What do you think?"

"I guess I was in that coma longer than I thought."

"Just come along, dear, and don't ask too many questions. I've waited a long time for nature to take its course."

In the meantime, Alex popped the trunk of her car and Micah reached in and pulled out two small suitcases and a brown shopping bag.

"How long is David going to stay with you?" he asked.

"A couple of weeks. He should be ready to go back to his apartment by the end of the month, but he'll still need intensive rehab every day as an outpatient."

"Did you see the paper today?"

"I stopped reading it days ago," she said. "David's safe—that's all that really matters to me anymore."

"A number of lawmakers are demanding congressional hearings to investigate fiscal agents and the way they administer present state and national health programs to make sure that if national health insurance does become a reality, it's administered honestly."

"It's hard for me to believe any of this ever happened."

"I've been thinking," Micah said, "it's been a rough few weeks. Maybe you should think about taking some time off."

"The idea sounds appealing, but at the moment a vacation is the last thing on my mind."

"You have the second two weeks in June off. Why not take advantage of it?"

"Where did you hear that? My next vacation's not until September."

Micah looked down and shuffled his feet. "It's been changed."

"What are you talking about?"

"Someone had it changed. It's now the second two weeks in June."

"I see," Alex said, stopping what she was doing to look up at Micah. "I'd love to know who my mysterious benefactor was."

Turning toward the car, he picked up one of the suitcases by grabbing the handle with both hands. "He asked me not to reveal his identity. What's important is that I just happen to have the same two weeks off," he said with some trepidation in his voice.

Alex reached up for Micah's shoulder and turned him back around. "What a coincidence. Where are you and Gabe going? Maybe Jessie and I will join you guys."

Micah stroked his chin. "As wonderful as that sounds, I was kind of thinking more of an adult vacation."

"By yourself?" she asked.

"Not exactly. I was considering inviting someone along."

"A woman?" she asked, taking the suitcase out of Micah's hand and placing it back on the ground.

"You act surprised," he said. "Don't you think I'm capable of planning a romantic getaway?"

"I have no doubt, but your vacation's only a couple of days away. A girl would need a little more time than that to get ready. When did you plan on letting the lucky lady in on your little plan?"

"Actually, that's what I'm trying to do right now. I just think I'm fumbling it a little."

Alex smiled. "No, you're doing great," she said, reaching up and interlocking her fingers around his neck. "What did you have in mind?"

"Have you ever been to Caneel Bay?" he asked, still having a little trouble looking directly into her eyes.

"I don't think so," she said.

"It's in the Virgin Islands. It's very restful . . . and romantic. They have long white sand beaches and . . ."

Alex tilted her head, went up on her tiptoes, and waited for Micah to kiss her. When it was over, she knew it was the perfect first kiss.